Autumn Whispers

An Otherworld Novel

YASMINE GALENORN

JOVE BOOKS, NEW YORK

THE BERKLEY PUBLISHING GROUP
Published by the Penguin Group
Penguin Group (USA) LLC.
375 Hudson Street, New York, New York 10014, USA

USA | Canada | UK | Ireland | Australia | New Zealand | India | South Africa | China

Penguin Books Ltd., Registered Offices: 80 Strand, London WC2R 0RL, England
For more information about the Penguin Group, visit penguin.com.

AUTUMN WHISPERS

A Jove Book / published by arrangement with the author

Jove Books are published by The Berkley Publishing Group.
JOVE® is a registered trademark of Penguin Group (USA) LLC.
The "J" design is a trademark of Penguin Group (USA) LLC.

For information, address: The Berkley Publishing Group,
a division of Penguin Group (USA) LLC.,
375 Hudson Street, New York, New York 10014.

ISBN: 978-0-515-15282-1

PUBLISHING HISTORY
Jove mass-market edition / October 2013

PRINTED IN THE UNITED STATES OF AMERICA

10 9 8 7 6 5 4 3 2 1

Cover art by Tony Mauro.
Cover design by Rita Frangie.
Map by Andrew Marshall, copyright © 2012 by Yasmine Galenorn.

This is a work of fiction. Names, characters, places, and incidents either are the product
of the author's imagination or are used fictitiously, and any resemblance to actual persons,
living or dead, business establishments, events, or locales is entirely coincidental.
The publisher does not have any control over and does not assume any responsibility for
author or third-party websites or their content.

ALWAYS LEARNING **PEARSON**

Dedicated to:
Tony Mauro, my cover artist.
Because people DO judge a book by its cover,
and my covers rock!

ACKNOWLEDGMENTS

Thank you to all my usual suspects: Samwise—my number one fan and the best husband I could hope for. My agent, Meredith Bernstein. My editor, Kate Seaver. Tony Mauro, my cover artist. My assistant, Andria Holley; my fan mail assistant and Street Team leader, Jenn Price; and my Facebook moderator, Marc Mullinex. To my furry "Galenorn Gurlz." Most reverent devotion to Ukko, Rauni, Mielikki, and Tapio, my spiritual guardians.

As always, biggest thank-you goes to my readers. Your support helps keep the series going. You can find me on the Net on my site: Galenorn.com, on Facebook at facebook.com/AuthorYasmineGalenorn, and at Twitter: @yasminegalenorn. You can also find an Otherworld Wikipedia on my website.

If you write to me snail mail (see website for address or write via the publisher), please enclose a stamped, self-addressed envelope with your letter if you would like a reply. Lots of fun promo goodies are available. See my site for info.

The Painted Panther
Yasmine Galenorn

It is when power is wedded to chronic fear that it becomes formidable.

ERIC HOFFER

Man, biologically considered, and whatever else he may be in the bargain, is simply the most formidable of all the beasts of prey, and, indeed, the only one that preys systematically on its own species.

WILLIAM JAMES

Chapter 1

I stood at the top of the ravine overlooking the waterfront below. Nestled on the front of Lake Sammamish, my destination was a sprawling behemoth of a house—like many in the greater Seattle metropolitan area, jokingly referred to as *McMansions*. Cookie-cutter design like its neighbors, the monster was a tribute to the high wages and high cost of living that came with this area.

Only tonight, all the money and success in the world wouldn't help the owner of the palatial estate. Tonight, the man who owned this house was going to die—and he was going to die the final death.

Behind me, in a sheer flowing robe that mirrored the twilight sky, stood Greta, my mentor, the leader of the Death Maidens. Petite, with hair the color of burnished copper, Greta and I bore the same tattoos, only hers were far older and more brilliant.

Emblazoned on our foreheads were onyx crescents, hers burning with a vivid flame. Mine sparkled a glistening black most of the time. An intricate lacework of black and orange leaves wound up our forearms. Hers were vivid. Mine had started as a pale shadow but now were nearing a similar intensity.

Patiently standing a few steps behind me, Greta waited as I contemplated the house. I was dressed in a flowing robe similar to hers, though mine wasn't sheer. I absently toyed with the tasseled belt girding my waist as I gauged the timing. This would be my fifth kill in the past month— or *oblition*, as it was called in Haseofon—and this time, I was on my own. Greta was merely supervising.

I'd been on a fast track the past eight weeks, spending a lot of time in Haseofon, the temple of the Death Maidens, learning to fight on the astral where we worked. And I'd been taking a high dose of the *panteris phir*, or Panther's Fang, to gain better control over my shifting into the black panther side of myself.

I was surprised the latter had been working so well, considering how little control I still had over shifting into my Tabby self. Greta told me that since Panther was a gift from the Autumn Lord rather than something I was born with, my half-human heritage wasn't a stumbling block to controlling the ability.

Now, I closed my eyes, listening for that internal sensor that would tell me the exact moment in which to move in. A pause . . . I lowered myself below my conscious thoughts, deep into my subconscious. And then I heard it.

Five . . . four . . . three . . . two . . . one . . . There it was, echoing in the corner of my mind. The gentle chiming of a clock as it counted down the last moments of Gerald Hanson's life. The clock—or sensor—was my guide, urging me on, directing me when to move in, at what precise moment to grapple with Gerald's soul and send it spinning into oblivion.

The only thing I knew about Gerald at this moment was that he was a lawyer, and his life was forfeit to keep the balance. Grandmother Coyote had called in a favor from the Autumn Lord, and Hi'ran had specifically directed that *I* be the one to take care of this. For whatever reason, I was to be the Death Maiden who attended his departure.

I glanced back at Greta. She remained impassive, waiting for my move, so I set out for the ravine and she followed me. We raced through the etheric winds as if we were meteors, shooting through the sky.

Movement on the astral still confused me, although I'd been here a number of times, but I was slowly getting used to it. And here it was that the Death Maidens paid their victims their last visits—on a tiny sliver of one of the astral planes reserved for our work and our work alone.

We were the last people our victims would ever see, the last faces they would know. Some, we escorted to glory and to great rewards for their courage and bravery. For others, we were the harbingers of doom, the final hand of judgment. And we could not be denied. We sent the latter into the churning pool of primal force, where their souls were cleansed, purged, and reborn as pure energy ready for use.

Gerald Hanson would be among the latter.

As the clock ticked down the last minutes of Gerald's life, I walked through the walls of his house, followed by Greta, until I was standing beside him. He wouldn't see me until it was too late.

Technically, I wasn't the one who would kill him. Oh, to the outer world, it would appear that Gerald Hanson had died of a sudden, massive stroke. In reality, the Hags of Fate would cut his cord that they had spun since his birth and that severing blow would trigger the stroke. Whatever sins Gerald had committed, they were great enough to earn him a one-way ticket into oblivion. His soul was so tainted that it could not be allowed to continue on the eternal cycle.

I stood beside him, waiting. There was no one else in the house except a little dog who was asleep on the sofa. The beagle would be well-cared for. I'd call Chase after I finished to make certain. This case—along with whatever notifications were necessary—would fall under the jurisdiction of the Faerie-Human Crime Scene Investigation (FH-CSI) unit. The FH-CSI would be involved because Gerald Hanson wasn't human. He was part werewolf—a fourth, if you wanted to quibble, but still enough to earn him a spot on the rolls of the Supe Community registers.

As the final seconds ticked down, I stepped forward, standing in front of him. A pause, then *three . . . two . . . one . . .* and Gerald clutched his chest, looking confused. I waited until he spasmed again, then went limp. As his body slumped on the sofa, his spirit rose to stand in front of me. At first, he looked confused, but then he saw me and jumped back.

"Where . . . who are you? What . . .?" He glanced back at his body and a slow look of understanding crossed his face. As he turned back to me, I moved in.

I grabbed his arm, and we vanished into a place where there existed only the swirl of mist and fog, as a thin silver crescent hung high overhead against the backdrop of stars. There was nothing familiar here, at least not to Gerald. There was nothing to comfort, nor to soothe fear or offer hope. Here, there was merely the whisper of vapor that flowed around us, and the cold shimmer of the stars. We stood there, between the worlds, and before he could speak I clutched both of his shoulders. His memories began to flow into my own, and I saw through his eyes.

Flash . . . A long hall stretched out in front of Gerald. On either side stood rows of cells. Cages with iron bars. The hallway was dimly lit and smelled like urine and feces. The faint sound of whimpering echoed through the air, but the smile on Gerald's face belied the blackness in his heart. As he started down the passage, a lovely Fae woman knelt in the center of one of the cells, her hands pressed over her face. As she heard Gerald's footsteps, she looked up, a plea filling her luminous eyes, but he snorted, and moved on. The woman would fetch a pretty penny, and there were plenty more like her out there. And plenty of men waiting to buy them . . .

Flash . . . Gerald sat behind a desk—a large oak affair that dripped with money and prestige. He was fiddling with a brief, but as he looked out the window, his cell phone rang. A man's voice on the other end of the line erupted in rough laughter.

"Number sixty-five needs a replacement. He broke his toy, *again*, and is willing to pay an extra fifty grand to find one who can take the wear and tear. You have one week."

As Gerald pressed the End Call button, he stared out the window, a faint smile crossing his lips . . . he loved his work. He truly loved his work.

Flash . . . Two men climbed into the limo, taking the seat opposite Gerald. One of them looked sullen; the other, afraid. Gerald rolled up the privacy window, cutting off the driver, then offered them a drink. As the men accepted the glasses and sipped, he leaned forward, waiting.

After a moment, he spoke. "I told you to handle the entire family. You *didn't handle the entire family* and now you've compromised our work." His voice was steely.

The taller of the pair shifted uncomfortably. "We don't do kids. I told you that in the beginning."

"And *I* told you what was at stake. I had to send in someone to correct your mistake. That wasn't a good way to conclude our business deal."

The smaller man began to shake and dropped his drink as he collapsed. The other man looked at Gerald, frantically clutching his throat, but within seconds, he followed suit.

The limo stopped, and Gerald opened the window again to speak to the driver. "Take us to the Cove. We've got a delivery to make." And with that, he settled back, opened a new bottle of bourbon, and carefully poured himself a glass as the car silently glided through the night.

I pulled myself out of his mind. The images were confusing, but the feeling behind them was a darkness driven by avarice. The desire for money, the desire for power. And the willingness to do *anything* to get it.

Repelled, I gazed into Gerald's eyes. He was scum, worse than scum, and I'd seen enough to know he'd buy and sell people without a second thought.

Nervous, he looked over his shoulder. "Where am I? How do I wake up?"

Ah . . . so he still didn't realize he was actually dead.

"You're on a one-way trip, Gerald. Time to let it go,

dude. Just consider me your angel of death." Before he
could do more than whimper, I laid my hands on him—
holding him so firmly that he couldn't get away.

He struggled, pleading, but his words fell useless. This
was my mission, and whatever mercy or empathy I might
possess vanished as my training kicked in. His spirit was
no match for my strength.

"Fires of the void, come forth to do my bidding. Cleanse
this soul and pass it through your center." The rite was second nature now—the ritual engrained in the core of my
being. Greta had taken me through the rites again and
again, and this time, I was doing it on my own, without any
help from her.

Gerald let out a sharp scream. "Please, don't—I don't
understand."

I let out a sigh. This was the part that confounded me.
They never understood—the ones who had been horrendous and brutal. They never understood the nature of cause
and effect—that actions brought consequences. How they
couldn't see this escaped me, but then again, if I had no
conscience, perhaps I wouldn't understand it either.

"Gerald Hanson, you sealed your destiny by your
actions. The Hags of Fate have made their decree. The
Harvestmen have agreed. Prepare to face the darkness of
the abyss."

I closed my eyes, summoning the karmic fire. A purple
flame washed over us, raging through his soul, crackling
through the mist and fog to electrify his energy. A wisp of
ash flew up from his aura, and then another, and then—
with a loud chatter of static, the flames raced through his
spirit, reducing it to harmless dust. Another moment, and
Gerald Hanson ceased to exist, forever obliterated. His
soul had been consigned to the final death. Only a fine
layer of ash remained poised for a second, then it, too, blew
away into the night.

I watched the astral wind sweep away the remnants of
everything Gerald had ever been, throughout all of his
lives, all of his cycles. The only thing left was a harmless,

benign energy. No trace remained of the person he'd been, no sign of the lives he'd lived. And then, with a final, silent *whoosh*, the lingering energy spiraled up and then returned to the central pool from which all things sprang.

As always, I felt oddly hollow, like a reed in the wind, bending but not breaking. Mournful, plaintive, but accepting of my place in this world.

I closed my eyes, willing Gerald's memories to fade, although I knew I would never be able to forget them. Death Maidens never forgot any of their kills, Greta told me, even when they numbered into the thousands. Everyone we took out remained as part of our own memories. We were historians, of a sort.

While his thoughts didn't make much sense to me at this point, I knew there was some reason the Autumn Lord had commanded me to be Gerald's doom. I wasn't sure what it was yet, but I had the uneasy feeling that, soon enough, I'd find out.

For now, I was stick-a-fork-in-me done. Turning my back on the ever-present mist and fog of this realm, I leaped back to where Greta waited. I hoped to hell we were done for the night.

Greta slipped her arm through mine as we journeyed back to Haseofon, the abode of the Death Maidens. She was so much shorter than me that it gave us a Mutt-and-Jeff look, but there, any resemblance ceased.

"You did very well. You've adapted quickly." She smiled up at me and I felt a tinge of pride. "Next time, I won't need to go with you. You're graduating, Delilah, although I'll always be here if you need me."

"I've tried." I pressed my lips together.

"You've done better than I hoped you would, and you've learned quickly. I'm proud of you."

At first, I'd freaked out when I realized that I'd been conscripted into the Autumn Lord's rule as one of his Death Maidens. But over the past couple of years my

naïveté had slipped away little by little. Oh, I'd stubbornly
clung to my eternal optimism, to the little girl/kitty cat
who didn't want to grow up. But when Shade, my fiancé,
had come into the picture, things began to shift. Half
shadow dragon, half Stradolan—shadow walker—Shade
existed in the realms of spirits and ghosts. Through being
with him, I'd finally grown used to the energy.

And over the past few months, I'd decided to embrace
the woman I was becoming, rather than long for the woman
I'd been.

Truth was: I felt proud to be pledged to the Autumn
Lord. I was his only *living* Death Maiden, and I was destined to bear his child one day, through Shade as the proxy
father. I could never again be the Delilah who first came
over from Otherworld. And *that* was okay. I didn't have to
give up believing in people, I didn't have to give up simple
joys and happiness or Cheetos or my undying fan-girl love
of Jerry Springer.

Instead, I fell into a comfortable balance.

"Are we done for the night?" I glanced at the cityscape
that unfolded in front of us. Though we were traveling on
the astral, we were close to my own world—the streets of
Seattle. Both realms were superimposed on one another. I'd
gotten used to that, too, and could see them both when I
didn't get too caught up in trying to figure out the logic of it.

Greta nodded. "Did you want to come back to Haseofon
to visit Arial?"

I thought about it. It would be good to see my sister—
my twin who had died at birth—but then I thought about
Camille and Menolly. They were waiting for me to return.
And the promise of a mug of hot milk and some chocolate
chip cookies was enough to make my decision for me.

"Not tonight, but tell her I love her and I'll see her soon."
I paused. "Greta, do you know why the Autumn Lord
asked for me specifically? To annihilate Gerald?"

She shook her head. "No, I truly don't. But he was very
insistent. He said it had to be you, and he said that Grandmother Coyote had come to him personally to request it.

The Harvestmen, they bow to the whims of the Hags of Fate. As does every creature."

Pulling away, she reached up and stroked my face. "Your crescent—it burns with the fires of Haseofon tonight. You made your first totally assigned kill without any assistance. And so your crescent has shifted and now the Autumn Lord's fires will forever burn brightly within it."

I reached up to finger the tattoo. I couldn't feel much change, but then again, I was used to wearing Hi'ran's sigil on my forehead. But once again, a fierce sense of pride swept through me.

"Thank you, Greta. For your help and your friendship."

She laughed, sounding like a schoolgirl rather than the ancient and fiercesome force that she was. And then, without another word, she vanished, and I willed myself home, and opened my eyes to find myself curled in my cat bed.

Blinking, I realized that I'd gone out of body while still in my tabby form. I yawned, arching my back up into Halloween-cat pose. I was in my favorite bed. Shaped like a tiger, with a striped tiger face and tail, the cushion was soft and warm. Iris had bought it for me.

From my vantage on the living room floor, I could see her sitting in the rocking chair, looking like an angry beached whale. Iris was two weeks overdue, pregnant with twins, and we were all tiptoeing around her. Roz was sitting next to her, trying to make her smile.

Camille was curled up on the sofa, next to Trillian, her alpha husband, and behind them, Smoky—yet another husband (out of three) leaned over their shoulders. They were poring intently through the pages of one of those huge coffee-table books, arousing my curiosity. But in cat form, I couldn't read the title.

Vanzir was huddled over the controls to the Xbox, and other than that, the room was empty. Menolly was off at work, I knew that much, but didn't have a clue as to where Morio, Hanna, Nerissa, Bruce, or my fiancé Shade was.

I crept out of my bed, stretched again, and flipped my tail high into the air. I loved the luxuriousness of being *cat*. My fur was long and silky, golden with faint stripes running through it, and when I shifted form, my clothes transformed into the blue collar around my neck. Iris had hung a bell on it, which annoyed the hell out of me and put an end to my bird chasing. Well, bird *catching*. I still chased. I couldn't help it, it was my nature.

I stopped in front of the fire to lick one of my paws, then shook my head and stepped delicately away from the nearest chair, giving myself room to transform. As I shifted, paws lengthening into arms, back arching, shifting, changing, transforming back to my two-legged state, I became aware of an ache in my lower back where I'd been training hard during the week. And the bruises throbbed where I'd tripped over a log in the forest while out on a run with Shade. I took my natural form, slowly rising to my feet.

"Welcome back, Delilah." Iris gave me a weary smile.

"Did you have a good nap, Kitten?" Camille asked, setting the book aside. Now I could see that it was a compendium of photographs from Finland, one that Iris had received as a wedding present back in February.

I yawned, then sat on one of the ottomans, pulling my legs up to wrap my arms around my shins. Leaning my chin on my knees, I frowned. "I didn't exactly nap. Greta came for me."

"That's right—you mentioned she might be summoning you again." Camille perked up. "That's five times in the past two weeks. Did you get to see Arial?"

I shook my head. "No, I decided to come back here instead. Tonight, I was assigned a target on my own. Greta supervised, but this time it was all up to me."

I glanced at her. If anybody understood, it would be Camille. She'd been through hell over the past year, and she'd been delving deeply into Death Magic with her other husband, Morio. She'd been playing in the dark a lot lately.

"On your *own*? How did it go?" Her violet eyes were

flecked with silver and I realized they'd been that way a lot lately, the further she dipped into the magic, and into her training as a priestess of the Moon Mother.

"I did what I needed to. But there was something odd. I don't understand yet, but I think you guys should know." And so I told them how I'd been specifically assigned Gerald's kill, and what I had seen when I looked into his mind.

"That's disturbing, but I don't see how it affects us, to be honest. We don't know where all of this happened, or who the woman is, or even what the hell is going on." She paused. "File it away for future reference. Meanwhile, Father called us through the Whispering Mirror. We've been summoned back to Otherworld tomorrow night for a war meeting. We leave here as soon as Menolly wakes up. And we're to bring Chase with us. And Sharah."

I frowned. "Why can't they just tell us what they need to through the Whispering Mirror?"

"Because something's up. I can always tell. Father gets those little pursed lines around his lips. No, we have to go and they want all five of us there. Shade said he'd come, and Trillian. The others will stay here to guard the house." Camille frowned.

"We really have to do something about the security situation here." It had become problematic, especially as our enemies grew more powerful.

"I agree. It's fine to leave some of the guys at home but we need to be able to head out in full force, especially now that Iris is about ready to pop." Even though Camille said it affectionately, Iris flashed her an irritated look.

"Girl, if I don't give birth to this pair soon, I'll be ballistic enough to rain terror over the entire city. I swear, these children are already plaguing me, still in the womb." Iris rubbed her stomach, letting out an exasperated sigh. "I'm two weeks overdue and these young ones are kicking up a storm. If they don't birth themselves soon, I'm going to forcibly evict them."

I stifled a laugh. During Iris's pregnancy, she had

become a volatile bundle of hormones. Everybody was crossing fingers it would be over and done with soon, but I suspected Bruce suffered the most.

Their house was snug as a bug, a two-story, four-bedroom cottage with plenty of room for the children—and others—when they started to grow. The guys had put the finishing touches on during the late summer months, and it was a hop and a skip away from ours. Iris and Bruce were firmly ensconced within it, but several times a week, they—or sometimes just Iris when Bruce was preparing for a lecture the next day—would join us for the evening.

I kissed her on the forehead. "It won't be much longer."

"And just what do you know about babies? How many have *you* had?"

Oh, she was grumpy, all right. I backtracked, fast. "You're right. I just hope for all our sakes that they make an appearance soon."

That brought a smile to her lips, and she ducked her head.

"Bruce has taken to hiding in the study after dinner, so I know he's feeling my temper, too." She let out a long sigh. "It will be over soon. Then I'll have two babies to raise and I'll get irate about other things." With a rueful smile, she leaned back in the rocker and closed her eyes.

I reached out and brushed the hair from her face. "Would you like me to brush your hair?" When I was in tabby form, I loved having my fur brushed. It was relaxing and I had the feeling, with the amount of hair our sprite had, she might just like it, too.

Iris gave me a quizzical look, then nodded. "Thank you. I'd like that."

Camille fished through her purse and handed me a brush as I gently removed the numerous pins and clips holding Iris's ankle-length golden hair in the coils that wrapped around her head.

"Sit, little mama." I pointed to the ottoman. She settled herself, with a little help from Camille, and I sat in the chair behind her and softly began to brush the long strands. After a moment, Iris let out a long, slow breath and her shoulders slumped gratefully. I took my time, sleeking over the glimmering tresses, thinking about my own hair. It had been long once, down to the middle of my back.

Should I grow it out again? But I'd changed so much, and my new style—short and spiky—fit the new me. No, long hair would be reserved for when I was in tabby form, and my tail plumed out in a delightful puff. Content, I returned my focus to Iris, and gave her a little scalp and shoulder massage in addition to the brushing. After about fifteen minutes, I gathered her hair back in a ponytail, looping it up so that it wouldn't trip her when she walked. She sighed, leaning back with a grateful smile and I hugged her.

"That felt marvelous. Thank you, Kitten. I really appreciate it."

I took a moment to put in a quick call to Chase about Gerald's dog. He wasn't there, so I left a message. As I hung up, the doorbell rang.

Camille answered. When she returned, she had a strange look on her face. Behind her followed a cowled woman in a long gray cloak. My blood chilled. Grandmother Coyote. And this time, she had come to *us*.

The Hags of Fate wove destiny, and they unraveled it. They measured out the cords and they cut them. They balanced good with evil, evil with good, order with chaos, and chaos with order. And, along with the Elemental Lords and the Harvestmen, they were the only true Immortals. They had existed long before the world had begun, and they would exist long after it ended.

That she appeared elderly was an understatement. Grandmother Coyote was both ancient and timeless. Her face mirrored a topography of ridges and lines, wrinkles on wrinkles, and yet she was beyond the scope of time, emerging from the very void to which the Death Maidens sent souls to be renewed and reused. Age was a misnomer, having no bearing on Grandmother Coyote because she was one of the few true Immortals. Though she looked like an old woman, she was so far from human that there was no comparison.

Iris paused, a hint of fear in her eyes. "Grandmother Coyote—what brings you here?" The fear was palpable in her voice.

Grandmother Coyote knelt down to gaze into Iris's eyes. "Be not afraid, young Talon-haltija. I am not here on your account. You have nothing to fear from me. Run now, to your home, and rest. The destinies of those who lie within your womb are only beginning, and you must have the strength and energy to run after them as they grow. There is greatness within you, and you, yourself, are as yet unrealized as to your place in the world. Be at peace."

A look of relief washed over Iris's face and she curtseyed, then glanced at Camille and mouthed "Later" before waddling out of the living room.

Camille motioned to a chair. "Won't you sit down?"

Grandmother Coyote lowered herself into the chair, leaning her walking stick against the arm. "I will not bother myself with chatter." A crinkle in her face substituted for a smile. "But I *will* accept a cup of tea. Camille, fetch me one."

Camille curtseyed, then hurried to the kitchen. I heard her fumbling around with the china and realized she was as nervous as I was. Grandmother Coyote never paid social calls, so whatever brought her to us had to be serious.

"Where is my grandson—so to speak?"

"Morio's off training," Smoky said.

I remained silent. The Hags of Fate spoke on their own time, according to their own agendas. It would do us no good to ask why she was here and I knew it. Like all cats, I could be patient when needed.

Smoky also seemed alert, on his guard. Trillian stood near the door, waiting for instructions. Vanzir put down the game controller and pushed himself off the floor, dusting his hands on his pants as he leaned against the arm of the sofa and nodded to Grandmother Coyote.

As Camille brought the tea in, Trillian took the tray from her and set it on the coffee table. He poured, as we gathered around. Grandmother Coyote accepted the cup and sipped the steaming liquid. Then, with a deep breath, she inhaled the fragrance. Finally, she set the tea cup on a coaster on the table next to the chair and looked around the room, her gaze falling on Camille.

"You cannot get rid of Rodney, my girl, as much as you want to. He's important. I know how much you hate him, but you have no choice. Unleash him at the right moment and he may save your life."

Camille gulped. I knew how much she hated the freaka-zoid bone golem that thought of himself as the love child between Rodney Dangerfield and Howard Stern—we all did—but she said nothing, merely nodding.

Another moment, and Grandmother Coyote cocked her head, turning slowly to look at the others. "Clear out. I need to talk to Camille and Delilah. Alone."

Oh joy. Just what we wanted to hear. "Are you sure they can't stay? You know they'll just find out later anyway."

"Of course they will, and you will be the ones to tell them. But for now, men, retire to the kitchen and do not return till you are summoned. And do not answer the door. I need to talk to Delilah, especially."

"Me?" *Oh, lovely.* Usually, when Grandmother Coyote had something to say, it was to Camille, but apparently she'd said all she had to say to my sister with the warning about Rodney. At least for the night.

"Yes, *you*." She waited while the guys silently cleared out of the room. They knew better than to argue with one of the Hags of Fate.

When they were gone, she continued. "While this matter will concern all of you, Delilah, you are the one who stands at the fulcrum this time—you will be the key to unraveling what you need to know when it is time. A balance has been upset and must be righted."

As she paused, a scratching sounded at the front door.

"What the fuck—" Camille moved toward the foyer but Grandmother Coyote stopped her.

"Halt. I brought visitors. They are here on my summons. You will meet them in a few moments." She paused again, then yawned. Her teeth were steely, cold and metallic, sharp as blades, looking like they could gnash bone into shrapnel. And I had no doubt they could—and perhaps they had.

A chill ran down my spine. I had the feeling that my work with Greta tonight had something to do with what Grandmother Coyote was talking about.

"What do you need me for?"

Grandmother Coyote touched her nose. "This cannot be discussed without me introducing my comrades. But you are correct in your silent surmise. This matter relates to your training as a Death Maiden—I cannot tell you how, yet, but know that it does. Secondly, this matter involves daemonic energies in the city *not* connected with Shadow Wing." At that, she nodded to the hallway. "Go now, let in my pets."

Daemonic . . . that wasn't good. But at least, daemons and demons didn't get along so well and were rarely on the same side. Which meant this might not have to do with Shadow Wing, the Demon Lord we were fighting.

I moved to the door, wondering who was waiting outside. It could be a troll or a goblin or a centaur or—just about anything. Knowing Grandmother Coyote, *anybody* could be on the other side. My stomach lurching, I yanked open the door.

There, on the porch, like stone statues come to life, stood two gargoyles. And they didn't look happy.

Chapter 2

❦⬦❦

I stared at the gargoyles. It had been a long, long time since I'd seen an adult gargoyle who wasn't in stasis. Back in Otherworld, they roamed free, unless they'd been captured. Since certain governments and individuals enslaved them to use them as spies, the gargoyles tended to steer clear of cities.

Woodland gargoyles—like our little Maggie—were seldom captured for this purpose, both because of their coloration and because they took refuge in the forest, hiding from those who would enslave them. Maggie would never be able to freeze into statue form—her race didn't have that ability.

But these gargoyles were of a different breed. Known as *granticular* gargoyles, they were able to enter stasis for centuries at a time, during which they would observe what was going on and feed that information to their masters. That they resented most of their slavers was well-known, but I had no clue how they felt about working for the Hags of Fate.

Large Cryptos, when they were full-grown they stood the size of a burro, with wings stretching out a good six to seven feet each side of their body. Like a dragon's wings, they were strong, though flight was magically powered. But they weren't ornamental—both dragons and gargoyles used them to steer and steady themselves in the air.

I stood back, allowing them room to enter. Folding their wings back, they maneuvered through the door, jockeying through the opening. They weren't exactly bipedal, but walked like gorillas on their back feet while they balanced with their front knuckles. As they silently passed by me, one of them looked up, into my eyes, and I fell into the dark brown depths. There was age there, and wisdom, and a long hint of sadness that touched me to the core.

I reached out, lightly running my fingers over the muscular shoulder that resembled moving stone. The gargoyle's gray skin was smooth, almost like velvet, but beneath the surface rippled flesh strong enough to break necks and bend bars and tear apart small trees. One of them gazed at me for just a moment, and let out a soft "hmm" before following his companion into the living room. A moment later, I joined them.

Grandmother Coyote stood waiting and the gargoyles moved to flank her sides. She draped a light hand on either back, and was speaking in a low, guttural tongue that I did not recognize. One of the gargoyles—the one I'd connected with—nodded to her.

She looked around the room. "What do you know about the granticular gargoyles?"

"Only what they taught us in school," Camille said. She did not mention Maggie, our baby calico woodland gargoyle. We kept her our secret as best as we could. We had too many enemies to let news of her trickle out. And while Grandmother Coyote knew about Maggie, we weren't sure what the granticular gargoyles would do if they realized we were keeping a baby at our house. Cryptos didn't always get along with each other and we weren't about to let anybody try to hurt her, or to take her away from us.

"Then you know the story that Y'Elestrial officials spoon-feed their subjects to keep the truth silent. Actually, it's not just your home city-state's doing. Only in Dahns-burg and some of the darker forests in Otherworld will you find the facts openly discussed. However, due to various treaties, King Uppala-Dahns has kept speculation to a minimum, even though it compromises the granticulars' lives. *Politics*." The word rolled off Grandmother Coyote's tongue with a sneer.

"So what *don't* we know?" I had the feeling we were about to find out something we didn't want to know, but since that was par for the course in our lives, why should this time be any different?

"Over the eons, the governments over in Otherworld have embarked on a clandestine operation to systemati-cally enslave the gargoyle race by suppressing the truth about their lineage and natures." Grandmother Coyote's eyes were dark and deep, shifting with flecks of the magic. When I looked at her long enough, I began to see through the age, through the body, into the immensity that lay beyond the surface.

She turned to the gargoyle on her left. "This is Mithra. He was born a prince in his world, until Lethesanar en-slaved him."

Lethesanar had been the queen of Y'Elestrial until her sister Tanaquar deposed her. She had been ethically devoid, an opium addict, a slave to her whims and emotions. Tanaquar was marginally better.

Camille curtseyed and I bowed to the gargoyle. We'd been raised to show respect to authority. Mithra looked surprised.

"You do not have to do that," he said, and his voice—guttural in his own language—was surprisingly soft in ours. "You are under no obligation to recognize our heri-tage. When we were captured, we lost the keys to our king-dom, to use a human expression."

"We *choose* to honor your birthright." Camille frowned, looking confused.

I knew what she was thinking. We'd been taught that gargoyles didn't have a strongly developed sense of intellect—that the Cryptos were, instead, like extremely smart animals who could talk. But Mithra's cadence, his very nature, spoke of a high acumen.

Grandmother Coyote cleared her throat. "Everything you were taught—at least about the intelligence level of gargoyles—is a lie. It was devised to allow the governments to keep control over the race, and to use them for their own ends."

I glanced at Mithra. He and his companion nodded. "But why hasn't this come out before? Why are the lies perpetuated?"

"Think of all the intelligence that the gargoyle race has gathered for the various governments back in Otherworld over the years. And what you do not realize—not till now, that is—is that there are secret societies over here, Earthside, who also know this and who also make use of it. They've had contracts in place with OW emissaries to buy gargoyles for their own uses."

"Why doesn't your race rebel?" Camille turned to Mithra. "Why allow this to go on?"

Mithra let out what sounded like a long sigh, but it came in a flutter of wings, the sound of wind howling through a stone arch. "We are too few. All gargoyles—combined species— do not make up a tenth of Y'Elestrial's population. We are rare. While we live long lives, as long as the Fae, we breed at a much slower rate. We are born ten males to every female, and a female may have one litter during her life, if she's lucky. Unless she's captive, used as a breeding machine."

Maggie's mother sprang to mind. She'd been held in the Subterranean Realms, as far as we knew, used to breed babies like our Maggie for demon food.

Gesturing to his friend, Mithra said, "This is my companion, Astralis. He and I were on a scouting mission for our father when we were captured. He is my brother, although I was the heir to the throne."

I considered what he said. It made sense—when you belonged to a race whose existence hinged on a small number of females, and when the population of your race was limited, it didn't make sense to wage war on your oppressors if you weren't systematically being destroyed.

"So you do your best to evade your captors, and to preserve your race." I met Mithra's gaze again and he nodded.

"We cannot change the thinking of an entire world without proving the governments who instill that mind-set wrong. And *that* task is, I'm afraid, more than we have the ability to tackle. As it is, we do our best to keep the entrance to our city warded so strongly that no one may enter." The look on his face spoke volumes.

"Has Y'Elestrial—or any other government—threatened to invade you before? To enslave all of your people?" Camille asked. While we knew the Court and Crown was corrupt, this was more than disconcerting. "I'm surprised it hasn't happened already, given what you're telling us."

Astralis shook his head. "If they were to do so, our actual natures might come to attention and they would not be able to keep the status quo. So they capture us, here and there, promising to leave the females alone. In return, our father looks the other way when they harvest."

Camille and I glanced at each other. This was hard to swallow, but given the nature of politics, I wasn't surprised. Saddened, but no longer surprised. Yeah, the naïve little girl was gone.

"Mithra and Astralis were harvested by Lethesanar years ago and pressed into service. King Virgil, their father, protested but the Opium Eater threatened to kill off the queen if he spoke too loudly. Since there were other children in the litter, he relented." Grandmother Coyote's lip twitched. "I approached her sometime back with an offer she dared not refuse. I freed them from her tyranny, but asked them to stay for a few years working for me, because I sensed a disturbance and wanted someone to watch over the matter."

"And now, Grandmother Coyote has freed us to return to our homeland after we tell you what we've discovered." The stone-solid countenance on Mithra's face softened and I thought I could detect a smile. "We have not seen our

family, or our city, in over eight hundred years. We were
first set to watch over Europe, then brought to this land a
hundred years ago."

"Lethesanar wanted eyes in the new world, and she
wanted them over here in this city." Astralis let out a soft
huff. "We were her most reliable. If we didn't fall in line,
she threatened to wipe out the royal family. Now, she is
gone, and we are free. Once we reach our city, neither of us
will ever set foot outside the boundaries again."

"Will you be able to reach home without a problem?"
The thought that they might be caught on their way home
set my stomach to churning, but I could see it happening,
all too easily.

Grandmother Coyote eased my worries. "Never you
concern yourself, young cat. I will make certain they
return home without incident. Now, before I ask them to
tell you what they have discovered, let me set the background of this tale for you."

Grandmother Coyote motioned for us to make ourselves
comfortable. As we settled into our seats, the gargoyles
leaned back, squatting on their haunches like I'd seen Maggie do a hundred times. Their wings were delicately tucked
back, folded to be out of the way, and when they stood still,
they looked made of the same stone of the buildings over
which they watched.

"Over one hundred years ago, a man named Michael
Farantino arrived in Seattle. He came from Italy, and he
was human. He was also rich. And he knew about Weres,
vamps, and other creatures. He also knew how to contact
demons and other creatures from the Sub-Realms. He did
so for his own gain, selling his services to the highest bid-
der. There are many things humans can do to benefit
Demonkin. Eventually, he built what is now one of the oldest buildings in Seattle. The Farantino Building. Once a
brick walk-up, now it's been modernized and turned into
office space. I felt it needed watching over."

"So I went to Lethesanar. Your former queen was deep in
the throes of her addiction and not amenable to my visit, but

as I said, she dared not refuse me." Here, Grandmother Coyote smiled, sending chills down my spine. Her steel teeth gleamed and I couldn't imagine anybody standing up to her. The Opium Eater must have been stoned out of her mind.

Apparently Grandmother Coyote thought so, too, for she laughed and shook her head. "She only protested for a little time. It did not take me long to convince her of the wisdom of bowing to my demands. I insisted she give me control over Mithra and Astralis. I chose them because I knew that eventually, they would need to return to their home in order for the balance in their city-state to return to normal. In the end, the Opium Eater had no choice. She did not like it, but her whims were not—and are not—my concern. By the by, remember, Lethesanar still lives. Never forget that—for she has a long memory for those who helped cross her."

A sly smile crept across her face and I caught sight of the predator that lurked within her. Not predator . . . no. *Instigator. Judge, jury, and executioner.* Grandmother Coyote was not afraid of her power.

"I replaced two of the statues on the building with the brothers, and told them to keep watch, to note the changes in energy, and there they have stayed these past eighty years and more. Until two nights ago, when the balance began to shift even further, and it became necessary to act." Here, she stopped.

Mithra cleared his throat. "My brother and I have done as requested. We've kept watch on the building and the comings and goings within. Over the years, there has been a steady increase of what we first thought of as demonic energy. It infused the aura of the structure, and during the past three years, that growth has been disturbing."

Astralis nodded. "Two nights ago, the strength of that energy grew again—so much so that we contacted Grandmother Coyote. Something big is waking. Something that could rock the city and surrounding areas. The entire building was being infused with demonic energy. *Or so we thought.* But we were mistaken. When the shift occurred, we realized that rather than Demonkin, the building's aura is infused with energy from the *daemonic* realms."

Grandmother Coyote nodded. "I'd first thought they were possibly in cahoots with Shadow Wing, but apparently not."

Daemons. She was right. Most of the daemons detested the Demon Lord's attempt to rule them. In fact, we were in unwilling cahoots with Trytian, one of the leaders in the daemonic realm who was over here, Earthside, leading a resistance faction against him. We didn't like him, or trust him. But like it or not, we needed his help, and the help of his kind.

When my sisters and I first were sent ES—Earthside—by the OIA—Otherworld Intelligence Agency, we knew we had been exiled to the backwoods. We had always done our best, but none of us was ever up for employee of the year, and Camille's boss had a long-time vendetta against her. He was determined to run her out. Thanks to his grudges against her, we *all* became targets.

One of the reasons we weren't so hot at our jobs was that we're half-Fae, half-human, and because of our mixed lineage, our powers can be erratic. Meaning, we fuck up a lot.

Sephreh ob Tanu, our father—full OW Fae—was a member of the Guard Des'Estar for most of his life. Back around the middle of World War II, on an ES mission in Spain, he met Maria D'Artigo, who was as human as they come. Sephreh fell head over heels in love with her, and swept her home to Otherworld, where they married, had us kids, and lived happily ever after until Mother fell from a horse and broke her neck, which ended any idea of Cinderella stories for the three of us girls. She left our father a widower and the three of us motherless at an early age.

Camille, the oldest, took over and did her best to guide Menolly and me, even though she was scarcely old enough to run a household. It was she who first knew our mother had died, and I don't think our father ever forgave her for playing the part of the messenger.

A Moon Witch and priestess, she's married to three

alpha men—a dragon shifter named Smoky, a youkai-kitsune named Morio, and Trillian, a Svartan—one of the dark and charming Fae. They make one hell of a powerful quartet. With raven black hair and violet eyes, Camille is hot. *Curvy pinup woman hot.* Busty, with hips, and thighs that could crush steel, she sports a wardrobe that would furnish half the fetish bars in Seattle and has an easy self-confidence that I've always envied. She is the owner of the Indigo Court Bookshop—which, like all of our "jobs," was the cover the OIA gave her when we first came Earthside. She loves it, though, even though she doesn't have much time to hang out there.

Menolly, the youngest, is the petite one. She barely tops five one and her hair color was—and still is—a mystery. Nobody in our family ever had the bright burnished copper she does. She wears it in cornrows beaded with ivory because the sound of the beads clinking together reminds her she exists. Vampires are silent creatures, and my sister is a bloodsucker.

Thirteen or so ES years ago, before we came over here, Menolly was on a mission. A *jian-tu*—or spy—she was scouting out a vampire's nest. Unfortunately, she slipped from the ceiling and landed in the middle of the vampires, which landed her in a world of pain and hurt. Dredge tortured her, raped her, carved her up, then killed her and turned her. After that, he sent her home to destroy us.

Camille managed to put a stop to his plans and Menolly spent a year in rehab, learning how to adjust to her new life. Or un-life as it may be. But we got revenge. Almost two years ago, he showed up here and we took the sucker out for good. Now, Menolly's married to a gorgeous werepuma named Nerissa, and she's also consort to Roman, a vampire lord and son of Blood Wyne, the vampire queen. And she owns the Wayfarer, the city's most happening bar. Or at least we think it is. Menolly's come a long way.

And lastly, there's me. I'm Delilah, the middle one. I'm a two-faced Were, with both tabby cat and black panther lurking inside. And, yes, I'm a Death Maiden. At six one, I'm athletic as hell, with short spiky blonde hair, and I'm engaged to a half dragon named Shade who has given me a new perspective on life. Every day I thank Bastus that Shade is in my life. And finally—finally, my sisters have quit treating me like a child. Probably because I don't act like one anymore. I ostensibly run a private eye firm above the Indigo Court Bookshop, though I seldom have time to take on cases, and I am the first to admit, I'm not the best person to hire.

As I said, when we were sent over ES, we mostly wanted to work our way back into the good graces of the OIA. And we've done just that and more: Now we *run* the Earthside division.

Along the way, we ended up smack in the middle of Shadow Wing's demonic war. Unfortunately, we are the ones standing first in line.

"And so we have a worrisome force waking." Grandmother Coyote turned to me. "I requested you be given charge of cleansing Gerald Hanson's soul for a reason, other than he's part werewolf."

I waited for it, somehow knowing what was coming. A glance at Camille's expression told me she was fast-tracking the same as me. But neither of us said a word out loud. Best not to interrupt Grandmother Coyote mid train of thought.

"Gerald Hanson owned the Farantino Building, at least for some time. And while Michael is long dead, Gerald was his great-grandson. His mother was from outside the family, of course, and she was the daughter of a werewolf and a human, which gave Gerald a few extra abilities, but he never was at the beck and call of the moon. The building is no longer in his family's possession, but they are still bound to it. And Gerald was connected to this last shift in energy. Whatever he was doing seriously upset the balance and it would have gotten worse, had he continued to live. Given all the disruption he's caused, we decided to forever eliminate him. Contrary to what is commonly believed, the

Hags of Fate are not omniscient. We know what we know, but the rest? A mystery."

"So Gerald is—was—connected to the daemonic energy." I frowned, thinking about what I'd seen in his mind. Some rough stuff, but it was hard to tell just how far it went. However, he'd upset the balance enough to get wiped out of existence, so whatever he'd done had been beyond bad.

"Yes, and I want you—and your sisters—to find out what's going on and put a stop to it. The balance is rapidly sliding out of sync and Gerald's oblition simply prolongs the inevitable. Whoever owns the Farantino Building has money and power, and movement on the web that threads through the universe indicates that he—and it *is* a he—will be making a play for more than the corner he has currently mucked out for himself."

Her voice was hushed and sent a shiver up my spine.

"You mean he's out for a power grab?"

"Yes, and whatever power he's trying to awaken can provide this for him. Unless you halt whatever lies at the core of this energy, the powers controlling Seattle will eventually fall under the reign of this veiled enemy. I can see no more than this, but it must not be allowed to happen." She stood, motioning to Mithra and Astralis. "Come. It is time to return you to your home." And with that, they swept toward the door.

The phone rang, and I picked it up as Camille saw them out.

"Is Menolly there?" The man's voice was vaguely familiar but I couldn't place it.

"No, she's at work. May I take a message?" I scanned the coffee table for a pad and pencil but there was none in sight.

After a pause and a whispered conversation on the other side of the line, the man was back. "Maybe you can help us. This is Tad, from Microsoft. You know, Menolly's friend, from the VA."

Vampires Anonymous . . . now I remembered the name. Tad, and his friend Albert, worked the night shift at Microsoft. They were vampires, and had both been turned around the same time. They managed to keep their jobs and their sanity thanks to Wade. Wade Stevens was the director of Vampires Anonymous, a self-help support group for newly minted vamps. Albert and Tad were geek boys and roomed together at the Shrouded Grove Suites, a new apartment complex specifically designed for bloodsuckers.

"What's up?" I had no clue what he might want. If it was vampire-oriented, it seemed that he'd either talk to the people at the VA, or the Seattle Vampire Nexus, or he'd just go down to consult with Menolly directly.

"We have a problem and thought maybe the three of you could help us." He sounded tongue-tied, but then again, Tad always sounded tongue-tied around women. The stereotypical geek boy.

I realized he was waiting for my response. A little irritated, I let out a sigh. "Go on."

"Can Albert and I come over? We're really worried about a friend of ours and wanted to know if you would look into it." He sounded so puppy-dog sad that I couldn't help myself.

"Meet us at the Wayfarer in twenty minutes. Menolly's there, she'll be able to join us." I could use some time on the town, anyway. And Camille would go with me, if I promised to buy her a drink.

"Thanks, Delilah." And with that, he hung up.

I turned around. "Get your coat, Camille. We have to head down to the bar. It's probably nothing but . . . you never know."

As we let the guys know we were headed for the bar, and that we'd fill them in on what Grandmother Coyote told us when we got back, my thoughts lingered over what she had said. It occurred to me that while we were out, we could stop at Carter's and see if he had any dirt on the Far-antino Building. Carter, half demon, half Titan, was a records-keeper of sorts, and if anybody would have info on this building, he would. We dropped on him unannounced too many times but he took it like a trouper.

Camille slipped into her new coat, a gothic blazer, and held up her keys. "Take my Lexus?"

I nodded. "Since my Jeep's in the shop, I think we have to."

About a week ago, my Jeep had started making knocking noises and I dropped it off at Jason's garage. I'd called today but it wasn't quite ready.

I slipped on my leather jacket and stuck my dagger in the boot sheath. I'd started carrying it there so that it wouldn't draw unwanted attention and so I'd always be ready. With as much shit as we got into, none of us felt comfortable going out unarmed. Ever since the Fae had started coming over to visit, the United States had relaxed its knife laws so we could openly carry long blades, but it still made some people uncomfortable, so I tried to be unobtrusive when I carried.

The sheath clipped neatly into the outer side of the motorcycle boots I'd picked up at the leather store. Shade had convinced me to try them, and I loved their sturdiness and badass look. They weren't high heels, but at my height, I didn't need the boost, and they would last through a number of ass-kickings. Lysanthra was a long knife but I had long legs, and so she tucked neatly into the sheath. My dagger was sentient and we were still developing a relationship.

Ready to go, we clattered down the porch steps into the rain-soaked night. Fat drops pelted down from the sky, where the crescent moon peeked out faintly from a crack in the boiling clouds. I shaded my face from the stinging droplets. The wind was whipping so hard that the rain was hitting us sideways, biting into any exposed skin. Camille winced and raced for her car with me right behind her. As she beeped the key to unlock the Lexus, I yanked open the passenger door and slid inside. She followed, seconds behind me, slamming the driver's door and fumbling to insert the key in the lock.

While our Fae heritage gave us more resistance to the elements than if we were purely human, it wasn't enough to take the edge off the night, and Camille hurried to turn on the ignition and start up the heater. The resulting air was cold, but it would warm up soon, and I pulled my jacket closed in front and zipped it up over the T-shirt I was wearing.

Camille waited for a moment to let the car warm up, then eased into the long driveway. Our house—a three-story Victorian—loomed like a Halloween house behind us, and the drive was long and wound through heavy trees and foliage on the way to the road.

We'd had the driveway paved during the summer—something we'd been reluctant to do, but it had become increasingly necessary. During the rainy season, we now had enough traffic coming and going that the road had become deeply rutted and after a few too many times getting stuck, we bit the bullet. Jonas, one of the Blue Road Tribe's werebears, had come out and done the work for us. He owned a private contracting company and we were glad to be able to throw some business his way.

As Camille guided the car along the paved drive, the rain pounded down, a driving force beating a tattoo against the roof. She glanced at me.

"You should call Carter and let him know we're on the way. But first we have to meet Tad and Albert. What do you think is going on?"

I shrugged. "Knowing them, it's probably a nonemergency. I know they're vamps but they still remind me of overgrown frat boys."

She shook her head. "Not frat boys—they aren't hip enough for that. Overgrown vidiots?"

Stifling a snicker, I tried not to laugh but I couldn't help it. "Roz and Vanzir would be just like them, if they'd been human to begin with."

Camille groaned. "No . . . Roz and Vanzir would be the frat boys who beat them up." And with that, she focused on navigating the slick roads, while I put in a call to Carter to let him know we were dropping by later.

Chapter 3

～❦～

The Wayfarer was crowded, as usual. The early focus of the inn and bar had been on OW Fae, when Menolly had been set up as an undercover agent for the OIA. But two factors had shifted the demographics.

First, Menolly now owned the Wayfarer. And second, the minute she'd been chosen by Roman to be his consort, bloodsuckers galore began to hang out at the bar. Menolly wasn't altogether thrilled with the change, but there wasn't much she could do about it. She did, however, insist on reserving the rooms in the B&B part exclusively for Otherworld Fae coming in to visit the area.

We threaded our way through the throng, up to the bar. Camille whispered something to me, but even with our heightened hearing, the noise of the crowd overwhelmed anything she was saying. I shook my head.

Menolly was on the phone, and she looked worried. By her side, Derrick Means, chief bartender and werebadger, was going at it full throttle, serving drinks right and left.

Digger, another bartender—a vampire sent by Roman to help—was also working up a sweat. Figuratively, of course.

The barstools were all taken, but I spied a booth that had just been vacated and made a beeline for it. Camille followed, motioning for Menolly to join us. As soon as she hung up, she hopped over the bar and joined us.

"Is something wrong?" By her expression, I had the feeling something was going on. "Did you get another letter?"

She shook her head. Two weeks ago, Menolly had received a letter from some law firm by the name of Vistar-Tashdey, offering a large sum of money from an unnamed client. Whoever it was wanted to buy the Wayfarer and the language had seemed semithreatening. Menolly had tossed the letter aside, but from the few times since then that she'd mentioned it, I'd gotten the impression that it had unnerved her.

"No, but . . ." She glanced around, then leaned in and lowered her voice. "I didn't want to worry you but I've received two threatening phone calls—the second just a few minutes ago."

Camille cocked her head, her gaze clouding over. "Who was it and what did they say?"

"I have no idea who it was . . . even whether it was male or female. The first time I thought it was some idiot teenager but now . . . I'm not so sure."

"What did they want?" From my vantage point, I could see Tad and Albert threading their way through the crowd. "Tad and Albert are on the way."

Menolly sucked on her lip. "Whoever it was threatened to burn down the bar and said that vamps deserved to charbroil in hell."

Before we could say a word, Tad and Albert appeared by the side of the booth. They'd already stopped at the bar for bottled blood, which they were sipping discreetly.

With a warning nod to keep silent, Menolly switched over next to us, allowing the guys to slide into the opposite seat. I glanced at Camille, who looked as worried as I felt, but this was not the time to discuss it. Tabling the threats for after our meeting, I turned to the geek squad.

The pair were unlikely looking vamps, that was for sure. Nerds to the core, they wore Microsoft T-shirts, and ripped— but clean—jeans. Slender and lithe, Tad had a ponytail that trailed down his back, touching his ass. He was soft-spoken and funny, one of those sensitive guys who would never be an alpha, but that you couldn't categorize as a beta male, either.

Albert, on the other hand, had been turned before he'd had a chance to shape up. He had a tidy beer belly on him. He sported a ponytail, too, though apparently he had just started balding when he'd been turned, so his hairline was receding. Last time we'd met him, he reminded me of the Comic Book Guy on *The Simpsons*. But this time, he seemed to have moderated his atttitude and had an almost pleasant look on his face.

They flashed us toothy grins. Their vampiric nature gave them an appealing feel and it flashed through my mind that they might actually be fun to hang out with; then I nixed that thought because even though I'd accepted my sister being a vampire, cozying up to the fangy set wasn't a good idea in general. Their glamour was all too easy to misuse and abuse.

"Hey guys," Menolly said. "How's it hanging?"

"Long and hard." Albert snorted as I blushed, but then his laugh slid away and a worried look filled his frost-colored eyes. "We have a problem."

"What's going on?" I pulled out my notebook and a pen. I always ended up typing our notes anyway, so I had finally put claim to the function of secretary for the three of us.

Tad blinked, his gaze coming to rest on my face. I recognized his expression. It was the same fear I'd felt when I was worried about one of my sisters. He leaned forward, lowering his voice.

"One of our friends has vanished. We're really worried about her." He pulled out his wallet and flipped it open, taking out a snapshot of a girl. She looked a little goth, a little geek, and was pretty in an odd sort of way. And then, as I looked closer, I knew what made her look strange. She was Fae—probably Earthside Fae.

"What's her name? Are you sure she didn't just go on vacation?" Always, always, get the mundane questions out of the way before chalking up a disappearance to foul play.

"Her name is Violet, and no, she didn't go on vacation. We're in the middle of deploying a new product. There's no way she could get time off right now. She hasn't come in to work the past two nights and I'm not going to be able to cover for her much longer. Albert dropped by her house when he left work this morning, before going home, but she didn't answer the bell."

Albert nodded. "I left a note on her door but I had to get home before the sun rose. When I dropped by again tonight before work, the note was still on the door, and still no answer. I have a key to her apartment—I feed her cat when she's out of town. So, I decided to make sure she hadn't fallen and hurt herself or something. There was no sign of her, and the cat was starving. I fed Tumpkins, and when I got to work, told Tad."

Tad cleared his throat. "That's when we decided to call you guys. We thought you might be able to find out what happened to her."

I glanced at Menolly, then Camille. "Was anything out of place? Any of her things missing?"

Albert frowned, then shook his head. "I didn't see her purse, but nothing else seemed amiss. Her bed was unmade and her nightgown was lying across the bottom. I glanced in her closet and there were two suitcases there. I suppose she could have grabbed a carry-on if she had to make a sudden trip, but she would have called me to take care of the cat."

"We're worried," Tad added. "This isn't like Violet. She's conscientious about her work, and she knows we need her. And she adores that frickin' cat. She would never let him go hungry if she could help it."

Menolly frowned. "It does sound odd. When was the last time you talked to her?"

"Near daybreak, night before last. She was at work. Last night, she was a no-show, and tonight. We're taking a long break here to come talk to you." Albert played with his bottle of blood, pushing it around in circles, the concern still washing across his face.

Camille bit into one of the pretzels from the snack bowl. "She have a boyfriend? Parents in the area? And when she left work, did she mention any problems that she'd been having?"

At the word "boyfriend" a scowl raced across Tad's face, but he shook it away. "She's been seeing some guy—his name's Tanne. He's from Germany, a writer."

"Got a last name for us?" I paused, pen waiting.

"Baum. Tanne Baum. Fir tree. Like the Christmas song. He's one of the Black Forest woodland Fae." Again, the grimace.

"You don't like him, do you?" I grinned, having a feeling the sentiment wasn't so much the Fae's nature but . . .

Tad let out a snort. "*Like* him? Not so much."

Albert gave me the faintest of grins. "He's jealous."

Even though that was a no brainer, I affected a surprised look. Camille let out a faint snicker, and Menolly stared at the ceiling.

"Jealous? And . . . why are you jealous?" Stupid question, but I knew better than to say what I was thinking, which was "You've got the hots for her, right?"

Tad shifted uncomfortably. "I . . . When Brenda broke up with me, I thought that I wouldn't ever find anybody I liked as much. But then Violet came to work in our group. I've never met anybody like her. She's vibrant, and witty. She thinks differently than any woman I've ever known. I think . . . I think I've been falling in love with her."

"Dude, you like her that much but you never asked her out?" Camille gave him a disgusted look.

"She's seeing this Tanne guy . . ." He squirmed. "I don't want to be responsible for breaking them up."

"*So what?* It's not like they're married, and besides, she's Fae. The Fae aren't monogamous by nature." With a sigh, Camille bit into another pretzel. "Humans, even when they're vampires, you guys are so uptight about sex. But, be that as it may, do you have Tanne's phone number or address?"

Tad swallowed the last of his bottled blood and wiped

his mouth, saying nothing. But Albert reached out, grabbed the notebook from me, and scribbled down both. When he handed it back, a wry smile on his face, I couldn't help but like him a little more.

"We sort of did some checking on the guy. Just to make sure he was on the up and up." Albert glanced at Tad. "Baum is what he says he is, that we know. He comes from the Black Forest and he's . . ."

"What Albert is saying is that the guy is intense, but genuine. And Camille," Tad said, looking straight at her, "if I thought I even had a *chance* of being part of her world in that way, even in a poly relationship, I'd jump for it. But I don't think she's into humans *or* vampires. When I'm around Violet, she treats me like . . . like a brilliant puppy dog. I'd have as much chance of bedding *you* as I would her."

His tone was so sad that my heart went out to him. He was willing to share, he was willing to put his heart on a silver platter, but the object of his attention had no clue and now she was missing.

Camille must have sensed it too, because she reached across the table and rested her hand on his. "You don't know that for sure, Tad. Don't underestimate yourself. You need to ask her . . . once she shows up again. She might surprise you."

Tad shrugged. "I guess. But mostly, right now, I just want to make sure she's okay. Will you guys check into this? We'd go to the police but they don't listen to vampires very much, and we want to keep this quiet until we know there's a reason to get them involved."

I glanced at Camille, who nodded. Menolly gave me the heads-up too and I turned back to Tad and Albert. "Sure. Give us what you have on her and we'll take a look around. We should go over and have a look at her place."

"I was going to take her cat home with me tonight, and leave another note for her. We can go now, if you like." Albert pulled out a ring of keys that looked hefty enough to KO a bodybuilder. He dangled them from his index finger. The next thing I knew, he winked at me.

Swallowing my surprise, I flashed him a bemused smile. "Let's go, then. You guys have rides?"

Tad nodded. "We'll meet you there, unless you want to ride with us."

Camille pulled out her keys. "Nah, we'll take my Lexus. Kitten, you have the address?"

I held up my notebook. "Right here. Let's book."

And so, we slid out of the booth. Menolly told Derrick she was going to be gone for a while, and we headed out into the night.

Menolly sat in the back while I rode shotgun with Camille. As the car eased out of the parking space, I flipped through my notes.

After a few moments, I looked up. "So, do we start with the threatening calls, or do we discuss Violet?"

"Violet," Menolly said. "I told you everything about the calls I can remember for now."

"Okay, then, we'll table the threat talk until we get home. As to Violet, if it weren't for the cat, I'd say she got bored and skipped town. The Fae don't always hold on to their possessions, especially ES Fae." Camille eased right onto East Aloha Street. "Where to from here?"

I glanced at the GPS on my phone. "When we get to Fifteenth Avenue East, turn left, then make a right onto East Garfield. Her house is located right after Garfield bends into Seventeenth."

Camille nodded, flipping the windshield wipers to high. The rain was coming down in sheets, and a crash of thunder broke through the night as lightning fractured the sky. The road was slick and traffic had slowed in response to the heavy rain, but since it was past rush hour, the streets weren't bumper-to-bumper, and following Tad's Porsche wasn't hard.

As we passed through the shops that turned into suburbs, the street began to wind and curve. The further we went, the older the houses grew; more weather-beaten but also with more character. Some of them were almost mansion-like, but they gave off an aged feel—not falling apart, but they had definitely seen the decades pass.

On Fifteenth, we passed by Volunteer Park, then as we approached Lake View Cemetery where Bruce Lee and his son Brandon were interred, we came to East Garfield Street and Camille turned right. East Garfield buttressed Interlaken Park. This was definitely a neighborhood that made perfect sense for one of the ES Fae to live in. Shortly before Auburn Place East, Tad eased into a driveway and we followed suit.

Violet's house was a cute little cottage, and from what I could see from the front yard, it backed up against the park. Chiffon yellow, the house stood out like lemon pudding, but ivy-covered trellises leaned against the front walls, giving them a gothic appearance in the gloom-soaked October night. The porch light was on. Tad and Albert waited at the front door for us to join them.

"I left the light on this morning before I left. It hasn't been turned off, as you can see." Albert inserted the key into the lock.

I had a momentary flash of curiosity, wondering why it was Albert and not Tad who had possession of Violet's spare key, given that Tad had the hots for her, but decided it wouldn't be diplomatic to ask.

As Albert opened the door and stood back, allowing us to enter, Menolly stopped at the doorstep. I glanced at her, puzzled, but Albert seemed to immediately understand because he crossed the threshold and turned around to face her.

"Please, be welcome and enter." His voice was surprisingly gracious and I suddenly understood. She had never been in the house and it was a private residence. It didn't take the owner to welcome her in, but merely someone on the inside. Hell, a maid could unbar the way, or even a child.

The prohibition to entry didn't count if the place was a publicly or governmentally owned institution—like a frat house or a dormitory or a hotel, which was why we'd been able to break into Dredge's room at the Halcyon Hotel and

Nightclub, and into the fraternity housing Dante's Hellions. Nor did the prohibition bar a vampire from entering an apartment building . . . he or she just couldn't break into the personal residences. Nobody was really sure what caused the force field, but it was there, and it worked.

Menolly crossed the threshold and Albert shut the door.

The house had an odd, empty air to it. Not the sense of abandonment when a place was left to rot and ruin, but of a flurry of a home whose owner had whisked away on vacation, or an unintended trip. Everything was neat and in order, and plants filled every spare surface of every table and shelf. They grew profusely, vining out like crazed groupies, their foliage thick and lush and vibrant green.

Camille lingered over one pot of flowers, gently fingering the leaves. "Violet is quite the gardener. Look at how beautiful and lush these are. Orchids like this are hard to grow for even experienced gardeners, but this one's branching out like it is on steroids."

The flower had five big blooms on it, the color of twilight, and while I knew squat about orchids, I did know enough to understand that they weren't the easiest plant to keep alive. But then again, for one of the woodland Fae, it wasn't at all surprising that her houseplants were thriving.

I glanced around. A cat was curled up on the sofa, staring at us. He was a gray and white fluff ball, with fur a lot longer than my own. Essentially, one gigantic tribble on legs. He yawned, and I smiled softly. This was his territory, and while my inner tabby let out a little hiss, the two-legged side of me that loved my own kind wanted to scoop him up and snuggle him and rub my nose in his belly. Camille did just that, laughing when he started to purr and lick her nose.

"I love this little guy."

"He's a keeper, all right." I scritched him between the ears and he softly patted my hand with one paw, claws in. "You're a well-behaved little munchkin."

I glanced around. The apartment was tidy. There were no dirty dishes, no scattered papers. Absolutely no sign of a struggle. As I crossed to the desk, Albert went into the kitchen and we heard the rattling of cans—most likely pet food. Tumpkins jumped out of Camille's arms and headed in the direction of the sound of the can opener.

A sudden thought crossed my mind and I turned to Tad. "The cat will be safe with Albert, won't he? There won't be any unnecessary . . . um . . ." Hallmark didn't make a card asking an acquaintance to please avoid draining the cat of blood.

But Tad got my drift. "Albert loves cats. Very few vamps manage to get close to felines, but he always does. They seem to know that he would never hurt them." By the soft look in his eyes, I could see he was telling the truth and it made me feel a lot more kindly toward Albert.

I slid into the chair at the desk and rifled through Violet's desk drawers. Even they were organized in what appeared to be an almost OCD manner. It was obvious she wasn't a smoker, nor did I find any booze or . . . I looked around. No books. There were no books in the apartment and no television. Oddly enough, the entire place felt devoid—except for the houseplants and the cat. In fact, now I knew what it reminded me of. It felt like a hotel room—impersonal.

I looked for a calendar but couldn't find one. "Do you know if she had a Day-Timer?"

"Nah, she used the calendar on her phone and synched it to her laptop." With a frown, Tad looked around. "Speaking of, I don't see her laptop anywhere, or her tablet. She might have taken them with her, wherever she went."

"Maybe in her bedroom?" I often took my laptop to bed with me to play games or answer e-mail before I went to sleep.

Blushing, Tad led the way. He stopped for a moment, staring at the bed as we entered. Covered with a gauzy spread, the bed was a king-sized futon, and a filmy night-gown made of spidersilk lay across the bottom. Two hooks had been drilled into the headboard, and velvet ropes hung down from them. One guess what they were for, I thought, trying to repress a smile. I'd seen Camille's toy box often enough. I knew restraints when I saw them, just like I knew that my sister liked to be tied up at times.

But Tad just stared at them, glaring.

There was no sign of any computer anywhere, but I did find something under the pillow. A journal, written in an ES Fae language. I flipped through it, able to pick out a word here and there, but my command of the dialect wasn't good enough.

"Camille, can you read this?" She could read a number of dialects, so I was hoping this might be close enough to one of them for her to muddle through, but she shook her head.

"No, but Aeval can. Let me take this, please. I'm due out at Talamh Lonrach Oll this weekend. I can ask her then if she will help me translate it." She tucked it in her purse.

Menolly was standing over by the window. "You know, her bedroom faces the park. And there are no curtains here. Anybody could hide out there in the bushes and watch her." She turned back to us. "Before tomorrow's over, somebody should check out there to see if they can find any footprints or signs that someone has been staking out her house."

The thought made me shudder, but I added it to my list of notes. "Right. I'd go out there tonight but we'd just mess up any prints in the dark. Tad, Albert . . . did Violet mention that there has been anything upsetting her? Anything out of the ordinary, at all? Think. Any little tidbit might be important."

Tad ran his hand over the nightgown and shivered. "She said something a few days back that struck me as strange . . . let me think for a moment to make sure I get it right." He mulled over his thoughts, then snapped his fingers. "I remember—she said that she was getting friend requests from someone online who made her nervous."

"Really?. She has a MySupe page?" MySupe was the equivalent to Facebook, even though most Supes used Facebook anyway.

"I don't know if it's Facebook or MySupe or what. She didn't say and I mostly hang out at Tech-Know-Katz, so I'm not sure."

"Hmm, we'll look into it." Camille frowned, then motioned for me to step out of the room with her. The look on her face set me on edge.

"I hate to bring up this thought," she said, once we were alone, "but, do you think Tad might have something to do with her disappearance? He's in love with her and she has never expressed an interest in him. She's dating someone he obviously dislikes. Maybe he broke . . . did something to her, and now is trying to cover it up? Or he feels guilty and wants to get caught."

At my expression, she shrugged. "Hey, it happens. Just saying . . ."

"I know, I know but . . . I don't think so. Maybe I still want to believe the best in people, but my gut tells me he's just as worried as I'm beginning to get. I could buy her running off to someplace without telling them, but not leaving her cat. Or her plants. Woodland Fae tend to treat their plants like children. And a dryad—or one of her cousins—wouldn't abandon her floral babies or fur babies."

She considered my point, then let out a sigh. "You're right. But if she didn't run off, then she was kidnapped. Or dragged away. What are the chances we're going to find her alive?"

I didn't want to think about that possibility. If she'd been the victim of a violent crime, chances weren't good that we'd find her alive. I already knew that much. But now I wanted to help.

"We'll cross that bridge when we come to it. Let's finish searching her apartment and then we'll head to Carter's. And tomorrow, we'll come out here and search the park out back of the house. She has no fence dividing the lawn from the ravine. Anybody could have been lurking out there." Another thought crossed my mind. "Can you do a Seeking spell to find her?"

Camille considered the thought. "I don't know if that's a

good idea. Remember the harpy? There's no guarantee and my Moon magic still fizzes out as often as it works. I'm willing to give it a go. I'd also have to gather the right components first. We'll see how it goes."

With that, we finished our unfruitful search. Camille clutching the diary, headed out into the night. Albert found a carrier and took Tumpkins home with him.

After promising the guys we'd call them the minute we found out anything, we dropped Menolly off back at the bar—she had some things to attend to there—and Camille and I headed to Carter's. The son of Hyperion, the Titan, and a succubus, the half Titan, half demon was leader of the Demonica Vacana Society, a group that watched over humanity and recorded interactions between the Demonkin and humans throughout the ages. Essentially, Carter was a demigod.

He had shoulder-length hair the color of Menolly's, and he cut a handsome figure, with horns that curved gracefully back like those of a ram's. He was able to pass in society by masking his demonic heritage when he chose to, but mostly, he stayed in his apartment, content to be a recluse. He was friendly and polite to us, but we never made the mistake of forgetting just how powerful he could be.

We parked outside the brick building that he lived in, and Camille stopped for a moment, closing her eyes.

"He's got his wards back up, strong as ever. His sorceress must have rebounded after Gulakah's bhouts and spirit demons dispersed."

For a while, every magic-using person in the area—be they OW Fae or human—had been in danger. The energy-sucking spirits that the Lord of Ghosts had summoned had turned the city into their private feeding ground and nobody who used magic was safe.

Now, things seemed to be returning to normal, although we'd learned that it would take quite some time before the increasing ghostly activity would scale back. Gulakah had spent eons increasing the connection between the angry spirits of the Netherworld and Earthside. The mess wasn't going to balance itself out in a few months, or a few years, even though he was no longer a threat.

As we clattered down the concrete steps leading to the basement apartment, the rain cascaded over the back of my neck. We seldom bothered with umbrellas because in Seattle, chances were good a rainstorm would be accompanied by windy weather. Umbrellas were sitting ducks for destruction.

Carter seemed to have a prescience about our visits; as usual, we waited mere seconds before the door opened. He stood back, graciously ushering us in. As we entered, the familiar comfort of the room welcomed us with its overly lush Victoriana décor, the aging upholstery that was still clean as a whistle, and the warm glow of the incandescent bulbs lighting the Tiffany lamps.

Carter was wearing his usual smoking jacket—this time a deep plum—and black trousers. Other than Roman, he was the only person we knew who could make a cravat look good. He waited till we were seated and then rang a bell.

A woman gracefully entered, wearing a stiff maid's uniform. She carried a tea tray filled with delicious bites of cake and cookies and scones, and then she brought back a tray with a chintz teapot and cups and saucers. As she poured, we took a moment to sink back in the overstuffed seats, and relax.

Carter motioned for her to leave, then turned to us. "I'm glad you came. I assume you have some questions for me, but let them wait for a moment. I was going to contact you tomorrow anyway. I have news for you, and I'm not sure just how you're going to take it."

One of his cats—he had three and adored them—jumped up on my lap. I had, when they were babies, attempted to drag them off in my tabby form because they were crying for their mama, but now Roxy, the cream and white fifteen-pound wonder who had been an adorable tiny kitten, landed in my lap with a thump.

I grimaced—she managed to hit a trigger point to a sore muscle, but the minute she started to knead, a soft spot in my heart flared and I found my territorial nature softening. I wasn't sure why, but lately I'd been more open to other cats. My hackles were less likely to flare.

Camille immediately took control of the cat, sweeping it into her arms and snuggling it. I grinned at her. She was an ailurophile, and while she loved her spirit kitty Misty that I'd gotten for her the preceding Yule, I knew she longed to have a real flesh-and-blood cat for a pet . . . and that did not include me when I shifted form.

Carter watched, an indulgent look on his face. After a few minutes, Roxy had had enough kisses on the head and snuggles, and leaped out of Camille's arms, wandering off.

I cleared my throat. "So, what's the news you have for us, and why do you think we might have some issues with it?"

Carter paused for a moment, then shrugged. "It's just . . . in doing some research locally, I ran across . . ." He seemed at a loss for words, and that wasn't like Carter at all. He was always eloquent, never tongue-tied.

I decided to make things easier. "Just spit it out."

"Well, I've run across someone—two people—I think you need to meet. Their names are Hester Lou Fredericks, and Daniel George Fredericks. They're brother and sister."

"Why do you think we need to meet them?" Camille looked as confused as I felt.

"The fact is . . . they are your blood cousins . . . on your mother's side."

As his words hit home, Camille and I looked at one another, incredulous. What we'd always hoped for had finally happened—our mother's blood family had come to light. Only now, I wasn't sure it was such a good thing.

Chapter 4

〜✿〜

As Carter's words fully registered, so did the shock of what he was actually saying. Camille stammered, but all she managed to spit out were a few little half-formed words. Surprised that for once I was the vocal one, I shook my head to clear my thoughts.

"Are you sure? Mother said she was an orphan."

"Just because you're an orphan, doesn't mean there isn't a record of your parentage. And just because someone *tells* you that you're an orphan, doesn't mean you really are." Carter gave us a long look, and the realization of what he was saying began to hit home.

Camille found her voice. "You mean . . . Mother *wasn't* an orphan?"

"No, she wasn't. You do have her last name—D'Artigo. Her adoptive parents decided to leave her that much of her heritage, which is surprising given the time period when they took her in. But Maria's parents didn't die like her foster parents told her. And they weren't best friends with Maria's parents."

Carter was holding a blue file, a thick one, and he set it down on the table, touching it lightly with the tips of his fingers. "How much do you want to know?"

I glanced at Camille. She gave me a short nod. "Everything, please."

The only thing we knew about our mother's lineage is that she was supposedly orphaned as a child and her parents' best friends had taken her in and raised her as their own. Our grandmother was supposed to have been a beauty, and our grandfather, a man of modest means but good character. Now, all that hung in the air, ready to fly out the window as the truth shed light on shadow.

With a deep breath, Carter motioned for us to drink our tea. He leaned back, the brace on his leg causing him to wince. Menolly had alluded to knowing how he got the injury, but she hadn't told us his secret and neither Camille nor I felt it our place to ask.

After a moment, he said, "Your grandmother's name was Theresa D'Artigo. She was fifteen when she gave birth to your mother. She wasn't married, and she wasn't engaged. In 1921, that was a big deal. Maria's father—your maternal grandfather—was named William Jones. He was a high school senior. His parents made sure their son never knew about Maria."

William Jones. The name hung on the tip of my tongue. After all these years, we were finding out about our mother's side of the family, but this all-too-human name sounded odd. I began to feel my emotions distancing themselves from the situation.

"Theresa was pressured into giving up the baby. In exchange for everybody keeping their mouths shut, William Jones's parents quietly paid off her family. There wasn't much she could do, I suppose. In human society, having an illegitimate child at that time was a tough row to hoe. Theresa's family kept her home, never telling anybody she was pregnant so she wouldn't be disgraced. Instead, they spread the story that she'd gone to visit relatives for a few months. Theresa had no choice in the matter—she was housebound and forced to obey. When she gave birth to Maria, her parents had lined up a couple wanting to adopt, and she gave in quietly. Theresa wanted her daughter to have a better life than she did. Back then, without the Net or even any prevalence of telephones, it was easy to keep secrets, and dirty laundry stayed buried."

"And that couple . . . they were the Wilsons? Maria's foster parents?" Camille looked shaken. I wanted to know what was running through her head but right now, my own thoughts were racing too quickly to sort out anybody else's.

Carter nodded. "Yes. Theresa did manage a few moments alone with them. She asked the Wilsons to please tell Maria that they had been friends with Maria's parents, and that the couple had died in an accident. Theresa didn't want her daughter ever thinking that she had voluntarily given her away, and she didn't want Maria to look for her."

"And they did what Theresa asked them to." That had been the story we'd always heard. Our mother talked about how she'd been orphaned by a car accident, and her parents' best friends took her in. She truly had believed every word.

I tried to imagine life back then and what it must have been like. Although a lot of people thought of Otherworld as technologically inferior and backward, it was—and had been for years—more advanced than Earthside on some social levels. And magic made up for some of the technology we lacked.

"They did. They were good-hearted people. They gave your mother Theresa's last name, but they also impressed on her that the only D'Artigos still alive who were blood-related to her lived in Spain. I suppose they felt the orphan story would both give Maria some comfort, and prevent her from looking for the truth. That's one reason why your mother went to study in Spain when she was in college. She assumed some of her mother's kin were still alive over there."

The realization of how hard life must have been for Theresa hit me in the gut. It was *still* difficult, Earthside, for single mothers. Though times were changing, a stigma remained to having a child out of wedlock. That stigma didn't exist in Otherworld because sex outside marriage wasn't an issue. Hell, for the most part, *sex itself* wasn't an issue.

"What happened to Theresa after she gave up our mother?"

"She finished high school. Four years after she gave birth to Maria, Theresa met a man named George Franco and they married. Eventually, they had five children. She never told George or her other children about Maria. Theresa and George died in 1965, when their plane crashed on a trip to New Jersey."

So our grandmother was truly dead. She would have been, anyway, given the time frame and human life span, but it brought home to me the difference our half-Fae heritage made.

"Can you tell us about Theresa's other children?" Camille bit her lip, looking ready to cry.

Carter reached over and tapped her hand gently. "Don't be sorrowful. The Wilsons adored your mother, they doted on her. As for Theresa and George, they had two sons and three daughters. Trey was born in 1928 and died young without leaving a family. Wilton was born in 1929 and he died during the Korean War. He never married either, though there is speculation he fathered a child on a South Korean woman . . . but that's never been tracked down."

I jotted down notes, even though I knew Carter would give us all the information. It gave me something to do with my hands and prevented me from feeling awkward.

"As for the three daughters . . . Sharon is still alive—she lives in Canada and has never married. She became a schoolteacher and is eighty-two now. Eve is in Ecuador and she had two children, and five grandchildren. She never returned to the United States after her parents died. She's seventy-eight. And Tansy was born in 1938. She had two children, and lived in Shoreline. She died in 2005 of cancer. Her husband died in 2008 of a heart attack."

"So our aunt Tansy . . . she lived here. We could have met her . . ." I frowned, staring at the words on the page.

"You said we have cousins in the area. Are they Tansy's children?" Camille straightened her shoulders and took another cookie.

He nodded. "Hester Lou and Daniel George Fredericks . . . Hester Lou was born in 1961. Daniel George was born in 1965. They are older than you, relatively speaking, though you outnumber them in actual years lived. But they're both still quite healthy and happy. And they both live in this area."

Camille stared at me, a question in her eyes. I could only answer it one way. I turned back to Carter.

"Do they know about us?"

He shook his head, then handed me a sheet of paper. "Walk softly, girls. This is bound to be a shock for them. They know about their aunts and uncles, but they don't know about Maria. And they do not know about you. I cannot tell you what to expect in the way of a greeting from them. There are too many variables."

Nodding, I took the piece of paper. "For good or ill, I think . . . it's time for a family reunion." I glanced at the sheet. Hester lived in Kirkland, and Daniel lived in Bellevue. We were sitting within half an hour's drive of two cousins we hadn't even known existed twenty minutes ago.

Camille shook her head. "This is one hell of a turn of events. I think I'm mildly in shock. But before we run off, hunting down family, we need to ask you a few questions about another matter."

I tried to focus on what she was saying, but it was hard to turn off my thoughts. Would they resemble our mother in any way? Had Mother taken after her father in looks, or Theresa? Would they welcome us in, or freak out and push us away? I tried to clear my thoughts and turned my attention back to the matter at hand.

"We need to know whatever you have on the Farantino building. There's daemonic activity going on there. Also . . . what was his name, again, Kitten? The man you were sent to . . . oblite? Is that the word?" Camille gave me one of her *buck-up-and-get-with-it* smiles.

I coughed, clearing my throat. "What we do to the souls we are ordered to cleanse is referred to as *oblition*. How we do it . . . is to obliterate them. Doesn't sound very nice but that's pretty much the long and short of it."

She shrugged. "We've all done a lot of not-so-nice things. It is what it is."

"True, that. And his name was Gerald Hanson. He was a lawyer at the Farantino Building, Carter." Quickly, we outlined what had happened during the evening, starting with my orders to take out Hanson, and ending up with Grandmother Coyote's visit.

Carter crossed to his desk, where he typed something into his computer. After a moment, he motioned us over. "I have a long history on the Farantino Building. I didn't realize that actual gargoyles were in stasis there, but I will annotate that little fact. Let me see what we have here . . . yes, the building was built over a hundred years ago by Michael Farantino."

"Hmm . . . hence the name of the building." Camille leaned over his shoulder and he glanced at her with a look that I hoped she hadn't noticed. Carter was part daemon, his mother a succubus, and there was a refined sensuality to him that bordered on scary.

"Yes, hence the name of the building," was all he said. "I'll note that Gerald Hanson was his great-grandson, and that Gerald died today." As he quickly typed in the information, I slid the dossier on our relatives into my messenger bag, and refocused my attention.

"Let me see . . . we have a lot of ghostly activity taking place in that area of the city—"

"Please don't tell us that the building is in the Greenbelt Park District!" A good share of our time during the last six months or more had been spent fighting ghosts and demons in that nasty little division of Seattle. The last thing I wanted was to troupe back there and deal with another haunting.

But Carter shook his head. "No, not at all. It's up in the U-District, actually. Near Forty-fifth Street, off of Eleventh Avenue Northeast. Old brick building."

The U-District? We had a center of daemonic activity hanging out in the University District? Oh wonderful, and how many college students had decided to go check out the weird-assed energy around the building? Just what we needed: amateur ghost hunters getting themselves in trouble. We'd already had that happen before and we didn't need it happening again. My thoughts must have shown on my face, because Camille snorted.

She stood, arching her back in a stretch. "Delightful. And how many humans have gone missing over the years around the area? Especially the college kids out to prove the spooks exist?"

Carter's answer surprised us. "Only a handful, and most of them were accounted for by all-too-human miscreants. Whatever the daemons are up to, I don't think it's the college kids who are in danger. There is a record of daemonic activity here, but so far, nothing is showing up on the radar as to what they're after."

"Well, that seems odd. No missing virgins? No gutted sacrifices lying around?" Daemons were cannier than demons, over all, but still . . . they were pretty ruthless and bloodthirsty.

"Nope." Carter grinned at me. "You want I should give you a long gory list of victims?"

Snorting, I shook my head. "You know I don't want that. You just surprised me. So if they aren't out to subvert or sacrifice the FBHs, then what do you think they doing?"

"That seems to be our job to find out." Camille accepted the printouts of the information Carter handed her. "Who owns the building now? We know that it doesn't belong to Hanson anymore."

Carter tapped a few more keys and up popped the info. "That would be Lowestar Radcliffe. There's not much here about him. He appears to hold a degree from Yale in business management, but background info is sketchy. Information says he was born somewhere in India. I have no idea if that's true. Picture of him looks odd but for the life of me, I can't tell you if he's mixed heritage or just an ordinary FBH."

We took the packet of papers and thanked him. As we headed for the door, he stopped us. "Girls, be cautious in approaching your cousins."

"Yeah, they may not welcome having mixed-breed relatives." I stared at the papers in my hand. We'd been called Windwalkers all our lives—a derogatory term in Otherworld, used for someone with no roots, often used for half-breeds.

"That's not the only reason." Carter limped over to us. He winced and I had the feeling his leg was hurting him more than usual tonight. "There are other reasons to be cautious. They may embrace you, but they may also want to use you. Or they may be no-good low-life types. You never can know, until you meet them. I didn't have time to vet the information."

Camille cocked her head. "So, how did you come by this in the first place?"

Carter blushed then—I'd never seen the demigod lose his cool and it kind of tickled me. It was his turn to stare at his feet. "I . . . it was a gift. Someone paid me to look into your background as a gift to you."

"Who?" The only person I could think of that might do so was Chase. "Was it Chase?"

But Carter shook his head. "The party in question asked to remain anonymous. And unless you feel like testing my powers, let it be. There was no ulterior motive. I would never do anything to deliberately hurt you, know that."

I stared at him, but his unflinching gaze was deep and dark and hid so many layers of power that I knew better than to push it.

"Very well. But, as grateful as we are for the information, if whoever paid you to dig it out becomes a problem in any way, then I'm holding you accountable."

Carter nodded, a bare dip of the head, and we left. Unsettled, I headed up the stairs first, Camille slowly following behind me. We didn't speak until we were back in her car, buckled in and ready to go. Then—and only then—we looked at one another.

"What do you think?" I was afraid to admit my hesitance, afraid I'd sound like the old Delilah—all timid and nervous.

But Camille surprised me. "I'm not sure about this. I've wanted this for years. Wanted to meet Mother's family. But it's always been a pipe dream. The fantasy of what would it be like if we were to find them—with all the long-lost love and family embracing that you see in one of those Lifetime victim-of-the-week movies. But life doesn't always work like that. Yes, Father and I are mending our fences, but there's a long way to go before I can fully trust him again. If ever. And how will he feel about this? About us meeting Mother's relatives?"

I bit my lower lip, chewing on it until I punctured a hole with one of my nonretractable fangs. Another by-product of being a half-breed werecat. "Does he have to know?"

"Of course he has to know. We can't just *not* tell him. Can we?" She looked over at me, the question hanging between us.

"What if we don't tell him until we meet them? Then we'll know if we should even bother. If they don't want anything to do with us, we can keep quiet about it. If they want a relationship, then we deal with that when it comes." It made sense to me. But there was another question we needed to answer first. "My concern is . . . do we want to do this? Do we want to even go there?"

Camille braked sharply as she was pulling out of the spot. She eased the car back next to the curb, disappointing a driver who had been waiting for the spot. He honked, but drove past.

"You think maybe we shouldn't? I thought you'd be beating down the door." She put the car in Park and turned to me.

I shrugged, not knowing quite how to phrase my thoughts. "I thought I would be too, but now that we're facing this as an actual possibility, the prospects of this end-

ing well . . . let's just say I'm not feeling the rosy scenarios
I envisioned all these years. I just don't want us to have any
regrets."

She pressed her lips together for a moment, staring at
the steering wheel. Then, quietly, she put her hand on mine.
"Part of me wants to say fuck it. We don't need them. But
we know that Mother never knew she had half brothers and
sisters. She never knew we had cousins. She didn't even
know her mother was alive. Don't we owe it to her memory
to find out what we can? To forge a link with her past, if it's
meant to be?"

It made sense when she put it that way. "I suppose. We
still have to tell Menolly. She'll no doubt have an opinion
on all of this."

Camille shuddered. "I'm not sure if I want to hear her
opinion, but you're right. Okay, so what next?"

"What say we drive by the Farantino Building, take a
look at it, then go wait for Menolly to come home. We can't
very well call . . . what are their names?"

"Hester and Daniel."

"We can't very well call them this late, can we?" I
glanced at the clock. It was going on eleven o'clock already,
and even though our bedtime was usually well after midnight, that didn't mean everybody else stayed up as late.

With a silent nod, Camille pulled back out of the parking space, and we were off.

The streets were empty as we eased into another parking
space, this time across from the Farantino Building. Brick,
it was six stories high from the looks of it. For some reason,
I'd expected a skyscraper, tall with chrome and glass, but
that wouldn't make sense if it had been built over a hundred years ago.

The building held a brooding old-world charm, almost
gothic in nature. The brick was weathered and in some
places had eroded away. A ledge between the fifth and
sixth stories sported a circle of gargoyles guarding the

building. I gazed at the line of stone statues, wondering if any others besides Astralis and Mithra had been actual Cryptos. Were any of them up there now, watching our car, silently perched there in constant observation?

The thought made me vaguely angry. What we'd been taught about gargoyles didn't jibe with the reality. I wondered why our father had never seemed concerned. He had to have known about the treatment of the granticular gargoyles, considering he was privy to government intelligence. And he'd always been so antislavery. Turning a blind eye to the enforced servitude of Astralis and his kind was yet another contradiction in our father's nature.

Camille unfastened her seat belt and slid out the driver's side. I followed, leaning on the top of the car. We stared at the building, waiting for a sign. For something . . . anything . . . to happen.

Although the Farantino Building was six stories high, who knew how many levels it had underground. The intricate carving around the ledge reminded me of knotwork braided into the stone, beautiful, looking far older than it really was.

Camille shaded her eyes from the rain as she looked up. "The building has a definite energy signature of strength and foundation. Whatever goes on in there, there are some major power players at work." She folded her arms across her chest and glanced back at me. "It makes me nervous, to be honest. I'm not sure what we're dealing with but it makes me think of old money and cognac and . . . like Roman, only far more ruthless."

Roman was ruthless enough. If whatever—or whoever—lurked behind these walls was more dangerous than he, I wasn't sure I wanted to get involved. But thanks to Grandmother Coyote, we didn't have a choice. I sucked in a deep breath and let it out slowly.

"There's not much we can do now. We might as well drop back to the bar and tell Menolly to get her butt home. We have a lot to tell her. And we need to go through the information Carter gave us about this monolith here."

As I shivered and climbed back in the car, I glanced up at the building one last time. The Farantino Building loomed over the neighborhood. It felt a whole lot bigger than its six stories. As a hint of Camille's clairvoyance broke through to me, I realized that the building itself was watching us. The damned thing was sentient, and it knew we were here.

Menolly caught sight of me as I peeked into the bar. It was still packed but the crowds had thinned somewhat. She strode toward me, her stiletto boots tapping hard on the floor over the sound of conversation and laughter. She was light and petite, but each step she took had a tremendous amount of force behind it.

I pulled her off to one side. "We need you to come home. It's not an emergency but we have . . . there's no way to explain it here. Carter had some news for us. The three of us have to discuss it—it's big."

"Another demon general hit the city?" She narrowed her eyes. "After Gulakah, we *know* Shadow Wing is going to be sending somebody bigger and badder in, and you can't get much bigger than a god."

"Yeah, it's just a matter of time. But no, this has nothing to do with Shadow Wing. It's purely personal." I really didn't want to go into it here. For one thing, if Menolly reacted badly, it could hurt her business. And I had no clue how she'd feel about the news. There really wasn't any reason for her to get pissed, but then again, vampires didn't really *need* a reason to get angry. And sister or not, Menolly *was* a vampire.

She cocked her head. "Is everybody okay at home?"

"As far as I know. Camille is waiting out in the car. Let Derrick close up and you come home now, or we're going to be standing here all night. You are going to want to hear this but it's not something I'm comfortable talking about in public." With that, I turned to go before she could ask any more questions.

Curiosity playing across her face, Menolly nodded. "I'll follow. See you at home. And be careful—it's slick out there, and the fog is rising."

As I headed back to the car, I saw her disappear into her office. By the time I was buckling my seat belt, Menolly had darted out of the bar, jacket slung over her shoulder, and was running for her Jag. We pulled out, with her following.

The district where we lived was about fifteen minutes away from downtown Seattle. On a good night, when traffic was light, we could make it in ten minutes, but with the roads slick from the downpour, Camille took it slow and easy. As we wound out of the city proper, we entered the Belles-Faire neighborhood.

Belles-Faire was a heavily wooded suburb that almost could be considered rural, but it was still part of Seattle. Just like Shoreline, Lake Forest, Bothell, and the dozens of other suburb cities on both sides of Lake Washington, the neighborhoods ran into one another in one massive urban and suburban sprawl.

As we rounded one bend in the road, Camille suddenly swerved as a blur raced across the road. The car skidded sideways—even though we hadn't been going a high speed, the road was slick enough to cause hydroplaning. Camille drove into the skid, and finally managed to ease the car onto the shoulder. She was breathing heavily, clutching the steering wheel. Behind us, Menolly had pulled off the road and was running over to us.

Shaking, I got out of the car as Menolly yanked open Camille's door and helped her out.

"Are you okay? What the hell happened?" She brushed Camille's hair back from her face.

Camille shivered, then looked around. "Something leaped out from the bushes by the side of the road. Did you see it?"

I squinted, looking into the night. There *had* been something—the blur—but I had no clue what it was. As I tried to puzzle out where it had gone, Menolly let out a shout.

"Kitten! Behind you!"

I whirled. There, behind me, peering out from behind a large cedar, was a pair of eyes. Brilliant green, they glimmered like a cat's eyes, reflecting the light from street lamps. But whatever it was, it was no cat. No Were, either. I could sense the presence of other Weres. And it wasn't the creature that had darted across the road, unless it had managed to recross without us seeing it.

"Is that Demonkin?" I asked softly, reaching for my dagger.

Camille slowly moved around the car to my left, and Menolly to my right.

After a moment, Camille let out a slow breath. "No, but I have no clue what it is. Feels Fae, but it's not any Fae I know about."

"Elder Fae?" The Elder Fae were highly unpredictable, beyond any sense of human behavior. They played by their own rules, and most didn't interact with FBHs or even those of us considered "regular" Fae. This was probably a very good thing, given some of the predilections the Elder Fae had for the consumption of human flesh.

"Possibly." Camille moved forward, slowly, holding her hands out. She inhaled deeply, closing her eyes, the magic beginning to swirl around her. As a flicker of sparkling light surrounded her hands, she reached out and a luminous glow began to emanate from her fingertips.

At the same moment, Menolly let out a grunt and went sprawling to the ground as a dark figure jumped her, holding tight to her back. The creature was bipedal, with the same luminous green eyes that were still staring at us out of the woods. About Menolly's height and weight, the creature seemed stronger than even her vampire nature. Menolly struggled against it, but the woman—it looked female—managed to hold her down.

I launched myself at it, grabbing it by the shoulders as it clawed deep into her arms to hold itself steady. At the same moment, a brilliant flash told me that Camille had let loose with whatever spell she had been prepping. The glimmering light flared in the woods. She had aimed it at the other creature, apparently.

I struggled with the one on Menolly's back. The skin felt leathery, but it wasn't like armor—more than that, it felt like a lizard's skin. I could swear it was demonic, except Camille hadn't sensed Demonkin energy and she was adept at that.

The creature turned its head and I saw that the features had a feminine bent. I was right—whatever this creature was, it was a *she*. But as her mouth opened, and she snarled at me with needlepoint teeth, I yanked my hand away from her as her lithe, supple neck bent at an angle that should have broken her spine but didn't. Before I realized what she was doing, she'd launched herself at my right hand and chomped down into the flesh, her teeth piercing the skin like it was butter.

The pain was excruciating and I let out a shriek. I yanked my other hand away and backhanded her with it as she let go of Menolly and reached for my throat. Menolly stumbled away and turned, grabbing the creature by the arm and yanking her away from me. She tossed her across the road. A chunk of my hand went with the creature, caught in her gnashing teeth. She landed hard, skidding along the pavement. Menolly pushed me toward the car. Camille was already backing away as the creature in the woods came barreling out, looking fit to kill.

Bleeding, I slammed the door and managed to fasten my seat belt. Camille slid into the driver's side and started the car, as Menolly headed back to the Jag. We couldn't fight these things till we knew what they were—but we knew they were strong and dangerous.

"How's your hand?" Camille asked, speeding up.

I winced at the pain. My hand was bleeding profusely. I tried to wrap it up with the tail of my shirt, but I bled through and was dripping onto the seat. The chunk of flesh that was gone wasn't large—the size of a quarter, but it was deep and I felt warm, almost as if I had a fever starting.

"I don't know. It hurts and it feels . . . itchy." As I thought about it, itchy was the word—burning, itchy, and tingling as if it were getting . . . "Oh hell, I think I think it had venom in it—or maybe some sort of bacteria."

Camille stepped on the gas. "We'll have Iris look at it. We don't want you getting blood poisoning. And we need to find out what the fuck those things are and why they're here."

We pulled into the driveway, Menolly right behind us. As we tiredly made our way up the steps, we could hear a commotion going on inside. Camille pushed open the door, letting me enter first.

The noise hit us—everybody seemed up and bustling around in a clatter. Roz was rushing around, carrying blankets, and behind him Trillian was carrying extra pillows.

"What the hell is going on?" I glanced around, looking for Hanna or Iris. Neither was in sight.

"Iris—she's gone into labor. She's in Hanna's room with Hanna and Nerissa. Mallen's on the way. Sharah's far too pregnant to come."

While Iris had gotten pregnant a few weeks before Sharah, she was overdue, and Sharah was nearing her own due date. I couldn't remember if she had one or two weeks to go, but while she was still working in the lab, she wasn't taking night shifts or field work anymore.

Camille turned to me. "Wait here. Mallen can tend to your hand when he gets here. I'm going to check on Iris." She hurried off. Menolly pushed me into a chair. Shade came rushing over, staring at my hand.

"Love, what happened to you?" He knelt by my side, gathering me into his arms. He was one of the most gorgeous men I could imagine, with skin the color of golden latte, and his hair was long, caught in a ponytail—honey colored with streaks of amber. He had a craggy scar along one cheek, and he was my height and sturdily built. He smelled like cinnamon and spice, and I felt safe when he was around.

"We got sideswiped by some sort of Fae on the way home—at least we think they are Fae. I don't know if they were waiting for us, or if we just happened along when they decided to pull their little stunt, but whatever the case, they are dangerous." I held up my hand. I was beginning to feel sweaty, and my stomach ached. "I think they have some sort of venom or bacteria, because I don't feel so hot."

Shade brushed my bangs away from my face and kissed my forehead. "Let me get you some water. Mallen is on the way. Relax and cover up, love."

Just then, Camille popped back through the doorway. "Where the hell is Mallen? Iris is crowning the first baby."

A thought hit me. "Where the hell is *Bruce*?"

Smoky frowned. "Iris said he'd be here in a few. He was out at the house. I'll go check on him." He headed toward the kitchen just as Shade reappeared with my water. The doorbell rang and Menolly answered it, leading Mallen in. Behind him was Chase, looking pale and shaken.

"Chase, what's going on?"

He shook his head. "I'm sorry to intrude at this time but I'm afraid I have some bad news. Menolly—I'm sorry to tell you this, but the Wayfarer . . ."

She stiffened. "Tell me. What's going on?"

"The Wayfarer is on fire. The fire department is there, trying to stop the flames, but they aren't hopeful. Chrysandra . . . she got caught in the smoke. She's in serious condition at the FH-CSI."

"Oh Great Mother, the threats were real." Camille paled as Mallen pushed past her, grabbing her arm.

"I need you to help me." He shook her lightly. "*Now.*"

As he dragged her after him, Menolly grabbed her jacket, still silent.

I stood, intending to go with her, but the room began to spin and the next thing I knew, I face-planted. As I hit the floor, my head buzzed like a hive full of angry bees had taken up residence there.

Chapter 5

❦

As I opened my eyes, I realized three things. One: I was lying on the floor. Two: The floor felt uncommonly good—nice and cool and smooth. Three: I didn't think I was supposed to actually be down here.

That's when the burning hit. My hand itched so bad I let out a croaking scream. I tried to sit up and found hands against my back, helping me. Shade was bracing me up. I shook my head, trying to clear the drone, but the buzzing grew worse, making it hard to even hear my own thoughts.

I squinted as Menolly knelt down beside me, Chase fretting behind her. "Kitten, Kitten, are you okay?"

"I . . . I . . . No." Truth being, I wasn't. I felt feverish and on pins and needles.

"I'll go get Mallen." She jumped up and disappeared from sight.

Shade gathered me up in his arms and laid me on the sofa. "Love, love . . . can you hear me? Delilah—can you hear me?"

His voice grated in my ears against the buzzing that

wouldn't shut the fuck up. It was beginning to annoy me. "Yes, I can hear you. Stop asking me that."

"You're burning up." Shade pressed his hand against my forehead.

A moment later, Mallen rushed back into the room, followed by Camille. The elf looked straight out of med school but he was probably several thousand years old, and he had a calm, cool demeanor that both felt aloof and yet comforting at the same time.

He leaned over me, touched my forehead, then straightened up. "We need to get her to the FH-CSI. She needs more care than I can provide here. Smoky can take her through the Ionyc Sea. Don't let Rozurial do it—he's not strong enough to carry someone in fragile condition. Smoky can offer more protection from the elements out on the Sea. So go. Find him *now*. I'll call ahead so they're expecting her."

Camille ran off.

Mallen turned to Shade. "Camille should go with her. Menolly—I understand that you're needed at the Wayfarer. We'll let you all know if anything serious happens with Iris, though I don't expect any complications."

Menolly looked ready to argue, but turned and headed out the door with Chase.

Shade worried his lip. "Who's with Iris?"

"My assistant, and Hanna and Roz. I have to get back to her—this is her first labor and with twins, it's not going to be easy. Someone find Bruce and send him in." Mallen stared down at me. "Get Delilah a cool cloth for her head until you can get her to headquarters."

At that moment, Smoky and Camille burst in.

"Smoky, take Delilah and Camille to the FH-CSI. A team will be waiting. Somebody—get your ass on the move and bring me Bruce. *Now*." With that, Mallen turned and headed back to Iris.

Shade kissed me. "I'll find Bruce, then join you at HQ. Go, love, and be safe."

I tried to kiss him back but the fever hit me again and I

started to pass out. The next thing I knew, the world was spinning—another period of darkness and I woke up in a bed in the FH-CSI.

I had no idea of how long I'd been out, but as I tried to push myself to a sitting position, Camille stepped into view and shoved me back down again.

"Stop right there. No moving. How are you feeling?" She ran her hand over my cheek, and I saw the worry filling her eyes.

I assessed my condition. Burning, itching hand? Still throbbing but much better. Buzzing in ears? Faint and muted. Feeling like hell? Check—still that.

"I'm better," I croaked out, my throat raspy. "Water?"

She nodded, holding a glass to me with a bendy-straw in it. As I sipped, the cool water raced down my throat, easing the harshness. After a few minutes, I could breathe better, and I leaned back against the pillow.

"What happened to me? I don't remember anything after Smoky picked me up to bring me here." I had a few vague images of someone grabbing my arm, and I thought I might have screamed at one point, but I had no other clue.

"You were phasing in and out, but you'll be okay. Be prepared though. You're going to hurt like hell for a while as you recover." Camille looked around, motioning to someone outside my field of vision. A healer joined her, staring down at me with a soft smile. She was Fae, and I'd lay bets she was part Goldunsan, from Otherworld. Her nametag read "Aswala" and she radiated a warm, welcoming energy.

"I'm glad to see you're awake." She fluffed my pillows and adjusted the blanket over me. "Do you know what happened to you yet?"

I gave her a brief shake of the head. "No, I just woke up. I'm not even sure . . . where am I?" I was pretty sure I was in the medic unit of the FH-CSI.

"You know that bite on your hand? Well, we know what

those creatures are now. And we now know that they have
a necrotic enzyme, like a brown recluse spider only worse.
It helps them digest the flesh they eat. If you hadn't gotten
your lovely self in here, you could have died. As it is, we
are able to counter that type of toxin, and you're on the
mend. But I won't kid you, the pain's going to continue for
quite a while, and you'll have a scar on your hand." Aswala
took my pulse and checked my heartbeat. Seemingly satis-
fied, she jotted down her findings in my chart.

The thought of a scar didn't scare me. Hell, both Menolly
and Camille had more than their fair shares of scar tissue. It
was my turn, apparently. "So what are they?"

"They are children of Jenny Greenteeth and the Dark
Dugald. Apparently the pair had several litters and it appears
that we have at least a small nest of them around here.
They're called dreglins, and they run in a pack." Camille let
out a disgusted sigh.

Jenny Greenteeth and the Dark Dugald were both flesh
eaters, and both were frightening and powerful members
of the Elder Fae. Singular, terrifyingly powerful Fae, the
Elder Fae were older than even the great Fae Lords. That
this particular pair had decided to get their groove on and
breed was both a sickening and frightening thought.

Jenny Greenteeth was similar to a kelpie, and far more
dangerous. The Dark Dugald was the leader of the barguests—
the Black Angus dogs, which were a lot like hellhounds. And
according to what we knew, the Dark Dugald was a hellion
and considered worse than a number of demons.

"Lovely. So now we have to track them down and get rid
of them. We can't let them just camp out and prey on anybody wandering by, and if they are flesh eaters, you know
they won't limit themselves to Supes. They'll go after
FBHs, if they haven't already." I wanted to get up and chase
after them, but when I tried, both Camille and Aswala
pushed me down again.

"You aren't going anywhere for another hour or two, until
we make sure you're stable. You seem to be responding well
to the antivenin treatment, and the healing magic. *If* you are

feeling better in a few hours, *then* we'll let you go home, but you have to go right to bed when you get there. No running around till tomorrow afternoon, and absolutely no fighting for a day or two. If you can't promise, we won't let you out."

I restrained a snort. "Sure, no problem."

Aswala leaned down to whisper in my ear. "We're going to make sure your sister and friends know about this so they can haul your ass back in here if you break your promise. Got it?"

Startled by her take-no-prisoners attitude, I stammered a "yes" as she gave me another shot of something and took Camille off to the side. I had the feeling Camille was getting an earful of Aswala's orders.

After she finished, I motioned to Camille. "What about Iris?"

"She was still in labor when we left. She probably has a while to go before the babies are born. I imagine we'll be home before then."

"Where's Shade?" I looked around, wanting my fiancé. My lover anchored me. Over the months I'd learned a lot about strength and self-acceptance from him.

"Remember? He stayed home to hunt down Bruce, who apparently wasn't around when Iris went into labor, and I gather it took longer than he expected. Bruce is never going to live that one down." Camille let out a laugh. "Smoky will be back to get us the moment he gets my call."

A few other memories began to phase back in that had been lost in the sudden onslaught of fever. I shot straight up. "Menolly! The Wayfarer!"

Camille hung her head. "She called half an hour ago. I won't lie—it's bad. They extinguished most of the flames, but the place is still smoldering. We won't know till morning how badly the bar was damaged, but it's not good. Menolly didn't have much to say. She'll be here soon, though. Chrysandra's fighting for her life, and so are several others—customers who were caught in the flames. We may never know how many vampires died—they would have been dusted by the flames if they were caught."

This time, I laid back down without being shoved. Chrysandra had been with the Wayfarer for years. She was there when Menolly took over and had helped her during the transition. She was easily the best waitress at the bar and she and Menolly had become friends.

"You don't think . . ." I didn't want to verbalize what was going on in my mind and I hoped Camille would understand what I was asking without me having to spell it out.

Her thoughts must have been running in the same direction because she sucked in a deep breath. "I know what you're thinking. I hope to hell Menolly doesn't decide to sire her."

"How close . . . how bad . . . is she . . ."

"Chrysandra's dying. There's no chance for her to pull through, and Menolly doesn't know that yet. I plan on being there when Menolly walks in to check on her. Maybe I can stop her, if her instincts get the better of her." Camille glanced up at the clock. "Speaking of, I guess I should go wait for her. You rest. And by the way, Kitten . . ."

"Yes?" I stared at her defiantly, knowing what she was going to say.

"Aswala told me what she told you. Don't you dare think of trying anything exerting for the next few days. Though, your hand is going to be hurting so I doubt you'll be able to do more than bitch and moan."

She sounded all too gleeful and I waved her out with my left hand. When she was gone, I looked down at my right hand. It was swathed in bandages, but at least it was still there. Necrotic bites could so easily cause gangrene, and I had movement and feeling in my fingers—all too much for comfort.

I shrugged, then flipped on the television, bored. The news was on and they were showing clips of the Wayfarer, engulfed in flames. I caught my breath, staring at the brilliant tongues of fire licking the building. Luckily, the shops next to it had been spared, but I had a sick feeling that morning wasn't going to see more than a pile of rubble where the bar used to be.

Wincing at the announcer's flippant tone, I changed stations until I found a nice, brainless rerun of *Jerry Springer*. I knew it was trash, and Camille and Menolly constantly teased me about it, but the truth was that I was a total fan girl and was crushing hard on the dude.

For some reason, he tripped my trigger and I fantasized getting locked overnight in a supermarket with him, and meeting in the junk food aisle where he'd drag me to the ground and fuck me like hungry bunnies.

By the time the "Shocking Family Secrets" episode was over, I was beginning to worry. Camille wasn't back yet and I hoped to hell there wasn't a crisis going on in Chrysandra's room. Since Aswala wasn't around to stop me, I pushed back the covers and slipped out of bed. A wave of dizziness and nausea hit me, but I pushed it down and headed slowly for the door, making sure my gown was firmly tied shut. An IV was in stuck in my arm, but it was hanging on one of those poles and I was able to roll it along with me.

The way was clear as I peeked out into the hallway, and I scurried out, holding onto the wall with one hand while I rolled alongside my drip-bag buddy. As I passed each open door, I glanced in—there weren't that many rooms in the medic unit and Chrysandra had to be here somewhere.

I was about to run out of hallway when I saw her—in the ER at the end of the corridor. The doors were closed but I was tall enough to see a group of healers next to Menolly and Camille through the windows. They were gathered around a bed that appeared to be cordoned off behind clear plastic curtains. One of the healers looked engrossed in casting a spell, another worked furiously at some machine to which she was hooked up.

I pushed through the doors and Camille turned, letting out a little noise. Menolly's back was turned to the wall and her shoulders were shaking.

"Don't even say it." I moved over to her side and turned to look at Chrysandra. "Oh Great Mother . . ."

Encased by what was—for all intents and purposes—a

plastic bubble, Chrysandra looked like she'd been spitted and roasted over a bonfire. Any resemblance to who she had been was gone, the skin largely burned away to reveal raw muscle and sinew covered in blisters and remnants of blackened skin. Her hair was gone. She was on a ventilator and a host of tubes were feeding meds and liquids into her. But what struck me as most horrific was that her eyelids and lips had been incinerated. She was so still, I thought she must have passed out.

I stared, unable to look away, then hung my head, the pain in my hand receding as I focused on my feet. I wanted to cry but the tears wouldn't come. I wanted to help but there wasn't anything I could do.

Camille placed her hand on my shoulder and I glanced at her. She silently shook her head and I turned back to look at Chrysandra. There was no way in hell she could make it back from this. A moment later, she woke and began to scream, but her voice was so strained that only a rough croaking came out.

"Can't they stop the pain?"

Camille shook her head. "They've given her what they can. She's too fragile to be transported right now, and even if she was at a burn center, all they could do is prolong her life for a few more hours. Maybe a day."

"Then why can't they help her die? Put her out of her pain?"

"She's human, Kitten. The FBHs have a problem with that concept. If she was conscious enough to tell them to stop . . . but she's not. She's caught in the pain, that's all that exists for her right now. She's dying and she's not going easy." Her words were whispered, but as she spoke, Menolly turned around, bloody tears slicing a trail down her cheeks.

"I want her to die. I want her to get out of that body, to be free from it. If you're worried that I might turn her, don't for a moment think I'd sentence her to eternity in a body so disfigured. But I can kill her, if they'd let me. I can take her out, give her release. All I need is a moment."

At that moment, the healer who was casting the spell stopped. "I can hear you."

Menolly faced him, defiant. "And you have a problem with what I said? Some fuckhead set fire to my bar—I know it was no accident. A murderer is responsible for Chrysandra lying here, dying. And there's nothing we can do to stop it, so I want her to go, to be free from this pain. And then, I will track down the motherfucking cocksucker who did this and I will make him pay—I will make him pay and pay with an excruciating and painful death."

"If I answered your question, I would be suspect." He stared at her for a moment. "She's going to go on in pain for too long. I can't remove the ventilator without permission from her family and we can't find any of them."

"That's because she left them behind. I've known her for years now and I have never heard her mention a single member of her family." Menolly held his gaze, and I could feel her glamour reaching out, trying to ensnare him.

But he was Fae, and he merely smiled, cool and aloof. "You know, I think I need to consult with the others. And for that, we need privacy. Excuse us for a few moments, please." He said everything he could not say aloud in one dark, deliberate look.

As he motioned for his colleagues to follow him, Camille whispered to me. "Guard the door." As I moved to keep watch through the windows, she pulled back the plastic for Menolly. I didn't want to look, didn't want to see what she did. She couldn't very well break Chrysandra's neck—that would be too obvious, so she'd have to drink her down and I couldn't bear to watch her sink her fangs into the burned flesh of the woman we called our friend.

But Camille swallowed and fastened her gaze on the bed. And even though I didn't *want* to see, I had to. Menolly was about to play the angel of death. And Camille and I . . . the least we could do was to stand witness.

The sterility of the ward, its pale cream walls and stark stainless counters faded into the background. The rise and fall of Chrysandra's chest, powered by the soft hiss of the ventilator, was the only noise as Menolly approached her side. This woman we had partied with. Watched movies with and shared appetizers. This woman, our friend, was here in front of us, but she was nowhere in sight. All that remained of her was a charbroiled living steak. The blood of her burns stained the sheets, flowers on snow, spreading their fatal blooms.

Menolly stood over her for a moment, then leaned down and whispered in her ear. Chrysandra began to breathe quickly, and with one last look, my sister bared her fangs and sank them through the crisped, flaking skin, searching for the jugular as she pressed her lips to Chrysandra's neck in one final kiss. Pressing her eyes shut, Menolly's tears raced down her face, their crimson drops falling to spread across Chrysandra's featureless cheeks and brow. The sound of life transferring from one body to another, the hush of pained breath moving to shallow pants to a faint, faint whisper and then . . . silence.

My shoulders began to shake as I watched Menolly slowly withdraw, her chin covered with burned flesh that had stuck to her skin, her mouth stained with the red of Chrysandra's life. She looked from Camille to me, turned and crossed to the sink where she washed her face, wiping her mouth softly with a paper towel. A moment later, the three of us were standing by Chrysandra's bed as the monitor shrieked out the lack of a pulse, the lack of a heartbeat.

The healer came running in. He pushed through the plastic without giving us a second look, and checked Chrysandra for a pulse. Then he listened for her heart, and lastly, he lay a gentle hand on her forehead, and I could tell he wanted to close her eyes but couldn't—the lids had been burned away.

He noted the time in her chart as his colleagues joined him. A few whispers later, they exited the plastic curtains and he stopped by Menolly's side.

"I'm sorry to tell you that your friend didn't make it. She died. Her burns were too extensive." He caught her gaze again, and compassion flickered across his face.

Menolly nodded. "If no one claims her body, I will. I honestly don't know where her family is."

Nodding, he turned away. "I'll make a note of that. Six others also died in the fire."

Menolly crouched down into a squat as she wrapped her arms around herself and began to rock. "No . . . no . . . no . . . what the fuck happened? Who did this and why?"

Camille stepped between her and the healer, pushing him back. "Keep us informed," she said brusquely. She took Menolly by the shoulders and drew her to her feet, moving her toward the door. Menolly allowed herself to be guided along. She did not resist, did not speak, a horrified expression branded on her face. And then we were in the hall and Aswala was there, looking ready to scold me.

I shook her off. "We need to leave."

"I have to see them. I have to know who died." Menolly's stammers were barely above a whisper, but they echoed through the still hall.

"You aren't in any shape—" Camille started, but let her words drift off. "All right. Delilah, go get dressed. You'll still be on bed rest till tomorrow when we get home."

Pain flared in my hand, digging deep, sending me leaning against the wall moaning. The image of a scalded Chrysandra came to mind. I couldn't fathom the pain she'd been in—it must have been excruciating beyond any scope of the imagination. I straightened my back as I headed back to my room. By the time I got there, I'd broken into a sweat, but I downed a glass of water, then another, and my stomach slowly began to settle.

Aswala followed me in, and silently handed me my clothes. She removed the IV from my arm and stood back, watching me.

"Your sister. She's going to need some counseling over this."

"Riiiggghhht. . . ." Menolly was about as likely to agree to counseling as I was to agree to a boob job. "That's not going to happen."

"It was her bar. She feels responsible. I could see it in

her eyes. Until they find the reason for the fire—and let's hope the reason is beyond her control—she's going to imagine the worst possible scenario."

"Oh, we're pretty sure this was arson. We have full reason to believe it."

"Regardless of that possibility, your sister is still going to blame herself. Trust me, I've seen this sort of situation far too often." Aswala opened my chart and scribbled something in it. "I'm releasing you, because otherwise I have a feeling you'll just sneak out. But get your butt home and in bed. You hear me?"

I nodded. "Yeah, I do. I just . . . we need to be home right now."

"I understand. Get dressed. And I want you to drink a lot of water over the next few days. It will help dilute what toxin still runs in your veins. The antivenin is helpful but it can't negate all of the poison."

I accepted the bottle of water she pressed in my hand and began to dress. All the quietude of the past couple of months had vanished in a snap of the fingers, in a quick gust of wind.

Aswala handed me a kit containing the healing salve to put on my wound, as well as a week's worth of bandages. Then, feeling I should say something, I caught her gaze.

"I promise to go home and rest. But our lives . . . there is seldom down time. We're . . ." And then I stopped. I couldn't tell her about Shadow Wing. I couldn't tell her about the war back in Otherworld. All I could do was shrug and give her a faint smile.

She held my coat for me. "I understand. Perhaps more than you know."

I headed out of the room, bracing my arm from time to time against the wall to steady myself. "Where are Camille and Menolly?"

"I imagine the morgue. It's—"

"I know where it's at." I waved her off. "Go do what you need to do."

I found the elevator and punched the button for the third

floor down and held on as the car descended to the underground levels. The Faerie-Human Crime Scene Investigation unit had the main floor, then three stories below ground. There was rumored to be another floor, lower still, but no one had ever confirmed it. Not even when I was dating Chase.

Riding in the quiet elevator, I stared at the nicely polished mirrors in the corner. I knew they housed hidden cameras and I realized just how pale I must have looked. Too fucking bad. There wasn't anything I could do about it right now except take it as easy as I could.

The doors opened with a soft whoosh and I stepped out. The morgue was straight ahead and I pushed through the double doors with a muted thud.

Here, the dead came to rest, limbo before their final consignment. Here, memories were severed. Blood and bone were mere leftovers of lives once lived and now lost. Death played no favorites, claiming the young and the old, the sick and the well. There was no get-out-of-jail-free card. And then my gaze fell on Menolly. She was standing in the middle of six tables covered with the snow white blankets of the dead. Sheets so pristine they made me shiver.

There *were* ways to cheat death . . . but at a high cost. Menolly had found out the hard way. Though eternity had not been her choice, she made the best of what she had. I wondered—could *I* do it? Could I face an unchanging existence, caught in my body, my soul trapped until either fire claimed me, the sun took me, or a stake plunged through the heart? Mortal thoughts, these, and not easy ones.

Camille had her phone out and was writing down the names of the dead as Menolly turned from table to table, the expression on her face fading from horror to disbelief. She was losing her ability to take it in—I could see it in her eyes. She'd reached overload and, for the first time in many years, fear flickered in her eyes. She began to back away toward the wall, whimpering.

"Camille!" I nodded toward Menolly and Camille dropped her pad and pen, softly moving forward. Menolly was crouching again, leaning against the wall, and the predator was coming to the surface. She looked cornered, like a mountain lion trapped against a cliff face.

"Be careful." I kept my voice low.

"Yes, I see." Camille didn't look back at me—she was close enough that she didn't dare take her eyes off our sister. When Menolly was in the grips of this sort of stress, her vampiric nature rose up, and it would be all too easy for her to attack those trying to help her.

"Call Nerissa. Get her on the phone. See if she's here. Chase may have dragged her in to talk to some of the customers at the fire—that's what she does."

I punched in Nerissa's number and she answered almost immediately. As Camille speculated, she was in the building—a boon for us—and I quickly explained what was going on. She hung up, on her way down before I finished.

And then, Camille was kneeling just out of arm's reach. Not far enough to save herself, but enough to give Menolly a second to clear her thoughts, should she attack. Camille held out her hands in an imploring gesture.

"Menolly . . . can you hear me? Menolly, honey, it's Camille. Your big sister. Remember me?"

The frightened, trapped look in Menolly's eyes flickered. She pressed against the wall, shaking her head. "Get out of here."

"No. We can't leave without you. You need to let us help you. Listen to my voice." And as she spoke, Camille's voice grew stronger. She didn't have the command voice down pat, but she could force a reasonable facsimile when necessary. "Menolly, I want you to listen to me. Do you hear me?"

"Leave me alone . . . just . . . leave . . ." Menolly stammered and fell silent. "Don't make me walk past their bodies again. What have I done?"

"You did not do this. It was a fire. You are not to blame. We know it was arson—you know this. Listen to me. You aren't at fault." Camille's voice grew stronger, but Menolly still resisted.

And then, from behind us, came a male voice. Chase.

"Menolly. Stand up. *Now.*" His voice rang through the room, echoing with authority. I shivered, staring at him. I knew he had some ability in this, but had no clue he had reached this level. I wasn't even sure if he recognized how well he was able to use a command voice.

Nerissa stood behind him, her eyes teary as she took in the scene. But she kept quiet, letting Chase take the lead. He moved forward, slow and deliberate.

"Menolly. Listen to me. Come back to us. Come back to yourself. Do you hear me? Answer me, now."

And just like that, Menolly's face flashed again and she turned to Chase, her face softening out of the predator's gaze. As she saw Nerissa, her expression crumbled. She folded then, not in defense, but in tears, and Nerissa ran forward, gathering her in her arms.

"My wife, my beautiful, wonderful wife, can you forgive me for this?"

As Nerissa led her through the field of bodies, holding Menolly's face to her breast so she wouldn't have to look at them, Chase gestured to Camille and me. We turned to follow, leaving the carnage behind.

Chapter 6

When we arrived home, it was nearing 2:00 A.M. We were ragged and beat but the first thing Camille did was make me lie down on the sofa while she went to check on Iris. Nerissa led Menolly into the kitchen where I could hear them talking softly.

"What gives?" Roz brought me a light throw and covered me with it.

"Seven people died in the fire at the Wayfarer, and Menolly is blaming herself since it's her bar." I leaned back against the pillows gratefully. I hadn't realized just how shaky I still was until we'd gotten to the steps and Shade had to carry me up. It felt awkward—I wasn't a small woman—but when he saw I was having problems, he had swept me into his arms without a word and carried me inside.

Roz's expression fell. He slowly sat down beside me. "No. That's going to kill her." He shook his head. "I wonder if I should go talk to her—"

"It gets worse. She received threats—two calls, one tonight, from someone threatening to burn down the bar.

She's going to be asking herself why she didn't take it seriously after the first one. And we're going to have to have an answer she can live with. Right now, Nerissa is with her. Give them some time. How's Iris doing?"

"Still no sign of the babies but we're getting closer and she's a trouper. Trillian and Vanzir, of all people, are helping Hanna and Mallen. They told me to stay out here. Apparently, I get too panicked when it comes to a woman in labor."

The look on his face said everything and I pitied Mallen trying to work around Roz, especially with his ill-disguised crush on Iris. Even though I knew Roz was seeing Hanna, I also knew they were just doing the friends-with-benefits thing, and that neither one was up for anything permanent.

Shade tapped him on the shoulder. "How about letting me sit next to my fiancée?"

Roz jumped up. He'd learned all too well what crossing a dragon was like—thanks to a thrashing that Smoky gave him early on. He walked softly around both of them now, even though Shade was only half dragon and a lot less possessive.

"I'll take a peek in the kitchen and see how Menolly's doing."

As Roz left the room, Shade turned to me. "I'm sorry I didn't make it to the hospital, but I had a hell of a time finding Bruce. Camille called me to tell me what was going down—not only with Menolly, but with you. We're going to have to find the dreglins and wipe them out, of course. How are you feeling, love?"

"Like I got hit by a burning hot sledgehammer. Actually, though, I'm a lot better. And . . ." My thoughts went back to the image of Chrysandra, lying there, burned to a crisp and still alive. "I'm fine. I just need a little rest, but I'm fine."

Shade wrapped his arm around my shoulder and pulled me to him, my head resting on his shoulder. "I know. I know. Sometimes, you see something that never leaves you. Sometimes, there's no way to erase a horror from your memory."

"She was in so much agony. She hurt so fucking bad and

they couldn't do anything to stop it. The healers were just going to let her linger, mired in the pain, until she finally died. We couldn't let that happen." I began to cry, the tears finally coming as I leaned into his arms. "I wanted to take her soul, right there. But I couldn't use my powers—Greta would have had my hide. I wanted to shift and let Panther rip out her throat—make it quick and easy."

"You wanted to give her release." Shade held me as the tears trailed down my cheeks. "I know. But healers have certain rules . . . they live by a code."

"There comes a time when death is healing in itself." I looked into his eyes. "Menolly killed her, and the healer let her do it. He knew. He knew that it would be a blessing. She had to finish what the arsonist started."

"We do what we have to. Every rule has an exception. Nothing in this world is black and white—not even Shadow Wing. There's always another side to the story, always another perspective. So, you know it was arson?"

"Not officially, not yet. But we know." I told him about the letter and the phone calls. "We have no clue what's going on. But somebody torched the place. There's no doubt in my mind."

"Fuck. Then we find who did it and we take care of them." Shade gently placed his hands on my shoulders and pushed me back to stare in my face. "I have something to tell you. Perhaps this isn't the best time, but I want you to be prepared."

Nothing good ever came from the words "*I want you to be prepared.*" But Shade was stubborn and if he wanted to tell me whatever news it was, he would do just that.

"Okay . . . let's have it. But I'm too tired to steel myself so if it's really bad, be ready for me to go to pieces." I waited.

"My sister is coming to visit next week. Her name is Lash. She wants to meet you." The way he said it told me exactly what was going down. His family had heard about me and they were sending a scout to find out just who the hell I was.

Once again, my stomach lurched. I cleared my throat.

"So . . . this is news, all right. Is she like you? Half shadow dragon, half shadow walker? Kind of helpful to know who my judge and jury is going to be." I still had no clue what the Stradolans—the shadow walkers—were, Shade had always evaded my questions, but I wanted to know just who was going to be giving me the once-over.

Shade knew when I was being sarcastic and he bopped me gently on the nose with one finger. "Lash isn't that bad. She's not coming here to . . ." He stopped, then laughed. "All right, yes, she's coming here to look you over, but I think you'll like her. And I think she'll like you. And yes, she is both shadow walker and shadow dragon. Though I came from an earlier clutch, so technically I'm her older brother."

I kept my mouth shut, but inside, my stomach was a fluttering lek of butterflies. If she'd only showed up a week ago, it wouldn't have been a problem. But now? With everything that had just gone down in the past day? Not so good. But I said nothing. I didn't want to make Shade feel bad. Instead, I adjusted myself against the pillows and rested my arm on the back of the sofa. The wound hurt like hell, but it would heal. Best to just let this little blip alone till I was actually facing it. Or rather, *her*, as the case was.

"I hope she likes chaos. If she's going to stay here, she's going to be subject to a whole lot of it."

Roz reappeared. "Nerissa took Menolly downstairs. I think she's going to apply a little touch therapy, if you know what I mean. Menolly seemed a bit calmer by the time they headed to her lair."

Just then, Camille dashed in. "Baby number one is here! Iris just had a little girl and everything looks lovely. I'll be back as soon as baby number two arrives." She vanished before we could say a word.

I looked up at Shade and, for the first time today, I laughed. "Go Iris!" A wave of relief washed over me as I realized that at least one thing was going right.

"For such a little thing, she has the strength of many men." Shade broke out in a smile and I realized that I hadn't been the only one worried about our Iris. Birthing twins—especially for first babies—was a rather daunting thought. But it was half over, and so far, so good.

"Iris is going to be such a mama bear to those babies. She's scarier than all of us put together when she's pissed." And Iris also had some pretty incredible powers. We'd seen her turn someone inside out before with her magic. And while it wasn't something she could do at the drop of a hat, she was not just *any* Finnish house sprite. She was also a high priestess of Undutar, with the tattoos and the scars—both physical and emotional—to prove it.

I scooted up, so I was resting half against the pillows, half against the back of the sofa, and took Shade's hand. I was starting to feel sleepy, and as he caressed my fingers in silence, the idea of a quickie crossed my mind. But before I could say anything, weariness took over, and the toll of the wound hit me. I closed my eyes and drifted off to sleep.

The next thing I knew, I was blinking to a thin stream of sunlight flickering through the curtains. As I shifted position, trying to cover my eyes, I realized that Shade had carried me up to our bedroom. He had arranged me on the bed so I wouldn't have a crick in my neck or lie on my injured hand or something that would have left me hurting when I woke up. I squinted against the glow, shaking my head as I yawned and rolled up to a sitting position.

Shade was in the recliner, his feet propped up, a soft smile playing around his lips as he watched me. He was wearing a black turtleneck, khaki cargo pants, and a golden hoop in one ear. A hunger in my belly woke up—it had been a couple days since we'd had a chance for sex. As I pushed back the blankets, my tank top brushed against my breasts, and I caught my breath. He noticed, and the soft smile turned seductive.

"Morning, pussycat." And with that, he was sitting next to me, his arm around my waist. "Mmm, you're all tousled and warm and soft." His breath tickled against my ear and I turned so he could kiss me with those thick, gentle lips. As he pulled me to him, pressing me back against the tangled pile of covers and pillows, I wanted nothing more than to slip out of the pajama bottoms and draw him between my legs.

As I lingered in his kiss, a sudden thought struck me and I gently pushed him away. "Iris—how is she? Did she—"

"Have her other baby? Yes." Shade laughed and helped me stand up. "And after you've had a shower and we've dressed your wound, you can go see the little mother and her twins. Those two have healthy lungs on them, that's for sure. You must have been exhausted, to sleep through all of the racket we had after the boy came."

"What did she name them?"

"I'll let her tell you that. I don't want to spoil her fun." Shade disappeared into the bathroom. A moment later he returned with a plastic bag. "We'll tape this around your hand. You don't want to get that wound wet, except for when we clean it. We're going to have to irrigate it. Camille gave me the instructions for your aftercare that the healers provided on your release."

I hadn't remembered that I'd been officially released. Too much had gone down with Chrysandra's death, and Menolly's meltdown. Shrugging out of my PJ bottoms and tank top, I padded toward the bathroom. As a rule, I took as quick showers as I could, and I never took baths. I detested water. The tabby cat side of me equated baths with punishments, but I also liked being clean and, except for the times when I *was* Tabby, I couldn't very well groom myself with my tongue.

But before I could reach the door, Shade waylaid me. "You feeling better?" He pressed his lips to my neck and, once again, the fire took hold.

I stopped in my tracks, then turned and draped my arms around his neck. "I want you."

I'd become a lot less hesitant about sex over the months with him. Chase and I'd never quite been the right fit, and Zachary and I hadn't stood a chance in hell, but Shade had taught me how to let go of my insecurities and become confident in my sensual side. Together with the Autumn

Lord—who worked through him—the pair had brought me into my own sexually. One day I was destined to bear the Autumn Lord's child, and Shade would be the father. We were a triad. I belonged to both of them, the way that Camille belonged to her three men.

Shade wrapped his arms around my waist, his lips pressing against mine, and I lingered in his embrace. His hands were soft against my skin, but the strength in his fingers gave me security, and I knew that as long as he was with me, he'd do everything he could to protect me and my family. Dragons were like that—they protected their own.

He slid his hands up my back, and I was suddenly ravenous. I bit his lip, sucking gently, as he slid one knee between my legs. Opening to him, I trembled as the hunger began to swell. Panther was rising, and she wanted her mate. I put my good hand against his chest and walked him backward toward the bed.

Shade let out a low chuckle as he fell back on the mattress, leaning on his hands as his eyes grazed me from head to toe. "You are so beautiful, my delicious pussycat."

"Pussy is hungry." My voice low, I motioned to his chest. "Shirt. Off. Now."

He obligingly pulled off his turtleneck, exposing those glorious pecs of his and the six-pack abs that looked so good on men. Shade was built, his chest muscular and thick. *Thick* applied to other vital areas of his body, too.

I let out a low growl, the hunger rising. "Pants, too."

As he unbuckled his belt, the hunger turned to ache, and I leaped on the bed, wrapping my arms around his chest as he kicked off his pants. He was already hard and waiting, and I slid my hand down his chest to that dark, delicious cock that was rising out of the thatch of honey-colored hair. As I took him in hand, he let out a groan and started to turn.

With a whisper, I squeezed just hard enough to make him stop. "Let me explore your body. I want to touch you." I swung around, off the bed, and knelt in front of him. He was barefoot, and I leaned down and gently kissed the tops of his feet, then trailed a line of kisses up the inside of his legs, alternating sides. Here and there, I nipped with my fangs, not enough to draw blood but enough for him to jump ever so slightly.

As I approached his thighs, placing my hands on the glowing skin, the strength of his quads rippled beneath my fingers and once again, I caught my breath at how beautiful this man was. He was not perfect, he had a number of scars, but there was a beauty of their own in those craggy reminders of battles past, a history of his life. I knew very little about his background, but slowly, in bits and pieces, he had begun to give up his secrets.

I trailed my fingernails gently over the taut skin as he spread he legs, and then I leaned in, slowly licking the length of his cock, drawing my tongue up the shaft, tasting his musk. I had to be cautious—nonretractable fangs meant I could do a lot of damage to a man, but Shade was half dragon, and it took more than the average slip of the tooth to inflict pain. I slowly placed my lips on the head, gently slid them over the top, my mouth open just enough so that the tips of my fangs barely grazed the skin as I swallowed him, deep into my throat.

He let out another groan and leaned back on the bed, his hands coming down to hold my head as I worked him, licking, sucking, sliding my tongue down the length of his shaft. I cupped his balls, then pressed my lips to the sensitive area that lay between them and his penis. He was thick, hard as a rock, with the veins ridging up, and he was driving me crazy.

"Enough. Get your ass up here." He leaned down and, hands beneath my arms, lifted me up and rolled me over so I was beneath him. His lips sought my breast, leaving a wake of kisses down my neck as he fastened onto my nipple. Sucking hard, he nipped just enough to make me yelp, then his lips continued their path down my skin, across my stomach, setting off a wash of explosions that spread from my pussy outward.

He nuzzled me, his lips pressing gently against my clit as he flicked his tongue around in circles, sliding two fingers inside me to stroke against the inner walls. I was slick, moist with wanting him, but before I could beg him to get the hell inside me, the roar in my head increased as his tongue became more insistent, and I found myself laughing as I came, the stress releasing in joy rather than tears. The shock of another jolt hit as I came again, but still he continued.

As the laughter died, I began to build up again, this time a serious, dark rolling thunder that echoed through me, sucking me under. The strength of his hands on my hips, the unrelenting stroke of his tongue gave me no chance to catch my breath, and so I rode the rising surf, teetering precariously as thought vanished, and only sensation remained. And then, a pause, just one second of clear thought and back under as a series of explosions ricocheted through my body, echoing out in concentric circles. I found myself floating in a space where I wasn't sure if I was alive or dead, whether I was even breathing.

And then, slowly, the world came back into focus.

I exhaled as Shade loomed over me. With his gaze locked to mine, he slid between my legs, searching for entrance. As he thrust himself inside me, deep and penetrating, the room began to spin again, and we moved slowly, his hips swiveling against me. Full, stretched, I sank into the hunger that blossomed again.

"Harder . . ." My voice was hoarse, desperate. "Don't stop. Please, don't stop. Fuck me *hard*." As the sex haze reclaimed me, I went under for the third time, a woman drowning in a sea of air.

Shade groaned, his eyes flashing as his skin warmed mine. Emboldened by his heat, I grabbed his shoulders and rolled him over, straddling him as I sank onto his cock, my head back as I rode him hard. He grabbed my waist, holding me firm as I leaned over him, my breast above his mouth. He tilted up, took my nipple in his mouth as my clit rubbed against the base of his cock.

Before I could peak again, Shade lifted me and rolled off the bed with me. We tumbled to the floor in a pile of blankets and I twisted over onto one hand—my good one—and knees. I braced my right elbow on a stack of books, keeping my injured hand safe.

Shade knelt in back of me, sliding his cock into my cunt, and as he began to thrust, Panther rose, not shifting me, but driving me on. I felt her staring through my eyes, and I looked up and there was Hi'ran, the Autumn Lord. My passion and my Liege, towering over us.

He held out his hands, and the smell of bonfire smoke rolled from them as the heart of the harvest ran through my blood. Hi'ran's energy sparked a flame so dark that it quenched every sensation of light except for the fires raging around us. Shade let out a low moan, for Hi'ran was also *his* master.

Together, the three of us formed a circle of death, a circle of life. We existed within a cloud of passion, cloaked in the swirling mists of the eternal autumn. The energy crackled around us, until—with a flash of lightning—the storm broke and I went soaring over the edge, crying out as I once again lost myself in the tumble of orgasm.

When I opened my eyes, I was sprawled in the pile of sheets, and Shade had rolled to the side. He was staring at me through veiled eyes, a gentle smile playing at the corners of his lips.

"Wow." I exhaled slowly. "That was . . . wow."

"Took the words out of my mouth, babe." He shoved a pillow under his head, then held out his arms and I rolled into them. "For an arranged relationship, I think we clean it up pretty damned good."

"From your lips to my heart." After a moment, I untangled myself from the warm nest and stood up. "Time to get myself scrubbed down and go see Iris."

Shade fixed the plastic bag over my bandage and I padded into the bathroom, grabbing my pumpkin spice shower gel on the way. I never lingered in the water, but sometimes the scents kept me under longer than the minimum required time to get clean. I lathered up, washed my hair, and then quickly toweled off and used my blow dryer to whip my short, spiky do into submission.

Shade made me sit quietly while he removed the dressing on my hand. The wound wasn't big, not in the scheme of things, but still a sizable chunk when viewed against the base of my thumb where it had come from. The dreglin had chomped down on the part of my hand right below my thumb, and the exposed wound was violent and red. The gaping hole oozed, but the wound hadn't spread and that alone told me the antivenin and magic were working. But it looked so gross that it turned my stomach.

As he irrigated the wound, I bit my tongue against the pain, which was bad enough for me to want to kick him a good one. He then applied more of the salve and dressed it, unfazed. Afterward, he taped up the bandage and motioned for me to stand up.

"Let's go see Iris. Then, Camille said you are due to go visit some park? What's that all about?"

As we headed down the steps, I said, "We didn't have a chance to tell anybody what went on when we got back last night. Wait till we're all downstairs and we'll fill you in. For now, though, I want to go see those babies."

The sun was still peeking through the clouds as we headed out the kitchen door. A pale glow hovered over our land, and the leaves that were still on the trees glistened. The raindrops from the night before that clung to the leaves and branches cast prisms as the sunbeams flickered through them. I inhaled the aroma of wood smoke from both houses. It was a comforting scent, caught up on the wind that gusted through. A gaggle of geese flew south, their mournful calls echoing in the morning air. Winter was on the way, and a sudden chill washed over me with a prescience of the dark days of the year looming down.

Bruce and Iris's house was beautiful. A tidy cottage, the two-story bungalow looked cozy, a pale blue with cream-colored trim. It had old-world charm, even though it was brand-spanking-new. The guys had done an excellent job on it, and every nail had been driven with care.

"Who's going to take care of Iris while she's recovering? Hanna's needed at our place." We were heading through the backyard, and it saddened me to see the gardens lying dormant now, barren and fallow for the winter.

"Iris has help, don't you worry about that. Her mother-in-law arrived this morning to look after her, along with a retinue. At Camille's request, a new group of guards came through the portal from Otherworld. Elves, from Elqaneve. They'll be posted around the clock to keep an eye on the O'Shea household."

"Her *mother-in-law*?" I remembered Bruce's mother. She was a lovely woman—a leprechaun like her husband and children—but there was a tiger hidden beneath that refined, gentle surface and I knew that I'd never want to piss her off. I hoped, for Iris's sake, that they got along.

"Um hmm. By the way, her title is the Duchess O'Shea. Somehow, we missed out on using the correct address during the wedding, and it did not go unnoticed. I was informed in no uncertain terms this morning that we better correct that." Shade snorted, but the look in his eyes told me that the title wasn't for show.

"Who the hell told you that? The Leprechaun brigade?"

"Smoky. And he was serious."

I blinked. "Who knew? Well . . . so Mrs. Mother-of-Bruce is actually a duchess? Bruce's parents are a duke and duchess?" I knew they were wealthy beyond anything we'd experienced, but I had no idea they were nobility. Bruce's father was a lush, that much had become apparent during their stay back in February. A *nice* lush, but a lush.

"That's right. In the Leprechaun Court, they are definitely among the titled. Bruce is officially Lord Bruce Golden Eagle O'Shea. Quite a mouthful, though I'm not sure how it all fits together, and I've learned it's better not to ask. Leprechaun lore is guarded close to the heart among their people."

He stopped as we reached the cottage. Two steps led up

to a spacious porch, with a swing just like on ours. Iris had a massive kitchen herb garden growing in pots that lined the edge of the railing.

As we reached to knock, the door opened. Bruce peeked out. He looked exhausted, but happy, and a giddy smile spread across the curly-headed leprechaun's face as he stood back to let us in. He looked like Elijah Wood, only with darker hair and finer features.

I flashed back to Iris's first date with Bruce, when he still dressed like a frat boy and had vomited on her feet after drinking too much booze. But now, he was a professor at the University of Washington, and the head of Irish Studies there. And he seemed to like dressing the part, with his tweed blazers and pleated pants.

He ushered us in to the living room, and there sat our beloved Iris. She was in the rocking chair, her ankle-length flaxen hair neatly braided around her head, and she wore a lace nightgown and robe. Her spiraling tattoos that bordered her face and trailed down her neck glowed with an indigo hue. Bruce stood behind her, his hands on the top of the rocking chair.

On the luxurious jacquard sofa sat Mrs. O'Shea. As in Bruce's mother. As in, apparently, the Duchess. The regal air she'd sported at Iris's wedding had only increased and she was dressed in a rich forest green gown with a delicate golden tiara crowning her wheat-colored hair. I could see where Bruce got his looks—it certainly hadn't been from his father. At either side of the Duchess O'Shea sat a nurse, each holding one of the babies. Obviously, Bruce's mother wasn't a woman who dove in and did everything herself.

I curtseyed to her. "Duchess O'Shea, welcome to our land."

She eyed me up and down, then gently smiled and extended her hand. "The hosts of my son's home are always a welcome sight."

Iris started to stand but I dropped to my knees by her side and shook my head. "No you don't, little mama. You stay in your seat and rest. I'm sorry I couldn't be here earlier but I . . ." I didn't want to bring up my injury but Iris wasn't stupid.

She pointed to my hand. "Yes, I've heard the story. Dreglins are dangerous. I'm glad you went to the healer. So, are you going to introduce yourself to my children, Kitten? Or do I have to do it for you?" Her smile broadened, the pride in her voice echoing through the room. For the Talon-haltija, the Finnish house sprites, motherhood was a high honor. And to be a priestess who was also a mother had to be pretty much at the top of the list.

I scooted over to the sofa. The babies were tiny, definitely tinier than FBH babies, but they were perfect and petite and lovely. I cooed over them for a moment—the girl was swaddled in a violet blanket, the boy in one that was sky blue. They were both awake, and their eyes—the same brilliant blue as Iris's—seemed to search my face. They were going to be smart, that much I could tell right off the start.

"You did good, Iris. What are their names?" I glanced back at Iris, flashing her a thumbs-up sign.

She giggled. "You'll laugh, but . . ."

"No, I won't laugh." I started to say "I promise," but I knew better than that. Knowing Iris, their names could be just about anything. And somehow, I doubted Bruce had had much say in the matter, his duchess-mother or not. I glanced over at him, and the soft grin on his face confirmed my suspicions.

Iris set down her teacup and joined me, wincing slightly as she walked. She leaned over the little girl and softly kissed her tiny forehead.

"This . . . this is my beloved Maria." She gave me a long smile and a well of tears swelled up from my throat. I gazed at her silently, unable to speak. *Our mother's name* . . . she'd given her baby our mother's name. At my look, she whispered, "I wanted to honor your family— because the three of you girls *are* part of my family."

Biting my lip I looked back at the baby. "Hello, Maria. Welcome to the world, little one. You have the bravest mother you could ever hope to have."

Iris chuckled. "Well, I would give my life for them, that is a surety. The boy, my strapping lad, is Ukkonen. I named him after the Sky Father, and after the wind. He will be a musician, I think. Perhaps a bard."

Laughing, I tried to keep from startling the babies. "You know all of that, already?"

"I do." She nodded emphatically. "And my daughter . . . my daughter will follow in my footsteps and serve the Lady of the Mists. Undutar has already spoken to me about this. Maria will be raised as an Earthside priestess. She will not go to the Northlands like I did." Her voice darkened. "No one, save for the goddess herself, could force me to give up my children the way I was snatched away from my home."

"Ukkonen and Maria. Iris, you did good, love. You did good." And then, I burst into tears and hugged her gently. When we'd first met her, she'd been under a curse, with a tortured past we had only learned about in dribs and drabs. Now, the curse was broken and she was getting her happy ending. Or at least, as happy as any of us could ever hope for.

"You get up to the house now, Kitten. Camille is waiting for you, and I need to rest." Iris returned to the rocking chair.

I stood, slowly, not wanting to leave. It felt like her life was moving along a different path than ours. Logically, I knew it was just that she was finding her niche. She was here, her home was here, and Bruce was more than happy to share his wife with us. But I still felt like things had shifted so far from the safe, tight-knit group we'd started as. Leaning down, I kissed Iris on the cheek.

"Little mama, if you need anything, *anything at all*, just let us know. Rest now." As Shade and I left her house, I looked up at the sky. Once more, clouds were coming in, thick and dark. A storm was on the horizon and I could feel it in my bones.

Chapter 7

The kitchen was jammed. Breakfast time had become a thriving bustle in our home, with the exception of Menolly, of course. Everybody other than Iris and Bruce was there. Smoky and Trillian were handing stacks of plates and dishes of food from Hanna, who was in charge of the counter, to Vanzir, who arranged them on the table. Camille was on the phone, trying to talk over the clamor. Nerissa had her head jammed in the refrigerator, looking for something while Rozurial filled juice glasses. Shade jumped in to help, while I slid through the chaos to sit by Camille.

Camille had one finger in her ear while pressing the receiver against her other ear and was shouting over the mayhem. And then, she let out a loud "Oh, fuck" and, at the tone of her voice, the kitchen quieted down. A moment later, she punched the End Talk button and looked up, mute sorrow on her face.

She inhaled sharply, slowly exhaled, and shook her head. "That was Chase. He's down at the Wayfarer. The fire's out, the embers are cold . . ."

"What's the damage?" Nerissa closed the refrigerator and approached the table, a guarded look on her face. She'd have to be the one consoling Menolly the most, even though we'd all be there.

Camille flashed her a bleak look. "Eight dead—they found another body in the remains. The bar is eighty percent destroyed. The fire marshal says a candle in one of the upstairs rooms tipped over, or something like that. It caught the curtain on fire and . . ."

"Oh crap. One of the guest rooms. Was the occupant one of the victims?" If not, then whoever it was had left the candle burning unattended.

"That's the thing . . . the door was locked, and there seems to be no record of a guest checked into that room."

"We were right. Arson."

Camille shrugged. "Yeah. I told them about the calls. Would be way too easy to cloak arson as an accident. And while there's a record of all guests, Menolly's office with the computer was a casualty. We have no way of accessing any of their names or where they came from. And you know, nobody's going to remember in this mess. Chase talked to Derrick and to Digger, but neither could help much."

"Do they have any clue whether any vampires were caught in the fire? Nothing would be left but piles of dust to mix with the ashes." Fire could destroy so much, including all traces that someone had once walked this world.

"We won't know for sure, ever, though tonight when the vamps rise, we might be able to figure out a few things. See if anybody was at the club with a vamp who has vanished. You know how that goes."

I nodded. "Yeah, sadly."

Camille attacked her stack of pancakes and sausage. "How are you feeling? How's your hand? You up to going out to Interlaken Park to find out if there's any evidence that Violet may have had a stalker?"

I held up my freshly bandaged wound. "It hurts. It's going to hurt. As long as I take it easy, everything should be fine. It doesn't look like it's spreading and I feel a lot better than last night."

She glanced over at Nerissa. "Tonight, we have to head to Otherworld. Menolly's going to have to know about the extent of the damage as soon as she wakes up. I think . . . we'd all better gather here around 5:30. Sunset is at about 6:30 for another week or so till Daylight Savings Time kicks in. We need to have as much info as we can on what's going down regarding the bar. Can you gather up everything you can find out while you're at work?"

Nerissa nodded. "Will do. I guess sometimes it's a good thing that I work for Chase's division." She finished up her breakfast—mostly, Menolly's wife ate a lot of meat, some vegetables and fruits, and a small amount of other foods. Her inner carnivore came out in spades. Earthside were-pumas were known for their high protein consumption. "Okay, I'm off. I'll be home before Menolly wakes up, and I'll see what I can find out. Chase or I will call you if anything comes up that we need to address right away."

As she gathered up her purse and threw on a jacket, the look on her face spoke for all of us. Telling Menolly that the fire had destroyed most of the bar would be bad enough, but we all knew the victims were the casualties that tore her to pieces. There was no way to cushion her heart from the death.

Nerissa had no sooner closed the door when Hanna turned around from the sink. "Someone needs to watch Maggie. I am to help the Duchess with Iris today, so the housework will have to wait."

She stood, hands on her hips, staring at us. Hanna was tough. When Hyto kidnapped Camille and carried her off to his lair in the Northlands to face torture and death, Hanna had helped her escape at risk of her own life. Camille had brought her home, and now Hanna lived with us and helped Iris out with the housework and taking care of Maggie.

I decided to delegate. "Smoky, you and Vanzir help Hanna today. Rozurial, can you and Trillian prepare for our trip tonight? Shade, come with Camille and me to check out the park?" And then, it occurred to me that—in the chaos surrounding the fire at the Wayfarer—we hadn't filled everybody in on what was happening. They knew something was up, given Grandmother Coyote and the gargoyles, but they had no clue about everything else.

"On second thought, let's start at the beginning . . ." I nodded to Camille, and we laid out everything that had happened the evening before.

"So, let me get this straight: A—Grandmother Coyote wants you to find out what's going down with the daemonic activity at the Farantino Building and put a stop to it. B— You have to track down a group of dreglins and exterminate them. And C—Tad and Albert want you to find out what happened to their friend Violet." Vanzir grinned at me. "That about it, pussycat?"

The dream-chaser demon liked to needle me, but his teasing had evolved into a fond playfulness rather than the edgy sarcasm that had at first prefaced it.

"That's about it. I honestly don't know what to think about Violet—there's still a nagging voice that says she just disappeared off on some trip, but I don't want to chance us being wrong." I glanced up at the clock. "Okay, let's head out. First, we'd better swing by the Wayfarer and see just what the damage is. Then we'll stop at the FH-CSI and I'll have them look at my hand. After that, we can do a little daylight surveillance of the Farantino Building. And then, over to the park."

As Camille polished off her breakfast, Shade began clearing the table. My mind was scattered, but in the back of my thoughts, I couldn't help but think that the dam had broken. Our lucky streak was over and we were back on the job.

Camille drove again. I was getting tired of my Jeep being in the shop but Jason was working as fast as he could, and we trusted him. Parts could only be ordered so quickly, and with three rush jobs ahead of mine, things had been poking along at a snail's pace.

We inched through the rush hour traffic. At this time of the morning, it was still bumper-to-bumper and would be for another hour. Camille had her iPhone plugged in to the dash and her playlist was blasting away. I grimaced. How anybody could listen to Nine Inch Nails at this time in the morning escaped me, but it was her car, so we listened to her music.

The morning gloom was thick and the rain heavy, and the streets were slick. Camille flipped off the music, just before an SUV swerved into our lane.

"Fucking idiots are out in droves." She slammed on the brakes as the SUV cut her off, nosing in where there wasn't room. The Lexus skidded to the right, and we almost crashed into a Mercedes parked in front of a coffee shop, but Camille managed to straighten out and avoid the collision. After that, she focused on the road, and Shade and I kept quiet.

A couple more near misses—both times a big hunking gas guzzler trying to shove into too tight of a space—and we were onto the street where the Wayfarer stood. Or what was left of it. We pulled in, parking in front of the smoking remains, and Camille turned off the ignition. We stared, none of us saying a word.

The fire hadn't spread to the neighboring buildings, luckily, but the bar was obviously gutted. I slowly unfastened my seat belt and opened the car door. The smell of smoke hung thick in the air, and the scents of charred wood and wet ash filled my nostrils. I sneezed, and Camille echoed me. She came around to stand by my left, while Shade flanked my right.

The yellow caution tape still surrounded the entrance, blocking off half the sidewalk. Derrick Means was standing there, staring up at the bar with his hands jammed in his pockets. His hair, usually in a ponytail, hung straight—as black as Camille's but with a shock of white streaking through it. He had eyes the color of my own—emerald green. He was damned good at his job. A werebadger, Derrick had quickly become Menolly's righthand man at the

Wayfarer, acting as both bartender and, at times, bouncer. Now and then he played the part of a sounding board.

He turned as we approached. "Fucking mess, if you ask me."

I nodded. "Yeah. It's worse than we feared. Menolly doesn't know yet, just how bad the damage is. We can't tell her till she rises tonight."

Derrick coughed, then spit on the ground. He wiped his mouth. "Going to break her heart. Does she know about Chrysandra?"

Camille let out a sigh. "Yes. All three of us were with her when she died. She didn't go easy, I'll tell you that. And Menolly knows that six others died—she hasn't heard about the eighth victim yet."

"The fire marshal says a candle ignited curtains in one of the rooms. I tell you though, it couldn't have. Nobody was in that room. The damned door was locked. They had to break it down. And I know for a fact we didn't register anybody into it—it hadn't been cleaned yet after the last guest left." Derrick scowled, kicking the wall with the toe of his heavy boot. "Did she tell you about the calls?"

We stared at him. So he'd had the same thought we had.

"You know about them?" I cocked my head to the side, squinting up at the second floor. Even from out here, it was obvious how heavy the damage had been.

"Oh, hell yes. But Menolly wouldn't let me report the first one, and the second—I was there when you were. I heard her trying to get info out of the freak. I'm convinced this was somebody's idea of payback. Who? I dunno. But somebody wanted to destroy the Wayfarer and they found a way to do it." The bartender shook his head. "And you just wait—two humans were among the dead. Their families aren't going to wait long before they lawyer up and sue Menolly's ass off."

That thought hadn't even crossed my mind. I didn't think it had crossed Camille's either, by the look on her face.

"What the hell . . . you think somebody might actually do that? What if it's found to be arson? Would she still be liable?" I hopped over the tape and cautiously approached the building. As I peered in the window, which was now an opening with a pile of jagged glass surrounding it, the inside of the bar was a surreal sight.

In the dim light, I could still see broken timbers from the ceiling that had come crashing down to the floor. The rows of booths were now piles of rubble, the tables and chairs were so much charcoal, and the bar—the beautiful hand carved bar—was a charred, ruined mess. The Wayfarer was a total loss.

I turned around. "Did the cops say when we can pick through the ashes to see what we can salvage?"

Derrick shrugged. "They told me that we can go back in, but we better have a demolition company come here first and remove some of the hanging beams. It's dangerous. Over eighty percent destroyed. But that means there may be a few things worth saving, and they said that the foundation of the structure is still viable. Menolly can rebuild, if she wants to."

"If it *is* legally deemed arson, we can collect the insurance. But if it's labeled an accident, then who knows what's going to happen. And if, like you said, the families of the victims sue . . . it could wipe out everything." I rubbed my head. "What are we going to do?"

Camille maneuvered over the caution tape and wrapped her arm around my waist, peering in. "You know as well as I do that the worst part of this for Menolly is going to be the eight victims. Money is only money. You can always make more. But lives have been lost and that's never easy."

"Yeah. I know." I knew she was thinking of Henry Jeffries, a regular at the Indigo Crescent—Camille's bookshop. He'd volunteered to work for her part time and the thanks he got for his trouble was a violent death come too early, meted out by our enemies. He had left a good share of his money to Camille, though, and she'd expanded the shop and rebuilt after it had been partially destroyed in an explosion, adding on a coffee shop next door.

But as far as keeping our Earthside livelihoods intact, we were batting a thousand, it seemed.

We stared at the entrance. I was tempted to go in, to find something to salvage in order to give Menolly a little comfort but Camille was right. The building, the bar . . . all of that would hurt, of course. But the people . . . their deaths would haunt Menolly for years unless we could prove to her that it hadn't been somehow her fault.

I glanced over at Derrick. "What are you going to do?"

"I'll wait here. The others will be here soon. We're going to dive in and start making some sense of this so that by the time Menolly gets here tomorrow night, it's not so horrifying. She's a great boss and we want to help out however we can." He gave us a two-fingered salute as we slowly returned to the car.

Shade was the first to speak once we were buckled in and back on the road. "If there's a question of money, not to worry. Between Smoky and me, we can make this happen. We talked about it this morning before the two of you woke up."

I glanced over my shoulder. "Love, you are so wonderful. And Smoky. But what we really need is for the fire marshal to find the evidence pointing to arson. We need the physical proof for Menolly's sake."

Camille frowned. "That's going to be difficult, especially if the fire marshal is on the fence about it. But . . . all right. If the fire started in a locked room, I guess our first question to ask is: Who had a key to that room? Who could have gotten in there? Could the lock have been picked? Was it an easy target? Considering it's a hotel room, essentially, I hope the answer to the latter two questions is *no*. Because having unsecured guest rooms? Not so good for business and you know the rumor mill would fly."

"I guess we ask Menolly who had the keys. Then, we ask whoever had a copy if they still have it. Maybe somebody stole one and it wasn't noticed." I pulled out my notepad and jotted stuff down. I loved my laptop but didn't trust my phone to capture the notes I was making. Camille, on the other hand, now used her phone for everything. I think she even slept with it near the bed, though I wouldn't put it past one of her husbands to turn the damned thing off when she wasn't looking.

"What next?" Shade looked around. "I don't think there's much more we can do here, at least not right now."

Slowly, I agreed. "You're right." Part of me was loath to leave the bar. It seemed callous to turn our backs and walk away, but what would we accomplish by staying? I tucked my notepad away and let out a long sigh. "Okay, it's off to the FH-CSI."

With a wave to Derrick, we turned, and left the burned out shell behind us.

The bustle was loud and noisy at the FH-CSI. Chase gave us a wave as we passed his office; he looked like he was in a meeting with some bigwig in a suit. He peeked around his office door.

"See you tonight, guys. I promised Nerissa that I'll gather all the information I can about the Wayfarer then, but right now but this meeting's one I have to take."

We waved him back into his office and headed for the medic unit. There, Sharah was bandaging up one of the officers, who looked like he'd been bitten by a dog. Blonde and timidly pretty, the elfin medic was ready to pop any day, like Iris, and looked harried and tired. She was also the niece to Queen Asteria, back in Elqaneve. She brushed away a stray lock of hair and flashed us a genuine smile as we entered the room, then slapped the officer on the knee.

"You're good to go. Just watch it next time, Dan. Dog bites can be dangerous, and it's worse when a hellhound is involved."

Camille winced. She'd been wounded by a hellhound before, and the acid in its bite had left quite a tidy scar on her. The cop merely nodded his thanks, pulled down his pants leg, and headed out without even glancing our way.

"You want me to check that hand?" Sharah asked.

I nodded. "Yeah, if you've got the time. You hear what happened last night?"

"Chase said that you were bitten by some sort of Fae, and then of course, all the commotion with the Wayfarer." Sobering, she motioned for me to take a seat. "I'm sorry about Chrysandra. She was a good person. Real class act."

"Yeah, she was. Menolly took it hard. Chrysandra was there from the start—from when Menolly first went to work at the Wayfarer." As I sat down, Camille and Shade headed out to the waiting room, giving us space.

Sharah and Chase made a good couple, and I had let go of any lingering sense of regret. They fit together. Shade and I fit together. Chase and I had not done so well and we made far better friends than lovers.

For a while, Sharah had been leery of my continued friendship with the detective, but it had been her pregnancy hormones talking, and she'd managed to get them under control. We'd had dinner out a few times—both couples together—and things felt like they were back to normal. Or rather, we were at a new normal—a comfortable one.

She unwrapped my dressings and winced. "Oh Delilah, this is a nasty bite. Must hurt like hell." Probing gently around the edges, she finally rose to fetch a jar of salve off the shelf. She motioned me over to the sink, where she used a cleaning solution and antibacterial soap to irrigate the wound.

"Well, it isn't spreading. It *is* necrotic in origin, but you caught it soon enough and the salve is doing its job. We seem to have neutralized the venom and all we have to do now is to keep the wound clean and bandaged and it will heal over. You will have a scar and there's going to be an indentation right here where the flesh is gone. I imagine it will fill in a little as it heals, but there's nothing that can really put that chunk of missing flesh back. Somehow, your attacker missed major arteries. The nerve endings might be a little dulled, but I don't think it will impede the use of your hand."

I winced as she dried it. "I feel like a jerk for even saying this, after seeing what Chrysandra was going through last night. But truth is? Great gods, this hurts."

"Don't even compare the two. Pain is pain. Yes, she was in agony but that doesn't mean this wound doesn't hurt, either. People make that mistake all the time—negating their own problems because somebody else has it worse. Now, if you said that directly to her? Yes, then it would be crass."

She sighed, pressing her hands against her back as she gently stretched. "We all have our trials. I'm afraid this will hurt for a long time—not as bad as it does now, but it's going to ache. While we can negate the toxin, we can't do anything for the pain without doping you up and I don't think you want that." She finished bandaging it and stood back with a sigh.

I gingerly rubbed my wrist, above the wound. "No, that's the last thing I need right now." Flashing her a rueful grin, I added, "Are you ready for tonight? You haven't been home in a while, have you?"

Sharah's expression crumbled and she sank into a chair, looking both uncomfortable and frightened. "No, I haven't. Thing is . . . I haven't told my aunt about the baby."

Okay, so I hadn't expected to hear that, but I understood her reasoning. If anybody knew how bad things were for half-breeds, especially among Otherworld nobility, it was my sisters and me. We had been teased unmercifully by a number of children in the Court back in Y'Elestrial, constantly called Windwalkers—a derogatory term for those of half blood among the Fae. I wasn't sure what the equivalent term was for elves, but it was probably just as mean.

"How will the trip through the portal affect you? Are you sure it's safe for you to travel right now? You say Queen Asteria doesn't know you're pregnant. If she knew, would she insist that you return home right now?" It occurred to me that if Queen Asteria knew the truth of the matter, she might give Sharah some leeway. I knew the portal probably would be safe enough, but if there was any doubt . . .

Sharah shrugged. "The portals shouldn't bother me. Honestly, while they feel like they rip you apart and stick you back together again, they don't. It may not be comfortable, but it's not like *Star Trek*. You know that." She grinned at me then. "But thanks for trying to give me an out."

I smiled back. "Yeah, true. And your aunt knows all about the mechanics of how they work. Seriously, do you think that word hasn't leaked back? Could Mallen have told her?"

She paled—and elves were naturally pale. "I never thought about that. He's my friend. He wouldn't rat me out."

Grinning, I said, "You've been over here long enough that you're starting to pick up the slang. Well, she's never mentioned it to us, but your aunt seems to be privy to a lot of secrets and it wouldn't surprise me that she's got operatives over here whom *none* of us know about. Whatever the case, you know that my sisters and I will stand behind you and Chase, even if Queen Asteria gets pissed."

With a nod, Sharah let out a long sigh. "See, the problem is this: I'm expected to eventually return home and marry into the Court. I'm her niece, and I'm close enough to the throne for things like marriage and breeding to matter. There aren't that many relatives left who are standing in line. But show up with a half-blood child? I have no idea what kind of reception I'll get. And the fact that Chase has a little elf blood in his lineage, well, that's not going to make all that much difference."

"Are things bad for half-breeds in the elfin court? When Camille, Menolly, and I were growing up, we were teased without mercy. Camille used to beat up on the kids who made fun of us, she tried to protect Menolly and me, but it never stopped." Visions of our childhood flashed through my mind, and I shook my head. Kids could be so damned cruel. For a long time the memories had haunted me, but lately, I found I could shake them away without the sting they once held.

Sharah caught my gaze and held it. "It's worse among the elves. Lineage means so much to my people."

"I didn't know that, but now that you mention it, yeah, I guess I can see how that is." The elves were proper and there was a sense of decorum about them that I could easily visualize verging into sanctimonious territory.

"Well, I guess we'll find out, won't we?" She gave me a rueful smile. "Thanks for backing us up, Delilah. Especially you. I know that it must feel odd with Chase and me being together but . . ."

"Not anymore. You two are much better suited to one another. At first, yes, it did feel a little awkward, but I'm happy for you, Sharah. And I love Shade. We're a matched pair. And I want Chase to be happy—and you make him happy, and so does the fact that he's going to be a father." I paused, not sure how far I should push, but in for a penny, in for a pound. "You know he would love to marry you."

"I know." She paused. "He's asked, and I was pretty sure that he told you I said no. I just . . . I don't want to tie him down to something he may regret. He's just barely beginning to discover his own powers. The Nectar of Life changed him, and there's no getting around the fact that he'll be going through this transformation for years maybe. It's impossible to predict just where he's going to end up."

"I know that." I leaned forward. "But one thing I've discovered over the years here is that humans—FBH's, if you will—they live uncertain and short lives. They are used to taking chances and risks because if they don't, they may face the end of their lives wondering what would have happened if they'd gone for the gold ring, if they'd jumped at this chance, or that opportunity. They don't have the luxury to stroll through life. And even though Chase's life span is now drastically extended, I think his mind is still caught up in that thought process. It's all he's ever known."

I'd never really thought it through before, but now that the words were out of my mouth it made so much sense. "Sharah, if the marriage doesn't work out, it's not permanent. Over here, Earthside, there really isn't any sense of permanence. If you guys find out that you aren't really meant for each other, you can separate."

Sharah bit her lip. "I hadn't thought about that. Back home, in Elqaneve, marriages are for life. Yes, they are usually marriages based on politics, and taking a lover is a common practice—though not quite as common as among your people—but I am expected to marry into the Court and produce children of my bloodline, and unless there is obvious abuse, I'm stuck with my husband for life. Somehow, I don't think this little one is going to be accepted." She rubbed her stomach. Tears welled up and she hung her head. "My aunt is going to say I disgraced my name. I know it."

Life back in Otherworld could be just as harsh as life Earthside. So many people had always thought of the Fae and elves as happy, peaceful creatures who lived simple lives, but that was a long way from the truth. We didn't flit around flowers, and even those who were woodland Fae, connected to the forests, were often ruthless and dangerous.

I leaned forward and rested my hand on hers. "Fuck 'em then. I don't use that word often, like Camille and Menolly do, but fuck them and the horse they rode in on. If they don't accept you, too bad. You've got Chase here, you've got us, and you've got friends. You're not alone, Sharah."

She lifted her head and I wiped the tears off her face.

"Thank you," she whispered. "That means so much to me."

"It's true." I sighed. "But I'd better get a move on. We have things to do before leaving for Otherworld tonight. See you this evening . . . and—whatever happens—we'll be there for you."

As I left, she began to disinfect the table on which I'd rested my arm. I paused, watching the elf for a moment, then headed to the waiting room. Camille and Shade were sitting patiently, Camille was reading a book—a mystery by J. A. Jance. Shade was writing down something in a small notebook. They both looked up as I entered the room. I motioned to them and they stood, following me out the doors.

When we were in Camille's car, I told them what Sharah had said. "She's scared out of her mind that Queen Asteria is going to be so pissed off she'll kick her out of the family or something."

"Well, I know how that feels." Camille frowned. Our

father had disowned her for a while, for a decision she had made. He was just now working his way back into our good graces and had apologized profusely.

"I told her we'd back her and Chase up, if the Queen gives her any flack."

"Hell yes." Camille put the car into gear and pulled out of the parking lot. "She and Chase are good people. I'm so tired of being pushed around by the royalty and I sure as hell don't intend to stand by and watch that happen to friends." She paused, and added, "While you were getting your hand looked at, I made a couple quick calls. Besides all of the offices in the Farantino Building, there's also a small coffee shop, probably to service the people who work there. But it's also open to the public. We can make a stop there, and get a feel for the building that way."

"Have you had a chance to look over what Carter gave us last night? The files on the building?" I had been in no shape to do so that was for sure.

She shook her head. "No, by the time we got home, I was as done in as everybody else. But we can do that . . . I guess when we get back from Otherworld. It doesn't seem pressing at this point so I think a day's delay won't hurt anything."

As we headed to the Farantino Building, I watched out the window at the heavy rains pounding down. We were in the thick of autumn now, and the energy was strong for me. Hi'ran loomed in my thoughts, and as I leaned back against the seat, soothed by the gray clouds and the gloom, it occurred to me just how far I'd come since we moved here. And it made me wonder just where I was going to end up.

Chapter 8

We found a parking spot right away, thanks to Camille's ever-uncanny luck at being in the right place at the right time. During the day, the Farantino Building looked even more imposing. The brickwork was intricate, the row of lifelike gargoyles lining the ledge giving pause. They had been made at a time when I doubted molds were used, and indeed, from even this distance, they seemed to have their own personalities and differences.

Camille leaned toward me. "They look real."

"Yeah. But wouldn't Grandmother Coyote tell us if there were more granticulars than just Astralis and Mithra?"

She snorted. "You want to bet on that? Grandmother Coyote? Secretive much, I think." Hoisting her purse over her shoulder, she opened the car door. "Let's get a move on. At least they aren't going to be on the lookout for us. Whoever *they* are and whatever their agenda is."

A mad dash through the rain and we were in the street-front coffee shop, called the Café o' Lait. It was small, but laid out in a precise manner that allowed for a surprisingly large number of customers to sit. I glanced around and led the way to a table near the back. I could see a hallway leading out into the rest of the building from there, and we had an unobstructed view of the rest of the coffee shop.

I motioned for Camille and Shade to have a seat. "What do you want? While I order our drinks, you can get a feel for the people in here. You're better at that than I am."

Camille nodded. "Order me a quad venti iced chocolate caramel latte, would you?"

Shade laughed. "Caffeine hound. I'll have black tea. Milk, two sugars." He pulled his wallet out of his pocket and handed me a ten and a twenty. "Better get us each a brownie, too."

Camille shook her head. "I'd rather have a roast beef sandwich, thanks."

I took the cash and headed up to the counter where I placed their orders, along with one for a tall hot chocolate and two peanut butter cookies for myself. As I stood there, waiting for the cashier to give me my change, I tried to start up casual conversation. "So, we just happened by and saw this place. How long have you been open?"

The cashier glanced at me. She didn't seem all that friendly, but she smiled briefly and gave me my change. "Several years. I just work here, though. I have no idea when they opened the coffee shop." She set a tray on the counter and slammed down a prewrapped sandwich on it, a small paper plate with the brownie and two cookies on another. "Here's your food. I'll bring your drinks over to your table when they're done."

And with that, she turned away and I realized the conversation was over. Ignoring the tip jar—which I seldom did—I carried the food back to the table.

"Apparently the cashier has either had a very bad day or she's not interested in casual conversation." I handed Shade his brownie as Camille unwrapped her sandwich.

As she bit into it, she winced. "Um, they aren't that interested in making food taste all that good either. This is okay but it's not going to win any awards for sandwich of the week. Either that or I'm spoiled by Hanna and Iris's cooking."

I tasted the cookies. They were nothing to write home about. "I guess they have a captive audience with the workers in the building." Glancing around, I tried to assess the clientele. "They all seem to be suit-and-tie, even the women have that dressed-for-success look. Think they all work here?"

Pausing as the waitress brought us our drinks, Camille waited till the girl went back to the counter before speaking. "I think so. And I don't sense any Demonkin, or even daemons—though I'm not as good at sussing them out as I am Shadow Wing and his kind. These people all seem entirely human to me." She looked perplexed.

"Then what? We just go wandering around the halls trying to figure out what's going on?" It wasn't like the building was a top security fortress, as far as we could see. "We can always say we thought our lawyer was in this building if somebody tries to stop us."

"Sounds good to me." She dropped the remaining half of her sandwich on the tray. "This isn't even good enough to finish." Picking up her drink in one hand, with the other she carried the tray over to the trash bin and we headed out into the hallway.

"Oh no, we're not conspicuous *at all*," Shade said, with a smirk on his face.

I smacked his arm. "Oh, shut up, you goober."

He grabbed my hand, entwining his fingers through mine. "A kiss in payment and I'll stop teasing you." His eyes were playful, and I leaned over and planted a soft kiss on his lips, once again grateful we'd met.

Camille laughed. "You two are cute. Now come on, let's get a move on before somebody tries to stop us."

The hallway led to a bank of elevators, and beyond that, several offices with windowed doors. The hallway was carpeted in a rich navy blue plaid, with green and red stripes running through it. A few potted plants were snug in the corners, and near the elevators sat a wrought iron bench covered with a blue upholstered cushion. Camille saw it at the same time I did and we both shuddered. Cast iron gave us nasty burns, though steel didn't affect us much. But touch iron too long with our bare skin? Led to a world of hurt.

We passed the elevators and I motioned for Shade and Camille to stay near them as I slipped down the hall to sneak a peek. There were five doors, as well as an entry to the stairwell. The first two offices simply had names on the doors without any indication of title or status or vocation. I jotted down the names quickly and moved on.

The third door, however, had two names: WILSON PRESCOTT III, P.C., AND REGINALD D. FAIRFAX, P.C., ATTORNEYS AT LAW. The fourth door had no nameplate, but there was mail stuck under the door. I wanted to pick it up and glance at the name but the chance of someone coming along and seeing me was too great. The fifth door had a sign on it that read JANITOR.

So two lawyers, a coffee shop, a couple unknowns, and a maintenance room. There was no sign that anybody saw me, but as I headed back to the elevator, two women who had been in the coffee shop were making their way into one of the elevators. They were giving Camille and Shade a long look, but then went back to whispering and laughing. As the doors shut, I quickly rejoined the others.

"Gerald Hanson's office must be on one of the upper floors." Camille frowned, looking around.

"Anything at all?" I looked at Camille. "If you can't sense anything, nobody can."

She sighed, then closed her eyes again and leaned back against the wall. A moment later, she shook her head. "Sorry."

"Shade?" I turned toward my fiancé. "What about you?"

He shrugged. A moment later, he softly said, "There are ghosts here, but they feel lost rather than angry or dangerous. I can't pinpoint them, nor can I sense anything else. But I can tell you this: I believe there's something blocking energy. Or rather, blocking the identification of energy. I sense a force field of some sort."

"Force field? Usually people put up a force field when they want to keep prying eyes out of their business. Can you sense the nature of it at all?" I frowned. Too bad Iris was out of commission. She was really good with things like force fields and illusion spells. Morio had some talent at it, but Iris was the one who was our expert. But right now, not such a good time to call her up.

Shade pursed his lips, then closed his eyes. After a moment, a breeze ran through the hallway but I was able to recognize that it was off the astral. Thinking Shade was responsible, I turned to him but he looked deep in trance and I didn't want to disturb whatever he was doing. I looked at Camille, touching her arm, and she nodded.

With a shiver, Shade's eyes flew open and he looked around nervously. "I think we'd better get out of here. I can't tell you why just yet, but this is not a safe place to be until we've done more research. Seriously, you and Camille? You need to leave this place. *Now.*" And with that, before we could speak, he slipped his arms around both our shoulders and pushed us back down the hallway toward the coffee shop.

We had almost reached the front door when my stomach lurched. I stopped at the same time as Camille, and subtly turned to look over my shoulder. She did the same.

Behind us, entering the shop from the hallway through which we had just retreated, was a man. He looked human enough, but there was something about him that was hard to pinpoint. He was suave—very suave, dressed in a suit that, from hanging out with Chase, I recognized as Ralph Lauren. The man had paired slim black dress trousers, which looked like expensive jeans, with a black leather sport coat. Beneath the coat, he was wearing a cobalt blue V-neck cashmere sweater that made his golden tan pop.

The man had incredible features. His tan looked so natural that I couldn't tell if it was his normal skin color, from the sun, or a very expensive tanning bed. And his hair was shaved close—not so that he was bald, but his buzz cut worked. The shape of his head seemed symmetrical and I found myself focusing on the tattoo showing through the pale layer of hair. I couldn't see from here what the ink portrayed, but it covered his head.

When I caught his gaze, his eyes stopped me. Pale green, the color of spring grass, they were ringed with a black halo, and his gaze was arrestingly sharp. He stared at me, then his gaze flickered over Camille and Shade, and he slowly, deliberately, headed in our direction.

I wanted to run. Panic welled up in my throat and, not knowing where it was coming from, I tugged on Camille's arm. She, too, looked alarmed. Shade must have noticed our reactions because he stepped between the approaching man and us.

"How do you do?" The man held out his hand. "I hope you're enjoying our little establishment here."

Shade nodded, ignoring the outstretched hand, but he did so with a smile to disarm. "We were about to leave, but yes, we needed coffee and happened to notice the Café o' Lait."

The man regarded Shade with quiet consideration. After a moment, his lips turned up at the corner, and once again, he glanced at Camille and me. "You have very lovely companions."

I could tell that Camille had taken an instant dislike to the man. As she opened her mouth to speak—no doubt to say something charmingly rude—I nudged against her, trying to shut her up. But Shade beat her to the punch.

"I'm afraid we have to be going." He smoothly turned and, once again, propelled us forward.

As we neared the door, the man behind us called out, "Please, do come again. And bring your lady friends. We always enjoy having beautiful customers grace our halls."

And then, we were out, crossing the street toward the parking lot. None of us spoke, but I was incredibly grateful that Shade was behind us. And I was also thankful that we'd parked in a lot, where it wouldn't be immediately apparent which car we were getting into.

The minute we settled ourselves in the Lexus, I noticed Camille began to shake. "What's wrong?"

"That man, he scared the fuck out of me. He's not human, I know it. He's nowhere near human. I think he might be daemon but I can't be sure. But . . . his energy? He's as dangerous as he is gorgeous. And that charisma he has? It's natural—like our glamour. There was no magic being used there." The words spilled out of her in a rush, and she clutched the steering wheel.

"She's right. He does have a natural charm." Shade looked around the lot. "And he is dangerous. Which is why I didn't let you say anything. We do not want to arouse his suspicions, given the building's nature, nor engage him in anyway—that much I can tell you."

"Dude, I wasn't going to be snarky, regardless of what you thought." Camille let out a long sigh. "I was simply going to tell him thank you and then leave."

"Either way, we needed to leave there. Fast. It looks like we can exit through the alley there. I'd rather not pull out on the street in case he's watching. He doesn't own the coffee shop, I can tell you that. Nobody wearing that suit owns a freaking coffee shop."

I glanced at them. "There *was* something seriously wrong about him. I think . . . I think we need to figure out who he is and what his connection with the building is. Because if there's a daemonic problem like Grandmother Coyote thinks there is, then I'll bet you anything that he's a big part of it."

"How are we going to do that?" Shade asked. "We can describe him to Carter but . . ."

"I'll tell you how," Camille broke in. "While he was talking to you, I managed to snap a picture of him with my phone. We can download it at Carter's and he can perform some of that tech mumbo-jumbo and see if he can come up with a facial recognition of anybody in his files." She stopped and grinned. "At least, that sounds about right to me."

"Get a move on, woman. The longer we sit here, the more time he has to come check out our license plate." Though his voice was gruff, Shade was smiling.

I had to smile too. "I'll make a detective out of you, yet. You can join my agency."

"Right. And you can shimmy back into those gold lamé pants Menolly had you in that one time, and go clubbing with Trillian and me." She snorted, easing the car into the back alley.

All the way to the park my mind kept racing over the man at the coffee shop. He was dangerous. He was rich. *Or could he be married to somebody who's rich?* But no. He exuded power and men like that didn't give over control to a rich wife. *They* kept hold of the purse strings, and *they* had the trophy wives and the eye candy on the arm.

I tried to shake the thought out of my head. We had something to focus on that might yield definitive results. And that would be the park. The rains could easily have washed away footprints, but my guess was that if anything else had been dropped, it would still be there, caught in the tangle of undergrowth. The park was thick with ferns and huckleberries and vine maple that grew between the trees.

When we reached Violet's cottage, it looked the same as it had. A thought struck me—something I'd done before and gotten Chase pissed out of his mind at me for, but too bad. It was a way to find out what we needed to find out and the only way anybody could bitch at us was if they found out.

I headed to the mailbox. Camille stared at me, a faint grin on her face, as I yanked it open and pulled out the stack of mail. It was obvious that it hadn't been picked up for a while. I tucked it into the car, Camille locked the doors, and we headed into Violet's backyard.

Interlaken Park was only a few yards behind the cottage, and a metal fence divided the two. But the fence was low and easy to step over. It would have been just as easy to break down, too.

I swung over it with no problem and so did Shade. But Camille, in her skirt and corset, eyed it with hesitation. It really wasn't that tall, but she could easily catch any number of laces or hems, or one of those teetering heels on it. Shade laughed and leaned back over the fence, picking her up as easily as he might pick up a feather. He quickly deposited her on the ground next to me.

Camille laughed. "Sorry. I didn't even think about a fence without a gate. Okay, let's have a look around. Where's her bedroom?" She shaded her eyes and gazed back at the cottage. I followed suit.

There—there it was, to the far left corner. And not all that far from here. It wouldn't be hard at all to see what was going on inside the bedroom if the lights were on and the curtains open. *Or if someone had night vision.*

I glanced around. "You take that patch over there. Shade, go back a little farther. And I'll look here. Check under ferns, under bushes, at the base of the trees. Look for footprints, debris—cigarette butts, food wrappers, cups, and the like. Anything that might give us a clue as to whether Violet was being spied on. If she had a stalker, she might have been abducted. And she might have been abducted at home, although Albert thinks her purse is missing."

"If anybody wanted to rob her via her ATM cards and kidnapped her from home, they would have probably stolen other stuff too. Though her laptop is missing." Camille shrugged. "Let's get busy."

As we combed the area, rain beat steadily down. Camille shrugged her capelet tightly around her shoulders and I turned up my collar. The trees offered some protection, but the drops still filtered through.

The cedars creaked in the wind, and the firs followed suit. The sky was getting progressively darker, even though it was barely past noon. The clouds banked up thick, and looming, and though the rain had been steadily pouring, thunder rumbled through the air. The ground shook with the echo of the clap, as a streak of lightning bolted through the sky, flashing so bright it blinded me for a second. I blinked, shading my eyes, and then began to hunt around. We were relatively safe here, out of the open, and if the storm got worse, we could always leave.

On the west coast of Washington State, the ground is wet most of the year. There's almost always a layer of moisture trapped in the fallen leaves and needles that turns the trails and soil in forests to a rich mulch-like consistency, which makes—if you're off trail—twisting an ankle fairly easy. It also creates a thick layer of loose detritus, and if you drop something, half the time it will disappear into the compost. And if you happen to drop something and not notice it . . . well . . . that's what we were looking for.

The ground here was covered with the usual mixture of sodden leaves, dead fir, and cedar needles that had dropped to make way for new growth next spring, and a plush layer of brilliant green moss. Mushrooms were everywhere— toadstools mostly, but I recognized a chanterelle here and there. Expensive taste treats, but we weren't here to collect wildcraft edibles.

I knelt down and began pushing the leaves aside, sifting through the mass of debris. The usual mixture of fungi, insects, and banana slugs. The latter were both cool and freaky: six-inch-long funky town mollusks that made their home up and down the west coast, eating plants, leaving a trail of slime.

A spider scuttled across my hand and I shook it away. Ever since my ordeal with the Hunters Moon Clan—a group of hobo werespiders—I tended to err on the side of caution around the eight-legged beasties, but then, before I could dwell on it, something caught my eye. A tamped-out cigarette. I had learned enough from Chase so that I didn't immediately pick it up, but instead pulled out a plastic baggie and used that to cover my hand as I lifted the butt. No lipstick, but that didn't mean it had to be a man. I dropped it in a second baggie, and held it up.

"Someone was here. These things don't just put themselves out. Comb this area thoroughly." I went back to scavenging and came up with a candy wrapper. Not for a candy bar, but for one of those expensive truffles. I added that to the bag. Then Camille let out a shout and both Shade and I hurried over.

She pointed to a footprint. It was caught in the moist dirt beneath a tree, shaded from the rain. While it was mildly eroded, it hadn't been washed away. I knelt down, examining it and looking around the nearby area. There was another partial print right near it, half in, half out of the foliage. Enough of it showed to tell me it was the matching print, the other foot.

I frowned. "We should take a cast, I suppose."

Camille joined me, cautiously squatting down in the mud. "What about calling Chase? He could send out a man to do that and it would be professionally done."

I glanced at her. "We can't. Chase would have to open an official file if we called him in and I promised Tad and Albert we wouldn't do that. Not yet. But if I get enough quick dry cement, we can make our own."

"I don't know if that's going to work—" She broke off as I pursed my lips and cocked my head. "Fine. But if we ruin the results, don't blame me."

Shrugging, I looked up at Shade. "I need you to run out and get us some quick dry cement. Hurry back."

He stared at the two of us, and it was impossible to read what his thoughts were, but the next moment, he was gone and we were alone. I marked out the corners of the prints with large enough rocks to keep us from plowing through them by mistake, then Camille and I withdrew beneath the trees, trying to avoid the downpour. It was silly, we were both soaked to the bone, but it seemed like a good idea at the time.

As we stood there, the park grew quiet, and I began to feel an odd sense that we were being watched. I glanced up and found myself staring toward Violet's bedroom window. It was an easy gander from here, but then . . . how easy was *here* to get to from the main park trail? Could someone just out for a stroll have dropped that cigarette?

"Come on, let's try to track his path." The *his* was automatic, even though we'd faced more than one female adversary.

I looked around. The undergrowth was so thick it would be hard going except for one direction, where it looked like the fern fronds on both sides had been crushed, as if somebody had walked between them. As I followed the line of trampled fronds, with Camille behind me, it led out into an open area that looked like it was used for picnics. Beyond that, a path looked like it wound through the rest of the park. We stopped, the pelting rain soaking us even further. Camille frowned looking back.

"You can't see her house from here," she said.

"What?" I was busy scouting out the area, trying to assess where the voyeur may have come from.

"You can't see her house from here. Unless somebody just happened to trample that path through the ferns, they couldn't see Violet's cottage from here. So either it was someone who stumbled on the area behind her house by mistake, or it was somebody who knew where she lived in relation to this area of the park." She smiled as I realized what she was saying.

"I'll be damned. You're right. Hell, you are *so* right. No, whoever was watching her house wasn't there by accident. I know it—my gut's tingling." And it was. That little voice inside was whispering, *Whoever set her up, they were watching her.* Which meant she had been stalked.

"I think so, too." Camille shook her hair back, her makeup smearing in the downpour. "Should we check the garbage cans over by the picnic tables?" She pointed to one of the wooden benches. "There's no guarantee that whoever we're looking for stopped there, but we're here and we might as well have a look."

We split up, tackling the four tables that were scattered around the clearing. There was also a barbecue grill, set in concrete, but that yielded nothing. Two large garbage receptacles and a recycling bin showed a mishmash of garbage, but nothing stood out of place to either one of us.

A few minutes later, I shook my head. "All we're doing

now is just getting wetter and wetter. Let's get back to that footprint. Shade should be here any time with the concrete."

We retraced our steps through the bushes, and by the time we arrived at our original spot, Shade had returned. He could travel between the worlds, but if he took someone alive with him, they didn't fare so well. Morio had been sick as a dog the one time Shade had transported him.

Shade was holding a bag of concrete—the quick dry kind—and a bucket. It had water in it already.

"You thought of everything," I said.

Shade grinned. "I filled it from her tap out back. Seemed a waste of time to wait till you two were back, and I figured if there was trouble, my Spidey-sense would be tingling." He'd recently discovered the Spider-Man comics—or rather, I'd turned him onto them—and he had developed an inordinate fascination with the superhero. I knelt down to examine the print again, as Shade began to stir the cement.

Camille stood back. "No offense, but I don't want to mess up my clothes. And you know me. If I can spill it down my bra, or on my skirt, I will."

I motioned her back as Shade carried over the bucket. "No problem. We can do this." As he poured the concrete, I smoothed it out. He'd also thought to bring a mini-tarp to cover it with until it dried. Speaking of . . . "How long till this stuff sets?"

Shade checked the bag. "For this amount? Probably twenty minutes. What do you want to do until then?"

Camille snorted. "I vote we wait in the car so we don't get any wetter than we already are."

That would give me plenty of time to go through Violet's mail. But there was one little issue. "Sounds good, but I don't want to leave this alone. I doubt whoever made it will return today, but . . ."

Shade rolled his eyes. "But if he does come back, he might realize someone is on to him and destroy the evidence. All right you two. Get your butts to the car and dry out, and I'll wait here. I'll bring the casts when they're done. Don't you dare drive off and leave me, though." He swatted my ass, then pulled me to him for a deep kiss. I melted in his arms with a contented sigh.

Camille was already on her way to the front yard, but I caught up with her. The minute we were inside the car, she turned on the ignition and jacked up the heater. She shrugged out of her jacket and I did the same, and we draped them in the backseat.

"When I first bought this car, I didn't want to get it dirty at all. Or water-stained or anything like that. Things have sure changed." She laughed. "Considering how many bloody injuries we've had to ferry around, I'm amazed it's in as good of a shape as it is."

"Don't you feel the tiniest bit guilty about how we got our cars?" I grinned at her, already knowing her answer. We'd gone down to the dealerships after Chase had taught us to drive in a free-for-all nightmare of a two-week time, and between Camille's boobs and our natural glamour, we had charmed the hell out of the salesmen. We'd gotten all of our cars at well below cost, with all the options we could want.

"No. Do you?" She glanced over at me, shaking her head.

"Well, no." I picked up the stack of mail and divided it. "Here, you go through this pile while I go through this one. Look for anything out of the ordinary."

"What would be ordinary for her?"

Damned if she didn't have a point. I scrunched up my nose. "Whatever seems out of the ordinary to you, I guess."

"Fine. But you know we're breaking federal laws by tampering with her mail." Camille pressed her lips together and I could tell she was trying not to laugh.

"Since when have you been concerned about breaking laws?" I stuck my tongue out and we got to work, flipping through the hefty stack of letters and fliers. The junk mail we could obviously discard, but the letters and bills were worth a look-over.

Camille held up one envelope. "She has a pretty thick credit card bill."

"Open it—that will give us an idea of her shopping habits and might lead to answering where she hangs out." I stopped at another envelope. It was from an online dating site— Supernatural Matchups. "I thought she had a boyfriend?"

Camille glanced over at the return address. "So what? I have three husbands. You're engaged to a half dragon and you also have the hots for an Elemental Lord. Menolly's married to a werepuma and she's also the consort of a vampire lord. Get my drift?"

"Yeah," I said slowly. "Violet is Fae. She's not likely to be monogamous, like you told Tad." I sliced open the envelope, using my pocket knife. A Spyderco Endura, my new blade was a handy affair, well-made. With a black nylon handle reinforced with fiberglass, and a lip that made it as easy to open as a switchblade, it had become my go-to knife for a dozen small jobs.

The envelope open, I slid out the paper inside. It was a listing of several matchups, but with no names. Instead, it gave a list of numbers, as well as links to the online videos for her to look at, along with information on the potential hotties just waiting to fulfill her life. The letter also included her user name, but no password.

I showed it to Camille and she gave me a long look. "Well, you're good with computers, and if you need backup, you can always call Tim. I say you go online, hack her password, and log in as her. Any one of these guys . . . or women, I suppose, might have found out her private information and been stalking her."

"Me, hack her info? No can do, but I'll bet Tim can." Wading through a bunch of lonely heart Supes sounded like *so* much fun. *Not*. Chances were, eighty percent of them were pathetic, or desperate. Just like bar hookups or produce-aisle stalkers. "Crap. Why do I always get stuck with the dirty work?"

"Because, my love, you *are* the detective, after all. Even if you don't take on many cases." Before I could protest, she laughed, pressed her hand to my cheek, and pointed toward Violet's cottage. "Here comes Shade. At least you aren't on the dating-go-round anymore. But you have to admit, there's nothing quite like the anticipation of meeting someone new. Of that first kiss, that first hookup . . ." She sounded almost wistful, but then laughed again. "Of course, when it goes bad it usually goes really bad."

With that, we set aside the rest of the letters as Shade returned to the car and we headed for home.

It was almost time to leave for Otherworld, where war was looming, and where Chase was about to be outed for sleeping with the Queen's niece, where Sharah was about to confront her aunt and perhaps be disowned forever, and where we hoped to hear any sort of good news on the demon front.

Chapter 9

By the time we reached home, we were ready for hot showers. But first, we gave the evidence we'd gathered to Vanzir and asked him to check with Carter on it, to see if they could figure out anything.

Camille took off to her room, looking for a bubble bath. Shade and I trudged upstairs to wash up and change clothes. Menolly wasn't awake yet, so we put off talking about the Wayfarer till we were refreshed.

By the time we came out of the shower, I felt halfway human again. The hot water had helped, but so had standing there after, aiming my blow dryer at various points on my body till the chill began to dissipate.

For Otherworld, I usually dressed in clothing that I'd brought from home, but now I stared at my closet, and for the first time since we'd come over I didn't feel like returning home dressed in a tunic and trousers.

I fastened my gingham pink bra and slipped into my Hello Kitty panties, then decided on a pair of formfitting low-rise jeans in dark blue, a gray thermal long-sleeved shirt, and my Pikolinos Brujas in chocolate.

The boots were knee-high, a Euro style that looked like a cross between motorcycle and cowboy boots. The straps and buckles were ornamental, but I loved them and they were so comfortable that lately they'd become my go-to boot. With the lower heel, I could maneuver through the woods as easily as I could stride down the street.

Shade pulled on his brown cargo pants, a black turtle-neck, and then his cowboy boots. He watched as I dressed, a barely concealed grin on his face.

"Sometime I'm buying you new lingerie," he said. "Maybe Powerpuff Girls instead of Hello Kitty? A step up, perhaps?"

I grinned back. "I think they're a little outdated. But Hello Kitty never goes out of style. At least with me." I pulled my shirt over my head, tucked it into my pants, and tugged on my boots. "Ready to go. Oh—hold on." I grabbed an espresso leather belt and fed it through the jean loops, then buckled it. "Okay, now I'm ready."

After a quick kiss, we headed downstairs, and by the time we neared the first floor, I could smell dinner. Bless Hanna's heart.

The kitchen was bustling, as it was almost every meal. Hanna had cooked up a big batch of fried chicken and mashed potatoes. Along with a salad, biscuits, and gravy, the food was spread along the counter buffet style. I grabbed a plate and loaded up, then slid into a chair next to Camille, who was busy working on a thigh and drumstick. She wasn't wearing clothes from home either, but instead a black satin skirt, a plum-colored corset, and a pair of stiletto patent leather Mary Janes.

We waited till everyone was seated, at which point Menolly appeared, awake for the night. She, too, was dressed in jeans and a button-down shirt. Her boots, though, were stilettos. It seemed we were all on the same page.

I motioned for Menolly to sit down at the table, for once,

instead of taking her usual place up in the corner of the kitchen. She liked to hang out near the ceiling, floating, where she was out of the way of the hustle.

"We have to talk about the Wayfarer." I gave her a long look, wondering just how to tell her that her bar was pretty much gutted. And that eight, not seven, people had died.

She held my gaze, those frosty eyes of hers turning grayer every day. Vamps' eyes did that after they were turned. No matter what color before death, they eventually turned pale and silvery. The stronger the sire, the faster the color change. And first with Dredge, and then when Roman had re-sired her, she had some of the strongest vampire blood in her system.

"I guess you'd better just blurt it out and get it over with." She braced herself as she leaned forward. I could tell she was desperate for good news, and it tore me up that I couldn't give it to her.

Camille reached over and took one of her hands. "It's not good."

I hung my head. "The Wayfarer . . . close to eighty percent destroyed. Eight people died, total. It looks like a burning candle ignited the curtains, in a locked room. We need to find out who had the keys to the rooms upstairs, and if we can account for all of them, then we have to figure it was somebody who picked the locks."

Menolly let out a little sound, and Camille grimaced. Vampires had incredible strength and the fact that she was holding on to Camille's hand meant she was probably squeezing pretty damned hard.

Trying to figure out a way to make things better, to shed some sort of hope on the issue, I reached out and took her other hand. "Derrick and the others were down there early this morning. They care about the Wayfarer. They care about you. They were down there to salvage what they could from the rubble."

Shade leaned forward. "And if you need money for rebuilding, well, I'm here." He glanced at Smoky, who inclined his head. "And Smoky. We are dragons, we have great resources."

Menolly's lips were pressed together, and she blinked furiously, trying not to cry. After a moment, she let out a soft murmur, then asked, "Do you have a list of the dead?"

I shook my head. "Chase will bring one tonight—if he has it ready. Also, it will take some doing to figure out if any vampires died in the fire. I imagine you and Roman will have to wait until anybody who frequents the bar comes up missing. There wouldn't be any remains left to tell, not with . . ."

"Not with vampires because fire burns to a crisp. You're right, of course." She looked at me, then over at Camille. "I don't know quite what to say. I'm . . ."

I started to say, *"Devastated?"* but realized it would be the wrong thing. Instead, I just let her words hang in mid-air, and so did Camille.

After a moment, Menolly pushed back from the table. "You guys eat. I'm going to make sure I have everything for our trip." Before we could say anything, she disappeared behind the bookshelf, back into her lair. I suspected she was crying, but when Menolly wanted sympathy, she'd ask for it. Right now, the best thing to do was let her be.

I bit into my chicken and was halfway through my meal when Menolly returned. Camille and I took the time to fill everybody in on our findings that day. "I don't know who that guy at the Farantino Building is, but Camille got pictures." I looked over at her. "Text them to Vanzir and he and Roz can take them down to Carter's while we're gone. He might be able to come up with a match."

"Good idea." She pulled out her phone and tapped it, and a moment later Vanzir's phone sounded a chiming sound.

He held it up. "Got them. I'll call Carter and see if he can meet us tonight. Meanwhile, how long are you guys going to be gone?"

I shook my head. "I don't know. Hopefully we'll be home

before daylight, because if not, Menolly will have to stay there for the day." I finished my food and pushed back my plate. "I guess . . . I'm ready."

Camille stood up. "Me too." The doorbell rang and she smiled. "And right on cue . . . Trillian, can you get that?"

As he moved to answer the door, Roz and Smoky began helping to clear the table. Roz pulled out Tupperware containers and began to put away the rest of the food, as Hanna rinsed off the dishes, getting them ready for the dishwasher.

"How's Iris?" I asked her, moving to her side.

"Tired. Birthing twins isn't easy work. But she's happy. Her mother-in-law is doting over her and making it hard for anybody to visit. I think she feels like it's a family matter."

I frowned. "Iris is part of *our* family, so if it's a family matter, we're going to be involved. But she won't put up with the hovering for long. Right now, she needs the help, though, so we'll let her decide when she's had enough."

Roz turned around. "Bruce and his family better not decide to take her away from here, I tell you that much." He went back to putting away the food.

Camille and I exchanged looks. We both knew—in fact everyone knew—that Roz had a crush on Iris, and he had for some time. He knew better than try to act on it, though. As an incubus, there was no way he could settle down with just one woman. In fact, when he'd been changed into his current form, it had broken up a very happy marriage. But his interest was apparent, and Iris knew too, and walked a careful line not to hurt his feelings.

Vanzir returned, Chase and Sharah behind him. She looked exhausted. Chase had a worried look lingering behind the smile. Nerves, no doubt. Tonight couldn't be much fun for either of them.

"Are we ready?" Camille gathered up her velvet jacket and purse.

Trillian picked up a duffel bag, which he slung over his shoulder. Dressed in black jeans, an expensive gray polo shirt, and a long leather duster, he looked ready for clubbing rather than for where we were going.

Shade slid into his calf-length duster—brown leather—and plopped an Aussie bush hat on his head. I shrugged on my leather jacket, and grabbed my backpack.

"I guess we're ready as we'll ever be." I glanced around, making certain we weren't forgetting anything. We'd leave the laptop at home, but take our cell phones for when we returned and were ready to be picked up at the portal. We were heading to Elqaneve instead of Y'Elestrial, so the portal out at Grandmother Coyote's land would take us directly to our destination.

"Who's driving us out there?"

"I will." Vanzir had managed to get his driver's license but he wasn't the best driver in the world, although he tried. We'd bought him a beat up old Chevy and he was content with the occasional jaunt into town. We knew he could travel through the astral on his own, so he didn't usually resort to travel-by-auto.

He picked up his keys and those swirling eyes of his flashed. They were impossible to pin down, a color that there was no real name for, and his spiky hair was platinum blond, in a David Bowie-as-Jareth style. He was punk in a way that punk had never been and wore the grunge jeans and ripped shirts to match.

As a dream-chaser demon, Vanzir could have easily come by far more money and charmed his way into a lavish lifestyle by draining others and confiscating their money, but he had been enslaved by Karvanak, a Rāksasa and demon general, as a sex slave. He'd switched sides when he met us, and although he was still a loose cannon, he had proven his loyalty even though he was no longer bound to us by an oath to the death.

We headed out to the driveway after Camille wrapped herself in between Smoky and Morio, turning from one to the other with long, lingering kisses. The sparks sizzled between them, and I could practically see the energy crackle in their touch.

As I glanced over at Shade, a warmth spread through my heart. I was finally beginning to understand the depth of connection that my sister had for her men, that Menolly had for Nerissa. I'd never really connected with anybody on that level before—not in a sexual, passionate manner, but now my feelings were waking up and I had begun to realize just how strong of a bond could form between two people. Or three . . . or four in the case of my sister. The feelings frightened me, to a degree, but I couldn't deny them.

Vanzir drove us the five miles or so to the woods where Grandmother Coyote lived. A patch of woods on the outskirts of Belles-Faire had long stood empty, and gods knew who owned it, but no development had ever taken place, no buildings graced the site. The forest was thick here, cedar and fir, vine maple and fern and huckleberries. As we crossed the grassy strip that ran along the road to enter the woodland proper, spiders stretched their webs from branch to branch, the big fat striped argiopes that called this neck of the woods home.

Their webs shimmered in the blustery night, withstanding the gusts that whipped through the woodland. Camille led the way—she had been here too many times for comfort, visiting the Hag of Fate, and each time she'd come home more shaken than she wanted to let on.

Chase and Shade helped Sharah along, and we moved slowly, making sure she didn't twist an ankle or fall. She was a trouper, never complaining, though I could tell it was hard going for her at this point in her pregnancy. I crossed my fingers she wouldn't go into labor before we returned. Trillian and I took the back, keeping our eyes open for any possible threat.

We pushed through the wet bracken, the sound of leaves squishing under our feet along with the occasional crunch of a breaking twig. A few minutes later, the thick undergrowth gave way, opening into a small grove. Circular, cushioned with the moss that so often overtook grass, the lea was open to the sky and a deep sensation of magic pulsed through the air. Even I could feel it, and I wasn't a witch.

A few barren oaks stood interspersed through the glade, and Camille headed toward one. She knew the way by heart now. We reentered the forest on the other side, and stopped at the base of a huge tree. A shimmering light around the trunk formed the outline of a door. Camille ignored it, but led us past, to the twin trees behind the giant cedar. There, between them, sparkled Grandmother Coyote's portal. And waiting patiently beside it, stood the Hag of Fate herself.

"You know the way." She hesitated as we approached her, then added, "Do your best to return safely. You are needed." And with that cryptic note, she fell silent.

Camille dipped gracefully into a curtsey. Trillian bowed as we passed by her, and I raised my hand in greeting. Grandmother Coyote caught my gaze and I thought I saw something flicker in her eyes—a warning, or a caution, but she motioned us through to the portal.

The portal crackled and snapped, the energy running between the trees like miniature lightning bolts.

Camille turned back to smile at us. "Here we go again. Let's do this." And with that, she stepped into the nexus and vanished.

Chase looked back at me. "Would you go with Sharah? I know she says it's safe but—"

"Chase, I'm right here. Don't talk about me like I'm deaf." She glared at him and he blushed, that scolded-puppy look on his face that I remembered all too well. After a minute, she laughed and shook her head. "Delilah, come on. Do as he asks, would you, so he doesn't freak out."

I stepped up, pushed Chase gently to the side with a snort, and took Sharah's arm. We plunged through. Instantly, the crackle of energy surrounded us, ripping us to shreds as we went hurtling between the worlds. A moment later, dizzy and my ears ringing, I stumbled out of the portal, Sharah still holding my arm. She looked vaguely queasy.

"You all right?" I was worried it might have spurred on labor, but she sucked in a deep breath, then let it out slow.

"Yeah, I'm fine. Like I told you, going through portals won't hurt you when you're pregnant unless you're sick or have some serious condition."

Camille was standing there, her arms folded across her ample chest, tapping one fingernail against a stone wall near the portal. "What took you so long?" Just then, Trillian and Chase appeared, and right after them, Shade.

The portal, along with several others leading to other cities in Y'Elestrial, was located in a cave near the Barrow Mounds that guarded the outskirts of Elqaneve. Guards bordered the cave, keeping watch on who entered and exited the portals. They couldn't prevent unsavory elements from traveling, but they could keep an eye on things if trouble appeared on their doorstep.

Trenyth was waiting for us. The advisor to Queen Asteria, the elf had been around almost as long as she had, and we all knew he was in love with her, but he would never admit it to himself, or to anyone else. Fiercely loyal, he would die for her, and it made me sad to think that he lived his life in a haze of unrequited love. But then again, perhaps she did love him. The elves were big on honor, as Sharah had said. Asteria probably couldn't marry someone who wasn't born to the throne—or at least born in the Court. I found myself musing that someday, when she was ready to step down, perhaps Trenyth could finally tell her how he felt. Maybe they had a future after all.

The Barrow Mounds had once been the home of an oracle. A seer, she walked in shadows, they said. Half elf, half Svartan, she was caught between worlds, both in lineage and in vision. But bandits had killed her during a raid. It was rumored that she had predicted her own demise. Now, her spirit haunted the mounds, and no grass grew over the dirt, nor plants of any kind. Stark, barren, the hill stood a solemn memorial to the unpredictable nature of life, and the oracle walked in the mists there, forever watching over her people.

Because of Sharah's condition, Trenyth had a carriage waiting for us. We piled in, and I felt a weariness that crept through me every time we portal jumped. It might not be hard on the body, but it still took its toll.

Sharah was looking anxious. Chase wrapped his arm around her shoulders and gave her a little squeeze. Camille and Trillian held hands, and I turned to Shade, who smiled and offered me his hand. I took it, leaning back in the carriage, staring at the open sky.

Here, it was autumn, like it was over Earthside. But it wasn't raining . . . yet. The night was overcast and the scent of wood smoke filled the air. The noblas stedas—horses that were originally from Earthside but had been bred in a different direction once they were imported into Otherworld—clopped along, their hooves clogging a steady tattoo against the cobblestones.

We passed through the city square, where the vendors were closing down their stalls and trailing home for the night. Eye catchers lit the streets, glowing orbs of light that were formed from the very magic of the air itself. They existed everywhere in Otherworld, and we thought they might be related to the will-o'-the-wisps over Earthside. But unlike the volatile ES Fae, these orbs silently held vigil, appearing at dusk, summoned by witches and sorcerers, to light the way through the darkness.

We had been over Earthside long enough now that every time we returned home, it was like moving from one lifetime to another. Regardless of their common origin, the worlds had evolved vastly different paths since their genesis brought about by the Great Divide.

At one time, the worlds had been united. There had been no Otherworld, merely Earthside with all the realms merging together. But as the demonic force rose from the Subterranean Realms, the great Fae Lords made a decision to divide the worlds and seal off the Sub-Realms. They created the spirit seal, an incredibly powerful artifact. And with their combined magic, the worlds began to fracture and split. A massive civil war broke out between the Fae who did not want this and those who did.

Known as the Great Divide, the fighting and the magic

burrowed through the land like a juggernaut, severing
realm from realm as it ripped through space and time to
calve off Otherworld and the Sub-Realms. The upheaval
created floods and set off volcanoes, and basically tore the
psychic structure of the Earth apart. On the physical level,
Earthside didn't look much different, except for the damage
caused by the quakes, flooding, and volcanoes, but its very
essence had shifted, and the world would never be the same.

Some of the Fae and elves chose to stay Earthside, while
a majority moved to Y'Eírialastar, our name for Otherworld. Once the move had taken place, a vast array of city-
states began to rise out of the wild lands.

From the icy Northlands to the sands of the Southern
Wastes, from the rolling waves of the southwestern Mirami
Ocean to the northwestern shores of the chill Wyvern
Ocean, Y'Eírialiastar formed a macrocosm. And within
that macrocosm, microcosms arose, containing every envi-
ronment from desert to swampland to waving plains of
grass to boreal forests.

Once the worlds had fully separated, the great lords
broke the seal into nine pieces and entrusted each one to an
Elemental Lord. Nine gems that—as long as they were
kept hidden and isolated—would prevent the worlds from
merging. It was an unnatural division, bridged only by the
portals, and those were kept heavily guarded and closed.
But through the millennia, the seals were lost and forgotten. They stayed hidden and safe, until the Otherworld
Intelligence Agency decided to open up some of the portals on a limited basis.

Shortly after that, the spirit seals started working their
way to the surface, seeking to reunite. Like twin souls
hunting each other down through the world, they did their
best to reunite.

So far, we've located eight of them, but have only managed to keep six of those out of Shadow Wing's grasp.
Every spirit seal he possesses means bad news for everybody. The problem is, if *all* of the spirit seals are reunited,
every portal will rip open, and travel between the realms

will be easy access. But even just possessing two of them means that Shadow Wing and his demons have an edge we'd rather he didn't. Every advantage they manage to attain ups the ante that the demons will be able to break through en masse. And that would be a very bad thing.

Queen Asteria's palace held an austere beauty. Its alabaster façade gleamed under the crescent moon, rising into a dome from which spiraling minarets overlooked the court. The intricate stonework of the walls was built to stand the tests of time; the stones mined from a quarry high in the Tygerian Mountains. There, the Tygerian monks walked barefoot over hot coals, and every rock, bough, and body of water contained a deep, resounding magic.

The elves were closer to the woodland Fae of Earthside than to our father's people. Slow to anger, but dangerous and fierce when roused, they blended in with their lands in a unification that was almost frightening in nature.

The gardens buttressing the palace surrounded the Court: rose gardens and topiaries and wild meadows where the grass grew knee-length. Now, during late autumn, the bushes were devoid of foliage. Every gust that blew past seemed to susurrate through the barren tress, rustling the skeletal branches. The scent of a storm loomed on the horizon. Even I could smell it.

"A storm's on the way in," Camille said, as if reading my thoughts. She looked uneasy and her voice began to tremble. "A bad one. Lightning and thunder . . ." Her Moon magic connected her to the weather in some ways, and she could sense storms and call on the lightning.

My stomach lurched. Panther rose up, her nostrils flaring, and I suddenly wanted to flee. I forced myself to remain in control. "Something's wrong. Can you feel it? Panther is prodding me to shift."

Camille leaned against one of the nearby trees, lowering herself into trance. A moment later she gasped and her eyes flew open. "This storm, it's alive and it's huge. I sense . . . a presence . . . a fury that rages forward."

Trenyth paled. "The seers have been predicting an event

that will shake Elqaneve to the core, but they've been unable to pierce the veil of what shadow looms over the city. If this is that threat, then why haven't they sensed what you are picking up?"

Camille shook her head, pressing her knuckles to her mouth. Fear welled in her throat. "I don't know—maybe I'm wrong. Maybe I'm picking up on something else and projecting it."

I broke in. "No. Panther is pacing. I'm doing my best to hold on, but it's not easy. Trenyth, listen to Camille. I don't know exactly *what* she's feeling but I know that she's right—something is coming and it's coming fast."

Trenyth leaned toward the driver. "Faster."

The driver picked up the pace as Camille closed her eyes again and held out her hands. They were shaking. "I'm crackling. I can feel the lightning on the horizon." She frowned. "Trenyth, could it be something other than a storm? Something . . . I don't know. Magic?"

He narrowed his eyes. "The moment we reach the palace, I'll take you to the seers. Queen Asteria will understand the delay." He fell silent, and the look on his face suggested to me he was hiding something.

After a moment, I tapped him on the knee. "Spill it. You look like you want to say something. Better to have it out in the open."

Trenyth let out a long breath. "It could be magic, yes. I don't like to speak of it in the open, but the reason we wanted to bring you in tonight is to discuss some unsettling events in the war. We have suspicions that Telazhar has scouts near Kelvashan, but all of our attempts to infiltrate have vanished. Add to that, we haven't heard from Darynal and his group for several weeks now. I fear that they were discovered." He glanced over at Trillian, who stared at him darkly.

Darynal was Trillian's blood-oath brother, and the two had a bond that went beyond family. They would lay their lives down for one another, and for those they loved. Darynal would protect Camille to his dying breath, if need be. Currently, he was in charge of a reconnaissance mission to the Southern Wastes, to find out what was going on with Telazhar.

Camille fumbled for Trillian's hand. "When was the last time you sent out feelers for them?"

Trenyth shrugged. "The seers have been trying to contact them daily. All efforts have come up against a veil." And that is all he would say as the carriage pulled up in front of the palace.

Trenyth lightly jumped to the ground and held up his arms, guiding Sharah down as Chase watched her from behind. When we were all standing on the marble walkway, he turned to face the sky.

"In truth, I have the horrible sense that something is, indeed, looming. And whatever it is brings death and destruction in its wake. I just pray we can stop it, before it manifests fully. Come, let us visit the seers." And with that, he gave one of the valets instructions to report to the Queen.

As we followed him up the steps, I heard Greta, from a long distance, whispering in my ear. "Prepare for duty," she whispered. "This is one call you will not want to answer. But you have no choice. Know that, Delilah. Because if you do not obey us, far worse damage will happen than the death you bring with your kiss. When you are summoned, answer the call and do not fail."

Startled, I let out a little cry and Shade turned to me. "Are you all right, babe?"

I shivered. "No, I'm not. And I can't possibly tell you why." How could I explain what Greta had just said to me? Though if anyone understood, it would be Shade.

He gazed down at me for a moment, then slowly leaned in and kissed my lips. "Whatever the path, I am here, my love. Whatever the path, whatever the fate. I am here." And then, as the sky seemed to darken and a faint swirl of clouds rolled in, we entered the palace of the Elfin Queen.

Chapter 10

❧❀❧

Trenyth led us past the turnoff to the throne room, down the wide, spacious corridor. The floor was a polished tile that shifted color every time I looked at a different section. Columns lined the hall, rising to the ceiling that towered over us, and eye catchers dotted the walls, caught inside of lanterns like soft glowing candles. The palace was beautiful, but at this point, we were focused on following Trenyth rather than on the décor. Chase and Sharah kept pace with us, and I had a feeling that Sharah was grateful for the delay.

We traveled through a set of double doors, then turned off the main hall into a smaller corridor, which led to a spiral ramp inclining down. The passage was about six feet wide, with a railing on one side. Even though the ramp was at a gradual slope, Sharah held to the railing as she cautiously followed Trenyth and Chase. Camille and I came next, Menolly and the guys in back. Another ten minutes of silent walking and we were at the bottom.

"We must be pretty damned far underground." Menolly broke the silence.

Trenyth glanced over his shoulder. "Yes, we are several stories below the ground. We keep the seers and the mages here, protected in case of war." His voice dipped on the last word, and he paused. "The last great wars Elqaneve was embroiled in were the Scorching Wars, and those were not on our territory. But we fought, sent legions to the Southern Wastes, when they were still oak and bracken, fern and soft grass."

My sisters and I had grown up hearing about the Scorching Wars, but Trenyth had actually lived through them. The realization of just how old he was began to sink in.

"Were you . . . did you have to fight?" I wasn't sure it was an appropriate question but I felt impelled to ask.

He turned to me. "I did, though I was quite young. So much blood flowed that it stained the sands red. I lost my brothers in that war—all of them. I watched as the sorcerers turned the vast plains that covered the area into dust and sand. The fires burned for years, scorching the land. Their magic was so powerful that it infused the air and is still caught in the rolling dunes. Things happen down there—and it is said that a great city lies beneath the dunes that vanished during the war, waiting to return."

The way he spoke made it sound as if the wars were yesterday, and I had the suspicion that—for Trenyth—they might as well have been. Just one more fact about our elfin friend that we had not known.

"And Telazhar led them, even then. Why? He's a necromancer. Why work with the sorcerers?" Camille's voice was soft. She was trying to keep from breaking the mood. She'd used the technique often enough that I could recognize it by now.

Trenyth gave her a gentle smile. "Don't play your glamour on me, young witch. I am too old and too experienced to be taken in by your beauty, as lovely as the gesture is." He sucked in a deep breath, then let it out sharply.

He continued. "Even then, Telazhar recognized the power in uniting forces. He crossed guilds. He was a master of bringing together disparate people and there was a point where the power shifted and he grabbed control, with sorcerers and mages following him slavishly. He enlisted the Brotherhood of the Sun, and played on their fear and distaste for the Moon Mother."

"Uniting through mutual hatred," Trillian murmured. "Always a powerful trick, if a distasteful one."

Trenyth nodded. "And he is repeating history. He has called on the sorcerers still angry at certain rules set up by Elqaneve and Y'Elestrial. Telazhar knows how to prey on the weaknesses of others. He uses truth, twists and perverts it, and spoon feeds it to his followers. And now . . . he works for Shadow Wing, and he's had a thousand upon a thousand years to hone his skills. He is danger incarnate, and he knows this."

We were all silent as the air seemed to thicken around us. Trenyth turned and once again, led us forward.

Another ten minutes and we entered what seemed the antithesis of the rest of the palace. Here, a soft dim light glowed through the chamber, and it was hard to see exactly how the setup was laid out. Silhouettes of tables and chairs were visible in the gloom, along with bookshelves lining the walls. This must be a study hall or something of the like, but right now it was deserted.

"Where is everybody?" Chase asked.

"Probably at the dinner hall. The mages employed by the Court work in two shifts and usually the night shift will not begin until midnight. The day shift comes on at the strike of noontide." Trenyth led us through another set of doors on the opposite side of the room and into another long, narrow corridor.

Here, doors lined the sides and I guessed we were in the living quarters area, but when we passed one room with an open door, the inside looked like Camille's study, and I realized these were private workrooms.

As we headed toward the end of the corridor, a young elf—well, he looked young, but truth was he could have been hundreds of years old—came racing down the hall. He skidded to a stop when he saw Trenyth and dropped to his one knee.

"Lord Trenyth, please, come quickly. There's something

wrong with Elthea." The elf was doing his best to keep from panicking, the war of emotions evident in his face.

Trenyth motioned him up. On the run, they started down the hall toward the end doors. We followed, while Chase and Sharah walked behind. I glanced back to see Trillian return to their side. Relieved they weren't left alone, I sped up and followed on the heels of Camille and Menolly. Shade had already vanished through the door.

We slammed through behind him, finding ourselves in yet another communal living room. But this was cozier, less austere, with leather sofas and rocking chairs and a cheery fire blazing away. In the center of the room, near a small seating arrangement, three elves were kneeling on the floor by the side of a woman. She looked middle-aged, which meant she had to be incredibly old, and she was seizing. Spittle frothed out of her mouth as her body convulsed, wracked in spasms. One of the elves was trying to turn her on her side, while another was murmuring some sort of spell, low and ominous.

Trenyth pushed aside the elf trying to help the woman and knelt beside her. "Have you called for the healers?"

"Yes, Lord Trenyth. They are on the way."

"What happened?" He managed to flip her over so the froth didn't choke her. As her body spasmed, he laid his hands on her and I had the feeling he was working some sort of magic.

The elf he'd pushed aside answered. "We were discussing what the . . ." He paused, glancing our way, and his gaze flickered back to Trenyth, who seemed to understand what he was about to say.

"It's all right. They're here to help."

"Thank you, my Lord. We were talking about the energy looming over the city when Elthea slipped into a trance. Her eyes rolled back in her head and she said, in a loud male voice, 'It's too late . . . we are here.' And then, she went into seizure."

At that moment, the healers burst through the room and took over. Trenyth moved back to give them space. I tapped

Camille and Menolly on the shoulder, and we moved off to the side. Shade followed.

"What the hell is going on?" I told them what Greta had said to me, figuring we'd better have everything out in the open.

Camille pressed her lips together and glanced over her shoulder at Elthea, who now seemed to be out of the convulsions, but was still unconscious. "The question is, who spoke through her?"

Trenyth joined us. "Come with me. This requires a visit. I normally would never allow you where we're going, but after what you felt, Camille, and what Greta said to you, Delilah, you must come with me. I'm afraid Shade cannot join us. We don't allow dragons in the restricted area. Nor Menolly, I'm afraid."

Menolly held up her hand when I started to protest. "It's all right. Shade and I'll join Trillian to help watch after Chase and Sharah. We'll be right here when you get back."

Without waiting for our answer, Trenyth hurried Camille and me through the room and out the back. He said nothing, hushing me before I could ask where we were going. We followed silently, rushing to keep up with him. His feet were flying, and while we could keep to a pace, it wasn't easy. Elves were lighter on their feet than the Fae.

The corridors went by in a haze of marble and magical light, and I lost track of the twists and turns as we wound our way through the palace. Camille gave me a strained look but remained silent. As we passed, no sound followed except for the hollow stroke of her heels against the marble, and the soft fall of my boots. We were a blur of motion, a whirlwind racing through the empty corridors. I had no sense of what time it was, though I knew it couldn't be later than eight o'clock ES time.

And then, we were there. Wherever *there* was. A solid gray door, carved in granite, stood before us. There was no knocker, and no handle. Trenyth motioned for us to stand back and began to incant a spell. The elvish he was speaking was older than time, older than I could recognize, and when I looked to Camille, she shook her head.

The ancient, sonorous rhythm of Trenyth's voice lulled me. He sang the words, on and on, weaving the magic through them. He was a charmer with a snake, a whisperer of horses, a tamer of all beasts and wild things, and his voice could cajole blood from the body, stones from the earth.

A minute passed, then another. On the third, the door shifted, slowly swinging inward. Trenyth let his words drift back into silence and nodded for us to follow him through. As we entered the room, I was surprised to see it was quite plain, not elaborate at all. There was a table in the center, and on that table, in a stand large enough to safely hold it, a glowing crystal orb. It was bigger than my head, bigger than a bowling ball, and it was emanating a brilliant blue light from its core.

The room was nearly empty, except for the dais and the orb. There were chairs around the table, tall enough to lean over to gaze at the crystal. The room was lit by eye catchers, softly glowing near the ceiling. Trenyth motioned for us to take a seat. Camille slid into the chair next to him, and I sat on the other side.

I wanted to ask what we were looking for, but a crackle sounded from the orb and the light began to spin. Camille leaned closer. I wanted to say "back away" . . . I wanted to shout "get out of there" . . . but there was no time.

The spinning blue light swirled into a vortex that rose over our heads. It spread out, clouds filling the room, flickering silver with sparkles of blue mixed throughout.

"Pretty . . ." Camille sounded entranced. She stood and reached up, as if to touch the mist. As Trenyth realized what was going on, he dove for her, as I tried to make my way across the table.

The clouds began to spin again, faster and faster, filling the room, expanding out, forks of miniature lightning flaring out to attach themselves to Camille. They began to attack her, racing up and down her body as she tried to slap them away.

Trenyth lunged, trying to protect her as I tripped over a hidden flange on the table and went skidding over the edge, hitting my chin on the floor. We all went down, with the lightning focusing on Camille. A moment later, as we scrambled for the door, the room shook and a sound like crashing thunder rolled through the air. The storm clouds we were facing shrank and vanished.

"Fuck, what's happening?" Camille managed to pull herself by holding on to one of the chairs.

I followed suit, realizing that the floor was rolling under our feet. "Earthquake!"

Trenyth panicked. "The Queen! I must get to her side!" He turned to us.

"Go—we'll find our way out. Just go." I shoved him toward the door and he stumbled out as the quaking went on and on. The sound grew from thunder to freight train, and I thought I could hear screams racing by, a blur in the mayhem.

Camille made her way over to the door, crawling on her hands and knees. "We need to get in the arch!"

But the door had swung shut again and there was no visible handle, no way to open it. We were trapped in the room. On the plus side, our nasty lightning storm seemed to be gone, but on the other hand—so did any escape. And the rumbling beneath our feet continued to grow.

"Get under the table, it looks strong enough to shield us." I grabbed Camille by the arm. We crawled under the dais, which was made of solid marble. If it cracked on us, we'd have one hell of a headache, but if it held, we'd be protected from falling debris. And given that the quake hadn't stopped, I doubted we'd get through without something breaking off and tumbling down from the ceiling.

The rumbling became more violent. Camille and I held on to each other, cowering against the center pedestal. I could hear her whispering something under her breath but couldn't tell if it was a spell or a prayer.

Rolling in waves, the floor rippled beneath us, like an ocean of marble, fracturing as a network of faults ran through it. And then, a loud crash, and out of the corner of my eye, I saw something thunder to the ground in a shower of dust. Another crack, and another shower of dust.

I had no clue how long the quake had been rolling through the palace. It felt like forever, like it would never end, and my stomach lurched with both fear and nausea. The worst boat ride in the world would be better than this. And then . . . slowly, the noise began to fade, and Camille squeezed my hand as the rolling slowed and—finally—stopped.

We waited for a moment, then scrambled out from beneath the table. The eye catchers were still glowing, but the dust clouded our sight. Only a few feet away, one of the stone figurines ornamenting the walls had tumbled to the floor, barely missing the table. It was big enough that it would have smashed us flat, for sure, if it had hit.

Coughing as the clouds of dust and debris filled the air, we stared at the destruction. The room was unrecognizable. Whatever decoration there had been lay in ruins, and the floor was a mishmash of broken marble. Camille inched her way closer to me and I took her hand, afraid to move for fear of setting off something.

Just then, an aftershock hit. Camille let out a scream as another one of the statues in the room toppled toward us. I grabbed her and ran, pulling her along with me by the wrist. Seconds later, the marble figurine landed right where we'd been standing, smashing into huge chunks and shaking the room.

"We have to get out of here. How are we going to get that fucking door open?" We skirted debris until we were at the door.

Camille stared at the huge gray obstacle. "I can get us out."

Her voice grim, she reached into her cloak and brought out her unicorn horn. A powerful artifact, given to her by the Dahns unicorns, it was one of eight in existence. The Black Unicorn, the father of the Dahns race, shed his body every few thousand years, and in return for playing the fire to his phoenix, Camille had been gifted with his hide and horn. It was an incredibly powerful weapon, with limited usage, and it needed to be recharged every month under the dark of the moon.

I backed away. "Get to cracking, then, because I doubt that will be the only aftershock we're going to feel."

Her gaze narrowed as she gauged the door. "I just hope I don't bring on the next one." She closed her eyes, sliding into trance.

I didn't understand the full mechanics of the horn, but I knew that there was a spirit inside of it, and that she'd caused havoc with it before.

A moment later, she raised the horn into the air, aiming it at the door. A wind seemed to rise in the room, growing steadily stronger. Another moment, and the floor began to shake again, though I didn't know if it was from another aftershock, or the powers from the unicorn horn.

Camille's hair rose in the wind, streaming back as if she were facing a giant fan, and as the tiles beneath the door began to collapse, creating an opening of about two inches below the door, the wind increased until it became a howling gale. I made sure I wasn't in the path of anything that might blow over on me, and crouched to the ground, holding on for dear life. How Camille managed to stand in the force of the winds she was raising was a mystery to me, but stand she did.

The doors creaked and shifted, groaning as they began to open. Slowly the winds pushed them inward. Inch by inch they moved, and with a hurricane gust, they slammed open so hard that the walls cracked, and a shiver of fractures ran through the gray stone, shattering the gates. Another huge cloud of dust swept into the air, blowing past us, from the rubble that cascaded to the ground.

As the winds began to die, Camille motioned to me. She looked dark, a dour expression on her face, and I wasn't sure what was running through her mind, but there was no time to sit around and chat. We headed through the broken remnants of the doorway, just in time for another aftershock.

This one was bad, perhaps as bad as the first one. I tripped, slamming against a wall. Camille went tumbling in the opposite direction as the world shifted. She landed hard and I heard her shout "Fuck!" but then we were plunged into darkness as all of the eye catchers faded and there was no more light.

The shaking continued, and all around us the sound of crashing stonework continued to reverberate through the air. I scrambled to get on my hands and knees, trying to regain some of my equilibrium, but up was down and left was right and it was one big blur of motion and sound.

"Camille? Can you hear me?" I held my breath, praying to Bastus that she would answer.

"Yes, I'm over . . . I'm here, trying to dodge the rubble." She sounded petrified, but at least she was alive.

"We need to get up to ground level. If this continues we're going to be buried alive. Which way did we come? Do you know where we are?"

After a moment, she answered. "When we first arrived, the room was to our right. So we need to make sure to head left if it's behind us." A pause, "Am I right?"

"Right? I don't—Oh! I know what you mean." I thought for a moment. We'd barely exited the room when this aftershock hit. I flailed around in the darkness, and found the wall. Following it, a few crawls forward gave me the opening to the room on my right. Okay, then, I had to turn around so the entrance was on my left. Then I'd be aiming on target. I positioned myself as best as I could, with the wall to my left shoulder, and then waited.

"Camille? Follow my voice. I'm pointing in the right direction. If you can find me, we can try to crawl out of here. Once the shaking stops, get the fuck up on your feet and we hurry as far as we can till the next one."

"Continue talking so I can follow your voice."

I didn't know what to say, so instead I began singing "Godzilla," by Blue Oyster Cult.

"Oh Kitten, can't you pick something else?" But there was an edge of a smile in her voice and the next moment, she was beside me. I got her positioned in back, just as the shaking stopped.

"Fuck, how long did that go on?" Camille's voice rose, and I realized she was standing up.

I followed suit. "Come on, keep your left hand against the wall at all times. We need to make certain we're not headed in the wrong direction." Without further chitchat, I started out.

"Delilah, be careful—if you go too fast, you might run into debris and hurt yourself—"

She had no sooner spoken when I hit my foot against a piece of what felt like marble that had lifted up from the floor.

"Fuck, oh fuck! Geez, I may have just broken my big toe!" I wanted to hop up and down as the pain raced through my foot, but I also realized that a broken toe was nothing compared to being buried under tons of rubble, so I sucked it up. "Be careful, there's a big block of marble right in front of you—well, as soon as I skirt it. It's. . . ." I paced it out until I was able to stand flush against the wall again. "It's five paces long. Six of yours, probably."

"One . . . two . . . three . . . four . . . five . . . six . . ." Camille counted them off and then grunted. "Yeah, that's about right. You okay? How's your toe?"

"Hurts like hell but forget about it." I tried to remember how long it had taken for us to get to this area. "Damn it, I forgot we came through so many turns . . ." I paused. There was an opening to my left. "Stay here for a moment. Don't move."

I turned, still keeping my hand against the wall. I distinctly felt the floor begin to slope upward. It made sense. There *had* to be more than one hallway leading up to the main floor. Hesitating, I realized we would never find our way back using the labyrinth through which Trenyth had led us. We had to take the chance.

"I think we should go this way. Make a left, turn at the corner," I called back.

"Done." Another moment and Camille was behind me. We headed on, trudging up the incline that was steeper than the one we'd originally descended to reach the seers' quarters. As we journeyed in silence, my thoughts ran to

Shade. He'd be all right—I was sure of it. He could shift into the Ionyc Sea if necessary. But what about Trillian? And Chase and Sharah? Sharah was pregnant. What if she went into labor due to this, in the dark and the mayhem? And Menolly . . . well . . . not much could affect her unless a beam struck her through the heart. She could be hurt but she would heal.

"You're thinking of them too, aren't you?" Camille's voice softly echoed through the darkness.

"Yeah. Do you think . . . Never mind." I didn't want to ask. I might not want to hear what she had to say.

"I know. Trust me, I know."

It was hard to gauge time, but after a while, the floor began to shake. "Drop! We don't want to be standing if there's another big one." I slid down the wall, keeping it to my left, and pressed against it. I could hear Camille's breath coming in soft puffs, as if she were trying to control her fear. Neither one of us spoke as the rumbling started again, but this time it lasted only for a little while—probably twenty seconds. Too long, but less than the first two shocks. The moment it subsided, I pushed to my feet again.

"Let's go. We've been lucky but who knows how much time that's going to continue?" And on we went, Camille murmuring a soft prayer for protection as we worked our way through the darkness. I hit my toes several times, but my boots were thicker and better able to handle the damage than Camille's sandals. Luckily I was able to warn her about the dangers.

And then, I seemed to see something like a light ahead. It was glowing brighter as we neared it. At first I thought it might be the moon, or a hanging chandelier that had been spared, but I suddenly found myself out of the hallway and in the middle of a large court, and I realized it was nothing of the sort. We were back to the main level of the palace. There were gaping holes in the roof—huge and yawning, but no moon shone down to light the way.

No, instead, the sky was lit up with red and orange streaks, like a ghastly aurora, as blue streaks of lightning forked through the night, illuminating against the crimson backdrop. Thunder rolled through the air like a wave of drumbeats, and fear stole into my heart as I watched the fiery display.

"The storm—it has broken." Camille came up behind me, wrapping her arm around my waist. "This . . . this is what I felt. It's a monster, a terrible, horrible beast." She moved beneath one of the holes and I shouted for her to get back, but she wouldn't listen. Her gaze was rapt, a blur of horror and awe, as she reached her arms into the sky and began to laugh.

"Camille—stop! Do not do this—you can't touch the power without bringing it down to rain on you!" I raced forward, knocking her to the side as a bolt of lightning ripped through the hole, striking where she had just been standing. I smelled smoke. Smoke from the left, smoke from the right. Queen Asteria's palace was on fire.

"Camille! Get up. The palace is on fire."

Camille shook her head, dazed. "What the . . . Holy fuck, I can't believe I almost did that. That . . . that . . . thing up there is alive. We have to get out of here now!" She scrambled to her feet as I glanced around, trying to find an opening to the street. And then I saw it, just ahead. We had to cross the courtyard, but off to the right, there were stone steps leading into one of the gardens.

"Come on—that way." I grabbed her hand so we wouldn't be separated, and we headed toward the opening. We were just clearing the archway when a huge aftershock railed the land. But this time, we could see what the hell was happening.

Outside, to the right of where we were headed, a lightning bolt seared down through the night, striking the ground with a force that must have far exceeded the trillion watts of the average bolt. It slammed into the soil, raping it deep, and the ground split where the fork burrowed in. And then, the steps buckled as the ground rolled.

That's what was causing the quakes—they weren't all aftershocks. The storm was attacking the city. And, according to Camille, the storm was an entity. I jumped off the steps, dragging her with me. We went down hard on the walkway in front of the palace, but I didn't stop to see if anything was broken. My alarms were ringing full tilt, and I grabbed Camille's wrist and yanked her to her feet. We took off through the grass, but she stopped me for a second to kick off her shoes. Then we were running again, putting as much distance between the palace and us as we could manage.

Behind us, a horrible rending split the night. Camille and I stopped, frozen in our tracks, as we turned to witness what was happening. The storm roiled over the palace—the entire city it seemed, but the central whirlpool centered over the Court. And then, out of the storm's core, a huge-assed lightning bolt appeared—this one as big as a vortex, as big as a tornado, slicing through the air with a piercing shriek. I stared, tears running down my cheeks as the point of the bolt struck the center of the palace. With a thunderous crash, the lightning split the marble dome, and the columns supporting Queen Asteria's court began to crumble. As they crumbled, the walls and roof disintegrated, and the entire structure imploded in a massive wall of dust.

Camille let out a strangled cry. "Menolly . . . Trillian!"

She started to run forward but I grabbed her, holding her back. "You can't go. There's too much danger. We have to trust that they'll get out of there."

"Chase, Sharah—you know they can't survive something like that." She was sobbing now, screaming at me. The anger in her voice was almost as frightening as the storm, but I knew she wasn't aiming it at me. But her magic, if she unleashed it . . .

And then, she reached for the horn. She thrust it into the air and looked up at the storm. "You fucker! You can't have them!"

"No! You can't use the horn—even the power of the Black Unicorn can't fight against whatever the hell this is! Camille, use your common sense. You'll only get us both killed." I wasn't getting through. The fury was rising in her eyes and I knew we only had seconds before she let loose with the full force of whatever power remained in the horn. And if she did that, she'd turn the eye of the storm on us.

"I don't want to do this!" I grimaced as I backhanded her a good one. My hand landed against her cheek with a resounding crack, startling her long enough that I was able to grab the horn from her. She raised her fingers to touch where I'd hit her—she'd have a nasty bruise, that's for sure—and then burst into tears, collapsing on the grass beside me.

As I knelt down, tucking the horn securely back in the pocket of her skirt, she gazed up at the sky, a horrified look on her face.

"What are we going to do? What the fuck are we going to do?"

I sucked in a deep breath. "I don't know. But we have to get out of the open. We have to get away from the city. Because I have a nasty feeling this is only the precursor to something far worse."

"You're right." The familiar voice washed over me like warm rain, soothing and clear. We looked up, and there, standing over us, was Trenyth. He leaned down to help Camille to her feet. "Come. I know some place we can hide." His face was strained, and he looked like he'd aged a century over the course of the evening.

Mutely, we followed him as he plunged into a side garden. Hell had broken loose, and we were missing loved ones, but the danger was too great. We had to regroup and sort out what this nightmare was.

Trenyth glanced at us as we entered a back rose garden. "Girls, war has come to Elqaneve. The sorcerers are here. And Telazhar is at the helm. We're under siege."

And with that, he paused by a trellis thick with branches, and pressed a hidden latch. The trellis opened, and he pushed us through into a hidden passage. Once again, we were on the run.

Chapter 11

❦❦❦

The passage was straight, thank gods, with none of the twists and turns we'd encountered in the palace. Trenyth rushed us along. Both Camille and I were hurt—bruised and bleeding, skinned elbows and knees, and Camille was running barefoot, but we ignored the discomfort, ignored the ache, because there was a monster outside rampaging at the gates, and we could feel the storm's breath on our heels.

Even here, I could feel the tingles of the storm attacking the city. Camille's hair was wisping out, almost like it was standing at attention. My arms were a map of goose bumps, and it felt like ants were marching across my skin.

Trenyth kept us at pace through the narrow corridor. It seemed to be entirely formed of hedgerows, even the ceiling, but as I squinted, I could see the faint outline of branches through the roof. They were so tightly woven that little light filtered through, but the brilliant colors of the storm were unmistakable. Trenyth led us with a pale light that sat on his shoulder, and I had no idea what it was—not an eye catcher, that I knew, but there was no time now for questions. No time for anything but running.

Finally, we came to a door at the end of the tunnel, and wasting no time, Trenyth touched the surface with his hand and it flew open, slamming back. He pushed through and we followed. We weren't near the palace, that much I could tell, but where we were, I had no idea.

As we entered what appeared to be a low-ceilinged room, Trenyth shut the door again and muttered a charm, and a faint blue glow raced around the edges. I had the feeling he had just sealed us in. The glow extended to fill the room, and we were bathed in the light, cool and sterile and neon. The room was square, with a door at the other end, and in the center of the room was a table and chairs. Cabinets lined one wall, and what looked like a well was in the corner.

Trenyth turned. "Sit down. Check your wounds."

We obeyed without question. Camille examined her feet and grimaced, but then yanked out what appeared to be a smallish thorn. She lifted her skirts. Both of her knees were covered with abrasions and her calves were bruised. Her elbows were bleeding from where she'd hit the ground a couple of times.

I hadn't fared much better. My arms were scraped, and I had a nasty bruise on my back where I'd tripped over some piece of debris. I realized that blood was dripping down my face, but the cut was small, near my left cheek. I wiped away the drops and settled into one of the chairs, grateful for the chance to rest.

We had been there no more than a moment or two when the ground echoed again, and began to roll. But Trenyth seemed unconcerned as Camille and I jumped for cover beneath the table. The rolling went on and on, but nothing in the room seemed to shake loose or even fall. A moment later, we crawled out after the shock dissipated. Trenyth motioned to the chairs.

"While we can feel the quaking in here, the fires and the damage cannot enter. This is a protected space. It was built to give the Queen refuge during a war." A veiled look clouded his eyes and his voice grew harsh.

I let out my breath, realizing what he was implying. "She's not here, is she?"

A pause. Then, a shake of the head. "No, I could not find her. I was headed back to look again, when I saw the two of you. And then . . . the palace went down." He pressed his lips together and the gentle nature that I'd always appreciated seemed to vanish. For one of the first times, I grew afraid of him. Trenyth grew in stature, rising up. Oh, he might be the same height he always was, but it was as if he had removed a cloak, and we were seeing the power that had been hidden beneath.

"Do you know what that thing is? That storm?" Camille turned a bleak face to him. She huddled beneath her capelet, which was now covered in dust and ripped into tatters from catching on debris.

Trenyth slowly shook his head. "I don't. Not for certain. But I know that Telazhar brought it with him, and the sorcerers conjured it. The storm is alive. You are right in that. And you felt it coming when our own seers could not. Had we only asked you over earlier, you might have been able to save us from this destruction."

Camille let out a little cry and I realized what was going through her mind.

"It isn't your fault. You couldn't have known. Trenyth, how could you say such a thing?" I turned on him, furious that he would lay such a burden on her shoulders.

But he simply shrugged and gave me a cool look. "I did not imply that she *should* have sensed it, nor that this is, in any way, her doing. I simply stated that I wish we'd thought to bring her over earlier."

"If wishes were pennies . . ." I pushed out of my chair, pacing the room. "What other resources do we have here? I see we have water."

"We have plenty of food. And there are sleeping quarters through that door, and a magical laboratory with spell components. There is a hidden exit through a storeroom. It is not large but we kept it well stocked, even through all the years of peace." He pinched his nose between his eyes and leaned on the table. "I have a headache beyond any I've ever had. This night . . . there will be so much death that comes from this."

"You said war is upon us. Do you mean Telazhar's army actually has breached the gates?" I frowned, trying to figure out how the hell we were going to get out of this one. First, we had to survive the storm. Then we had to make our way through the city to the portals, hoping they were still intact. That was, providing there weren't sorcerers and their army running wild through the streets.

"As I said, we lost track with Darynal and his group a few weeks ago. We were getting ready to send out new scouts, and we called you in to tell you what was going on. But . . . it's obviously too late." He glanced up at us. "But I forget myself. You have loved ones who were in the palace. We cannot go outside again until the storm withdraws, but the moment it has passed, we will begin searching."

A thought occurred to me. A horrible, terrible thought. "Menolly—if the storm does not pass before dawn . . ."

Camille gasped. "We have to get over there, storm or no storm. We have to find her. We can't sit safe in here while she's out there. While Chase and Sharah are in danger."

Trenyth let out a slow breath. He took her hands, but his voice was clear and cool. "Don't hold too much hope. We'll scour the grounds, but you saw what happened to the palace."

"We have to hold hope. It's the only fucking thing we've got." Camille shook him off and crossed to the well, where she got a drink of water. "The storm. If the sorcerers following Telazhar raised it, where the hell did they find it? Is that thing a creature that they invoked from a different plane? Or did they just decide, *'Hey, let's build a magical construct—a monstrosity of a storm. Boy, the fun we could have with that!'* How the hell can we fight it if we don't know what it is?"

Tensions were strong. Trenyth had slipped into a quiet place, where he had locked his emotions in a box. And

Camille's temper was rising. Not a good mix. And me? I was caught in the middle. I tried to sort through what we were facing. We had to find the others. We had to find Queen Asteria. We had to make certain Menolly was protected when dawn broke. Which brought up another question.

"What time is it?"

Camille whipped out her iPhone and I groaned. I hadn't even thought about doing that. But then she let out a growl. "Totally fucked. Won't work. It should at least tell me the time but the storm fried it, I think."

I checked mine. Blank, dark screen. "Yeah, same here. Trenyth, how close are we to midnight?"

He shook his head. "Believe it or not, it's barely eleven, Earthside time. You came across around seven. The storm came in at . . . eight?"

Only three hours had passed? It felt like a lifetime. "That gives us some time with regards to Menolly. She was with Trillian, Shade, Chase, and Sharah. They were all together in the seers' living quarters. How hard is it to find? And just how far below ground was it?"

Given a question he could tackle, Trenyth let go some of his dour demeanor and a bit of the elf we'd come to know peered through the gloom. "It's not difficult, at least when the palace was standing. But it's probably the equivalent to three stories below ground. Who knows if the hallways accessing the lower levels are still standing?"

"They were when we escaped." Camille frowned. "But . . . that was before the strike on the palace."

Trenyth let out a huff. "I apologize, by the way. I was wrong to be short with you. I'm just worried . . ."

"You don't know where the Queen is. And she is your first duty." I didn't say, *"And your love . . ."* but I was thinking it. He loved her. And even though he could never have her, he couldn't imagine her not being in his world.

He nodded. "Yes. It is my duty to protect her at all times. And I failed."

"But you can't be with her at every moment. No one can ever be there 24/7. It isn't physically possible, nor emotionally healthy. She has bodyguards. Surely they will help her." The edge had gone out of Camille's voice. Now, she just looked tired.

When Trenyth didn't answer, but looked to the side, she pulled out the unicorn horn to examine it. "Wow. I guess busting us out of that room discharged all the energy. I couldn't have turned this loose on the storm even if I'd tried. I'm going to have to recharge it before I can use this again."

"Put that away," Trenyth said sharply. "Even though we're protected here, who knows what magic the sorcerers have at their disposal? They may be able to sense powerful artifacts, and even when the horn isn't charged up, the essence it contains is ancient and magnetic."

"Putting it away isn't going to help, since it means just stuffing it back in my skirt. But yeah, probably best not to make access too easy. Though, if any sorcerer wanted it, all they have to do is fry me to a crisp. And considering the nature of that storm, I doubt they'd have much difficulty." She tucked the horn back in the secret pocket she'd had Iris sew into most of her traveling skirts.

Trenyth motioned for us to stay put, as he left the room. When he was gone, I turned to Camille.

"What the fuck do we do, then? Sit here?"

"I don't like it any more than you do, but he's right. When you think about it, if we go out there while the storm is still rampaging, we're going to probably die. I doubt if we could even make it to one of the portals without chancing being caught in the destruction. I suppose . . . we can't do anything else but stay here." She toyed with the hem of her skirt. "I could, however, attempt to go out on the astral to contact Smoky."

I felt the blood run from my face. "What if that storm is on the astral? You don't dare do that."

She gave me a look that I was all too used to seeing. "I know that. But do I have a choice? Our sister is out there, in that rubble. And Chase. And Sharah—who is about to have a baby. And . . . Trillian. I don't want to lose any of them."

"Not a good choice. Camille, for once, listen to me. I'm not even risking going out to find Greta. *It's too dangerous.*" I stressed my words, hoping that this time she wouldn't think of me as her little sister, but instead that she'd take me seriously.

As she was about to reply, Trenyth returned. The look on his face told us everything, and my heart sunk.

"The storm is still raging. There's nothing left. As far as I can see, only rubble. I can hear the screams of people who are trapped, but there's no way to get to them. Utter carnage." He looked so shaken that I slipped out of my seat and went over to guide him to the table.

Camille took his hand, helped him sit down while I brought him a drink of water. Then, I peeked in the cabinets. Rations, food that stored well. I found a cured ham and sliced off several pieces, as well as a loaf of hard bread, not stale but baked for keeping long periods. I made a makeshift sandwich and pushed it into Trenyth's hand, then went back to make more for Camille and me. Though my stomach was in knots, I realized I was starving. And having channeled the power of the horn, Camille had to be as well.

We ate silently. The meat was too salty, the bread too hard, but it was food and we needed the energy. Trenyth finally wiped his lips on the hem of his robe. He looked at us.

"You girls should rest. Sleep now and I'll wake you up in a couple hours. There's nothing more either of you can do until the storm starts to clear."

As we stood, the floor rolled again and Camille stumbled. I caught her, and we rode out the quake. Trenyth wanted to show us to the bedchamber, but I nixed that.

"I have no desire to get caught in a back room. I don't care how safe you say this place is. We'll sleep on the floor out here." I turned to Camille. "You agree?"

She nodded. "Yeah. I want to be within inches of the door, to be blunt."

Trenyth pointed to the door at the other side of the room. "At least bring in some blankets to cushion and cover you.

The floor is not comfortable, but with a thick quilt, you should be okay."

There were two bedrooms, a storeroom, and another room that seemed to be a makeshift bathing chamber with a toilet. Camille washed her face and I followed suit. We cleaned up as best as we could, then headed into the first bedroom we came to. We were too tired to pay much attention to the rest of the room except the bed, but I did notice that the door contained arrow slits and slid into the wall instead of opening the usual way. There were heavy latches that could be thrown. A glance over my shoulder told me the room was expensively furnished. Probably the Queen's chamber for emergencies.

And she's not here now. Which could mean very bad things for the Elfin race. I brushed away the thought, trying to stay focused. Camille grabbed several pillows while I took hold of the comforter and we returned to the main chamber.

There, we spread out the quilt and pillows. Without a word, we laid down and, under Trenyth's watchful eye, fell into uneasy slumber.

I stretched out, steam rising from my nostrils. My body ached, but the blood rolled through my veins, and my fur rippled as I yawned and snuffled. More and more, I found my panther form comfortable. I was used to the strength of my muscles, the heavy thickness of my paws, the hunger to hunt that never quite left me. As I inhaled deeply, the astral breeze filling my lungs, a song lured me from somewhere in the mists. I cocked my head, listening to catch the direction.

There, off to my left. I turned and began to jog through the jungle. By now, I knew that I was on the etheric plane where my panther roamed. I had no clue as to why I always landed in a jungle when I was in panther form, but my astral jaunts were far different than when I was in two-legged stance. And when I went out as a Death Maiden, I found myself in a different dimension as well. The number of layers making up the universe never ceased to amaze me.

I raced through the jungle, the smell of moisture thick in my nose as I loped through the undergrowth. Even though I knew I was out of body, I could still feel the air rushing through my lungs; intensely oxygenated from the towering trees and rich, lush undergrowth. A trickle of water sounded somewhere near, a waterfall by the sound of it, blending with the voice that lured me on.

On I ran, through the trees that scraped the sky, through the vibrant ferns and flowers spilling over onto the narrow pathway. When I was out here, it felt as though I could run forever, prowl forever, hunt forever.

I turned off to the right as the path forked, and soon found myself at the edge of a cliff overlooking a river that raged below. White water churning, the rapids were thick, promising to sweep away anyone who dared enter their territory. A long tree trunk stretched across the river, a yard wide, forming the only bridge to the other side.

I slowed, cautiously making my way out onto the tenuous bridge. The trunk seemed firmly set, and in cat or panther form, I was sure-footed and confident. I didn't look down. I'd learned the hard way in tabby form when I was leaping from cupboard to cupboard that looking down? So *not* a good idea. When I made it to the other side, I turned back, looking downriver. The forest ran on and on, and each time I came here, I found myself in a new part of it. I had no clue where *here* was, and when I had asked Greta about it, she had refused to answer.

Still, the song lured me forward. The unending rainforest was humid, but here, near the ground, the heat stayed around eighty degrees, and the air was still. Heat rises. Up in the treetops, the temps could soar well into triple digits, with hot winds gliding through to sweep the perfumes of the jungle into a heady, intoxicating whirl.

The song grew louder, and then, I was through into a clearing and I knew where I was. I'd been here before, and the sight before me scared the fuck out of me, because I knew what it meant.

There, before me, rested a dais—a circle built in bronze, jutting out of the ground—and covered in glyphs and runes. Surrounded by the jungle, this place was sacred to the Death Maidens. This was where we brought heroes to die.

And there, on the other side of the circle, stood Greta. She waited, watching a figure who was kneeling in the center of the dais. I found myself shifting back into two-legged form, dressed in my robe. Flowing to the ground, loose and lovely, the material of my gown was the color of twilight.

I sucked in a deep breath, not wanting to look closer at the dais. I knew what was coming—but not *who*. Inside, a horrible feeling began to rise. I knew this person, though I had no sense of his or her name yet. I knew this person, and it would be my job to kill them. I knew this person, and I would be facing my worst nightmare when I turned to look them in the face. I had dreaded this day since I first began to understand my nature as a Death Maiden. The day I'd be required to take out someone dear to me.

I slowly walked up to the dais and the first thing I noticed was that my victim was a woman, but she was wearing a long gown, and a veil covered her face. *Please don't let it be Sharah. Please don't let Chase lose the woman who has captured his heart.* The refrain echoed over and over in my heart.

As I set foot on the bronze circle, a reverberation echoed through me and I knew that this would be no angry death. There would be honor here. This was why she had come— to be honored, revered, to walk through death's doorway and escorted to the halls of the valiant.

I stood in front of the figure, as the sky overhead echoed an aurora of brilliant blues and greens. Glowing orbs rose up around us and I recognized them as will o' the wisps, as a thousand voices joined in a lament so ancient that the language had been lost in the veils of time.

I stood tall, facing her, weariness dropping away as a surge of energy flooded through me. The smoke of bonfires lighting the hills, the drumbeat of time, the flutter of autumn leaves on the wind, the flurry of storms on the horizon . . . it was the harvest come to bear. The light touch on my shoulder told me Hi'ran was standing behind me, but I steadied myself, continuing to look at my quarry.

And then, without a word, without a protest, she reached up and pulled the veil back from her face.

The plants, the trees, the animals of the forest gave a collective gasp. The air fluttered as the lament grew stronger. And I stared into the face that I had come to know too well.

"Your Majesty . . ." I started to kneel but could not.

Greta's words from a recent training session echoed in my memory. *A Death Maiden supersedes royalty . . . supersedes all nobility and title. To us, all are equal, all come before us as they were born—without title, without class, without rank. All who come before us are here to die. Whether they die in obliteration, or are taken to the halls of the revered depends entirely on how they lived their life. Remember this. We only kneel to the Harvestmen, and to the Hags of Fate.*

Queen Asteria faced me, a serene look on her face. She stood here, on the cornerstone of death, as she had lived in life: dignified, in her power, and accepting what could not be changed.

I stepped up to her. She was so very old, ancient beyond her days, and I could not imagine what she had seen in her life. Tonight, I would find out. Even though I was to escort her to her glory, I still had to break the soul-connection she had with life.

"Delilah, you do me a great service." Her voice was steady. "I hoped, if this were to be the time, that I would be worthy of this honor."

"Your Majesty—" What the hell could I say? I fumbled for words, my heart breaking. I didn't want to do this, but there was no choice, there was no quarter to which I could retreat.

She tipped her head, in a fashion I had seen her do a dozen times over, and shook her head. "It has all been said.

I understand. Please, though . . . look after my niece for me? She has a long road ahead of her, with what waits in her path."

Again, I started to say something, but there were no words. "I promise."

Sucking in a deep breath, I stepped forward, holding out my hands. She took them, her wizened face suddenly looking tired, and I could feel how very much she needed to rest. I clasped her fingers gently, feeling the slow pulse of her life ebb and flow. She was hurt, that much I could tell, and in pain.

I leaned in to place my lips against hers, and the kiss became a blur as our auras merged. I gazed into her eyes as I kissed her, the hands of the clock sweeping backward, first slowly, then at a great pace. The moon rose, and set, and then the sun—racing widdershins across the sky—and the moon again, until a blur of days and nights became a streak of time against the void.

Flash . . . a glimpse of Trenyth, and my heart rises, filled with love and longing and the knowledge that I can never have him. The desire to throw my crown away and run off into the wilds with my advisor almost wins out, but there is always duty, always honor, and it weighs heavily on my heart.

Flash . . . a glimpse of the night sky, and a longing to let go and be free. Daily duties grind the day into dust, and the years into ashes, and there exists only the slow march of time with no break, no reprieve.

Flash . . . The Scorching Wars are over, and Telazhar stands before the tribunal. I am the only member pleading for his death. The others relent and sentence him to the Sub-Realms. But I know, deep inside, that he needs to die. He looks at me directly—I was the only one speaking for his death—and he winks. A goose walks over my grave then . . .

Flash . . . and I am standing by a lake. The world is fresh and young, and I wonder, did we make the right choices in calving off Earthside? In leaving everything we ever knew behind? But there were so many dangers, and surely now, they were forever put to rest. The demons are safely locked away, and the portals are barred. And we have a world to explore . . .

Flash . . . I stare into the mirror. The heavy coronation dress—a glimmer of sparkle and light, of spidersilk and flower blossoms, trails behind me. I am not ready for this. I am not secure in my abilities. How can I ever fill the shoes of my mother, Queen Lia, who was recently killed by assassins?

Tears form in my eyes, but my cousin, Lent, shakes his head. "You must never show fear, never show doubt. After today, you hold the keys to the kingdom in your hand. You must learn to sweep your emotion under the rug and pretend it doesn't exist. For you will be the living Court of the Elfin Kingdom. You are the throne. You are no longer a person, but an icon. You owe this to your mother."

And I hear his words and obey. I know no other way. This was what I was born to do. This was what I must do. And so . . . I put aside my sorrow, and I tip my lips into a smile. I'm beautiful, and I'm brilliant. *And I swear to my mother that I will become the shining star of the Elfin world, and never let my people slide into despair* . . .

As I pulled back, I looked into Asteria's eyes once more. And there, I could see her life laid out, road lines on the map of her face. She smiled, then, and reached up to remove her crown.

"Heavy is the head . . ." She softly dropped it to the bronze dais, and shook out her hair. "Shall we go then? I am ready. Let us take this life of mine and emblazon it on the pages of history."

Still holding tight to her hands, I let out a slow breath and smiled. She was ready, and as much as I dreaded the next moment, I turned and walked her to the center of the dais. Where she was going, I could not follow—I was still alive, and the guardians of the Silver Falls would not allow me in. She stood in the center and began to let go of my hands. I caught my breath in my chest, not wanting to let go, wanting to hold on to her, to keep her here.

"You have to let go, Delilah. You have a life to live. There will be great challenges ahead. You must not let Shadow Wing and Telazhar win, and now—the seals . . . they are running free. You have to let me walk into the past, while you move forward."

Crying in earnest, I felt her fingers slip away from mine. She began to fade, shimmering in a crystalline light that sparkled around her shoulders and head. It was so bright, it almost blinded me, but still I watched, unwilling to turn away, unwilling to let her go without proper witness.

Queen Asteria laughed, then, and she sounded free and easy and happy. And then as I watched, she faded away, her hair blowing in the astral wind, looking young again and strong. As the light paled, and went out like a candle, the forest let out a collective sigh, and fell into mourning.

A murder of crows rustled out of a nearby tree, their cries echoing in the night sky. As they went winging overhead, I reached up, as if to capture one in my hands. The scent of fire rose on the wind, as autumn fully took hold, and the season of death descended.

"How can we possibly win this battle?" I whispered.

And Hi'ran, still standing behind me, turned me around and gathered me in his arms. He pressed his lips against mine and kissed me, drinking me deep, drinking me down into the dark, carrying me into the depths of his season where skeletons danced and spirits sang, and the melancholy tombs gave up their dead for one night each year, to visit the living and remind them that all flesh is mortal, that all life comes with a price tag at the end, that all war claims its heroes.

I wept then, in his arms, and he loved me deep, laying me down on the dais, and parting my gown. He reached down, to stroke me with autumn's sweet and dangerous touch, and everywhere I looked a shower of crisp leaves fell in a shower around us. I opened my legs, wanting him, hungry for his passion. We could not meet on the physical plane—there, Shade was my lover, and Hi'ran's proxy, but here, Hi'ran could enter me, stroke me in fire, take away my pain with his pleasure. Here, we could fuck into the oblivion and freedom from pain that my heart sorely craved.

Into the night, we moved against one another, slowly at first, then furious in motion, until my sorrow was spent, and I was comfortably, peacefully, numb.

Chapter 12

⤜✦⤛

"Wake up. Delilah, Camille—you have to get up."

Trenyth's voice echoed through my foggy brain. As I sat up, the memory of what had just happened washed over me and I realized that I knew something that neither Trenyth nor Camille did. Queen Asteria was dead. And I had guided her through the veil.

I sat up, yawning, more tired than I had been when I laid down. The question of whether I should say anything weighed heavily on my mind. If I told Trenyth, it would save him fruitless hours searching for her. Hours that he could put toward helping others. On the other hand, would he blame me for her death, even though it had been the attack that had caused it? And if he did, would he *kill* me? I was pretty sure he could take me out without blinking.

"Camille, can I talk to you for a minute?" I turned to Trenyth. "Let us take care of personal needs and then . . . well . . ."

"Fine, but hurry. You were out for three hours." He nodded and we headed down the hall to the bathing chamber.

At least it had a bathroom of sorts, and while we took turns, I told Camille what had happened.

She stared at her hands, soaping them in the chill water at the basin. "So, she's dead. What the hell is that going to mean for Elqaneve? And . . . oh fuck . . . what about the spirit seals? Delilah, the Keraastar Knights! Where are they? You know Telazhar is aiming to find the seals and if the Knights were caught in the rubble . . . We don't even know where Queen Asteria kept them hidden."

I was shaking with both fear and weariness. The stress we were under had gone from *meh* to *horrendous* in the course of one evening. "I don't know. I have no clue where she kept the Keraastar Knights cloistered. What the hell do we do?"

The Knights were formed by Queen Asteria, who had been protecting the spirit seals we'd managed to gather. Each knight was bound to a seal, and what she was planning, we did not know. One spirit seal we'd stumbled on was still unbound, and so it, too, was floating around. Until this moment, eight of the nine had come to light and we'd managed to keep hold of six of them.

Five of our friends had been conscripted into service— Venus the Moon Child, the Rainier Puma Pride's former shaman, Benjamin Welter—a disturbed young man, Luke—Menolly's former bartender, and his sister Amber, and Tom Lane, who was actually the Tam Lin from legend. He was a broken man, after so many thousands of years, but he still carried the spirit seal with honor.

"We've got to get word to Father and Tanaquar. They can help. But the way things are going, I don't even know if there will be a city to save. The storm . . . Delilah, that storm is one of the most terrifying entities I've ever felt. Worse than Gulakah and he was a *god*." She gave me a pale, strained look. Tears ran down her cheeks but they were silent, as if she didn't even know they were being shed.

"Do you think I should tell Trenyth about Asteria? He loves her so much. How can I break his heart?" I hung my head.

"We have to. The pain will be there whether you tell him now, or whether he finds her body in the rubble. Best to prepare him, I think. And though he'll be heartbroken, he's professional enough to focus on the job at hand. Come on, let's go." She turned to the door and we headed back down the hall.

Trenyth was waiting in the hall for us, but before we could speak, he hustled us toward the storeroom. "Come on, we have to get out of here now. Save whatever it is for later. We have to move."

We burst through the storeroom door that led to another chamber, which had a magically sealed door to the outside. Trenyth broke the seal with a single slam of the hand against the door and again, I wondered just how much power the advisor had hidden away. We had never really had the chance to see him in action, or to ask him what his specialties were.

When he opened the outer door, Camille and I clung together, not knowing what we'd be seeing. It was going on close to midnight. Surely the horrendous storm had to have broken. How long could it last? How long could the sorcerers keep fueling it? But a little voice inside whispered doubts. *How many sorcerers are you talking about? A dozen? A hundred?* Telazhar would not arrive with a short deck. No, this was all out war and so they'd be prepared. And they'd caught Elqaneve—and us—unprepared.

And now, Queen Asteria was dead.

We stepped out, and the storm was still raging. As far as we could see, the landscape was dotted with fires, raging in brilliant oranges and pinks and crimsons. *Magical fire.* Was this the Scorching Wars, all over again?

There were no buildings standing, save for the one we'd come out of, and that was only by the fact that it was hidden behind an illusionary barrier. But, as Camille and I looked around, the devastation began to sink in. The palace was in rubble. The outer buildings were so much wreckage, splintered beyond any hope of recognizing what they had been only hours before.

"We have to find your sister and friends, and the Queen." Trenyth glanced at the sky. The churning clouds seemed to be thinning, but now they were streaking smaller bolts of lightning down to set off the tallest trees.

"Trenyth—stop!" I grabbed his arm. "Queen Asteria is dead. While I was asleep, I was summoned to Haseofon. I was . . . I had to . . ." I stopped, staring at him bleakly and, after a moment's hesitation, blurted out. "I was assigned to escort her through the veil, in an honored manner, to her ancestors."

He stared at me for a moment. Then, without a word, without showing a clue how he felt, he turned back to the palace. "We must focus on finding your sister and we absolutely have to find Sharah, if she's alive. She's the Queen's niece. Technically, she's an heir to the throne and who knows how many of them are alive? There were only two or three others in line before Sharah. And with the devastation this storm has wrought . . ." He trailed off.

But the thought was enough to send me into a tailspin. Sharah had mentioned this. She could end up being the next queen of Elqaneve. And what would that mean for her and Chase and their baby? *If they still live,* the voice of fear inside me said. *If they made it out.* And what about my love, Shade? While I had little doubt he could survive, there was also Trillian. So many factors. So many chances for death.

"Let's go. We'll have to chance the storm, but it seems to have let up some." Camille headed toward the palace, trying to avoid the pieces of debris that could cut her feet if she stepped wrong.

We ran through the darkness, past bodies charred by fire, hit by shrapnel. Everywhere, the screams of the injured rang out and my heart ached because there was nothing we could do for them. We ran through the hail of lightning bolts, the ravages of the magical thunder, skirting trees, skirting debris, skirting chunks of marble and stone that had been blasted when the palace went down. The sky lit the night brighter than the moon ever could, but even so, the storm was moving to the west, moving away.

By the time we reached the palace, the strikes were few and far between. I looked around nervously, wondering where the sorcerers actually *were*. Surely they weren't around the corner. They had no need to put themselves directly in the line of fire—magic traveled across long distances. And why not send in the grunts first, to take care of those left standing? Which meant, chances were that before morning a contingent of mercenaries would show up on the outskirts of the Elfin city. They'd want to get in before Y'Elestrial or Dahnsburg could send help.

Camille shouted and leaned on my shoulder, raising her foot. She yanked out a sliver of glass and tossed it to the side. "I need shoes."

I let out a long breath. "Yeah. Hold on."

There were several corpses near us and I shivered as I approached them. This was so surreal that I barely knew what I was feeling. But one of them—a woman, who had been struck by a piece of granite, had feet near Camille's size. And she was wearing a pair of leather moccasins. I quickly, silently, yanked them off her feet and without looking at the dead woman's face, handed them to Camille. She said nothing, looking mutely at me. But she put them on and we continued on to the palace.

The steps were broken, but still accessible in some places. The tons of stone and alabaster, of metal and wood that sprawled before us were daunting. Smoke filled the air from the still-burning fires, and dust hung heavy, choking us as we neared the shattered palace. Up was down, front was back, and it was hard to remember where anything had been.

Trenyth led us on, as we approached the behemoth that had been Asteria's pristine court. Camille was crying, but her tears were silent and slowly ran down her face as she shook her head.

Trenyth's lips were pressed together, as he grimly assessed the area. After a moment, he pointed to the left. "That way."

And we were off.

Making our way through the rubble was a nightmare. So

many death traps, so many blockades. *Here a body, there a body. A pile of what was once a royal statue, now ground to rubble and ash. Skirt a fire that burned brightly, showing no sign of stopping—and don't look because the fuel may just be a pile of corpses. The scent of burning stone, the scent of burning flesh. The greasy feel to the air because so much soot was flying loose. A bonfire to rival all bonfires, a testament to destruction and death, to hatred and greed. And there, to the right, that had been the throne room . . .*

Trenyth stopped suddenly, and looked to what appeared to be the shattered remnants of the throne room. It was buried under the rubble, under the fallen roof. If there had been anyone in there, they had to be dead. And Queen Asteria had been there, waiting for us. Her body was now entombed in a thousand tons of stone. After a moment, he turned back to our path and we moved onward.

"Here," he said after a long while of edging around piles of debris. "I believe . . . this should be where we turned off to head down to the quarters containing the seers."

We slowly approached what would have been the entrance, but now it was buried under a pile of stone and wood. And there was no way in.

"Fuck." Camille stared at the barred entrance.

"I echo the sentiment." I shook my head. "What now? What the hell do we do? How do we . . . I'm so lost here, I can't even begin to see the light of day."

Trenyth sucked in a deep breath. "I am going to tell the two of you what to do and I want you to obey me. Do you hear? I am acting head of Elqaneve for now."

Both Camille and I mutely nodded. We knew when were in over our heads and Trenyth needed our cooperation. He'd been through battles before, and we—we'd never come close to experiencing something on this scale.

"You are going to return to Y'Elestrial and contact Tanaquar." A cloud passed over his face.

"We can talk to our father while we're there," I said. "He'll be able to help somehow." Even as I said it, I knew how lame it sounded.

"Girls . . ." Trenyth shifted uncomfortably. "Your father . . . he . . ." He paused and we read the story on his face.

Don't say it. Don't say it. If you don't say it, it's not real.

Camille let out a little cry and her hand flew to her mouth as she turned to him. "He's here. Isn't he? He came to meet with us. He was waiting for us, wasn't he? With Queen Asteria, in the throne room."

Trenyth nodded. "Yes. I'm sorry."

A sucker punch to the gut and we were down for the count. But the night had numbed me so hard, so far, that the shock of the news washed like water on a duck's back, rolled over me and off again. Camille's tears stopped and she stood there, mute.

I was the first to find my voice. "If Menolly and the others survived, surely they would think of heading to Y'Elestrial. And remember, Shade can transport through the Ionyc Sea. He could have . . ." I let the thought drift off.

"You're right of course," Camille said, her voice so soft it was barely a whisper. "We'd better get to the portals before the armies come in. Because you know they've got to have a force marching this way. Trenyth, come with us?"

He shook his head. "I cannot. I will find someone to take you to the portals, though. It's likely to be dangerous on the roads." At my pleading look, he rested a gentle hand on my shoulder. "Delilah, you know that I would go if I could, but I'm in command here. And the Keraastar Knights are scattered—if we don't find them and get them away from here, Telazhar will have a damned good chance of getting the rest of the spirit seals before the week is up."

I nodded. "Yes. Yes . . . we'll go now, then. Who can we take with us?"

"Wait here." Trenyth hurried off, and Camille and I stood, hand in hand, mute. There was nothing much we could say. Within moments, he was back with a guard in hand. "Take them to the portals leading to Y'Elestrial and make certain they get through. Do you understand?"

The elf, his uniform torn and blackened from the soot, nodded. "With my life, Liege."

"Good, because their lives may depend on yours. And if they die and you live, your life will be forfeit. They are that important."

Not even looking fazed, the guard simply nodded and then, silently, he led us out of the palace, and we were off and away into the night.

The journey to the portals was devastating in itself. Elqaneve lay in ruins, the city ablaze with fires that burned too bright to be sparked from normal lightning. Everywhere, houses were razed, forest was burning, and people were dead or dying. Those who seemed unharmed sat in shock, or milled aimlessly. We passed through them, silent and without trying to help. There was nothing we could do. Nothing we could say. They did not stop us, nor try to speak.

And so we made our way to the Barrow Mounds, still no sign of invasion, but my intuition told me it would happen soon. The guards were at their posts, but they quickly told the one leading us that they had barred anyone from entering or leaving through the portals. I didn't hear what he said to them—my mind was churning on overload, and Camille was just as quiet.

Within minutes, however, we were hustled toward the portal pointing to Y'Elestrial, and then we were in, and a whirlwind later, we emerged into our home city.

As we exited the portal, the soft glow of eye catchers surrounded us, and the silence and sense of peace was palpable. It washed over us like a wave, and before I could help it, I was weeping, on my knees, exhaustion and despair my cloak. The guards took one look at us and rushed to our side. Camille sucked in a deep breath as they gathered around us.

"Elqaneve is fallen. We need to speak to Her Majesty immediately. We are His Lordship Sephreh ob Tanu's daughters. Take us to her now."

And without a question, without a protest, the guards swept us into a carriage, and we were on our way to the

Court, under a night sky that was clear and crisp, and the only smell of smoke was from the hearth fires in the houses that we passed by.

We were escorted into a private chamber. The Court and Crown was far more ostentatious than Elqaneve could ever have hoped to be, but it still made me catch my breath when I saw it. After the destruction we'd witnessed, my cynicism seemed to have flown the coop. Camille and I walked into the room to find ourselves facing a mirror that spread across one entire wall. I stared at our reflections, only now realizing how we looked.

We were bruised and battered, black and blue over our arms and faces, with crusted blood here and there—whether it was our own, or from some stranger we touched, some body we brushed against, it was hard to tell. Soot stained our torn clothes, and my hair—blond and spiky—was streaked with it. Ash and dirt joined the mix. Camille looked down at her moccasins and let out a yelp. They were covered with blood. She yanked them off, but a quick look at her feet showed only minor cuts and scratches. We truly looked like we had emerged from a war zone.

A glance around the room showed no one else in attendance, but a tray with water and wine and fruit and cheese was prominently placed on a table. We sank onto the edge of one of the leather benches, and I was grateful that the material could be wiped clean. We wouldn't stain the upholstery, at least.

In the back of my mind, I heard a cynical little voice say, "Who the fuck cares about upholstery?" but there was still a part of me that wanted to be polite.

Camille reached for a piece of cheese and a cracker. She glanced over at me. "I have no clue what we're supposed to do now. We warn Tanaquar and then . . . what?"

"We could go out to Father's house. See if Menolly is there."

She nodded, eating slowly. "Good point." But our talk

was all so much chatter. I felt broken, frozen by a sense that the world had just crashed down. Humpty Dumpty fell off the wall, and we were staring at a pile of scrambled eggs on the sidewalk.

A moment later, the door opened and Tanaquar, Queen of Y'Elestrial, swept in. Tanaquar was tall, with hair the color of flames that fell to her waist. She was tanned, and her eyes glowed with a light mirroring the golden glow of the sun. Beautiful, she looked a lot like her sister—the Opium Eater, whom she deposed in a civil war not too long before. We had thought the destruction from that war horrendous, but it was nothing—*nothing*, in comparison to what we had just been through.

Tanaquar stared at us for a moment, then held up her hand when we started to rise in order to curtsey. "Stay your selves. There is no time for decorum now. My advisors are on the way in." She paused. "You know your father was in Elqaneve." By her tone, she knew we knew.

I nodded. "Yes. We do know. He's missing."

She merely waited until her flock of advisors joined her. They sat around us, in a half circle, three men and two women, as well as the Queen.

Sucking in a deep breath, I looked at Camille. And then, together, stumbling over events because they had become one big blur, we told them about the destruction of Elqaneve. When we finished, all the energy seemed to drain from me, and I leaned on the arm of the bench, exhausted.

"We're missing Shade, Trillian, Chase, and Sharah, and . . . apparently, our father." I stared at the Queen, unflinching. "Queen Asteria is dead."

"And so . . . we are on the eve of war. And Elqaneve is fallen, and a reign that lasted thousands of years comes to a horrifying end." Her voice was soft, but her words still pronounced the death knoll on the Elfin city. She turned to the man on her left. "We hold a treaty. Kelvashan is under siege and their capitol city, destroyed. Go now, marshal the army, and prepare to march in aid to to the elfin lands. We will use the military portals. There is no time to spare."

At that moment, a messenger burst into the room. He skidded to one knee in front of Tanaquar. "Your Majesty, I bring news. A huge contingent of soldiers has been spotted marching on the road to Elqaneve. They came out of the Tygerian Mountains. They are armed and said to be at least a thousand strong. They have not reached Kelvashan yet but are expected to breech the borders by morning."

Tanaquar turned to her advisors. "Go and prepare. Marshal the armies to begin leaving before the night is out. We *must* be there to meet the enemy."

As they left the room, Tanaquar and her bodyguard alone remained. She waited till they were gone, then turned back to us. "So, my friends . . . I can offer no solace except that we will do what we can. Telazhar cannot capture the spirit seals. The danger grows with every hour."

"We will go in search of them, Your Majesty." A familiar voice echoed through the room and we turned.

Trillian was standing there, along with Smoky, Shade, and Rozurial. Trillian looked banged up pretty bad, but he was alive. Camille let out a little cry and ran over to him, throwing herself into his arms. He kissed her, pressing his lips to her hair, her face, her neck.

"Menolly? Chase and Sharah . . . are they all right?" Her voice was shaking now, and I was as afraid to hear the answer as she was.

Trillian nodded. "Yes, my love. They're all right, though Sharah went into labor."

"I traveled through the Ionyc Sea to fetch Smoky and Rozurial. They returned with me and helped rescue the others. Everyone's safely back Earthside now." Shade held out his arm and I slid into his embrace, wanting never to leave the shelter of his protection.

Camille glanced up at Trillian. "Did you . . . did you happen to see our father anywhere? He was in the throne room with Queen Asteria and . . . she's dead. She was crushed under the rubble, as far as we know. As far as Father . . . we have no news. We don't know whether he was . . ."

Her lip quivered and she sucked in a deep breath. The

fact that they'd been just starting to iron out their relationship had to make this doubly hard. He'd disowned her for a while, and she'd walked away, accepting his decision but not knuckling under to his prejudice. They'd just made up a few months ago, an uneasy truce to see if they could forge a new bond. And now, this.

"We will look, my wife. We will go to Elqaneve and look. I am a dragon, these goblins cannot harm me." Smoky tipped her chin up, smiling. His hair rose up and stroked her shoulders gently.

"You don't know—you don't know what it was like!" She broke away and turned to me. "They don't understand how . . ."

I stepped up by her side. "Guys, she's right. Trillian, you have no clue what was going on while you were trapped down there. The sorcerers, they raised a sentient storm. It was massive, far more massive than anything I've ever seen. That . . . thing . . . destroyed the city. It wasn't an earthquake—not a natural one. Those damned lightning bolts went barreling into the ground, setting off the shaking. The storm was alive, malevolent. If Telazhar and his cronies can do that, what else are they capable of?"

Trillian caught my gaze and slowly shook his head. "We must find the Knights. If we don't, then everything we've been working for goes down in ashes. Because if those loons that Asteria set to wearing the spirit seals break free and are unprotected, there is no hope. They aren't bred to fend for themselves over here. Venus, maybe—he's a wily old shaman, but the others? Helpless babes in the blazing wood. Telazhar will find them, of that you can be sure. And he will take them to Shadow Wing, who will destroy their souls and take the seals. And then . . . he will be all but unstoppable."

Camille and I looked at each other, mutely. They were right, of course. "We can help—" she started, but Smoky shook his head.

"No, wife. You cannot. Trillian has been a mercenary in Queen Tanaquar's army before. I'm a dragon. Rozurial can travel through the Ionyc Sea and he's armed to the hilt. The three of us will stay here. You must return to Earthside. We cannot be worrying about you or it will distract us."

Reluctantly, I saw the value of what they were saying. "Fine. But you have to let Trenyth know that Sharah is alive. She's in line to take the throne if the other heirs are dead. Tell him, please."

Smoky inclined his head. "Then, we shall be off, before the armies marching on Elqaneve arrive there."

I wondered how he knew just what was going on and opened my mouth to ask when Shade held up his hand. "No, love. I know what you are going to ask. Trenyth actually found a Whispering Mirror still intact. I do not know where, but he found one. He told us everything, including the soldiers marching toward Elqaneve. They know scouts who weren't in the city, who survived, got word to them."

I wanted to slap him. To ask why he hadn't told us that in the beginning, but considering the trauma and chaos of the night, I didn't have the heart.

Tanaquar stood and we all curtseyed and bowed. "Then, I accept your help, Trillian, Smoky, and Rozurial. You will leave for Elqaneve immediately. And the rest of you—go home. Go home and be safe, and wait for word. Even here, the roads are too dangerous to send you out in public—we cannot know who might be lurking. So I will send you a guard to escort you to a hidden portal that leads Earthside." With that, she turned and left the room.

Camille was whispering to Trillian and Smoky, and I could tell she was upset but we were all too tired to fight, to argue, to even cry.

I glanced up at Shade. "You are staying with us Earthside?"

"Someone has to protect the house, and so I will stay. And Vanzir and Shamas and Morio. But the elfin guards must leave for home—they will be needed there. Perhaps Camille can ask Aeval for additional support from the Earthside Fae to guard the house." He pressed his lips against my forehead, and I wanted to lose myself in him, to forget the events of the past six hours.

I could not believe it was still *today*—this morning seemed a million miles away. Everything had seemed so normal, and now the world stood turned on its head. Like an extended nightmare, when I closed my eyes, all I could see were the endless fires and lightning strikes amid a cloud of dust and soot. *Too much. Too much.* I wanted to turn back the clock, to pretend this had never happened. But nothing would ever erase the memory of the storm as it rained down death.

The door opened and a guard peeked in, motioning for us to follow him. Camille let go of her men and joined Shade and me. Her lips were set in that determined look that I knew covered up a well of pain and fear. But she shook out her hair and stood proudly.

"Be safe, my loves. Be safe, Rozurial. Return to us under the watchful eye of the Moon Mother." She turned and walked toward the door, not looking back.

I raised my hand in salute, and joined her, followed by Shade. Silently, we left the room, and just as silently, followed the guard down the hallway and into another chamber—a small library filled with scrolls, and a writing desk and chair. He walked up to a relatively bare wall and, in one quick motion, pressed a brick. A passageway sprang open and we followed him through into a narrow stairwell, which led down, spiraling into a lower level with a simple bed, chair, and table. A guard was standing at attention and after whispering with our guide, he motioned for us to turn around. Another moment, and we turned back to see a door to yet another secret chamber. In this chamber, a portal waited, like the one in the Wayfarer.

The guard hustled us into the portal, and the next thing we knew, the world shifted, the veils parted, and we were sailing home.

Blinking, I realized we were in Grandmother Coyote's portal. And she was there, softly smiling, waiting for us.

"So the tide has turned, girls. And there is death and

destruction imprinted on your souls. Bear in mind that all
that was, all that will be, is dictated by a thin scale. The
universe metes out its will. The gods play their hands. And
we—the Hags of Fate and the Harvestmen, we wind the
skeins of all life. But even we follow rules, and we are gov-
erned by the balance of order and of chaos. I will help you
as I can, but things will grow much darker before there can
be light. And the night—the night has just begun."

And with that, she motioned for us to go, not giving us a
chance to ask her any questions. We stepped out into the
star-filled night. It was late, very late now, and nearing
dawn. Menolly would still be up, and I wanted to get home
in time to reassure myself that yes, she was okay. That
Chase and Sharah were all right.

The trek back to the clearing was wet and soggy. Rain
poured down, but the scent of the cedar and fir and moss
and mildew soothed me as we pushed through the undergrowth. As we came into the clearing, we could see Vanzir.

He was waiting for us, leaning against his car, the headlights on to guide us. For the first time, the snarky look was
gone from his face, and I could see real fear in his eyes. He
straightened up as he saw us.

The sound of a jet winging overhead filled my ears and
it felt sweet and safe—a far cry from the echoing thunder
of the storm. But how close would that storm be to us? How
long before Telazhar found more of the seals, or took control of the portals in Elqaneve and filtered his sorcerers
through here to gate in the demons?

Too many questions. Too much danger ahead. I slipped
into the backseat of the car next to Shade, while Camille
settled in front with Vanzir. He started up the engine, and
as we settled back against the seats, he eased the car out
onto the road. But, even though I felt my eyes starting to
close, the spin of the wheels on the pavement seemed to
whisper, *"Death . . . death . . . war is come and you are
right in the path."*

Chapter 13

❧❧❧

When we walked through the house, it felt like we'd been gone a million years. A million miles. Morio was there, waiting for Camille. Hanna had filled the table with steaming food. The quiet sound of Maggie playing echoed from the living room. Everything seemed so surreal that I didn't know what to do first.

Camille looked equally at a loss. She cocked her head, and said, "What . . . it feels like we need to be doing something. How can we just walk back into our lives and go on as if nothing were happening over there?" She sounded mildly hysterical.

Morio glanced at Shade and nodded. "Okay, you two. First things first. You both need baths and food. Then, we'll sort out what comes next. There's nothing you can do for anyone in Elqaneve tonight. You've done all you could. You'll just make yourselves sick if you don't get some rest."

He bundled Camille off to their rooms, and Shade slid his arm around my waist and we started the long haul up the stairs, watching as Morio and Camille vanished onto the second floor. By the time we reached our bedroom, I felt so exhausted I could barely walk. I wearily dropped to the bed, wanting nothing more than to pass out. But Shade wouldn't let me.

Instead, he began to undress me, and I let him. Normally, I didn't like anybody fussing with my clothes, but I laid back, letting him slide my boots off. Then he unzipped my jeans and eased them down my legs. Next, he slowly inched my panties off and added them to the pile.

"Give me your hand." His warm gaze held me, and I obeyed. He pulled me to a sitting position and motioned for me to raise my arms. Off came the sweater, and then the bra. I sat there, naked, assessing the roadmap of bruises lining my arms and legs. There were also plenty of them on my torso, and I knew Camille had fared just as badly.

"How's your hand?" he reached for my bandaged hand.

I stared at it. "I forgot about it." And so I had. The pain of the wound seemed minute compared to everything that had happened.

Shade cautiously removed the bandage. The wound was sore and red, but it had not spread and seemed better than when Sharah had bandaged it earlier. He irrigated the wound, cautiously scrubbing the skin around it, then medicated it and fastened it with a new dressing. A plastic bag over the top, snugly fitted to my wrist, would ensure that it didn't get wet.

"Come on pussycat. Let's get you cleaned up." He led me into the bathroom, and even though I didn't care for baths, I welcomed the sight of the steaming tub of bubbles. My aching muscles also didn't like the thought of standing up in the shower, and so I eased myself into the tub, leaning back, trying to ignore the sensation of motion that always made me queasy when water lapped around my body.

A moment later, and Shade was scrubbing my back, still in silence. I closed my eyes, but the rolling clouds, the flashing lightning, lit up my memory and I began to panic. I jerked to a sitting position, trying to breathe.

"Love, love . . . are you all right? Delilah?" Shade had hold of my hands.

"The storm . . . the storm." And then, I was crying, weeping, as I wrapped my arms around my shins and rested my head on my knees. "It was horrible. It was so . . ." I lifted my head slowly, staring straight ahead. "If this is what war is like, how do men live through weeks and months and years of it? How do you live in that much fear for so long without going crazy?"

Shade stroked my hair, then my face. "You don't. Every war takes a toll. Even tonight, even what you and Camille went through . . . I'm sorry, my sweet, but it will be with you forever. I doubt you'll ever be free of that memory. That's what war does to people, whether you escape near the beginning, or you see utter destruction for years on end. There's nothing to be done but learn to live with it. To learn to face the fear and not run."

As he took the shampoo and rubbed it in my hair, holding me gently as I lay back for him to lather and rinse, I thought about all the people we knew who had been to war. How, even though we were on the verge of demonic war and had been fighting demons for what seemed like forever, we had seen nothing yet.

And Shadow Wing's armies would be worse than Telazhar. The death that we'd seen rain down from the sky today was a pale shadow to what the Demon Lord could do if he broke through. We'd need to be at the top of our game. We'd need to push aside the apprehension and make certain that our worst fears didn't happen.

By the time I was clean, the numbness was beginning to seep out of my soul. The hot water, Shade's gentle hands . . . the feeling of being home, helped to cushion the pain. My body ached. I was hungry and tired but ready to face whatever came.

"I guess . . . food next. And then, we see how Sharah is doing. And then . . . to sleep?" I looked at my lover.

Shade held out the towel. "It will get worse, Delilah. It will get far worse before it gets better. But we have an advantage. We have something to lose. And you always fight harder when you've got someone to protect, or something to lose."

And with that, I toweled off, brushed my hair, dressed in my sweats, and we headed down to the kitchen to regroup, take stock, and figure out what the hell we were going to do after that.

Menolly was anxiously waiting to launch herself at me when I entered the room. In an uncharacteristic move, she slammed into me for a hug, then—to my startlement—leaned up to plant a quick kiss on my cheek. It was over before I could say a word, but that she had been able to bring herself to show physical affection to someone other than a lover spoke volumes.

Camille was already at the table, tucked into a silk robe, and she cradled a cup of tea between her hands. A plate of cookies in front of her remained untouched, but she had a hamburger on her plate, and it looked like Morio had gotten her to eat a few bites.

The kitchen felt eerily devoid of life. Without Iris around, and without Smoky, Trillian, and Roz, the noise level was at a bearable level and everything felt too calm.

Hanna put a burger in front of me, and a big glass of milk. "Get your sister to eat," she said. "She needs her dinner."

I toyed with my food, not that hungry either. But we both needed to get something in us, so I motioned to Camille. "She's right." As I lifted my hamburger to my lips, I paused and looked at Menolly. "Do you know everything? Well . . . you can't know what we went through, but you know Queen Asteria is dead?"

Menolly nodded. "Yeah, I know she's gone." After a moment, she continued. "Nerissa is down at the station with Chase. Sharah went into labor as she came out of the Ionyc Sea. Smoky did the best he could but it's not the same as going through a portal. It really hit her hard."

"Is the baby okay?" I sat up, alarmed.

"We don't know, but the fetal heartbeat is strong. I last talked to them about twenty minutes ago and she's dilated six centimeters so it's going to be a while yet. She's narrow-hipped and Mallen said that may be an issue, but so far, so good. Nerissa is keeping Chase occupied."

Relieved that at least one thing was going right, I nodded. "After everything we've experienced, I have to say I was scared to even ask."

"I can't imagine what it was like where you were." Menolly played with a bottle of blood, taking care to wipe her mouth as she drank her dinner. She was fastidious, and often complained about vampires with messy habits.

Camille let out a sharp breath. "We're all at the 'can't imagine' stage, I think. We saw things last night that I never want to see again, but I have the horrible feeling that we haven't seen the last. If that's what war is like, then we have to fucking make sure they don't break through the portals." After a moment, she looked at me. "Shade's heard, but the others . . ." She looked at Menolly. "You may know some of what went down, but unless you were there, you really can't imagine."

So, once again, we told our story. I was tired of telling it, the images were too fresh in my mind. And I could see, by Camille's expression, they were haunting her as well.

Menolly's jaw dropped as we told her about the storm, and what it had been like. Vanzir's face remained expressionless but he leaned forward, pushing his beer out of the way. Lately, he'd gotten into drinking microbrews, and while the alcohol didn't affect him, he liked the taste.

"I'm going to tell you girls something and I want you to listen." His eyes whirled, kaleidoscopes in the dim light of the kitchen. "War is war. War happens and has always happened, and will always happen. As long as there are men, as long as there are demons, as long as there are gods and dragons and the Fae, as long as there is greed and anger, hatred and desire, lust and passion, there will be war."

He stood, hooking his thumbs in the rope belt holding up his low-cut jeans. "Only one thing that is a certainty:

even in the most insane of times, you have to go on living your lives. You have to carry on your daily activities as much as you can, because if you don't, the enemy wins. If you lose track of what makes your life important, then you give them the chance to fuck you over, upside down and sideways. You forfeit and they screw you."

We stared at the dream-chaser demon. Vanzir had been soul-bound to us under a geas with a death threat, but that had been broken during an emergency that had set into motion a horrible chain of events, culminating in giving Hyto, Smoky's psycho father, the chance to capture Camille and torture her. He'd chosen to remain with us, though, in the battle against the demons.

Camille was the first to speak. "He makes a good point. I guess that's what we do, then. We can't sit around here worrying. I can't sit here 24/7 wondering if Smoky and Trillian will come out of this okay. Or if Telazhar will capture the Keraastar Knights. Until Trenyth contacts us again, we have to go on with life."

I ducked my head. Vanzir was right, and so was Camille. Straightening my shoulders, I swallowed the desire to curl up in a ball and hide. "Then that's what we'll do. Menolly has a bar to rebuild. And we have to find out what happened to Violet, as well as mopping up whatever mess is going on over at the Farantino Building." I paused, then opened my mouth. "It's just . . . everything seems so mundane, so minute compared to what we just came through."

Camille stared at her plate and listlessly picked up her hamburger. "Hanna's right. We need food. You know, when Hyto kidnapped me, after everything that happened there, I wondered how I would ever go back to normal. I mean, I still have nightmares where he's . . ."

A pause, then she continued. "Anyway, at first I wasn't sure what to do, how to act. But by picking up the threads of my routine, by doing the things that life demands of us every day, I began to find my way back to myself. And I realized that there is no going *back* to normal. You create a *new normal* for yourself. It's like coming off a path to a much bigger one, where there are more factors. But you learn how to navigate this one just like you learned how to navigate the one you were on."

Menolly picked up her thread of thought. "True. We were at loose ends when we first found out about Shadow Wing. It felt like we were on a rock slide, going down fast. But we adapted. And now, we will adapt again. Hell, you think I didn't have to face some of the most grueling adaptation of my life when Dredge turned me? When the OIA took me in and taught me how to regain control over myself? There was no shred of my old life left, I thought. But I was wrong—you two were there, and Father, even though I knew how he felt about vampires. But he was a link to the old world, and I used the three of you to merge the two paths so that I didn't feel like an alien."

Hanna bustled over. "You are all correct. I had to do this too—when Hyto captured me. I had to learn how to adapt to try to keep me and my son alive." Her face fell; it was obvious she was thinking about Kjell. He'd been about fifteen when Hanna had been forced to kill him. Even though there had been no real choice, the fact that she'd poisoned her son to keep him from a worse fate still hung heavy on her conscience.

She placed her hand on Camille's shoulder, and Camille gently took it and kissed it. The two had formed a bond, and Hanna had been instrumental in helping Camille escape before Hyto killed her. Together, they'd made their way down a frozen mountain high in the Northlands, hiding from the psychotic dragon who was bent on destroying his son and my sister.

Hanna kissed her gently on the top of her head, then motioned to the food. "Eat. You cannot fight these monsters if you are undernourished. Then, you must sleep. You two are exhausted, and also, Miss Menolly, dawn is near and you should be in your lair." With a scolding cluck, she pushed the bowls of salad and fruit, and a plate of cookies toward us.

Camille and I ate, and my appetite flared. We wolfed

down our food, once we got started. But halfway into the meal, I felt myself fading. Camille wearily put down the rest of her cookie.

I said it for both of us. "If we don't get to bed, we're going to keel over from exhaustion."

She grunted. "I'm so tired I can't even nod my head. It's almost five in the morning and we've been to hell and back."

Menolly kissed us both lightly on the forehead. "I will see you when I wake tonight." She vanished down the stairs, shutting the heavy bookcase door behind her.

With Morio and Shade's help, we made our way upstairs. Camille and Morio hived off to their rooms, and it seemed strange to see her only with the youkai. Her quartet was incomplete, and she looked fragile and shaken.

Shade and I finally reached the third floor.

"I didn't think I was going to make it up that last set of steps. I can't believe I ache so much." Wearily, I dragged myself over to the bed and face-planted on it.

"How about I rub your back?" Shade tugged on my pajama top.

I let out a muffled grunt. "I'm too tired for sex."

"I said rub your back, not fuck your pussy." He laughed, low, and leaned down to land a kiss on my neck. "I love having sex with you, but woman if you think I'm going to push for a roll right now, when I *know* what you've been through, then you don't think very highly of me."

And so, he turned on soft music, and dimmed the lights, saying nothing, letting me decompress. As exhausted as I was, I couldn't shut off the images in my brain, or the memories of facing Asteria. She'd been so beautiful and radiant, so insanely strong and dignified. It had been both an honor and a great heartbreak to be the one assigned to escort her through the veil. And then, there was the worry over Father. I didn't want to let myself even go there, but I could feel the fear hanging like the proverbial sword over my head.

I'd thought myself cried out, but once again, tears trickled down my face; they were slow, and I didn't bother wiping them away. I just let them absorb into the pillow-case, unwilling to deny them.

Shade tugged me out of my PJs and draped the sheet over my torso. He began with my feet, and I let out a little sigh as he worked the tension from my ankles, my toes, and up my calves. When he came to my back I was half asleep, but I could still feel his knuckles digging deep into the knots that had settled into my muscles.

And then he was rubbing my shoulders, stroking my skin, and I became aware that he was soothing my aura somehow, calming the stressed parts, feeding energy into the places where I was drained dry. I started to ask him a question, but found my tongue refusing to work, and I suddenly realized that I was in trance. Had he hypnotized me? Had he cast some sort of dragon or Stradolan magic on me? Whatever the case, I decided to give in and just go with it.

Another moment and I felt my breathing deepen, and then the blissful arms of Morpheus dragged me down and took me under in a wave so murky and frothing that there was no denial, no retreat. Only the blessed oblivion of darkness and sleep.

When I opened my eyes, it was close to noon. I wearily pushed myself to a sitting position. Shade was nowhere to be seen, and pale gray rain splattered in drops against the window. I slipped out from under the covers and shivered. The room was chilly, and I pulled a robe over my PJs and padded over to look outside. The sky shimmered, silver interspersed with thick black clouds. But this storm, it was natural, and I could feel the difference. It didn't frighten me, this Seattle gloom. I pushed the window up to let the scent of rain-soaked cedar seep through the room as I quickly dressed. Olive-colored cargo pants, a V-neck sweater in mustard, and a wide brown leather belt, and a matching pair of brown leather boots finished the outfit. By the time I brushed my hair and teeth, I was starting to feel like I might make it through the afternoon in one piece, without having another meltdown.

As I headed down the stairs, Camille came out of her room. She was wearing a purple satin low-cut vintage dress and over it, a black waist cincher. A pair of black chunky-heeled granny boots paired nicely with the outfit, but one glance at her and I knew we'd both changed. There was a haunted look in her eyes that mirrored the way I felt.

We headed downstairs, saying little. Hanna met us at the foot of the stairs. "Sharah, she has had her baby. She's asking that you come to the station as soon as possible. She says it's very important. And Mr. Chase, he's very upset. He's waiting for you in the living room."

Chase was here instead of by Sharah's side? Fuck. What had happened now? Before we even thought of food, Camille and I turned toward the living room. There, we saw Chase pacing.

"What's going on, dude? How are Sharah and the baby?" I slipped over to his side and gave him a quick hug, but it was obvious how tense he was—his back was stiff and he looked pissed out of his mind.

"I need your help! I can't stop them, can I? They said I have no choice—and that she has no choice. Like fucking hell!" He was babbling.

Camille held up her hand. "Slow down and tell us what happened. Start at the beginning, and first things first: are Sharah and the baby all right?"

He stood there, clenching and unclenching his fists. "Sharah is all right—it was a hard labor, but she's okay. And our daughter is fine." He paused, and the look that crossed his face was priceless. But the next minute, it was replaced by a black cloud. "But that fucking Trenyth—I'd like to wring his neck."

"What the hell happened?" And then, I knew—or at least I suspected. "She's . . . they want her to return to Elqa-neve, don't they?"

"Like hell she's going to. After what went down there yesterday?" He seemed to lose steam and dropped onto the sofa, hands on his knees as he stared ahead with a bleak look. "Trenyth came to the hospital this morning. He said she must return. She's the only living heir and she has to take the throne."

"Sharah is going to become Queen of Kelvashan? What about the baby? And you?" I had thought this might happen.

"They won't let me come with her. And . . . they won't let her bring the baby. They said that she'll have to leave her with me, here. Because the Elfin Queen cannot have a half-breed child at the Court." His voice was thick with rage and I thought he was about to burst a blood vessel. "Even though she's a newborn, they're intent on separating our family."

"Fuck. The. Elves." Camille whirled and marched toward the table. She grabbed her keys and purse. "We'll grab lunch when we're out. Meet you at headquarters, dude. And we'll do everything we can to put a stop to this."

Although I didn't share her optimism, I followed her to the door, stopping long enough to snag a jacket and my backpack. Chase, a grateful look in his eyes, followed us out to his car. As he headed out of the driveway, Camille and I followed him.

"Fuck, we didn't get a chance to check in on Iris," she said, glaring at the rain. The water ran down in sheets, glazing the window as the wipers washed it to the side. "I can't believe we didn't stop in to say hi to her. She's going to think we forgot all about her!" She slapped the steering wheel with one hand.

She sounded so upset that I knew she was triggering off last night. "Iris won't think anything of the sort. You know Hanna will have told her about what's happening—she's a smart cookie."

Camille let out a short sigh. "I know. I know. I'm just . . . this is so fucked. I know we have to focus on what's going on here, on what we've promised to do, but all I can see is the heart of that storm. It was evil . . . purely maleficent, and the feeling—the energy of it got under my skin. I can't shake it. Somehow, it hooked into my aura and I can feel it with me, around me, even though I know it's not."

There was nothing I could say to that. Instead, I stared at Chase's car in front of us. "Did he say what they named their daughter?"

"I don't think so. I think he was so upset he couldn't think about anything except protecting Sharah. And what the fuck, anyway? Not letting Sharah take her baby with her? I guess I can see how they would forbid Sharah to bring Chase as her consort, though that's going over like a lead balloon, I can imagine. But to abandon her child? What the hell is she supposed to do?"

"You tell me. Elqaneve . . . Kelvashan as a whole . . . they are steeped in antiquity. They are far more proper than the Fae, and they change only in slow, slow stages. I can't imagine Trenyth being happy to deliver this news. Maybe we can talk some sense into him."

The road sped by in a watery blur as the rain pounded down. Neither Camille nor I felt much like talking, though I did mention briefly to her that we might want to interview Violet's boyfriend—Tanne Baum. She giggled then, and I couldn't help but join her. Our mother had sung "O Tannebaum" to us over and over when we were little, and even though I knew it was juvenile, the thought of a grown man—one of the woodland Fae at that—being named after a Christmas tree seemed to spark off a much needed tension release.

As we came to the FH-CSI and pulled into the parking lot, Chase was already bounding up to the doors. We followed him through, for once hurrying to keep up with *him*. He slammed through the doors, then into the medic unit, with us hot on his heels. There, Mallen was arguing with Trenyth, while a group of guards kept watch. They saw Chase and stiffened into what I recognized as a battle stance.

I leaped forward, grabbing Chase by the arm and swinging him around. "Dude, if you engage them in this mood, they won't think twice about taking you down, and if they take you down, all the Nectar of Life in the world won't help you. You'll be dead and gone. You capiche?"

He glared at me, but stopped in his tracks. "You'd better do something, then, before I do."

"We'll do what we can. No promises. We have no control over the Elfin government, you know. We have a treaty with them—Y'Elestrial does, but there's nothing covering this sort of mess. That, I can guarantee you." I pointed to the doors. "Go now. Sit in your office and talk to Yugi while we try to sort out this matter."

He grumbled, cursing a blue streak under his breath, but then he turned and stomped out to go talk to his second-in-command. As the door closed behind him, I turned around to find Camille already in an argument with Trenyth.

"How the fuck can you do this?" Her hands on her hips, she leaned toward him. "Sharah just had a baby. *Today*. Do you understand? And Chase is that child's father."

Trenyth folded his arms. No need to read body language on that stance. "While I value and appreciate your input, and your loyalty for your friend, there's nothing you can say to change this matter. Understand: by morning light, the entire land of Kelvashan lies in ruins. Elqaneve has been flattened, and still the storm moves on, crossing our land as it strikes village after village. The forests are burning. The dead number in the tens of thousands. We are desolate—and there is a good chance that, unless enough soldiers from other lands arrive, the goblins who are on the march to our city gates will take our lands. Within one night, we have become a dying race."

Camille fell silent.

I shuddered. "Tell us, then, why do you need Sharah there? Isn't that going to put her in danger?"

He frowned, staring at the floor. "Yes, of course it will. But you must understand that the people need someone to look up to and to lead them. I am a puppet, I was Queen Asteria's right hand, but I am not the leader they long for. Sharah—even if she doesn't have the experience the Queen did—she has the blood of royalty flowing in her veins. Our people will believe in her. They will follow her, and they will take heart enough to fight the coming darkness."

"But why can't she take her baby? And why not Chase?" Camille pleaded with him, but the Elfin advisor simply shook his head.

"She cannot bring a half-breed into Court. These are not my choices, girls. I would not see a problem with it, but this is the way of our people and there has been so much disruption in the past twenty-four hours, that one more shift will dishearten them further. If Sharah returns now, we can deal with the impact of her child later, once things are settled. This does not have to be forever. Merely until our people are free of the coming threat. We may not have a palace, but we can have a Queen again."

"I will do it." Sharah's voice came from the door. I jerked around to see her, sitting in a wheelchair, her face a tangle of emotions.

"What? But what about—?" I stared at her, but then I let my words drift off. Her gaze was filled with enough anger and loss already, without me adding to it. And she was afraid—I could see that.

Another emotion was wrapped up there, one that I— and especially Camille—understood all too well. *Duty.* She had a duty to her people. To her aunt. To her country and land. We had grown up the daughters of a guardsman, and the code of honor, of fulfilling one's obligations, had been drilled into us from the time we could barely talk. Sharah knew her duty, and if it meant giving up that which was most precious to her, she would do so. For the good of her people. For the good of her land.

"Who will take care of your child?" I walked over and knelt down beside her.

"Trenyth, send a wet nurse through, and a nanny. They will stay with Chase and our child. Also, guards. I do not want my family left unattended." As she struggled to stand, wincing, Trenyth knelt at her feet.

"Please, remain seated, Princess Sharah." He snapped his fingers at one of the guards. "Do as she commands, and alert the portal guards that we will be returning, and that the Queen-Elect will need transport and healers."

I knelt by Sharah's side. "Who will tell Chase?"

She winced. "I will. He is my beloved, and the father of my child. We have to pick out a name before I go home. Can you please get him for me? I'll be in that room over there." She pointed to an empty office.

With a sinking heart, I headed to Chase's office, dreading every single step along the way.

Chapter 14

The news went over just about like we'd expected it to. I'd asked Yugi and a couple of the other men to join us so they could keep Chase from throwing a punch at Trenyth, but when he stalked out of the room where he'd talked to Sharah, the stark look on his face said everything. He slammed past Trenyth, into another office, rattling the walls with the force of the door.

Sharah wheeled herself out, looking pale and weary. "That didn't go over well." She met my gaze. "Delilah, he's going to need you. He's going to need all of you over the next months. He's angry and he threatened to keep our daughter away from me forever, since I'm *not going to look after her*." She rubbed her temples. "I told him to name her whatever he liked, that I'd love whatever he chose."

I glanced over her head at the room. "Is he coming out?"

She shook her head. "I wouldn't bet on it. Not till after I leave. He's just upset. I understand—I'm upset too. But with what happened? My people need me. I knew there might be a chance this day would come, but I hoped the call wouldn't be for me."

She reached out for my hand, and I took it, squeezing to calm her trembling. Tears were glistening in her eyes. I leaned close.

"I'll watch out for them. We all will. And you can always call us, we'll find a way to get your daughter over there for a visit. I promise you this." I lifted her hand to my lips and kissed it gently, then smoothed her hair back. She was doing everything she could to hold on; I could see it in her eyes. She was trying her damnedest to remain calm. Which was just as well because when she ascended the throne, she would have to wear a mask in public. The Queen wasn't allowed to show fear, or doubt, or loss. She had to be strong, she had to be the anchor for the populace.

And with Sharah's hormones . . . a thought crossed my mind, and before I thought, I blurted out a question. "What are they going to do about your milk?"

She ducked her head. "The healers can give me herbs to stop it." But the pain when she answered made me wish I'd never brought up the subject.

"Then you won't . . ."

"Be able to breast-feed? No. I cannot do that when I'm trying to put all the pieces back together again. My city is shattered, my homeland lies smoldering in ruins. They are taking me away from my child . . . I have lost everything, and soon, I will be alone and in charge of a nation that I never wanted to lead." She sounded on the verge of emotional collapse, and she didn't look all that hot, either.

I wanted to urge her to fight them, to say no and walk away, but the memory of what we'd witnessed, the utter destruction, hung heavy in my mind. I squeezed her hand tighter.

"We will be here for you. We will do everything we can to help you. And we'll look after Chase. He'll come around. He's just scared and hurt right now, and afraid of losing you. I'll make him understand. I promise." I had no idea how I was going to fulfill that vow, but I was determined to do my best.

Sharah let go, slowly. "Thank you. I wish . . . I wish you were my sister. I wish I was part of your family." She blushed when she said it—elves generally weren't that expressive.

I hugged her. "You are," I whispered. "Chase is my brother, so you are my sister. Always."

And then, as I stood back, she motioned to Trenyth, and they wheeled her away to prepare her for traveling. She stared ahead, a numb expression on her face, but I knew her heart was torn to pieces.

I glanced at Camille, and she nodded to the room where Chase was still lurking. Without a word, I headed over and pushed through the door.

Chase looked up. His dark eyes were filled with anger and he was sitting stiffly in a chair. The room was obviously a break room for the staff, with a coffeepot and some cookies on the counter. I found a mug and poured him a stiff cup of the steaming coffee, then shoved it in front of him. Turning a chair around, I straddled it, swinging one leg over the side.

As I settled down beside him, he stared at me dourly. "What do you want? I really don't feel like talking right now."

"Too fucking bad. We're going to talk. Or rather, *I'm* going to talk and *you* are going to listen." I let the words sink in and, at his startled look, added, "The mother of your child is being carted away. She's making the most difficult decision of her life, and you are sitting here like a whining idiot. You cannot let her go with you in this mood or so help me, Chase, I'll slap you silly."

He brought his fist down on the table. "What the hell am I supposed to do, then? She's leaving me and . . . she didn't even want to help name our daughter. She's abandoning us—"

Aha, the core of the matter. Chase had abandonment issues, and he was projecting them onto Sharah. He'd been so terrified about not being a good enough father, and now that he was faced with raising the child alone, his fear was coming back full force.

"Like hell she is."

"What the fuck are you talking about? She's leaving—and our baby's just born."

"Get it through your head, Chase. You've fallen in love with someone who isn't human. Who isn't remotely human. On top of that, Sharah is a princess. She's a member of royalty. And said royalty just vanished in a buttload of flame and fire and tumbling tons of stone. Sharah has to go home or her people won't have any hope. They won't have anyone to look up to. Every country must have a leader, and she's the only one left, Chase."

"But . . . her child . . . our baby . . ." Chase looked hurt, but by the sound of his voice, I could tell that he understood the circumstances. He just didn't want to face them.

"You suck this up and you deal with it. Sharah's hurting enough without you giving her crap. You saw what happened over there—well, you were trapped and *didn't* see the worst of it by any means. But I was there. Camille and I saw what went down and let me tell you now, we'll never, ever be able to get the images out of our heads. People were dying right and left, Chase. Our father is probably among the dead—we haven't heard from him, and he was last seen with Queen Asteria. Who, by the way, is lying crushed under a thousand tons of stone and wood."

He winced, staring at the ground, but I could see the stubborn line of his jaw and I realized he wasn't quite ready to budge yet. Pausing, I tried to think of another way of getting him to own up to what was going on.

"Listen, if Sharah was in the ES army and had to go to combat, you'd stay home and take care of the kids, right?"

Still silent. Exasperated, I smacked him on the shoulder—not hard, but enough to get his attention. *"Right?"*

Apparently, I'd dislodged the last bit of resistance.

"All right, already! Enough." The glint in his eyes shifted and he deflated. "I get it, Delilah. I just don't like it. But yes, I get it." Straightening his shoulders, he looked over at me. "I didn't totally fuck it up, did I?"

"You will if you don't get your ass out there now and tell

her good-bye and that you'll wait for her and take good care of your daughter. Your daughter as in the child you *both* produced, and whom you will not turn against her."

Standing, I yanked him to his feet. "Get moving, Johnson. Before I kick you in the ass again."

He wiped his mouth, then turned toward the door. "Delilah," he said over his shoulder, without looking back. "Thanks. Kick me in the ass any time I need it, okay?" And then, he was off and jogging down the hall.

I followed more slowly. Chase and Sharah had a long, hard road ahead of them and a lot of obstacles working to block them. But he didn't need to know that right now. He just needed to do what was right for the moment, and deal with the consequences later.

Camille and I wandered over to the nursery—or what had been turned into a nursery for the baby. She was tiny, and delicate, with Sharah's nose and ears, but Chase's shock of dark hair. The nurse let me pick her up and it felt strange to hold her—she was so small. I tried to imagine having one of my own. It would happen, one day, the Autumn Lord had made that clear, but for now, I was content to leave it to the future. Too much danger surrounded us to ever think about having a child until we'd dealt with the demonic war.

I glanced over at Camille. "What about you? You still not interested in this?" I motioned toward the baby.

She laughed. "Only from a distance. I really . . . there's *no pull*. I know Smoky wants one, but you know, even the chance of us finding a way to interbreed is remote. And having a child because somebody else wants you to, when you're not ready? Beyond stupid. I'm not mother material. I mothered you and Menolly most of my childhood. I'm done with that. Now it's *my* turn. I'd make one hell of an auntie though."

With that, I brushed a kiss across baby Johnson's forehead and handed her back to the nurse. We returned to the nursing station just in time to see Chase leaning over Sharah to kiss her. She caught my eye as he hugged her, and smiled. It was a rough, wan smile, but it was a smile. And then they wheeled her away, and Sharah was gone.

I glanced at Camille. "I guess . . . we'd better get a move on."

"First, you get your hand looked at." She pushed me toward where Mallen was standing, looking over a chart.

He rebandaged my hand. "It's healing well. Keep it clean, and keep using the salve. Replace the dressing twice a day. You'll have a scar, definitely, but you'll live."

And with that, we headed out. We had work to do, and I had a feeling we'd have a lot more work as the days went along.

In the car, as Camille drove, we made a list of what we needed to do. Take care of the dreglins, hunt down Violet, deal with the Farantino mess—whatever that was. And over-shadowing everything was the specter of losing our father and the threat of the Keraastar Knights being captured.

"We need some good news soon." I tapped my notebook.

"I think we may have gotten our little bit of it in that Iris and Sharah had their babies safely." Camille pulled over to the curb, parking. She pointed to the Supe-Urban Café, which Marion Vespa, a coyote shifter and friend of ours, had just rebuilt after arsonists destroyed her restaurant and her house. "Let's grab breakfast and talk."

Marion saw us the minute we entered. She and her husband had stayed with us after the fire, and we had a long history before that. We considered them extended family.

"What will you have? Just coffee today?" Marion was unusually chipper, but then again, the gaunt, lanky woman wasn't very taciturn to begin with. You wouldn't want to fuck with her, but, overall, she was a good-natured person.

"Breakfast, actually. I know it's lunchtime, but we haven't eaten yet." Camille glanced at the menu, but we always knew what we wanted when we stopped in at Mari-on's. A brilliant cook, she made the best biscuits and cin-namon rolls around. "I want one of your big biscuits, a side of sausage, and a cheese omelet. Also, yes, coffee—a triple iced latte, please."

I didn't even need to look at the menu. "I'll have a cinnamon roll, scrambled eggs, bacon, and a big glass of milk. Also some rose blossom tea." Marion served a delicate herbal tea consisting of rose blossoms, cherry, and some other herbs that she wouldn't disclose from her secret recipe. It was fragrant and fruity and soothing, all at the same time.

Marion gave us a sharp look. "What's wrong? I know those faces, and they are not happy faces."

I glanced at Camille, who shrugged. "There's been trouble at home—back in Otherworld. We're kind of trying to keep it quiet for now, because . . . well, because it's just a good idea, but the Elfin lands? They've been decimated. And we were there to see it happen." I must have looked bleak because Marion stuck her order pad and pen in her pocket and pulled up a chair.

"I'd say that sucks but that's the understatement of the year." She frowned. "Hey, aren't you guys investigating the disappearance of a Fae girl?"

"How did that news get out?" It seemed that none of our secrets were safe anymore.

"Tad told me. Don't look so surprised. He comes here to pick up goodies for his coworkers. Just because he can't eat Danishes doesn't mean that his buddies at work can't. When he was here yesterday, he asked if I'd seen a coworker of his—she comes here a lot. I said no, Violet hasn't been in lately. Then he told me she hasn't been seen around for a while, and that you are investigating for him."

Tad needed to learn how to keep his mouth shut, I thought. But then again, he was worried and just trying to help. And the fact that Violet came here regularly and hadn't been around for a few days helped confirm that she just seemed to have vanished.

"Yeah, we are. Since she was a regular here, you don't have any insights, do you? She hang out with anybody that

seems suspicious? Look worried last time she was in here?"
I pulled out my notebook.

Marion leaned back in her chair. "Violet's been coming
in on a regular basis for . . . oh . . . a year give or take a few
weeks. Of course, we didn't see her during the time the
café was being rebuilt, but once we reopened our doors,
she was here again. Sometimes she comes in with her coworkers, other times she's with some guy. He's a dark type,
as in he feels shadowy. Fae, tall, blond, taciturn. Doesn't
talk much except to her. And . . . once in a while I'll see her
with an odd person. Almost always Supes. She doesn't
hang with FBHs, it seems."

The blond Fae was probably her boyfriend—Tanne
Baum. But the others? "Do they seem like they're on a date?
When she comes in with the people you don't recognize."

Marion shrugged. "Hard to tell. Maybe. I don't really
pay that much attention to the comings and goings of my
customers. Okay, then, I'd better get your orders in." She
stood as I jotted down the information.

After she headed to the kitchen, I glanced at Camille.
"We have to break her password. Remember? Her letter
from Supernatural Matchups? And we need to talk to that
boyfriend of hers."

Camille nodded. "How are we going to break into her
account? You're handy with a keyboard but let's face it, you
aren't a hacker."

"No, but we know someone who is." I grinned. "Tim is
mighty handy." Tim Winthrop was a friend of ours. At one
time he'd been a female impersonator while he put himself
through college. Now, with his degree in computer science,
he'd opened his own consulting business. He also ran a lingerie shop, though he hired someone to work there. We'd
been at his wedding, and his husband, Jason, was a
mechanic and he was the one working on my Jeep.

Camille snickered. "Tim is a whirlwind with a computer. Give him a call while I run to the bathroom."

As she left the table, I pulled out my cell phone and

punched in Tim's number. He came on the line within two rings. "Hey, Tim. Got a favor to ask. Need you to hack an account. We're following up on a missing persons case and need to get into her account on Supernatural Matchups."

Tim laughed. "I just love how you assume I'll happily dive into your illegal investigations."

"Well . . ." I paused, not knowing how to respond. "Um, will you do it? I'll have Hanna make you cookies."

A snort, "How can I resist such a desperate ploy? Okay, but they'd better be peanut butter chocolate chip, and I'd better see more than just a couple dozen."

"Deal. I'll call you with the info when I get home. And, thanks." I hung up before realizing I hadn't even asked him how he was. But when Tim found out what was going down, he'd understand.

Camille returned as Marion brought over our drinks. She set them in front of us. "Your food will be along shortly, girls." Then she was off again to welcome a large group of werewolves who had just entered the café.

"Tim said sure, for cookies. I need that letter to give him the info."

"I think it's still in the car, to be honest. What else do we have to do today?" She took a long drink of her latte. "I need this. Caffeine."

I stared at the page, doodling a stick man in the corner. "We still haven't told Menolly about our cousins. We need to do that tonight. We should ask Vanzir if Carter found out anything about the cigarette butt or footprint casts we found at Interlaken Park."

Camille nodded. "Doesn't it seem weird to sit here talking about all this crap? Father's missing, the Keraastar Knights are vulnerable and scattered, and Elqaneve is trashed. Sharah's on her way home to become a queen . . . Chase has a baby and no one to help him with her. I know they'll provide a nanny and wet nurse but . . ."

I glanced up at her. "Speaking of Chase, what do you think about asking him if he wants to stay with us until everything gets sorted out? We could put him in the parlor.

Hanna will be there to oversee meals and what's one more mouth at our house? If he has a nanny and wet nurse, Hanna wouldn't need to bother with the baby. We'd just need to make sure Maggie can't get in there."

Camille cocked her head. "I dunno . . . we've got a full house as it is. And do we really want him there when we're always under Shadow Wing's bulls-eye?"

She made a good point, but . . . "He's going to be a target anyway, since he's known to be Sharah's lover and has her child. In fact, who's to say some zealot elf with a grudge toward Windwalkers won't try to kill the child? I promised Sharah I'd look after him."

After a moment, Camille shrugged. "I'm fine with it. I'm sure Menolly will be too. Are you sure Shade will be okay?"

"You mean because Chase used to be my lover? I doubt if Shade has any worries in that department." And truth was, he didn't need to. At least for me, Shade was twice the lover Chase had been.

"Okay then. So we ask Chase to move in. After we eat breakfast, let's drop by Carter's to ask if he's had any luck with the cigarette and the footprint casts. And then, let's start hunting down the dreglins. We'll need help. I wonder if Ivana knows anything about them."

"Oh, you *have* to be kidding. Not *her* again, especially after what we found out about her when we were hunting down Gulakah." I shuddered. Ivana Krask—the Maiden of Karask—gave me the creeps.

Ivana was one of the Elder Fae. They were all entities beyond the realm of mortals, and they played so far out of social niceties that it was amazing they even tried to coexist with humankind. When you had dealings with them, you had to watch every word, every phrase, because it was easy to seal yourself into a deal that was most definitely not in your favor. They weren't always evil, though some like Jenny Greenteeth, the Black Annis, and Yannie Fin Diver, were definitely not on the best-behaved list. Mostly they were chaotic, and they played outside of human rules.

Camille shook her head. "Let's face it, Ivana is our best touchstone for finding out what we need to about the dreglins."

"And you really think she's going to give us information on other Elder Fae?" I still didn't buy it, but then again, I didn't like Ivana. "Fine, you call her. I don't want any more to do with her or her garden of ghosts than I have to."

Camille dialed her number as Marion set our food in front of us. It still amazed me that one of the Elder Fae had a cell phone. But then, the world didn't run on fairytales, and reality was much stranger than fiction could ever purport to be. A few seconds later, she glanced at me and pointed at her phone.

"Yes, Ivana? . . . Yes, it's the Witch Girl . . . Um hm. That's right. Listen, we were wondering if you would meet us. We have a deal to propose."

Ivana did nothing without recompense. We just had to watch what we offered her, because if there's one thing the Elder Fae could do, it was twist the meaning of words. Especially when there was a deal involved.

"Yes, we can. We'll see you there in an hour." Camille hung up. "I agreed we'd meet her in the park in an hour."

I glanced outside as I tore off a piece of the cinnamon roll. It was so good, I thought I'd just have to buy a second for the road. "It's pouring rain."

"I'm not going to melt and neither are you. Now, let me call Carter and see if he's going to be home." She stabbed one of her sausage links and ate it down before she picked up her phone again. A few minutes later, we were set to meet with Carter at around 4:00 P.M.. We finished our meal and I ordered a second cinnamon roll to go, then we left a good-sized tip and headed out to the car.

"We still have half an hour before we need to meet Ivana. Can we stop by Jason's and see if he's done with my Jeep?" I was getting really tired of relying on others for my rides.

"Sure thing." She scooted out of the parking spot and we were off.

Fifteen minutes later we pulled into the parking lot at

Jason's garage. We headed into the office and he was there, poring through some parts catalogue. Jason was a fine-looking man, dark and bald, his skin the color of coffee. He and Tim had been together for a number of years now, and he treated Tim's little girl like his own. She was somewhere around six or seven now, and while Tim's ex-wife still had issues with him, she never took it out on his relationship with his daughter. He got her every weekend, and did his best to be a good father.

Jason smiled when he saw us come in, waving. He'd finally come to accept Tim's involvement in the Supe Community, and even accepted that Tim's best friend was now a vampire. Erin Matthews—Menolly's "daughter." In fact, we'd met Tim through Erin, when she still owned the Scarlet Harlot and both he and Camille had shopped there.

"Hey girls, what's shaking?" Jason turned around and grabbed a set of keys off the pegboard behind him, tossing them to me. "Don't even ask. Your baby's ready."

I laughed. "You're the best! What was wrong with her?"

"Do you really want to know, or do you just want the bill and the lifetime guarantee?" He snickered, pulling out his ledger.

I laughed. "Got me there. Okay, I trust you. How much do I owe you?" I pulled out my wallet and took out my credit card.

He grimaced. "It wasn't cheap, girl. I had to order a lot of parts. Whatever the hell you did to it, I'd like to know. Or maybe not. Anyway, bill comes to nine-hundred fifty-eight dollars and thirty-nine cents. And that's *with* your friends and family discount."

I coughed, but handed over the credit card. Jason was a good guy, and he didn't stiff anybody. Which is why he had repeat clientele, and a damned fine reputation. As he rung up the service, I turned to Camille.

"I'll take my Jeep and follow you. I've missed her."

"I had that mess on the side of it detailed, girl." Jason gave me a smile. "You've had that bad cover-up job on there too long."

I gaped at him. "But that had to cost . . ."

"Shut your mouth, sugar." He winked. "I will not let one of my friends carry around the memory of a hate crime."

Back in February, shortly before Iris's wedding, my car had been the victim of a hate-filled graffiti artist who had tagged it with, *"Go home, Faerie Sluts!"* in red paint. I'd covered it up the best I could with spray paint but it never had looked right. Now, the door matched the rest of the paint job—a turquoise blue.

I hopped over the counter, surprising Jason, and gave him a quick hug. He froze at first, then hesitantly returned the embrace.

"Damn girl, you are strong. I can feel your muscles through that jacket." He grinned at me then.

"You're pretty fine, yourself. Those are some big guns you have there." Jason was built like a body builder and I had no doubt his biceps were *ooo-baby* worthy. "You work out a lot?"

He nodded. "I do. In fact, I teach Thai boxing. You interested in learning?"

I cocked my head to the side. I'd always wanted to take up one of the Earthside martial arts classes. "How much time is required? If I'm out on a case, or have to be in Otherworld, am I going to get kicked out for not showing up? I don't want to commit to something that I might have to flake out on."

He pursed his lips, smiling. "We could schedule private lessons. Then we can reschedule as needed. When you have the time, it would be best to go for two classes a week, plus keeping up with your regular workouts."

I slid my credit card back in the holder. "Sounds good. I'll give you a call later tonight or tomorrow to talk some more. Thanks, Jason. Tim has himself a good man."

"I know, love. I know." And then he shooed us out. "I have work to do. And I know you do, too. Off with you now."

As we left the shop, I glanced back. "I hope to hell he and Tim weather knowing us. I'd hate it if—"

"Don't say a word. Don't even think it. They will be all

right because we need them to be okay. I can't handle see-ing another friend hurt. Not now. Especially not with Father missing."

As I climbed in my Jeep and started her up, enjoying the purr of her motor, the rain turned to hail, the pea-sized ice balls bouncing off the hood and windshield, covering the pavement. I followed Camille out onto the road, the silver of the sky glimmered like light shifting onto layers of crin-kled foil.

We headed to the park to meet Ivana, and all the way there, I couldn't stop thinking about Father. Had he man-aged to get out? Was he searching for us? And if he had, surely he would have contacted us by now—or contacted Trenyth.

Was he trapped, unable to escape? Would he die, starv-ing to death, while rescue workers frantically tried to dig out those who lived through the carnage? Or was he already dead and buried, at the bottom of a heap of rubble?

I tried to keep my focus on the road, to shove the thoughts out of my mind. Worrying wouldn't speed up finding him. Worrying wouldn't do anything but interfere with what we were supposed to be focusing on.

Our father was a guardsman most of his life. He had been fully prepared to give his life in the line of his work. When he'd become Ambassador, even for the short time it had lasted, he had been prepared to give his life in service to Queen Tanaquar. And now, as head of the OIA, Other-world Division, there was the chance he'd be killed. He'd known the risks, and he'd taken them.

Just like we knew the risks when we joined up.

Just like we knew the risks when we chose to fight the war against Shadow Wing. We could have gone home to Otherworld. We could have let Smoky take us all away to the Dragon Reaches where we would be safe. But we were bound to our honor, to our duty. And we took our responsi-bilities seriously. No, we all knew how precarious life was, and we never took it for granted.

At the same time, we were ready to lay down our lives

in this battle. All of us—my sisters, our lovers; even Iris and Hanna. We knew what we were facing, and we still pressed on. We'd lost friends along the way and every time it hurt like hell, but what else could we do?

And so, if Father was dead, we'd weep and we'd mourn, but we would accept it as part of who he was, and what he did, and what he stood for. And we would carry on, through the dark nights of war, as we walked through the fires the demons were pushing before them.

Chapter 15

❧❧❧

Ivana Krask was waiting in the park. Camille and I darted through the rain to where she was sitting. The Maiden of Karask was dressed like a bag lady. Her face was a gnarled map, covered in burls and knobs. She had a pointed chin, reminding me of a bird, and her eyes were beady, sharp, and piercing. But we now knew just how illusionary her appearance was. Underneath that shabby persona was a brilliantly powerful Elder Fae who could shatter our hearing with her voice, who could rise up like a beautiful and terrible monster.

She stood, her polyester muumuu shifting under the too-large coat. Her silver hair was tucked under a scarf, which barely kept it under control. The staff in her hand made me nervous. That damned thing could suck up spirits right and left. Ivana collected them for her garden of evil ghosts, where she tortured them, feeding off their pain for magic.

Camille gave her a sharp curtsey and I bowed. Always paid to be polite when you were standing in front of someone who could make mincemeat out of you. A sharp wind blew by and Ivana laughed, raising her staff.

"A ghostie on the wind, come to me, my pretty. Come to the Maiden." And with a *zap*, her staff lit up and we saw something wispy filter into it. A sharp wail sounded, though it was so high-pitched that any FBHs around wouldn't hear it. They might feel a flash of fear, a sense that something wasn't right, but they'd just shake their heads and move on.

We watched her smile, her razor-like teeth sparkling. She licked her lips and turned her beady stare to us. "Witch Girl and Pussy Cat. Too bad my Dead Girl is sleeping, for I would like to converse with her. I like dead things."

"We seek a deal, if you would be willing to listen." Camille knew the pattern better than I did so I kept my mouth shut. It was dangerous to dabble with the Elder Fae unless you knew what the fuck you were doing, and I was the first to admit that I was clueless about effective bargaining.

Ivana sat down on the wet bench, motioning for us to join her. Great, time to get our butts soaked. But we did as she asked. Again: you don't quibble with those who can make you look like a dust mote.

"What say you, Witch Girl? What do you want from the Maiden of Karask? And what will you bargain with? Bright flesh would guarantee you a deal, you know." Her crafty smile reminded me of a crocodile.

"We are *not* going to give you bright meat. *No bright flesh!*" Camille stared at her sternly. Ivana was always trying to get us to bargain with babies. The fact that she meant it, and that she actually ate them with relish made us even more leery, but the Elder Fae lived so far outside our realm that there was no way to get through to them how bad of an idea this was. We just refused every time she hinted around.

"Then state your deal and I will see if it tickles my tooth." Ivana glanced past her, coyly looking at me. "Standing back, are you, Pussy Cat? Afraid of the Maiden, perhaps?"

Involuntarily, I scooted over on the bench, moving away. I didn't have any desire to be the focal point of this conversation. I decided my best course of action was to remain silent.

She sniggered and turned back to Camille. "State your deal, Witch Girl."

Camille cleared her throat. "Prime beef flesh, for information that will benefit us. I will tell you what I want to know. If you have the answer, payment will be ten pounds of tender steak."

Ivana sighed, frowning. "You drive a hard bargain. No bright flesh, today. If you were to throw in a chicken and some tasty fishes, we could strike a bargain. *If* I have the information and choose to share it." She leaned back, seemingly unaware of the puddles of water that raced down the bench.

"Very well. Ten pounds of beef flesh, a chicken, and a salmon. We want to know how to kill dreglins. What makes them vulnerable? And do you know where any might be hiding around here?"

Ivana cocked her head, a smile playing over those thin lips, which made her seem even more nerve-racking. "So, old Jenny's offspring have made the leap? They are here, are they? Jenny and I, we are not such good friends. We fought, long ago, over the same man. I finally decided he was not sweet enough for so much blood to flow and let her have him. She feasted well that day. But, she also made an enemy, and we have never been on terms."

Camille held out her hand. "Seal the deal?"

Ivana accepted, shaking with a dark twinkle in her eye. "Witch Girl, you have too little fear. Or too much need. But yes, we seal the bargain. I will tell you what I will, and then you bring me the meat."

"How do we kill them?" Camille wiped a strand of her hair out of her face, where the rain had plastered it to her cheek.

I pulled out my notebook to take notes. Granted, the pages were getting wet, I was soaked through, and the whole day was a soggy mess, but I wanted to be sure we remembered everything.

"Dreglins . . . they are tough little bitches. They have a nasty bite to them, too." She paused, then looked at my arm. "Perchance the Puss has found that out?"

Couldn't pull much over on Ivana, that was for certain. I held up my hand. She'd outed me, so no use in lying to her. "Yeah, one bit the hell out of my hand. Hurt like of a son of a bitch, too."

Ivana nodded, touching her nose. "Dreglins, they are dangerous and not very intelligent. The bloodline . . . they inherited the hunger, but not the smarts. And Jenny, she just keeps popping out the litters. I surmised it would only be a while before some of the kits found their way over to this side of the world. Their venom comes from their father."

"So they hunger for blood and flesh, and they don't reason well. What else should we know about them?" A fat drop of rain landed on my nose, slowly trickling down to the pad of paper.

"They are quick, and can hide. You could not see them because they are like chameleons—they can shift color when they are in the forest. In fact, my dearies, you might think of them as the komodo dragons of the Fae world." Ivana grinned. "They have the venom to go with it. So yes, they are fast, easy to conceal, venomous, and deadly. The best way to catch them is to lay a trap and then have at them with your blades and magic. They cannot resist quick and easy meat—on the hoof, though. They don't scavenge, not often. So you find a good plump wench and put her out in their territory, and they will sniff her out."

"You mean, use live bait. Lovely, and who are we going to get for that? And where do we find them? Do you know where they are?" Camille looked slightly squeamish. Live bait meant the chance of losing someone.

Ivana tapped her staff on the ground three times. She closed her eyes. As we watched, a clew of earthworms came out of the ground, and Ivana leaned down to the writhing mass and whispered something to them that we couldn't catch. A few moments later, they burrowed back into the soil.

"We will wait now." She held up her hand for silence. "Can you feel the beat of the soil? The message is being passed along."

I wanted to ask her how the hell a bunch of worms was going to come up with an answer for us but decided to forego irritating her. Magic is as magic does, and the Elder Fae worked with the forces of the world in a way even we couldn't pretend to understand. But my thoughts must have shown in my expression, because Ivana pushed herself to her feet and before I knew what was happening, she was standing in front of me.

"You do not worry yourself, Puss. But since your curiosity has your cat, I will tell you. The worms . . . think of them like telephone lines and wires. They are the medium, not the messenger. The messenger is my voice, gone searching, seeking. It hunts for our quarry." She leaned down and tapped me on the nose with one of her talon-like nails. "Do you fear me, Kitty? Do you turn into a fraidy-cat when you face a fear?"

I was starting to feel uncomfortable. I had grown out of a lot of my timidity, and shifting into Tabby? Didn't happen so much anymore. But that she could see into me spooked the hell out of me. Then again, she was Elder Fae, and when she shed her disguise, she was freaking scarier than the Fae Queens, and that was going some.

Ivana let out what sounded like a purr, then laughed and turned back to Camille. "I frighten your sister, but she knows . . . she knows." She paused, staring at the ground. "I hear the pulse of the world. My message is answered." Leaning down she whispered something and the wrigglers burst out of the ground. Ivana tilted her head to one side, listened, and the worms vanished again, back into the soil, burrowing deep.

"Your dreglin children are hiding in the forest, two miles east from where you encountered them. There you will find their lair, and there are five of them. Be cautious, my girls, they are deadly and clever, if not overly intelligent. You will need to walk softly. They sleep during the day, so you may have better luck finding them during the sun's waking hours."

I sucked in a deep breath. "Daylight? Then we can't take Menolly with us. And the guys are off in Otherworld . . . well, we have Shade, Morio, and Vanzir. But if they go with us, we won't have anybody to watch the house."

Camille smiled. "About that, I made a phone call. Aeval promised to send me guards, just as soon as she can make a decision on who would be safest."

"Well then, that works. But first . . ." I turned to Ivana. "Where do you want to meet us so we can fulfill our bargain?" One thing I knew, it never paid to welsh on debts to the Elder Fae.

Ivana pursed her lips, grinning. "Oh, my Puss. You learn quickly. I will ramble out to your house. Call me when you have the treatsies and I will come. If you are not home, just leave it on the porch and I will leave a note that I found it. And Witch Girl, you drive a hard bargain. I hope the information is worth it. The fighting will be difficult, but that is not my affair. Now, for bright meat, I would happily join you. You have seen my true form, you know what I can do."

For a moment—just a moment—the glamour lifted and she rose so tall she seemed to blot out the sky. Brilliant and beautiful against the gloom, her long silver hair flowing around her, and her eyes glowing like a warm merlot. She was pale as a moonbeam, and I dropped to my knees, gasping. The only other time we had seen her true form was in her hideous garden of ghosts.

As quickly as the mask had vanished, it returned, and she was Ivana the bag lady again. Without a word, she touched her nose, turned, and wandered off through the park.

I looked over at Camille, who was watching her leave, the same look of awe on her face that I had felt in my heart.

"I wish . . . I wish we could be friends. I wish I could hear her stories." Camille's hushed voice echoed in the stillness of the afternoon.

"Are you so certain you want to hear what she has to say? Be careful what you ask for. You may just get it." I shook my head to clear my thoughts. "Come. We still have to stop at Carter's before we go home."

And so, we returned to our cars. As we drove the short distance to Carter's, all I could think about was how so much of life was hidden under an illusion. We all wore our masks, and when we took them off, was it to reveal yet another mask, or was it perhaps the truth of our heart? How did we know if the person we were looking at in the mirror was really us—or just another façade?

Carter was waiting for us. As usual, he had a tray of steaming tea and cakes ready. I'd long finished my second cinnamon roll so I was very hungry, and Camille seemed just as famished. We ate while he was in the back, tooling around with something, and by the time he came out again, our evidence in hand, my stomach had stopped rumbling. I was mildly embarrassed because I'd eaten five of the little cakes and three tea sandwiches, but Camille had done just about the same amount of damage to the tea tray and she seemed perfectly nonplussed.

Carter put down the casts and smiled at the sight of the empty plates. "Good, I'm glad you liked the tea cakes. I was hoping you would. I tried a new recipe and wanted to see what you thought."

The idea that the be-horned half demon, half Titan had been baking made me let loose a peal of giggles. Camille followed suit. At his befuddled look we tried to explain but the tension we'd been under picked that time to break and we were off and howling. A few moments later, we managed to get hold of ourselves, but he just grinned and waved our explanations away.

"It's quite all right, girls. I get the gist. And no, I do not wear an apron, and yes, I love to cook. Someday I shall invite you over for dinner and make you my specialty— beef bourguignon. And then there will be no twittering." He arched his eyebrows and we burst into giggles again, but this time he joined us.

After a few moments, he leaned back and crossed his good leg over the one with the brace. "I have some answers for you about your casts and the cigarette, but they also netted more questions."

Once again, I pulled out my notebook but he shook his head. "I've printed out the information for you. Here's the thing—the cigarette? Whoever smoked it is purely human. No Supe blood whatsoever. Hard to tell with the casts but the energy coming off them? Human. However, there is something attached to this person. Some energetic binding . . . much like you had with Vanzir for a while. This human is bound to a daemon. Not a demon—but a daemon. But who and why, I cannot tell you."

Camille frowned. "Possession? Could it be someone who is possessed?"

Carter shook his head. "No, it isn't that. The human is capable of making his own decisions. And it *is* a man. Now, the fact that you were asking about daemonic activity in the Farantino Building seemed like too much of a coincidence, so I did a bit more sleuthing. And I came up with several pieces of information."

We both leaned forward. One of Carter's cats leaped onto my lap and I absently stroked her, but then she jumped down and went to Camille, who scooped her up, rubbing her face in her fur.

"You mentioned that Grandmother Coyote told you that Michael Farantino had connections with demons and the like. So I did more research into his background. It seems his grandfather was a member of a cult in the old world—Italy. They weren't Strega—the Italian witches—but some FBH tradition that had passed down through the years. I discovered that the Farantino family was heavily involved in a magical war with another prominent clan in their village, which was started over a territorial dispute."

"That sounds all too familiar." I shook my head. "Clan fighting, family turf wars, they're common as rabbits in Otherworld. We saw them a lot between members of the nobility, though quite often the attacks were subtle."

Carter nodded. "Yes, and they aren't much better here. As a result of this particular feud, one of the Farantino women was cursed. In retaliation, the patriarch of the family made a deal with a daemon, bargaining his family's freedom in exchange for help and a grab for glory. And so, as the Farantinos rose to power, the other family faded their curse vanished, broken under the weight of their downfall. Eventually, the Farantino family was deeply involved in daemonic activity and the tradition was passed down. The children were bound to the daemon at birth, and they grew up in his service. Everything they did was affected by this daemonic activity, and if they didn't pay proper tribute, they were ground to dust by poverty and ill health."

Camille frowned. "So Michael Farantino was a part of this family and he grew up steeped in daemonism. It would make sense for his building to be infused with this energy then."

"That means Gerald Hanson was immersed in the tradition, too." It made sense—his soul and memories had been too cold, too calculating.

Carter nodded. "Yes, and Michael passed the building on. Eventually, his great-grandson, Gerald Hanson came to own it, and I believe he was intent on carrying on his great-grandfather's work. Grandmother Coyote is correct, a dark force is connected to that building and I'm not sure what it is, but it's ancient and powerful, and linked to the daemonic realms. Whatever is behind it still sleeps, but that doesn't mean it will continue to do so. Meanwhile, there are lesser, though still vile, energies connected to the building. And I'm sure that Gerald managed to open several gateways before you sucked his soul into the abyss. Especially since he's got a fraction of Were in him."

Camille and I looked at each other. So we had a long-running fam-trad focused on daemonic worship. Fam-trads—family traditions—both in Otherworld and Earthside, could be highly dangerous. They tended to be insular, and they tended to be volatile.

"What could they be waking up? And if the Farantino

family no longer owns the building, why are the energies still continuing?" It didn't make sense to me. Since the building had been sold, the daemonic hold should be lightening up.

"There's the rub. I did a facial features match on the picture you snapped of the man in the coffee shop." Carter's expression faded from inquisitive to concerned. "Damned if it's not Lowestar Radcliffe—the current owner of the building. So I dug into his background a little further."

"What did you find?" I was almost afraid to hear. It seemed like all the news was bad lately.

"Radcliffe shows up in a number of financial journals. Very successful man. But . . . and here's the rub . . . he seems to have just arrived one day, bought the building, and moved into Seattle. He supposedly has a history with Yale—a degree in business management—but damned if I can locate the files. He was supposed to have been born in India, but again, no birth certificate. Lowestar Radcliffe might as well have just appeared out of nowhere."

Camille frowned. "That doesn't bode well. Either he went to great lengths to cover up his tracks, or . . . or I don't know what. You can't become that successful without leaving a trail. Do you know why he bought the building?"

Carter shook his head. "No. Just that the deed suddenly transferred hands. Gerald Hanson was the owner and he stayed on. I looked into his financials, and there was no indication he was in trouble on that level, so there had to be some reason that he gave control of his great-grandfather's prize possession to someone outside the family. Find out why, and you may find out what's going on."

"Here's another question to answer: why would Gerald stay on if he sold the building? But wait, did he actually *sell* the building? Or did he just deed it to Lowestar?" Camille asked.

Carter tilted his head. "That's a good question. I didn't actually look at the deed. Let me see what I can find. Give me till tomorrow, if you would. I'm expecting company for dinner tonight." By the way he said it, it was obvious that he was talking about a date. Which sounded ridiculous, when you considered that he was essentially a demi-god.

Braver than I, Camille snickered. "Who's the lucky lady? Or man?"

Carter gave her a sly smile. "No one you know. But if things work out, you may get to meet her in the future. Your scaly-winged husband may know her—her name is Shimmer and she's from the Dragon Reaches. And that is all you need to know for now."

"You're dating a dragon? Since when?" Camille was teasing, but Carter's expression smoldered.

"Oh girl, don't press your luck. Or I might just . . ." He paused, and the look passed. "You will know if and when I decide you need to know. Now run along, and take the information that I gave you. Oh, and have you contacted your cousins yet?"

I shook my head, deciding to take the focus off Camille. She needed to learn how to be more diplomatic. Although I certainly couldn't provide much of an example.

"No, we haven't even told Menolly yet. We will tonight, though. With the Wayfarer burning down, and with the destruction in Otherworld, we've had too much on our plates. Our father is still missing, too." The last, I hadn't intended on letting slip out, but slip out the words did.

Any snark or danger on Carter's face vanished. His shoulders slumped and he leaned back in his chair. "I'm sorry, truly. I hope you can find him, safe and in health. As to the Wayfarer, I will ask around. Perhaps someone has heard something. And Otherworld? There are no words for this matter. Not now, not with what's going on." And with that, he stood to show us out.

We were on the street when Camille's cell rang. She motioned for me to wait before I got into my Jeep while she answered.

"Hello? What's up? . . . What did he say? . . . No, no—we're on our way home. Fifteen minutes, maybe twenty depending on traffic . . . Don't do anything until we get there." She hung up and turned to me. "We have to get home. Morio said there was a call through the Whispering Mirror. Trenyth wants us to contact him. He said that he has some news for us, but he wouldn't tell Morio what it was."

Her voice was shaking. I reached out to take her hand. Two of her husbands were in Otherworld, as well as Rozurial. What if something had happened to one of them? Or what if Telazhar had captured one—or more—of the Keraastar Knights? Given that there was an army marching on the city, any number of things could have happened.

"Let's go. You okay to drive?"

Camille nodded. "Yeah, I just want to be home." She jumped in her Lexus as I swung into my Jeep. We headed out, and I had the feeling neither one of us was paying much attention to the road as we wound through the rain and the traffic to Belles-Faire.

By the time we got home, everyone—including Iris and Bruce—were gathered in the living room. Morio had brought the Whispering Mirror downstairs from Camille's study. He shrugged.

"I just thought it might be a good idea to have this here. At least for now, considering everything that's going on."

Hanna brought in tea and cookies, and the smell of spaghetti bubbled on the stove. Menolly had woken up and we gathered in the living room. Camille stared at the mirror.

"I suppose I'd better call him and find out what's going on." She bit her lip, gnawing on it until Morio tapped her mouth.

"Stop that. You can't help anything by hurting yourself. Do you want me to put in the call?" He kissed her forehead, gazing deeply into her eyes.

"No. No, let's just . . . let me get this over with." She settled herself in front of the mirror, activating it with the magical password.

I snuggled close to Shade, and he draped his arm around my shoulders. He leaned down to whisper in my ears.

"Whatever happens, you will be all right. Your sisters will be all right. We will weather through this."

I kissed his hand, feeling the warm promise of his love seep into my heart. "Thank you, thank you for being here."

Camille caught her breath as the mists in the mirror lifted. Trenyth appeared, looking tired and wrung out. We waited for him to speak.

"Girls, are you all there? Menolly—is she there?"

"I'm here." Menolly couldn't be seen through the mirror, though she could talk through it.

"Good. I have news for you. First, Sharah has been . . . as you say, fast-tracked. She took the throne this afternoon and is the new Queen of Elqaneve. For the first time since before the Great Divide, the Elfin race has a new leader."

That wasn't exactly grounds for celebration, given the circumstances. Be that as it may, at least the elves had someone to look to for guidance, as inexperienced and young as she was.

Trenyth shifted in his seat. "The goblin forces are nearing the gates of the city. But the armies of Y'Elestrial are here to face them with us. There will be bloody war before the morning light hits. We have set up a temporary headquarters in a protected area. Before you come over to Elqaneve again, let us know so we can whisk you away. We can't give out the location because we are still too vulnerable—not until we've fully reinforced our defenses."

There was something he wasn't telling us, but knowing Trenyth, he would get around to it in his own time. I squeezed Shade's hand, waiting.

Trenyth's gaze flickered as he glanced down at a paper in his hands. "Camille, your husbands and friend are hunting for the Knights. So far we do not believe that Telazhar has captured any of them, but neither have we discovered where they went. We do believe they're all in hiding. They were instructed, if something should ever happen, to run for the hills and forests, and hide."

"Then Smoky, Trillian, and Rozurial are all okay?" Camille's voice was shaking.

With a nod, Trenyth smiled softly. "Yes, they are all right. I spoke with them about an hour ago. They are spending the night here before going out hunting again." He paused again and I could feel something hanging.

And then, he dipped his head. "I have other news. We discovered Queen Asteria's body. She was crushed beside her throne. She will be laid to rest tomorrow. We have no time for formal rites and ceremonies. She will be placed in the Barrow Mounds, where the Oracle lived."

I pressed my hand to my lips. We knew—hell, I had escorted her out of her body, but it was truly real now. She had been found, and she had passed into history, and the Elfin race would have to march on without her wisdom.

Trenyth motioned to someone out of sight of the Whispering Mirror. Trillian came into view, and Trenyth moved to let him take the seat in front of us. "Girls . . . Trillian, please."

We waited in silence. The air in the living room felt thick, as if something tangible—palpable—was hovering around us. Camille scooted close to Morio and he placed his hands on her shoulders.

Trillian gazed at Camille, holding her gaze. "My love, I have news for you and your sisters." He let out a long sigh. "I thought to visit your father's home in Y'Elestrial. I traveled there via the portals this morning. I went to your family shrine . . ."

The room felt like it was beginning to spin. Camille let out a faint cry and Menolly lowered herself to the floor, moving to take my hand. We stood, crossing to stand near Camille. Everyone backed away, letting us have space.

"What did you find?" Camille's voice was so faint that we could barely hear her.

"My love . . . your father's soul statue. It's shattered. Sephreh ob Tanu is dead. Your father is dead." As Trillian spoke, the room fully started to spin on me.

I shook my head, letting out a whimper. Father had been a constant in our lives. He'd been there from the beginning and for some reason, I'd never thought he'd die. He was hard on us, and his honor was both his downfall as well as his foundation, but he'd always been true to his beliefs.

Camille shook her head. "No . . . no . . . we just started to repair our relationship. He can't be dead . . ."

"Are you sure? Are you sure it's his statue?" Menolly asked.

Trillian nodded. "Yes, I'm certain. I don't know where his body is, but if he was in the throne room near the Queen, we're sure to find some evidence as the recovery efforts continue. The dead . . . they are everywhere. Elqaneve has suffered a serious blow and thousands have died. In the city, in the villages, the devastation is horrendous. Delilah and Camille saw the storm. The aftermath? It's terrifying how powerful the swath of destruction is."

I closed my eyes as the room began to phase in and out. And then, for the first time in a while, tension and stress hit me and I found myself shifting. Tabby rose up, taking over for me, and the next thing I knew, I was racing up the stairs, heading for the protection and comfort of my kitty condo. The pain was still there, but it felt more removed, and as I hurried into my playroom, I leaped up to the carpeted perch, crawling into the hidey-hole box.

I snuggled deep into the light fleece blanket that Camille had thought to stuff in there, hiding away from the worry and stress and pain. Closing my eyes, I purred to comfort myself, trying not to think about the people I loved, or the people I had lost. Before I knew it, slumber claimed me.

Chapter 16

❧❧❧

I'm not sure how much later it was before Camille and Menolly found me and gently pulled me out of the kitty condo. I woke with a start as Menolly gathered me into her arms, whispering comfort in my ear. After a few minutes, I began to relax and Menolly put me on the floor and I shifted back, slowly, leisurely, so it didn't hurt. As I stood up, it hit me again. Father's soul statue was shattered. And that could mean only one thing.

"How long was I . . ." It pissed me off that stress could still send me turning into Tabby. I wanted to be more responsible. What if something like that happened during a fight? But then again, it always seemed to be family stress that set it off.

"About ten minutes, Kitten. Not long." Menolly sat down on the edge of the sofa. She picked up one of my cat toys and began playing with it. She swung the mouse by the tail, staring at the floor. "So, can we be sure he's dead? Could his statue have shattered any other way?"

"It could have been accidentally . . . or even deliberately

broken, but why would his be and not ours?" Camille
shook her head. "He was last seen in the palace, with
Queen Asteria. I think we have to accept that he's dead. I
guess . . . I guess we contact Aunt Rythwar and tell her
about Father. I'll do that, tomorrow. I just . . . not tonight."

I wanted to cry, but mostly I felt numb. So much had
gone on that the whole past couple of days seemed like a
vivid, painful nightmare. We sat there for ten minutes,
twenty, none of us saying a word. Tears were too dangerous
to give in to right now. Mourning would come later, when
we'd had time to adjust.

"Do you remember how he used to take us to the falls
every chance he got? Delilah, you hated those outings, but
I loved them. I loved swimming in the pool, and pretending
I was a mermaid." Camille shuddered as she spoke, but her
words made us all smile.

"I just hated the water. I loved going places with you
guys." I gave her a wan shrug, but the memory of the sunlight on the grass stood out, a ray of light in a dark, dreary
evening.

"I wonder how the pond looks by moonlight. We could
go back there . . ." Menolly twirled my toy mouse by
the tail.

After another silence, I realized we still had to tell
Menolly about our mother's kin. No time like the present,
and maybe, in some way, it would help.

I looked up at her. "This is a hell of a time to bring it up,
but . . . speaking of family, Carter told us something a couple days ago but it got shoved to the wayside with what
went down in Elqaneve."

She grimaced. "Oh, what *joyful new*s does he have for
us now?"

Camille leaned over her shoulder. "Apparently, our
mother has blood kin that live in the area. Long story short:
we have two cousins living near here. Alive. They're in
their forties, and they are full FBH."

Menolly's jaw dropped. "What? I thought she was an
orphan."

"Apparently not . . ." We told her what Carter had found out.

Camille sighed. "So, the question is, do we want to contact our cousins and tell them about Mother?"

A pause, then I looked up. There was no doubt in either of their eyes. "Of course we do. I don't think we have a choice."

"Do you have their number?" Menolly gazed at me, evenly. I realized it was a dare.

"Right here in my notebook." I pulled out my notebook where I'd written it down. "You want me to call now?" Somehow it seemed wrong to call right after we'd gotten the news about Father's soul statue, but I had begun to realize that there would never be the right time. Not with our lives. There would always be something going on, always some battle brewing, some friend or loved one missing or dead. That was just the way our existence had become.

Camille handed me the phone and I stared at it for a moment.

"Before I call them, let me contact Tim and give him the account name and URL for Supernatural Matchups so he can start trying to hack into Violet's account. We need to know who she was hooking up with."

"Good idea." Camille leaned back on the sofa, crossing her legs. She sounded weary as she reached down to unbuckle one of her stilettos and toss it on the floor. We all looked worn out, and I had the feeling we'd be a lot worse off before we got better.

I put in the call and five minutes later, Tim had written down the information and promised to do his best to break in. As I hung up, I stared at the phone in my hand. No more procrastination. We'd made the decision to do this thing, and we might as well get it over with. If they didn't want to talk to us, we'd be no worse off than before. And if they met with us and rejected us, well, we couldn't make people like us. Blood didn't automatically garner acceptance; we knew that all too well.

I punched in the first number. I was running on autopilot, but when a woman answered the phone, a rush of hope washed through me.

"Hello, I'm looking for Hester Lou Fredericks. Can you tell me if I'm calling the right number?" I paused.

"This is Hester. Who's calling, and what can I do for you?" The voice was so friendly and open that it lifted my heart. I wondered, what did she look like? Was there any sort of a family resemblance? I looked most like our mother, and my mind began to whirl in a thousand directions.

"You don't know me, but my name is Delilah D'Artigo. I don't know how to explain this, but . . . we're related. We're cousins. My sisters and I would like to meet you." How the hell I thought I could explain this over the phone, I had no clue, but maybe if we met and were face-to-face, the words would come.

A pause. Another moment and then, "Of course. Would you mind if we met in a coffee shop? It's not that I don't want to be hospitable but . . ."

"No worries. We understand. Would you and your brother—we know about him, too—be able to meet us this evening?"

It seemed we might as well make the date as soon as we could. I half wanted to get it over with so we didn't sit wondering how it would go down.

Hester let out what sounded like a snort. "I don't know if I'll be able to get hold of Daniel, but I can meet you. There's a Starbucks on Fiftieth and Lexington. I'll be wearing a chartreuse shirt. Can you be there in an hour?"

I glanced at the clock. It was six thirty now. "Yes, we'll meet you in an hour. And Hester . . . thank you." I handed Camille back the phone. "It's set. She knows my name so we'd better go through with this."

We stared at one another for the next minute, then, in a flurry, we beat a rush to make ourselves presentable.

An hour later we walked into the coffee shop, not sure what to expect. Camille was decked out in her usual—a black bustier over a warm plum skirt and ankle boots with mile-high heels. Menolly was in clean jeans, a turtleneck, and knee-high brown leather boots. And I'd changed into a pair of pair of cargo jeans, a pale green sweater, and a black denim jacket. We were about as good as we were going to get, given the circumstances.

On the way over, Menolly had gotten a call from Derrick that hadn't helped any. The salvage operations for the Wayfarer had yielded very little. It was going to be a complete rebuild from the foundation up. And he dropped the bomb that a lawyer had come sniffing around but had been close-mouthed.

We were all worn out, and when Camille had suggested going dreglin-hunting after our meeting here, neither Menolly nor I were much in the mood. It was too soon after what had happened.

The coffee shop was buzzing with wired java-junkie Seattleites. We didn't have coffee back in Otherworld but since we'd come over here, Camille had gotten hooked but good on it, and she drank enough to bring a grown man to his knees. The smell of freshly baked cookies filled the air, and the warm lights and hustle of chatter felt like a welcome retreat.

I glanced around, looking for someone we might recognize. Hester Lou had said she'd be wearing a bright green shirt, and within seconds, my gaze landed on the only chartreuse-ensconced woman in the place.

We knew she was someplace in her forties, but she looked fit. Skinny as a rail, with blond hair like mine tied back in a ponytail, she didn't have a speck of makeup on that I could see, and she was sitting next to a red-headed woman, also lean and athletic, who had her hand on Hester's arm. I had the feeling they were more than good friends.

We headed over toward them, and Hester looked up.

"Hi, I'm Delilah, your cousin." I smiled at her, trying to sound natural.

Her eyes widened as she stood, and she let out a little noise that sounded all-too catlike.

"You have to be kidding. You can't be . . . I thought you

said we were related. If you expect me to believe we're cousins, forget it. None of my aunts are young enough to have girls your age."

I glanced at the others as we sat down. "This is going to take some explanation." We introduced ourselves. Hester's friend was Sue Ann, and as I'd thought, they were married.

After an awkward pause, Camille spoke up. "Our mother, Maria D'Artigo, was Theresa D'Artigo's daughter. She was born in 1921, when Theresa was fifteen, and adopted out to a couple because your grandmother was a teenaged unwed mother, and that didn't go over so well."

"You are telling me that your mother was seventeen years younger than my mother? You expect me to believe that?" And then Hester stopped, tilting her head as she examined our faces. "*Who are you?* What do you want? You're not fully human."

"You're right on that count. Our mother, Maria, fell in love with a man named Sephreh ob Tanu . . ." As I said Father's name, I choked, and bit my lip, trying to keep my composure.

"Our father was from Otherworld. He's one of the Fae. He took Mother home with him and she had the three of us. She was half sister to your mother, Tansy. So that makes us cousins. We're all over sixty Earthside years old." Camille gave her a long look, open but not bringing up her glamour. We didn't want to charm our way into a relationship with Hester Lou. It had to happen naturally.

After a moment, Hester let out a long breath. "So the rumors were right. Grandmother had a baby when she was young. My mother did some genealogical research and something led her to that conclusion. I don't know what because I never took much of an interest in the subject. But she always maintained that she had a half sister or brother somewhere. Mother didn't find out until after Grandma died and couldn't ever confirm her suspicion."

Sue Ann leaned forward. "Hester, they are of your blood. I can sense it. I can see it—there's a connection." She leaned toward me. "You . . . you have the strongest bond with your mother's spirit." Shaking her head, she sat back. Sue Ann wore snug jeans and a tank top, and her motorcycle boots caught my eye. Her hair was pretty much the same cut as mine, though she looked older. But she was also FBH, so her years would wear far more on her than ours on us.

Hester glanced at her, then back at us. "Sue Ann is psychic. She's seldom wrong, and knows her stuff. Let me put in another call to Daniel—he was out when I called earlier." This time, she got ahold of Daniel. "He'll be down in twenty minutes. Why don't we get something to eat? When he gets here you can tell us about your life, and your mother."

Her demeanor was cautious, but she believed us. We bustled around, found a bigger table, and got food and drinks. At one point, Hester Lou came over to me. She was about my height, and she looked tough, but not worn out. She reached up and brushed my hair out of my eyes.

"It's so hard to believe that you three are all older than I am. Than Daniel is. We're close in age, you know. My brother is . . . well . . . he's trouble at times but I love him." With a glance over at the table where Menolly sat waiting, she added, "She's a vampire isn't she?"

I nodded. "She went through hell on earth. Or Otherworld, as it was. She's been a vampire for close to fifteen years. Camille's a witch and priestess. And I'm a werecat. I had a twin, Arial, but she died at birth." I didn't know how much to tell her, but figured that it was a safe bet she would find out about our abilities eventually.

"It must be something, having powers like that. Of course, like everybody else, I know about Otherworld and vamps and Weres but . . ." She paused and wiped her eyes. "To know that we have blood kin on the other side of the veil. Your mother and my mother were half sisters and they never knew about one another, and that makes me sad. My mother was so sure there was someone out there. She said she just had a feeling. She looked and looked but could never find concrete evidence, and by then Grandma was dead."

I let out a soft mew. "You have other cousins, right? That's what our informant told us."

Hester nodded. "Most of them we haven't met. My aunts live scattered around. For some reason, they weren't close. My mother told me that there were family *issues* at play, but she wouldn't talk about them."

Camille let out a little laugh. "We know all about family issues. Trust me, in Otherworld? Being half-human? Not such a good thing."

Sue Ann bit into her scone. "I guess prejudice is everywhere."

Hester nodded. "Sadly, I think that's true. My mother wasn't happy that I'm gay, but she finally accepted it. But I doubt my other aunts would."

"I'm bi, and married to a woman." Menolly finally decided to join the conversation. "I'm also a vampire. My father couldn't accept the latter." She lowered her eyes. "You'll have to forgive us. We just received word today that our father is probably dead. We're a bit shell-shocked."

I was glad Menolly brought it up. I wasn't sure I could handle saying the words out loud without breaking down.

"And you still came to meet us?" Hester looked a little confused.

I cleared my throat. "In our lives, we've had to learn how to juggle multiple emotions as well as events. We do not lead a safe life, nor an easy one at this point. We belong to the Otherworld Intelligence Agency, and actually, we run the Earthside Division."

Sue Ann broke into a smile. "Government agents, huh? I was a marine up until a few years ago." She pulled out a chain from beneath her tank top. Dog tags dangled at the end. "I was discharged due to a combat injury that left me with a weak knee. It gives out without warning, but damn, I did my duty and put in my time for my country." She leaned over and planted a kiss on Hester's cheek. "I keep telling Hester that some of us are made for fighting. And some aren't."

I found myself liking my cousin and her wife. They

were open, but not overeager, and neither seemed like they'd take much guff off anybody for anything.

Just then, the door to the shop opened and a rather short, thin man entered. He was around Hester's age, with a shock of tousled blonde hair that was the same color as mine. He seemed easy in his body, his movements were fluid and graceful, and I had an odd feeling about him as he walked up. Not bad, just odd. His eyes were a piercing blue, shrewd and clever, and a hint of a sarcastic smile played across his lips.

Hester waved him over. "Daniel, you are not going to believe this. Meet our cousins from Otherworld. It seems Mother had a half sister she never knew about."

As Daniel cocked his head, giving us a bemused look, Hester launched into what we had told her. When she had caught him up, we took over, telling them both about Maria and Sephreh's meeting, and how he swept her away to Otherworld, how we came along, and finally, how mother had died, how and why we'd joined the OIA, how Menolly had become a vampire, leading to us being sent over Earthside.

When we finished, we sat back and waited.

Hester let out a long whistle. "This morning when I woke up, I never expected to be here, tonight, listening to all of this. But somehow it feels the most natural thing in the world." She glanced over at Daniel, who gave a noncommittal nod. "We know what you do, let us tell you a little about us. I own a coffee shop in Kirkland. We host local artists now and then. It's called All The Perks. And Daniel is a private buyer."

I glanced at him. "What's that mean?"

He gave a little shrug. "Clients want to procure certain items that are difficult to come by. They hire me, and give me a set price limit. I find it for them for a commission. I make a tidy living."

It sounded odd, but a number of stores had personal shoppers so why not private clients? Celebrities had them, and there was nothing to say that someone who had money and was in a time crunch couldn't do the same.

Daniel winked at me. "I love my work and I'm good at it. I look at it like being a form of personal assistant. Now, tell us more about Otherworld. We're all ears and I know I'm dying to hear more."

Something about him struck me as off, but he was likable, and Camille seemed at ease with him. She was like a litmus test for freaks. So, I chalked up my feelings to all the stress we'd been under and let it go. We talked late into the night, and when we parted, we had exchanged numbers, e-mail addresses, home addresses, and a big round of hugs. As Hester Lou threw her arms around me, I suddenly flashed back to being a little girl, with my mother hugging me. And I knew right then, I could trust this woman.

As we left the coffee shop, I stared into the night sky. The rain had let up and the stars were shimmering overhead. I should have felt tired, tired from the mess back in Otherworld and from hearing the news about Father, but now I felt wired. It was like I was watching a movie in which I was starring. Maybe it was a coping mechanism, or maybe it was how exhaustion manifested in me, but I was charged up and ready to go.

"I've changed my mind. Let's go get the dreglins." I turned to the others. "I know they're active at night, but I'm ready for a fight. We can swing by home and armor up. Menolly's here—she obviously can't go to work tonight." As soon as I said it, I bit my tongue. I hadn't meant to be so thoughtless.

But she just shrugged. "You're right. And I could use a good ass-shaking. I'm in no mood to sit at home and twiddle my thumbs."

Camille let out a small sound. "I'm in. But let me change clothes. I don't want this outfit messed up."

Within ten minutes we were home, and another ten saw us changed and ready. Morio wanted to go, but Camille nixed his offer.

"Listen, you, Shade, and Vanzir have to protect the

house and Iris. Shamas will be home soon, but still . . . the elfin guards had to go home to Elqaneve, and Aeval's new guards aren't due till tomorrow morning. You *can't* come with us. But we've fought monsters before without you. We can take on a few by ourselves now."

Morio glowered but Camille cleared her throat and put her hands on her hips, and he quieted down. Shade harrumphed but he, too, kept quiet. Vanzir just snorted.

"We're on our way. We'll call if we get into trouble. One of you take Nerissa and drop over to make sure Iris and her family are okay. Hanna, take care of Maggie." I gave Shade a quick peck on the cheek and we were out the door.

It was only a few minutes' drive to where we'd encountered the dreglins before, and we parked off the road, on a turnout near where we'd fought them before. Two miles east, Ivana had said.

"I wish I'd been able to go with you," Menolly said. "I kind of like Ivana."

I stared at her. "Are you crazy?"

"Maybe, just a little. But she's who she is, you'll have to give her that. Ivana doesn't change for anybody." She laughed. "In fact, I know it sounds nuts but given other circumstances, I bet you Ivana could become a good friend, as long as we could keep her off the topic of baby-eating."

"Yeah, I was saying something like that earlier but Delilah didn't like the idea." Camille let out a curt laugh. "Hey, this is the first time in a while that the three of us have been out bashing monsters on our own, without the guys along." She grinned, shaking her hair back out of her face. "Kind of a chance for the three of us to reconnect."

"The family that slays together, plays together? Bonding through bloodshed?" I had the worst desire to giggle, but stifled it as we headed off the road and into the woods, heading due east.

Two miles, Ivana had said. With our abilities to navigate through the forest, it wouldn't take long. We could move faster than FBHs and we had a lot more endurance, and a better ability to navigate during the night.

The October night was chilly and I pulled my jacket tighter. For once, Camille had chosen an outfit that wouldn't get caught in the bushes—she was wearing her cat suit, which looked better on her because of her exaggerated curves than it had on Emma Peel of *The Avengers* TV show. A low-slung silver belt held her dagger, and she had traded in her stilettos for a pair of stylish suede boots.

"You giving up on the spikes?" I asked with a laugh.

She snorted. "After our skirmish with the storm, and trying to get through the rubble, I've decided that going into a fight in heels isn't the best idea. If I land in one by accident so be it, but deliberately heading out? I'll figure out some sort of outfit that works for me and for battle."

Grateful for the lack of rain, at least for the moment, I pushed through the bushes. Menolly stopped as we neared a clearing.

"Let me turn into a bat and fly up ahead. I want to check out the general vicinity. Just hide over there by that cedar until I get back." She motioned to one of the ancient trees that towered up through the wooded area. Cedars were thick in this area, their scent cut through the air with a sharp tang in the rain-soaked forest, and they smelled clean and fresh.

"You're just loving the fact that you're able to transform into a bat so much easier now that Roman re-sired you. His blood certainly did a number on you."

Neither Camille nor I added that we still weren't sure about the vampire lord, and that we weren't sure if we trusted him. But there was no going back, and he had helped us more than once, so we had agreed not to present our concerns to Menolly. We all had too much stress as it was.

She laughed at me. "Whatever, Kitten. I'm just glad I can do it right now, instead of flying like I'm drunk or trying to drive a stick for the first time." She closed her eyes, and within seconds, a very tidy pretty bat hovered above us, then she silently glided off into the night.

Camille and I crouched beneath the cedar. It was cold, and we huddled together. The sounds of the forest echoed through the area, the dripping of rainwater off trees, the soft hooting of an owl somewhere near. Creatures lived in these woods, and not just the Fae. Snakes—though it was too cold for them at this time of year—frogs, coyotes, and sometimes a stray mountain lion or two. Squirrels and lizards and slugs and all of the critters that inhabited the woodlands of the Pacific Northwest.

Camille leaned toward me, kneeling on the ground. "You know, this is helping. I still can't believe Father's dead, but with his soul statue shattered, I don't think we have any choice but to believe it. I know this sounds horrible, but better it be in pieces than re-formed like Menolly's did when she became a vampire. Father couldn't handle the transformation. He'd walk into the sun." Her voice shook, but it could have been the cold causing it.

I nodded, balancing in a squatting position by bracing myself against the tree. "Yeah, I realize he couldn't deal with it. We were always aware this could happen. We never knew if he'd come home from a mission, from a battle. We've been prepared for this since we were little girls. I guess that he went in duty would make him proud."

Even as I said it, I knew it was the truth. We'd always worried when he was away with the Guard Des'Estar. There had always been the chance he wouldn't come home, and so many times we waited on pins and needles for him to walk through that door and reassure us he was okay. The odds had finally caught up to him, and by default, to us.

"So, when are we going to contact Aunt Rythwar?"

She sucked in a slow breath. "I'll do it tomorrow. Give her one more day. We can send word to Smoky or Trillian to contact her. I don't think we should leave home right now. There's too much going on. I don't feel comfortable making a trip to Otherworld just to notify her, even though she is his sister."

"Speaking of sisters, what did you think about our cousins? I liked Hester Lou, but I'm not sure what to think of Daniel." Something scurried over my hand and I shook it off. Probably a spider of some sort, but we'd all learned not to react loudly when on a mission.

"He's hiding something—that much I can tell you, but I don't get any negative feelings about him. Just . . . he's crafty." There was a hint of a smile in Camille's voice and I knew instantly that she'd taken a shine to him. "I'm intrigued and I want to know more."

"I have a feeling we're going to find out. Hester, especially, seemed to cotton up to the idea that we're kin. I have to admit, it cushioned the blow about Father—just a little." I honestly didn't know if I was trying to make myself feel better, but just saying the words gave me false courage.

"We're going to have to get used to this. We've lost friends. We've lost family. It's part of life and as much as I hate to sound fatalistic, considering what the fuck we're up against, we're lucky we haven't lost more people. We have our husbands and wives and fiancés, we have Iris and Hanna and Maggie. We've lucked out. So many things can go wrong so easily." She rapped lightly on the tree. "Knock wood we continue in that luck."

I was about to say something else when there was a blur in the air and then we saw Menolly, hovering above us. Another blur and she transformed back into herself. It was hard to believe she'd made so much progress; she'd been such a klutz when she tried to turn into a bat before Roman's intervention.

"I think I know where they are. The nest of them is going to be tough and we have to avoid getting bitten. Delilah got lucky with her bite—it's healing up, but there's no telling if the next one won't be worse."

"Should we wait till morning and come back with the guys?" Camille asked.

Menolly shook her head. "They took out somebody tonight. I don't know who but they're eating the woman's remains." She grimaced. "We can't chance letting them get another victim. Who knows how many people they've killed so far?"

Camille frowned. "I can't use the horn again—not until it's recharged under the new moon. I didn't even bother bringing it. I could call down a storm and I have my Moon Mother magic."

"What about a death magic spell? Do you have anything that might work on them, that you can cast without Morio around?" I wasn't sure just how entwined they were on the energy, though I knew Camille had some power on her own in that sphere.

She snorted. "I could try but there are no guarantees."

"There's no guarantee with your Moon magic either. In fact, your fuck up ratio seems to be pretty strong with it." I meant it playfully but it came out a sharp jab. With an exasperated sigh, I apologized. "Sorry, I don't mean to sound like a bitch."

"Don't sweat it. You're right. The question is, will death magic even work on them? They're magical beings, children of the Elder Fae. Does that make them Elder Fae in their own right, or are they a hybrid?"

"Well, I can try to drain them of blood." Menolly frowned. "But I can only attack one at a time. Luckily, their toxic venom won't do much on me. Delilah, you have Lysanthra? Can she do anything?"

I had still only tapped the surface of my sentient dagger's powers. We were in tune, and on occasion she surprised me with a new move, but it was haphazard at best.

"I don't know. Fuck, why didn't we plan this out better? I feel like we're right back to playing the Three Stooges."

"Maybe I can help." The voice took us by surprise. We turned around and there stood Vanzir. He grinned. "Don't even say a word, girls. Shade sent me. If he can't protect the house, nobody can. So just keep your yaps shut about me being here and let's get to work. I can attack them and they probably can't do a whole lot to me, not with their actual venom. They can hurt me but, then again, I can hurt them." Here, he laughed, and it took on an ominous tone.

Vanzir's powers had shifted since he and Camille had their unwilling tryst and the Moon Mother had stripped them away. They had been returned to him changed, altered in ways that even he didn't understand. It seemed like we were all going through our metamorphoses and none of us knew where the light at the end of the tunnel was.

"I brought someone else with me," he added, looking at Camille. "You're not going to be too thrilled but tough titty."

She slowly stood. "Who?"

Out of the shadows, from behind Vanzir, stepped a pale-skinned, dark-haired man. He was handsome, but had an otherworldly look about him, angular and harsh and glittering.

Camille let out a groan. "You didn't."

The man snorted. "Don't look a gift horse in the mouth, *Lady* Camille."

And with that, Bran, the son of Raven Mother and the Black Unicorn, stepped fully into view.

Chapter 17
❧❦❧

Menolly stepped between Camille and Bran. "Thank you for coming. We can use the help."

I couldn't help but think that when Menolly had to be the diplomatic one, something had gone to hell. But Bran and Camille had developed a hostile relationship, even though they'd been ordered to work together, and from what she'd said after her training sessions out at the Court of the Three Fae Queens, things weren't getting any better. She couldn't read Bran, couldn't read how he felt about the fact that she'd killed his father—even though it was by divine design. And his mother, Raven Mother, had long been after Camille to come join her in the Otherworld Forests of Darkynwyrd.

Bran gave Menolly a short, studied glance, then turned back to Camille. "Aeval bids me to come help you until your men are back from Otherworld. She sent several of her guards to your house tonight and they are patrolling the boundaries. I will stay with you for a few days until you have things settled back to normal."

"Like hell you will. I doubt you'd enjoy our hospitality."
Camille's eyes narrowed and she let out a little growl.

"Oh, trust me, I shall. Aeval commands it. Do you wish
me to return to Talamh Lonrach Oll and inform Aeval that
you decided to defy her wishes?"

A threat was implicit in his voice and I wanted to slap
him, but decided that wouldn't be the best move. This was
between Camille and Aeval, and chances were, the Fae
Queen would win hands down. I knew it, Bran knew it, and
by Camille's smoldering look, she knew it too.

"Fine. Just don't get in my way." She glared at him,
relenting. "You willing to kill the children of Elder Fae?"

His nostrils flared, but a thin, razor smile appeared on
his lips. "I have no qualms about killing anything or anyone
I need to. Why do you think Aeval is putting me in charge
of her armies?" And with that, he pulled out an extremely
sharp looking short sword. It flared with a pale, shimmering light. I realized it had been charmed in some manner.

Vanzir pulled out the magical stun gun we'd taken off a
dead guard during a raid when the Koyanni had been kidnap-
ping werewolves to make Wolf Briar. He'd developed a love
for the weapon, and had found alternative ways of recharging
it now that the Energy Exchange nightclub had vanished.
Especially since Vanzir had been the one to implode it.

I readied Lysanthra and she sang in my hand, crooning
to me in a voice only I could hear. Dumbfounded, I turned
around and realized she was responding to the energy in
Bran's sword. He simply stared at me, with a sardonic
smile on his face.

"You like that energy, do you?" I whispered to my long
dagger.

So very much. Like recognizes like, you know. The
voice was clear as a bell in my head.

"By chance, you wouldn't have anything new to show
me, would you?"

Perhaps not this night, but soon . . . you never know . . .
And the whisper faded away as she glimmered lightly in
the night air.

Menolly led the way since she had already scouted ahead. I swung in behind her, then Camille and Bran, and Vanzir at the back. I was spoiling for a fight, and I could tell Camille was too. She seemed pissed out of her mind but she moved silently alongside Bran.

We slid through the undergrowth, as stealthily as we could, and I kept my eye on Menolly's back. She moved in silence, totally focused. After a few minutes, she held up her hand and I motioned behind me, coming to a halt. A brief pause, then she started again. Another moment and I found myself on the edge of a clearing.

The ground was plush with a layer of mulch, a combination of wet leaves and fir needles and detritus from the autumn foliage that the trees and shrubs had shed. The chill of the night filtered through and I could see my breath in front of me, as the clouds drifted across the moon, blotting out the light at one moment, then baring the silver crescent into the open.

Menolly softly moved to the left, staring out at the group of dreglins who were hunkered over the remains of a body, feasting. With iridescent skin that changed from blue to green and back to blue again, they were sleek and hairless, and totally naked—allowing us to see their sex. I thought they might have scales, but it could have just been a trick of the moonlight. Lean and taut, they were muscled but wiry, and they ate like ravenous animals. Ripping out chunks of the woman's gut, they dangled the intestines above them, eating them like spaghetti, their faces smeared with blood and bile. It was worse than watching zombies—zombies were killing machines, they ran on autopilot. These creatures were cunning and crafty. Ivana was right, they were dangerous, and even from here I could feel how they delighted in destruction. Jenny Greenteeth had an appetite for flesh, and so did the Dark Dugald, and they'd passed it in spades to their children.

Menolly glanced over at me, and I looked down the line. We were all poised on the edge of the clearing now, and the dreglins hadn't noticed us, so wrapped up in their gruesome meal they were.

Lysanthra began to vibrate in my hand. She was spoiling for blood and I was about to give it to her. But Menolly would go in first, disrupt them and take down one of them. Vanzir motioned that he'd go in second. Again, he stood a better chance of not being harmed by the dreglins' toxins.

We waited, then, in an imperceptible flicker, Menolly leaped out into the group. She said nothing, gave no war cry, just went for the throat of the biggest one. As she landed full-frontal on it, she knocked the woman to the ground, taking her down.

Now, speed was our ally. Vanzir moved in quickly, firing at the nearest dreglin with the stun gun. The energy bolt hit hard and center, and the dreglin was knocked through the air, a good two yards, to land on his back. Vanzir turned the gun on the next one and fired, and I realized he was trying to give us an advantage by getting the drop on them.

I rushed in after him, toward the one he'd shot first. I landed atop the creature, bringing Lysanthra down square, full force. The blade slid neatly through the dreglin's chest, but to my horror, there was no blood. What? Didn't these things bleed? Then, as a thin trickle started to flow, he lifted me up and I found myself soaring through the air to land against a stump. I screamed as a sharp rock jammed into my lower back. It didn't penetrate my jeans or jacket, but I could already tell I'd have a massive bruise there.

I pushed to my feet in time to see Bran take on one of the dreglins as, once again, Vanzir shot the one who I'd been fighting. He went down again, and this time, Vanzir shot it twice more and it stayed down, twitching. But that meant he'd used five—maybe six—bolts and the stun gun only held ten charges.

Camille seemed to be assessing the situation and I could tell she was prepping a spell, trying to stay out of the way. Smart girl—she'd never be able to take on these creatures in a physical fight.

Bran danced toward his quarry with a grace and strength that stunned me, his movements precise, incisive.

He was beauty-in-action to watch, and I found myself mesmerized by how fluid he was. Camille was staring at him too, and I had the feeling she had never seen this side of him. I also had the feeling she didn't like being forced to admire him for any reason.

He darted to the side as a female dreglin—with the breasts to prove it—lunged toward him. Turning in midair, Bran brought his blade to bear and it glimmered with a brilliant purple flame. The sword whistled as he spun, cleanly slicing through the dreglin's neck like a hot knife through butter.

The woman didn't stand a chance. One moment she was leaping forward. The next, her body continued on its arc as her head went tumbling to the side. The flame attached to the sword cauterized the wound instantly, and the blood stopped flowing as soon as it had started. Bran stepped to the side as the body lurched forward, then fell, spasming as it hit the ground. The head rolled to the side, eyes wide open, staring up at the night sky.

Menolly's dreglin went down for the count, and Vanzir had finished off the one on the ground in front of him, so that left two. I launched myself at my attacker again, and Bran moved in from the right. Camille sent a spell reeling toward the last one, but the energy bolt arced up and looped, heading back toward her with a vengeance. She screamed. Bran stopped in midstep, whipped around, and launched himself toward her, taking her down just before the bolt hit.

The spell zoomed past and collided with the tree behind her, sending a shower of sparks and flame up in the side of the trunk. But the wood was too wet and it quickly burned out.

Seeing that she was safe, I turned my attention to my opponent. Blood oozed out of the wound but it was slow and thick, and I realized they had a far different make up than we did.

As I aimed Lysanthra toward the creature, Vanzir shot him from behind. He stumbled, turning to see who had attacked him.

I stared at him, openmouthed. "Dude! You could have missed and hit me. What the hell? Watch out!"

"I could have, but you'll notice I didn't." With a laugh, he shot again and the force knocked the dreglin forward. Menolly dove in for the attack. She landed on the man and, in a flurry of fangs and blood, he was dead.

I hurried back to Camille, but Bran had once again interceded and the last dreglin was sprawled on the ground, headless like her sister. We had killed them all. Correct that: *Bran, Vanzir, and Menolly* had killed them. Camille and I'd done shit. Feeling oddly irritable, I let out a low growl but then decided that—with or without our help, they were dead and we were all okay, and that's what mattered.

"Is that all of them?" Vanzir asked.

"Yeah, at least according to Ivana. But that doesn't guarantee more won't sneak over here." I wiped my dagger blade on a rag that I'd stuffed in my pocket before we left home.

"We'll worry about that when it happens. If it happens." Camille sighed and turned to Bran. "Thanks. You saved my life. I would have fried myself royal if you hadn't knocked me out of the way."

He gave her a long, cool look and a hint of a smile tipped the corner of his lips. But it wasn't a smile that made me comfortable. It was too cunning, too sly.

"Can't have Aeval's pet taking a powder due to her own fireball, can we? She'd have my hide. Then again, my mother would tear her to pieces if the Queen of Shadow and Night harmed me and we'd have a full-scale war on our hands. And once my father grows into his new body and returns to his full glory . . ." His voice drifted off as he let the words hang.

Camille stared at him for a moment, then turned away. Menolly interposed herself between the two, though she said nothing, and Bran abruptly headed back out of the woods without so much as a "good-bye" or "see you later."

We stood there, looking at the dead bodies, then at each other. The corpses of the dreglins were starting to smoke a little, and as I leaned down, I saw them oozing the pores. They were . . . no, it couldn't be.

"They're melting." I frowned. "We haven't wandered into Munchkin land, have we?"

"My guess is that toxin releases in their bodies when they're dead and somehow cause a highly increased rate of decomposition. I'll bet in half an hour there won't be anything left but bones, if that." Vanzir eyed one of the bodies and nudged it with his toe, pulling away quickly as the flesh began to split.

I picked up a stick and poked one of the corpses with it. The flesh had already started to fall away and I grimaced as the branch drove a hole in it and a gush of pus and ooze ran out.

"Okay, then, we just leave them here? No burying, or anything gross like that?" Camille shuddered. "The clouds are moving in, the rain should take care of washing the slime away."

The dreglins were oozing around the edges, the flesh putrefying as we watched. Skin flaked off, muscles and tendons began to bubble and liquefy, pooling into gelatinous mounds of frothing tissue that foamed over the bones. We stood, watching in an awed silence as the dreglins disintegrated into jellyfish. Only instead of floating through the sea, they oozed back into the earth for good.

As the bones began to follow the flesh, we turned and walked away. At the end of the day, nothing would remain to mark their existence.

By the time we headed home, it was near midnight. But as I got in my car, my phone rang. I glanced at the Caller ID. Tim.

I fastened my seat belt as I punched the Answer button. "Hey, Tim. What's up?"

"I cracked her password. Texting it to you after I hang up. But let me tell you, that place is as bad as Cupid's Arrow. I had a quick peek around the site and there are as many creeps in the Supe world as there are among my kind." He chuckled. "If you ever break up with Shade, I don't recommend you dip your toe in that wading pool."

"I promise. I won't dip my toe or anything else." Grinning, I leaned back against the seat. Tim was a comfortable friend and I loved hearing his voice. I heard someone talking to him.

"Oh hey, Jason wants to know how you like the Jeep?"

"Tell him he did a great job, and thanks for the detailing on the door. Nice to have my baby purring like new again."

"Good. Well, I'm off. I have some late work to get done and Jason wants to go out for coffee—a twenty-four hour Starbucks opened near our house and we can walk there."

"Okay. Be careful, dude. There are monsters in the dark."

"I know that all too well since meeting you. But even before you opened up the portals, we had plenty of monsters of our own, honey. Some of them are called bigots." He signed off and a minute later, a text came through with Violet's password.

I turned the ignition, then headed for home. The day's events had started to catch up with me, and by the time I pulled in the driveway, I could barely think. I tumbled into bed and the next thing I knew, I was out like a light.

Shade was gone when I woke up, he'd left a message that he had some business to attend to and would be back by dinner time. Missing him, horny and lonely, I moped around, but by the time I came down for breakfast, I felt relatively refreshed. A shower had cleaned any residual gunk off me that I had been too tired to pay attention to the night before.

Camille was sitting there with Iris, who had a relieved look on her face. Iris beamed at me.

"It's so good to get out of the house for a little while. Camille's been filling me in on everything. I can't believe how the world falls apart when I decide to take some time off." She was joking, but turned serious. "Delilah, I'm so sorry about your father."

I blinked. I hadn't even begun to visit the pain that I'd locked away inside, and I suspected neither had Camille nor Menolly. Right now was not that time.

"Thanks." I leaned down and kissed her. "How are you, little mama?"

"Tired. I have a nanny—the Duchess insisted on hiring someone. But I am sore and achy, and my nether regions still feel like I passed a couple of watermelons. Birthing's not easy and don't let anybody tell you it is." She chuckled. "But my Maria and Ukkonen are doing well. They both have extremely healthy lungs and they know how to use them. Bruce is a deer in the headlights, but he's feeling his way along."

"And how do you get along with your mother-in-law?" Camille set a cup of herbal tea and a plate of cookies down in front of Iris.

I rummaged through the refrigerator. "Where's Hanna? No breakfast?"

"Make it yourself. I gave Hanna the day off and she went shopping." Camille fixed herself an iced latte and sat down at the table with what looked like a leftover plate of spaghetti.

Iris cleared her throat and glanced around. "The Duchess . . . I've never met such a bossy woman. But she is kind and she loves her grandchildren, and so far she hasn't tried to change my house décor, so we're good. That's one thing about sprites and leprechauns, we respect the connections others have to their homes."

I found some leftover turkey breast and pulled it out, slicing it and slapping it between pieces of French bread, and slathering it with mayo, mustard, and ketchup. I added three slices of cheese and called it good. Pouring a big glass of chocolate milk, I sat down at the table with them and bit into the sandwich.

Camille pulled out her phone and tapped on the screen. "We have to pay Ivana's debt today. I called her and told her to come by this afternoon. And did you want to ask Chase if he wants to move in here?"

"Chase, move in? What is this, a boarding house? He can stay with Sharah—she should be having that baby any day." Iris looked a little put out and I thought that, even though she had her own home now and it was only a minute or two away, she still missed living with us and being queen of the household.

I glanced over at Camille, then back at Iris. "I guess we missed telling you. Sharah had her baby and because Queen Asteria is dead, she's now the Queen of Elqaneve and they made her leave the baby and Chase behind. He's a single father, for the moment."

"The entire world is falling apart around my shoulders and I seem to have no clue." Iris shook her head. "Well then, he can't possibly take care of that child on his own."

"Sharah sent a nanny and a wet nurse over Earthside," I started to say, but Iris waved me quiet.

"Nonsense. I'm producing an abundance of milk. I can wet-nurse his baby as well as my own. We have two guest rooms, and Chase can stay in one, and the nursery can hold a third baby. The Duchess loves children of all makes and models, she'd probably be overjoyed to add another one to her care while she's here, and it will keep her busy."

By the wicked grin on Iris's face, she had an ulterior motive hiding behind that cunning smile. "You call him right now. That way he won't be taking up your house space, and Bruce will welcome the male company. I'm afraid the estrogen factor is getting rather strong for him."

I grinned. "Whatever you say, Iris. I'm not going to argue." I dialed Chase's number. He was quick to answer, but he sounded groggy.

"Delilah, what's up?" There was an edge to his voice and I had the feeling he was already going down for the count.

"I have an offer for you from Iris and I think you should take her up on it, at least for a little while." I quickly outlined her proposal. "So you'll have a babysitter for . . . what did you name her?"

"Astrid, after Asteria. It seemed the thing to do." He

sounded hopeful as he said it, and I had the feeling we wouldn't have any trouble convincing him to hie it on over.

"You'll have a babysitter for Astrid, and Iris can nurse her. You will get more sleep and you can feel safer about leaving her during the day. What do you say?" I was a little hesitant. After all, Iris hadn't consulted Bruce yet, but then again, Iris was Iris and we *all* did what she said.

Chase let out a long breath. "Bless that little sprite. Tell her I accept, and I'll do whatever I can to lighten the load. And that way, Astrid won't be alone either . . . she'll have babies her own age."

"I don't think right now that matters so much, but you know? Hard to tell. When can you come over?" I nodded at Iris, who let out a broad smile.

"Does she mind if I pick up Astrid and bring her over now? I can stop on the way home tonight to get a suitcase with some clothes for me. But wait—I'll have a gun in the house. How does she feel about that?" Chase hesitated. He had to have his gun, but I also knew he respected others' feelings about the subject.

I sat down my phone and turned to Iris. "Here's the deal. He has to keep his gun with him. Will that bother you? If not, he'd like to bring Astrid—his daughter—over right now."

Iris didn't even blink an eye. "Chase knows what he's doing and it will be a long sight before those children are out of their cribs. I have no issues with it. Tell him to get his hindquarters in gear and bring that lovely baby over."

I told Chase what she said and he promised to be over in an hour. After I punched the End Talk button, I turned my attention back to my sandwich.

"Are you sure this won't be too much work for you, Iris?" Camille forked a bite of her spaghetti but Iris reached out and touched her hand.

"Is that cold?"

"Yes." Camille blushed. "I don't mind it cold."

"We'll see about that. You get right over to that stove and heat it up, Miss." Iris started to stand up, wincing. "If you don't, I will."

"You sit down!" Camille jumped up and carried her plate over to the microwave. "I'll heat it, but don't you even dare get up." She popped it in the microwave and punched the Express time button for two minutes.

"I swear, I move out and everything goes to hell." Iris frowned. "We'll have to figure out a way to streamline the workload in both of our households. Hanna is doing her best but things are getting out of hand. I think she and I can put our heads together and come up with a *plan*."

The way she said it, made me nervous. "What do you have in mind?"

"You just leave all that up to us, Delilah. We'll figure something out. Meanwhile, I'd better get back to the house and make sure the Duchess hasn't decided to buy me new furniture. When Chase gets here, you bring him and the wee one down. We'll get a bassinet set up—we have an extra."

At my look, she blushed, right through her tattoos on the sides of her face. "Well, you never know when you'll need a spare."

And with that, she gently eased out of her chair and headed out the kitchen door, back to her house.

Camille watched out the window, making sure Iris arrived home safely. "Somehow, if it's possible, I think Iris has gotten bossier since she gave birth."

"You're telling me. Man, she's going to be a pistol when she gets back on her feet. I guess we'd better prepare Hanna when she gets back."

The two women had come to a truce about who controlled what, especially since Iris had moved into her own house, but Iris still claimed our home as her territory too, and it led to some awkward interactions at times. They never really argued, but as Hanna got more comfortable, she also wanted to take more responsibility. I was wondering how the hell they'd come to some suitable arrangement, but knowing the two of them, they'd find a way.

Camille sighed. "I need to contact Trillian and have him go talk to Aunt Rythwar. Want to come with me?"

I didn't, but since she was offering to do the dirty work,

the least I could do was offer moral support. It was hard enough thinking about Father, let alone talking about him. We headed into the living room. The Whispering Mirror was still set up downstairs and we'd probably leave it down here for easy access as the war progressed. I dreaded finding out what was going on back in Elqaneve. By now the goblins had probably reached the city and we could only hope that Tanaquar's forces had made it in time to repel them.

Camille settled herself in front of the mirror and it flared to life and she stated her name. Voice activated, only our voices—and those of our husbands—would allow access. The frame was woven in a silver knotwork of delicate roses and leaves, and the glass was normally covered in mist, but when Camille said her name, the mist cleared and we could see a dark room. There were no windows in sight and the only illumination seemed to come from the eye catchers that hovered along the walls at regular intervals. A soft chime sounded, and a moment later, Trenyth appeared. He looked tired, harried even, but at least he was alive.

He slid into the seat in front of his own mirror and let out a soft sigh. "The war is on in earnest. The goblins have breached the gates of Elqaneve and are scattered throughout the whole of Kelvashan. Tanaquar's armies reached our side shortly before the goblins, so they spread out and the fighting is echoing through our lands."

Depressing news. But at least Tanaquar had sent her armies in advance and we'd been responsible for getting the news to her. That made me feel a little bit better. "What of the Knights?"

Trenyth's solemn look didn't change. "So far, your men have not been able to track them down. We have no idea if the other side has got hold of any of them." He winced and rubbed his head. "If they do, we are . . . as you put it . . . fucked."

Hearing that come out of Trenyth's mouth was shocking, but then again, nothing had been normal since we'd first come over Earthside.

"How's Sharah doing?" I asked.

"She's coping. Postpartum depression has hit her pretty hard, especially since she can't be with her baby. It's not going to be easy, this transition. She never expected to reach the throne, and nobody expected her to so she wasn't trained in the nuances of the Court. Or rather, she didn't bother to learn. We're having to fast-track her training."

"Well, tell her that Chase and Astrid—her daughter— are moving here. They'll be staying with Iris and will be a lot safer than if they stayed at Chase's apartment for now. It's not permanent but we'll sort that out later."

Trenyth gave me a faint smile. "She'll be happy to hear that. I know it's been weighing on her heart and her mind."

"Is Trillian there?" Camille asked. "We need him to . . . we need him to go find our Aunt Rythwar and tell her about our father. And . . . have you found his body yet?"

Her question hit me in the gut and I gulped back a sob, but Camille was maintaining and I'd be damned if I'd be the one to need comforting this time. She'd already carried us through Mother's death. We weren't going to put her through doing the same now that Father was dead.

"No girls. I'm sorry, we haven't found a trace of him yet. But his soul statue . . . well . . . I wouldn't hold out hope if I were you. As for Trillian, he's in the back room. They're preparing for another scouting mission today. A few of our seers escaped and they are trying to locate the Knights."

Another thought hit me. "Amber—she had a baby! Did . . . do you know . . ." How could I ask? How could I ask if they knew if Amber's baby was dead. One of the Keraastar Knights, Amber had ended up with her brother Luke—Menolly's ex-barkeep—in Otherworld, chained to the yoke of the spirit seals. And there, she'd had her baby. Nobody knew if her possession of the spirit seal had altered the baby while it was in her womb, but it was just something we assumed we would find out as the child grew.

Trenyth gave me a bleak look. "I don't know. Delilah, there are so many missing here that we will never have a true picture as to how many of our people have died. The toll is massive. Whole villages were wiped out by the storm. And now the armies are descending, and the sorcerers will surely come behind them. The Moon Mother is sending her Dark Moon Sorceresses to fight by our side."

Camille shifted in her seat. "Is Derisa going to be leading them?"

Derisa, the High Priestess of the Moon Mother, had held the position for who knows how long. But Camille was being trained to be the High Priestess of the Moon Mother's sorceresses—the priestesses who followed the Dark Moon. Derisa would lead the witches who followed the Bright Moon. Derisa would stay in Otherworld, while Camille was to stay Earthside and lead the new acolytes here. Or at least, that was the current plan.

"No, she cannot. She is too valuable. But there are Dark Moon sorceresses of great power and one of them, Seith, will lead the helm. They will drive forward to Kelvashan in two days' time. And the King of Nebulveori is sending warriors. Dahnsburg has an army on the march to our lands, and Svartalfheim is also dispatching a legion. If we can hold out for another week, we will have a formidable force."

Camille stared at Trenyth for a moment. "Will this leave their lands open to attack?"

He paled. "No, we have thought of that and insisted they send only those they can spare. Why? Do you sense something?"

She closed her eyes, and then, with a sharp cry, leaned over, clutching her head. "I see the same vision I did when I reached Elqaneve. The storm—it did not dissipate. It still lives, and it waits. They have chained it—this is no storm, Trenyth. It's a creature they've constructed. It takes the shape of a storm, but it's like a golem of sorts. And they have it ready to use again."

"How are you tuning into to this? And do you know where it will strike next?" Trenyth stood. "I will send word immediately if you can pinpoint it."

She sucked in a deep breath and lowered herself deeper into trance. I could feel the magic settle around her shoulders as her head dropped forward. "There is a city to the northwest . . . they will go after Svartalfheim next. They seek to enslave the sorcerers of Vodox's realm."

Her eyes flew open and she leaned forward, clutching the sides of the table. "Hurry, Trenyth. They are on the march. I don't know how I am tuning into this, but *trust me*. They will attack soon. Warn King Vodox. I don't know how they can protect the city but he has to try."

Trenyth paled, but he nodded. "What did you contact me for? Hurry, and then I will rush to send word to Svartalfheim."

Camille shook her head. "No, go now. Do it now. What we wanted can wait. Just protect my husbands and our friend Roz. But go, warn Vodox. If he does not erect a force field, his city will go down in flames, as sure as Elqaneve was destroyed."

And with that, she signed off, and the mirror fogged over again. I looked at her, horror filling my heart. "Telazhar . . . he can't be stopped, can he? He's laying waste to Y'Eírialiastar all by himself."

She shook her head. "Not by himself. He carries power from Shadow Wing, and the armies of disgruntled sorcerers. But he can be stopped—I have to believe this. If not . . . then Otherworld is lost to a war far more deadly than the Scorching Wars, and Earthside will be next. Once he breaks through, he'll be able to use his sorcerers to gate in the demons. They'll rip apart the portals one way or another. And the worlds will be a feeding ground for the damned."

Chapter 18

❧❦❧

We were a solemn pair by the time Chase arrived. Nerissa was with him, carrying Astrid, while he held the diaper bag, a stroller, and a bag full of toys. The kid could barely see the world and he already was showering her with stuffed bears and dolls. I repressed a grin, not wanting to say anything to squash his enthusiasm. He looked like he'd lost a lot of sleep though, and I had the feeling that he wouldn't stay in very good shape for long if he kept trying to do this all on his own, wet nurse and nanny or not.

The baby was fussy, and Nerissa immediately headed over to Iris's with her. Chase dropped into a chair in the kitchen, his dark eyes flashing.

"I never expected it to be like this. I thought Sharah and I would move in together and . . ."

"And you'd be a happy little family." I rubbed his shoulders. "That would be ideal, Chase, but the sooner you accept that it's not going to happen that way, the easier it will be to adjust. Life sucks, sometimes."

Camille handed him a cup of coffee and a Danish.

"Everything is in a mess right now. We just have to weather through. Iris will be a huge help and she'll look after Astrid like she will her own. You know that."

He nodded, the dazed look lifting just a little. "I honestly don't know what I'd do if she hadn't made the offer. I feel like she just threw me a lifeline and I'm holding on for dear life. And Sharah's only been gone since yesterday. Last night was horrible. Astrid wouldn't stop crying and the nanny—who is one bitch of an elf—couldn't quiet her down. By three this morning, I was ready to kick that elf's ass to the curb."

"Astrid wants her mother. But she has her daddy and that will make a huge difference. Sharah's not having a field day either." Camille told him about our conversation with Trenyth. "The world has gone to hell and we're all just going to have to hold on as best as we can. I'm mostly worried about the Keraastar Knights. Smoky and the guys *have* to find them. If Telazhar finds the seals first, we're all doomed."

On that gloomy note, she offered to help Chase carry his bags over to Iris's, leaving me to sort out what to do next. Now that the dreglins were squared away, it was time to get back to hunting for Violet. I opened my laptop. Might as well start with the Supernatural Matchups site, now that I had her password. By the time Camille returned, I was into Violet's account and poking around.

"Why don't I call Tanne Baum and see if he'll talk to us?" She pulled out her phone. "You find anything yet?"

"Not yet. Go ahead. See if he'll meet us this afternoon." I shook my head. "I'm trying to figure out how to navigate her account. There are a gazillion different links and I want to make certain I don't do anything to alert the site owners that I'm hacking in. Especially if they might be in on her disappearance."

As I puzzled through the menu, the doorbell rang. Camille went to answer it. She returned within seconds and motioned for me to follow her. There, on the front porch, stood ten soldiers, dressed in the colors of black, indigo, and silver.

"Aeval sent us guards for the house."

I scanned their faces. They weren't as friendly as the elves, by the looks of them, but they also looked more feral and dangerous, which was probably a good thing considering what we were facing.

"Welcome, and thank you."

The leader of the group, a stalwart, stoic warrior who carried a thin, light blade that looked as glitteringly sharp as his eyes, tapped his heels together and gave us a curt bow.

"Kendris, at your service. My men and I will do our best to protect you and your family, Lady Camille. We will die in your service, if need be. If you will just show us the lay of the land and tell us who lives here and who your safe visitors are?"

Camille glanced at me. "Go back to the website. I'll call Tanne Baum from out here. I've got his phone number in my contacts." She led the warriors down the steps as I headed back inside, glad to not be the one wandering around in the scattershot of rain.

After pouring another glass of chocolate milk, I hunted through Violet's account. She had a prime-level membership, which meant she could peruse all the videos available, as well as all the text listings. I glanced over the settings on her profile as to what she was looking for in a partner.

She'd checked the classifications for lovers and friends with benefits, but apparently was not looking for a long-term relationship. She'd also checked the box for polyamorous, but she was straight, not bisexual. She wasn't open to anybody other than Fae—no Weres, vamps, humans, or other races. Which made Tad's assertion that she wasn't interested in him more likely to be true.

Under her interests, she'd listed computers, gaming, dancing, hiking, camping, gardening, rafting, and a number of other outdoor activities. Violet didn't drink, she didn't smoke, and refused to try drugs. She had checked the box for kink, but in the designations, she had excluded some of the grosser activities—no water sports or bodily wastes. Also, she wasn't into S&M, however, she was open to bondage, and slave-play.

She'd uploaded a video a couple weeks ago that had already been viewed four hundred times. A listing offered statistics as to who—by nickname only—had looked at it. As I studied the stats, I noticed that the same user had viewed the video thirty of those times, all before Violet had disappeared. The rest had watched it once or twice. Noting down the nick of her most avid fan, which was Hot-Bod24, I watched the video.

Violet was pretty . . . long dark hair with brilliant green eyes. She was slight, but looked fairly strong, and I had the feeling she was a tough little cookie. Her voice was soft, and alluring. No wonder Tad had been attracted to her, there was something primal about her—seductive but not overt. Definitely a geek girl—as much as one of the Fae could be—she had the same glamour that all the Fae do, regardless of background or interests. Even the Fae who were hideous by human standards possessed a magnetism that was hard to deny.

Next, I did a search on HotBod24.

Well . . . according to his profile, HotBod24 was a guy, and his picture had a Fae look to it, but something felt off. His profile seemed too streamlined, almost generic, and if there's one thing that the Fae weren't, it was generic. Even those of us who were half-breeds had some oddball quirk that made us who we were.

The more I studied his picture, the more I had the feeling the account was a cover up. And the fact that he didn't have a video posted seemed odd, too. I did a quick perusal and, as far as I could tell, at least 75 percent of the members had some sort of live footage available.

Next, I opened up Violet's account e-mail. There were five e-mails from HotBod24, all sent within the past three weeks, all asking her for a meetup. They became more insistent with each one. They weren't slimy, which some of the other letters were, but again, something nagged at me that I couldn't put my finger on. I checked her Sent Mail.

Bingo. She'd finally agreed, after writing two hesitant letters. They'd scheduled a meeting for . . .

Hell. She'd agreed to meet him at the coffee shop at the Farantino Building. At 4:00 P.M., the day she had disappeared.

As I stared at the e-mail, Camille entered the kitchen from the back porch. She was flushed from the rain, and wet.

"I got them squared away—one is on duty at all times watching the rogue portal out . . . what's wrong?" She cocked her head. "What's going on?"

I crooked my finger. "Come look at this. I found out Violet was having coffee with one of her contacts from Supernatural Matchups the day she vanished. Look at where she agreed to meet him."

Camille peeked over my shoulder. "Oh fuck. Fucking hell."

"Yeah, that was my reaction. What now?"

She shook her head. "I don't know what to make of this. But if she is involved with daemonic activity, it can't be all that good." She glanced around. "Where's Shade?"

"He's taking care of some sort of business. He left a note that he wouldn't be back till dinner time. What about Morio and Vanzir?"

She shrugged. "Morio was gone this morning too. Left the same kind of note. I'm not sure about Vanzir. He never leaves much in the way of messages."

I let out a little laugh. "Gee, the house feels empty. Wait—who's taking care of Maggie today?"

Camille's eyes opened wide. "Fuck, I don't know. I thought she might be with Shade." She jumped up and me, hot on her heels, headed into Hanna's room.

As we skidded into the tidy bedroom, we stopped short. There was Vanzir, playing on his Game Boy while Maggie was laughing in her playpen. She was dancing with her Yobie doll, and she moophed softly when she saw us, and held up her arms.

"Camey! De-ya-ya!" Her smile cut through the gloom

and I lifted her out of the playpen while Camille leaned over Vanzir's shoulder.

"Thank you—we thought she'd been left alone."

"Hell no. Nobody leaves the Magster alone." Vanzir flashed us one of his rare smiles free of sarcasm. "What's shaking besides your boobs, chickie-pooh?"

Camille snorted. "Hey, I can't help having curves. And I don't remember you complaining . . . On second thought, never mind." She sobered and took Maggie from me. "We found out something disturbing."

"No—really?" And snarky Vanzir was back, but that was the way we were used to him. Anything else seemed out of place.

I told him about Violet and HotBod24 and the Farantino Building. "I have the feeling we're poised on the tip of the iceberg here."

"I'll have a talk with some of the guys down in the Demon Underground. I can do that now, if you take Maggie." He stood, cinching his belt. His jeans were skintight and ripped, and his undershirt was torn. He looked like a retro punk rocker, but he wore the look well.

"Go, but don't be too long. Hanna's not here and if we have to run out . . ." Camille stopped.

"Right. I'm off then." And he was out the door before we could say another word. We followed, Camille carrying Maggie while I dragged out her playpen. Hanna had removed it from the kitchen so she could wax the floor and forgotten to put it back. After settling her in with her toys, I glanced at the clock.

"Time for her morning cream drink. She gets her meat for early breakfast and Hanna always prepares all her meals in advance now, so it's easy to see when she's been fed." I pulled her bottle of cream out of the fridge and poured it into a bowl, then stuck it in the microwave for one minute. Maggie was learning to eat solid gargoyle food, but she would still get her cream dream several times a day for another few years till she was fully weaned onto solid food.

The mixture of cream, sage, cinnamon, and sugar smelled comforting and familiar as I took the warm bowl out of the microwave and put it down into Maggie's playpen. She eagerly began to lap it up, and I watched her.

"It's hard to believe that someday she'll be as big and large as the granticulars." Maggie was so cuddly and oddly proportioned that I couldn't imagine what she'd look like when she grew up. "I don't think I've ever seen a woodland gargoyle, other than her."

"We should make a trip to Thistlewyd Deep. I know there are pockets of woodland gargoyles there." Camille patted Maggie on the head, then returned to the table. "I'm going to call Carter and see if he's found out any more info on Lowestar Radcliffe and Gerald Hanson's deal for the Farantino Building."

"Sounds good, but hey, we need to buy the food to pay Ivana. She'll be here this afternoon, expecting her meat treats, and the last thing we want to do is piss off one of the Elder Fae. I'll stay with Maggie if you head to the store and pick up the meat. Unless you want me to go."

"No, I'll do it." She grabbed her purse. "I'll be back in a few. At least we have guards here."

As she headed out the door, pulling her jacket on, I wandered into the living room. The relatively peaceful days of the past few months were gone, broken. I thought about turning on the TV to watch some mind-numbing trash but for once didn't feel like it. So I put in the call to Carter. He was home, as usual.

"Carter—things are heating up with the Farantino Building. Have you found out anything more on the deal between Radcliffe and Gerald?"

I dropped into the rocking chair, propping my feet on the coffee table. Iris and Hanna both would kill me if they saw me do that but neither happened to be in the house right now.

He rifled through some papers and I heard the tapping of keys. "Yes, actually. I have it . . . *right here.* Okay, it looks like when the deed changed hands, it did so for the nominal sum of twenty-five dollars. Which means either Gerald didn't need the money, or Lowestar has something on him, or perhaps both. I also did some more digging into Lowestar's background and there is no record of him being born in India. In fact, he's either far older than he appears or has ancestors by the same name, because the first record I can find of a Lowestar Radcliffe is . . . guess where?"

My stomach knotted. "Italy."

"Right, he showed up right around the time that the Farantino family began to rise in power. Then he vanished again until he showed up in Seattle. The information as far as his appearance in Italy is sketchy but from what I can tell, he was labeled a "foreign supporter" of theirs. But nobody ever specified where this particular foreigner was from."

Carter paused. "I have a bad feeling about this, Delilah. We know there's daemonic activity attached to the building and there has been since Michael Farantino first built it. But there's something going on there—and Grandmother Coyote is never wrong. If something big is waking up, I have a hunch that Lowestar is directly related to it."

"More than that." I told him about Violet and the meeting at the coffee shop. "There has to be more than a coincidence there. I can't imagine there *not* being a connection."

"Then there may be . . . Hold on . . . Let me check on something and call you back in five." Carter signed off.

While waiting for him to call back, I wandered in to check on Maggie again. She seemed lonely, so I sat on the floor and pulled her into my lap. We cuddled for a moment, and she pushed Yobie in my face for a kiss. I hugged her, staring down into those soft gentle eyes. Her long lashes fluttered as she yawned and I realized it was time for her nap.

"Come baby, let's put you to bed." I carried her into her crib and she yawned again, then closed her eyes and fell asleep without a fuss, clutching Yobie. Once I was certain she was snoring up a storm, I tiptoed out of the room just in time to field Carter's return call.

"Okay, I have some interesting news. Guess where Supernatural Matchups is headquartered?"

I groaned. "In the Farantino Building."

"Right. And guess who was not only in charge of fielding their legal issues, but who also had stock in the company?"

A chill ran through me. "Gerald Hanson."

"Right again."

And then, an image from Gerald's memory flashed through me. "Fuck. Fuck, fuck, as Camille would say. I think I know something but I need to put it together. Please, don't go anywhere. I need to think about this and call you back when I've sorted it out."

"I have a lunch date, but that's not till two o'clock, so I'll be here till then. And you can catch me again after five." With that, Carter signed off.

I wanted Camille to get back. We usually worked well as sounding boards for each other. As I strained my memory, the door opened and she toted in a couple big bags.

"Don't say anything for a minute," I told her, grabbing the bags and carrying them into the kitchen. "I know something, but I need to figure it out. Sit down while I try to find the words."

Camille slipped off her coat and sat down at the table as I paced. Quickly, I filled her in on everything Carter and I had discussed.

"Okay, so, what's running through my head is this: when I was in Gerald's mind, I saw a Fae woman, in a cell. She was locked up and Gerald was thinking about how much money she would bring. In another memory, he was talking about replacing a *toy* and whatever it was, was expensive. What if Supernatural Matchups . . ."

"White slavery." Camille paled. "He was selling that woman."

"Right! What if Supernatural Matchups is a cover up for a sex slave operation? And what if they are finding their merchandise through the dating site?"

"But if he was running it, then when he died . . ."

I snapped my fingers. "But he's not running it. I need to check something." I jumped back on the laptop and scanned through the Supernatural Matchups site again.

The dating service had been formed . . . "They started the company the same year that Gerald sold the building to Lowestar. Lowestar's the one in charge of it. I'll bet you anything."

I quickly tapped out a few inquiries into the search engine and sure enough, the Washington State Secretary of State's site gave me all the information I needed. Under the Corporations Division, I was able to find out that the president of Supernatural Matchups was, indeed, Lowestar Radcliffe. Gerald Hanson had been VP. There it was, in black and white pixels.

"Here—look at this. One guess as to what's happened to Violet."

"I wonder if she's still alive." Camille peeked over my shoulder. "But this can't be what Grandmother Coyote was talking about with something ancient waking up. This is new, and as far as things go, yes it's bad but it's not the worst thing we've gone up against."

As we were puzzling things through, Vanzir burst through the door. He actually looked flushed, as well as soaked through to the skin.

"Okay, here it is. I talked to Trytian—"

Camille bristled. "Fuck, just what we need. Bring *him* into this."

"Listen, toots, you want information fast? You go to the person most likely to know. So I did." He folded his arms across his chest. "You want to hear what I have to say or not?"

"Yeah, yeah, go on." I tossed him the hand towel off the counter. "And wipe up, you're dripping all over Hanna's clean floor and she'll kill you."

"Big fucking deal." But he quickly wiped up the water and muddy footprints he'd tracked in. "Okay, here's the scoop. Trytian knows perfectly well who this Lowestar Radcliffe is."

"And how does he know?" Something in Vanzir's tone told me we weren't going to like this.

"Lowestar *is* your daemon—a very high-placed, intelligent, and powerful daemon. He doesn't like Shadow Wing but he's not working with the resistance. But he *is* out to carve himself a niche here Earthside, and he's always out for his own agenda."

My stomach dropped. "He's really the daemon. The one who the Farantino family pledged themselves to."

"Then why didn't I catch it when we were at the coffee shop and met him? I knew there was something uneasy about it, but none of us caught it—not even Shade." Camille rubbed her knuckles on her arm.

"He's powerful and old and probably very good at shielding his energy. Apparently, he's been attached to the Farantino family for a couple of hundred years. Looks like he's been using them to establish a home base for himself. He also happens to be leader of a cult, and their focus is . . . ?" Vanzir leaned against the table, waiting.

"Let me guess." Camille paled. "They're trying to wake up something that's been sleeping for a long time?"

Vanzir nodded. "Spot on. And that *something* would be an ancient demi-god named Suvika. He's one of the triple lords of vice and debauchery and he's been sleeping for millennia. Lowestar Radcliffe happens to be the high priest of the cult. Trytian told me that the Farantino Building is probably—not guaranteed—but most likely, a temple dedicated to bringing Suvika out of his slumbering state to rejoin the world of the waking. And when he does . . ."

I sighed. "Let me guess. The mighty will fall, Suvika will rise up and take control, and Lowestar, his prize priest, will reign in terror. Old story, heard it before."

"Actually, no. They aren't out to control the world, just sort of . . . take over the corporate structure. Suvika is also, not so conversely, a lord of business. I think Lowestar may be combining his love of debauchery with his love for money and he's aiming to become the Donald Trump of hedonism."

With a snort, Camille dropped into a chair. Tears ran down her face and I couldn't figure out whether she was laughing or crying. After a moment, she caught hold of herself and wiped her eyes.

"Great, we're taking on big business now." She sobered. "Put two and two together and this makes sense. Lowestar is running a white slavery outfit. He is high priest in a cult that worships a demi-god of vice, debauchery, and business. What better way to marry several loves while trying to bring your patron god back to the world of the waking? But that means he's probably trying to get his hands into other businesses. Quite possibly, the threats against the Wayfarer—trying to intimidate Menolly so she'd take the lawyers up on the offer to sell? We need to know how deep his pockets are, and what holdings he's invested in. If he's been meddling in human affairs for a long time, there's no telling what he has control over."

"And think . . . waking the demi-god of vice and business? That's going to put a big monkey wrench in the balance. No wonder Grandmother Coyote wanted us involved. I wonder why she picked me, specifically?" I frowned. "But honestly, it doesn't matter because we're all in this together. So . . . now that we know this, how does it help us find Violet?"

"If she's still around to be found. He's in the business of selling people. Supernatural Matchups is focused on the Supe world, so we can assume—though we may be wrong—that he's interested in procuring Supe men and women. I guess the place to start would be to find out who's going to replace Gerald. They'll have to have a new lawyer and soon. Lowestar will have to replace him."

Vanzir shifted. "I'll get on that. I can go visit Carter again."

"Please. And tell him everything we've learned."

As he headed out the door, I turned to Camille. "You think we'll be able to find Violet alive?"

She pressed her lips together. "I don't even want to bet on that. Thing is, alive or dead, she's never going to be the same. I can tell you that from experience." A cold look passed over her face, and once again, I knew she was flashing back to Hyto and the torture he'd put her through.

"We'll bring them down." I put my hand on her arm. "We'll stop them."

"Maybe, but the corporate world is thick and fast with corruption. It's that way here, just like it was in Otherworld. The nature of the beast. I'm not holding out a lot of hope for much of anything right now. I guess our biggest hope is to put a stop to the cult, and prevent the reemergence of Suvika."

I sat beside her and leaned forward, propping my elbows on my knees. "Is it just me, or does it seem like the harder we fight, the worse it gets?"

With a shrug, she shook her head. "The world is a complex web, Delilah. There is no answer to that. The deeper we go, the darker things get. But we have to keep trying. Too many people need us for us to ever give up."

"Then, it's simple. We don't give up. We don't lose. We get knocked down, and we try again. We dust ourselves off and we fight the good fight." I laughed. "Easy, huh?"

And then she smiled, her face lighting up. "That's the spirit. So yes, we fight on. And now, let's get this meat outside for Ivana. Because as you say, we don't want to welsh on our debts to the Elder Fae. So *not* a good idea."

As we carted the meat out to the appointed place, the rain began to pour in earnest. I gazed up at the silver sky. We were in for a long, hard winter. I could feel it in my bones.

Once Hanna was home to watch Maggie, we decided to go through with our plans to meet with Tanne Baum, even though we now had a handle on what was going on. He was gruff on the phone, with a thick German accent, but when we met him at the Supe-Urban Café, he was handsome, tall, and blond as spun platinum. He was also pleasant—far more pleasant than I'd thought he'd be.

"We wanted to talk to you about Violet." I wasn't sure

how to launch into what we thought had happened to his girlfriend.

Camille had made a valid point on the way to the restaurant that we should make certain he wasn't in on the slavery operation before we spilled our suspicions to him. The last thing we needed was for Lowestar to get wind that we had puzzled out what was going on.

Tanne cast a long look at us. "And I want to talk to you. I know who you are. And I know you're looking for Violet. Know this: She lives."

I almost choked on my drink. That was the last thing I'd expected to hear. "Since you know who we are, and that we're looking for her, let's skip the formalities. How do you know she's alive? Do you have any proof? We came here to ask if you've heard from her lately."

He tapped his forehead. "*I know.* She and I are linked. I know she's in trouble, though I don't know what kind, but I also know she's alive. If she dies—I will know that, too. We have been through certain rituals together."

Camille inhaled sharply. "Like the rites of Eleshinar Trillian and I went through together."

"I know what those are . . . Slightly different, but yes, the same principle. You will find her?"

"Well, it helps to know she's alive, but if we could ask you some questions?" I frowned, but Camille gave me a nod and I could tell she believed him.

"Whatever I can do to help." He played with the scone in front of him. "I do love her, you know. Tad is jealous, but truly, she has no taste for vampires. He would not stand a chance whether or not I was out of the way."

I decided to bypass the whole jealousy issue. "Then tell us what you know. When did you last see her? And where? Have you noticed anybody suspicious hanging around her house?"

We talked away the afternoon. Tanne was engaging, without any of the angst that Tad and Albert showed. He was polite, and very European in action. Even the Fae from over the other side of the pond were different than the Fae on this side of the ocean.

By the time we finished, we had a pretty good feel for the guy and we both believed him and we liked him. He didn't play games, didn't bother with challenges unless they intrigued him. He didn't have any jealousy toward Albert and Tad, and in fact, treated them like teenagers. And even though he knew she still lived, his loss and worry were obvious. But none of the information we gathered from him was anything we didn't know, except the fact that she lived.

Approaching him about the dating site was a gamble, but it turned out to be okay.

"I know she hung out there. We don't have an exclusive relationship. In fact, we have playmates together." He shrugged. "It's our way."

"Not an issue. I have three husbands." Camille pointed to my notebook. "But can we get their names, just in case?"

After he gave us the names of everybody he could remember—a tidy list, at that—he leaned back. "Do you think . . . do you think you'll be able to find her, to save her?"

I glanced at Camille. She caught his gaze and stared for a moment. He hung his head and turned to me.

"We'll do everything we can," I whispered. "Since we know she's alive, there's a chance. If you pick up anything more on her, let us know. We'll keep in touch."

As he stood to go, he gave us a curt nod. "I understand. Thank you for not sugarcoating matters. If I can sense anything more—if I can somehow reach out and touch her— I'll call you immediately. There are ways . . . they require preparation but the Fae of the Black Forest have many secret rituals and I can perform some of these. They are dangerous at times, but I'll do anything I can for her. Violet is special. She's . . . she's Violet." And with that, he turned and left the restaurant.

Camille and I finished our drinks, not knowing what else to do.

When Marion came by, she brought a plate of cookies.

"By the hangdog looks on your faces, I think you need these." She set them down on the table.

"Thanks." As Marion left, I turned to Camille. "So, what next?"

"Honestly? I have no idea. I guess . . . we eat cookies, then go home, and decide how we're going to stop a demigod from waking up to take over corporate America. We know that Violet's alive, so we do our best to figure out where the fuck they're stashing her."

"Or if they've sold her already." I stared at the table, tapping it nervously with my nails. "Trouble is, Radcliffe isn't the worst menace we're facing."

And on that sober thought, we ate cookies.

Chapter 19

Ivana had picked up her meat by the time we got home. We trooped in the house, dropping our stuff on the bench in the hallway. Morio was sitting on the sofa, sorting through a bunch of papers. He glanced up as we filed into the living room. Shade was leafing through a book, Chase was sitting in the rocking chair, holding Astrid, and Vanzir was playing with Maggie on the floor.

The scene looked so peaceful and quiet that it was hard to believe that we were back in the fray. But neck deep, we were. Vanzir had filled Morio and Shade in on the day's events.

"How could anything get this convoluted, this fast?" I grimaced. "Three and a half days ago everything was on an even keel. Now? We have demons on the left, daemons on the right, and sorcerers in the middle. We're sinking fast, Captain, and I don't think we have a bucket large enough to bail us out of this situation."

Shade shook his head. "I don't know, Matey, but the universe is like that. So what do we do next?"

Camille and I consulted our lists.

"Well," I said, looking over our notes. "All we have to do is discover how far Lowestar Radcliffe's reach extends, and see if we can to find Violet. At least we know she's alive, but we have to move on this and move quickly before he sells her out from under us yet. Tanne Baum will get back to us—he's going to try some ritual to see if he can locate her or find out more information about where she's being kept."

"We need to research Suvika; figure out what his powers—and vulnerabilities—are, and hopefully how to stop Lowestar from waking him up." Camille slid onto the sofa next to Morio.

"Oh," I added. "Also—we still don't know if there are any vamps missing from the Wayfarer fire, and we have to start talking rebuilding."

Camille sighed. "I need to take Violet's journal to Aeval to see if she can translate it. And we haven't contacted Aunt Rythwar yet to tell her about Father. The Keraastar Knights are still missing. Sorcerers are marching on Svartalfheim and overrunning Elqaneve."

"And let us not forget, Shade's sister is visiting in a few days. I think that about sums it up, don't you, Camille?" I gave her a helpless look and she nodded.

"In other words, life as usual." Chase attempted a joke but it fell flat, and he sighed. "I miss Sharah. I know I should be thinking about how she's doing her duty, how she's being selfless and leading her people in a gods-forsaken battle, but damn it, I miss her. She should be here with her baby. Or they should have let her take Astrid with her, even if they wouldn't allow me to go along." He nuzzled his daughter and kissed her lightly on the forehead.

I pulled a chair up next to his. "I know it's not going to be easy, Chase, but life never makes that a package guarantee, you know. But you have your daughter, and you know Sharah loves both of you. And . . . you can keep Astrid safer than Sharah can right now."

He shrugged, but a shy smile crept over his face. "Iris is

wonderful. I can't believe she took us in, and her with two babies of her own. They are cute munchkins, aren't they? And she seems so sure of their place in the world. I wish I could see a safe future for Astrid. But when I try to look ahead, it's all . . . just a blur of what might be."

"That's because your abilities don't seem to include prognostication. But Chase, you have other gifts. And they will come out the more time goes on. You can help make the future safe for Astrid." Camille stretched out her legs and stared at her shoes. "I am thinking, even though it's barely near dinner, of crawling into a nightgown and hanging it up for the day." After a moment, she whispered. "I miss Smoky and Trillian."

Morio set down the papers and wrapped his arm around her. "So do I, love, but they will return safe to us."

I glanced at the clock. "Menolly should be up at any moment—"

"Beat you to it, Kitten." Menolly entered the room. "Why so solemn? Who . . ." She stopped. "Bad joke, not even going there." At that moment, the doorbell rang. "I'll get it." In a minute she returned, an envelope in her hand. At my look, she shrugged. "For me. I have no idea who it's from—messenger delivered it."

As she opened it, the Whispering Mirror chimed and I motioned for Camille to stay put. "I'll answer it." I took my place in front of the mirror. "Delilah here."

"Fuck! This is a notice that I'm being sued by one of the victim's families! One of the FBH's families." Menolly let out a growl even as the fog lifted in the mirror.

I was facing Trenyth, who looked exhausted. I'd never seen him look so rough. "What's wrong?"

Camille and Menolly crowded in behind me.

"Girls, I'm glad you're here—Menolly, are you there too?"

"I am."

"I don't have much time. We are under siege and the fighting is rough. I wanted to let you know two things. One, you need to head to Grandmother Coyote's portal as soon as we finish talking. Trillian is on his way over with Luke and Amber, and Amber's baby. You need to keep them safe—along with the spirit seals. We don't dare let them stay in Otherworld at this point. You have to hide the seals there, and they cannot be removed from Luke or Amber at this point."

Camille paled. "How do we keep them safe here?"

"I don't know, figure out a way." He choked a little. "We lost Tam Lin to Trenyth's forces. Shadow Wing now has another spirit seal. Benjamin and Venus are still missing. Smoky and Rozurial are hunting for them like madmen."

I thought, quickly counting. "What about the seal we sent you from fighting Gulakah?"

"I'm sending it with Trillian. You must hide that, as well."

"Then . . . we have three seals. Two are missing, and Shadow Wing has three now. They've evened up the playing field, at our expense." The thought that Telazhar had managed to catch Tam Lin made me breathless. I could not imagine what torture they would put the man through. If he was lucky, they'd kill him outright and take the seal.

"And we still have one remaining undiscovered." Camille hung her head. "This is beyond nightmare status."

"What of the war?" Menolly rested her hands on my shoulders.

Trenyth pinched the bridge of his nose. "Camille, your vision was correct. The storm-creature has been spotted near Svartalfheim. I managed to get word to King Vodox and he is doing everything he can to protect the city. At least he wasn't caught unaware. His sorcerers are massing to fight against it. There will be fire raining from the skies before midnight."

A soldier appeared over his shoulder and whispered something in his ear. Trenyth nodded. "I must go—I . . . I have to go. Sharah is all right, please tell Chase she's safe for now. And that her people rally to her feet." And with that, the fog returned and the mirror fell silent.

We sat there for a moment, silent, digesting all the information, then Menolly grabbed her keys. "I'm heading to the portal. Delilah, bring your jeep. Camille, work with the others to figure out where the hell we're going to stash three spirit seals and two Keraastar Knights. Let's go."

Grandmother Coyote was waiting for us, and she led us back into her forest without a word. There, in the shadow of the trees, Trillian stood, along with Amber and Luke. Amber was holding her daughter, who was almost a year old. She hadn't been born when I last saw Amber, and I had no idea what she'd named the child. I hadn't been sure we'd ever see them again, and moved forward to give them a hug, but paused at the look in their eyes.

They'd changed. Whatever Asteria had been doing with them had changed them. They smiled, both of them, but the smile was distant and there was a sense of aloofness there, almost a feel of regality. They also looked somewhat shell-shocked, and they were covered with dirt and leaves and soot.

Trillian led them forward and I gave him a brief hug. He patted my back as he embraced me. "I'm sorry about Sephreh," he whispered. "I never wanted for that to happen, as much trouble as I had with the man."

"I know." I smiled sadly and nodded toward Amber and Luke. "How are they?"

"Rough. I'll tell you what we know once we're back at the house. How's my wife?"

"Missing you and Smoky. About as shaken as we all are. Let's get them home and figure out what to do in order to keep them safe." Menolly and I guided them back to our cars. Menolly drove Amber, Luke, and the baby, while Trillian rode with me. We didn't talk much. Trillian looked exhausted and the smell of smoke clinging to him reminded me too much of Camille's and my escape.

As we drove the short distance back to the house, I thought about what Chase had said—about not being able to see ahead. Right now, I was glad I didn't have the sight. Camille had helped Svartalfheim prepare for war, but I didn't envy her the horror of that knowledge burned into my thoughts. And what must it be like to be Grandmother Coyote, to see all the threads and balances? To have to balance out good with evil, light with shadow? To deliberately weave discord into the web? Somehow, being an assassin for the gods—reaping the souls of the dead—seemed easier.

Camille and the others were waiting, along with Nerissa who had gotten home from work, and Shamas.

Amber and Luke didn't say much, they seemed uncomfortable and so very changed. Menolly shook her head at me when I tried to talk to them, and I left my questions unasked.

"We thought for tonight at least, we can keep them in your lair? Nerissa can sleep upstairs tonight. Hell, the safe room still has to be standing at the Wayfarer—it was built to survive just about any disaster. But now, I think it would be too easy to access. I'm worried about the portal down there in the rubble of the basement, too." Camille glanced over at Menolly. "I know it's a sore subject, but we can't tiptoe around it. Not with everything that's happening."

"It's all right, Camille." Menolly shrugged. "My bar was torched, eight people died, and I'm being sued. But compared to what's going on back home right now? Kind of puts things into perspective. As for the portal, Tavah is keeping an eye on it for us. She's stationed herself down there. I doubt if anybody's going to mess with a vampire hiding out in the dark ruins of a basement."

"I had a thought." Camille glanced at us. "But I need to talk to Smoky. What if we take the Keraastar Knights to the Dragon Reaches? They owe me one, and they promised to help in our war against the demons. Smoky's mother—Vishana—would do what she could to help us, too. Perhaps they can stay at Smoky's family home."

"That's a brilliant idea." I smiled. It felt like we'd caught a break for the first time since our trip to Elqaneve. "How can we get in touch with him?"

"I'll call through the Whispering Mirror tomorrow and talk to Smoky. But for tonight, Luke and Amber should be safe here. Menolly, you and Nerissa want to take them below and make them comfortable? The baby . . . we'd better not separate her from her mother." Camille turned to Hanna, who was home and bustling around. "Can you make dinner now? Something easy—spaghetti or a casserole."

Hanna nodded and hustled toward the kitchen.

Trillian yawned. "I'm exhausted. I'm going to take a shower and get some clean clothes on, then I'll tell you over dinner what we found when we went out hunting for the Knights." He headed upstairs. Camille looked like she wanted to go with him, but instead, she stayed with us.

"If Shadow Wing has three of the spirit seals, we know he's going to use them together. They may not be able to break through all the portals here, not with just three, but the power compounds with each one. We're in for a world of hurt, I think. And you know he's going to send somebody new through sooner than later." I kicked the ottoman.

"At least the daemons and demons don't like each other. Which means, though we're fighting on two fronts, Lowestar won't be likely to join up with Shadow Wing. He's got too much invested here Earthside to want to destroy it."

Vanzir shrugged. "Trytian doesn't like Lowestar either, for what it's worth. He's offered an olive branch—well, as much as he can. He'll give us whatever information he finds on Radcliffe and his cronies. Because you know if there's one daemon over here praying to Suvika, there have to be more."

I picked up the letter Menolly had dropped on the table. Sure enough, it was a notification for a lawsuit. "We have to find a lawyer. Anybody know any good Supe lawyers?"

Chase nodded. "I do, actually. I've talked to several of them over the years. Tomorrow, when I go into work, I'll get some names for Menolly." Astrid started to fuss. "She's hungry. I'm going to run her out to Iris's and I'll be back afterward. I think I'd better sit in on what's going on." With a little kiss on her forehead, he headed toward the kitchen, holding her like she was a fragile piece of crystal.

My phone rang and I moved to the side, out of the line of conversation, to answer it. It was Albert.

"We were just wondering if you've had any word on Violet yet?"

I could hear the concern in his voice, but there was no way I could tell him what we suspected. "We have some leads, but it's going to take a while. Meanwhile, Albert, you'd better take good care of her cat for her, please. I don't think . . . we don't think . . . Violet went off on her own voluntarily."

A thought struck me. "Listen, can you discreetly—and I do mean discreetly—ask around. See if any other Fae women went missing? Or Supes or . . . just put your ear to the grapevine to see if you catch news of any other missing persons, especially among women."

"That doesn't sound good."

"It isn't. But right now, I can't tell you any more than that. Except—you and Tad, don't you go poking around. This is bigger than you think, and dangerous, and we need you guys to mind your manners and leave the detective work to us or you could endanger a lot of lives. Do you understand?" Perhaps it was pouring gasoline onto fire, but I had to make certain they understood that this wasn't a Hardy Boys mystery where they could run out and play detective.

After a pause, Albert answered. "I get it. I'm not sure what's going on, but I get it. We'll keep our noses out of it, and I'll take care of Tumpkins. Please though, if you can, save Violet. I know what monsters are lurking out there in the night." A hush, then, "I *am* one of the monsters."

My heart went out to the programmer. "No, Albert. Vampire or not, you're one of the good guys. So is Tad, and so is my sister Menolly. To be a monster—that begins in the heart. It's a choice."

But even as I said good-bye and put my phone away, a little voice inside whispered, "No, Delilah. There is evil in the world, and you are facing it every day. There are monsters who come from the depths, who live in anger and hatred and desire . . . and they are born to it."

"What you thinking, fuzz bucket?" Vanzir tweaked my

elbow, and I shook myself out of the dark reverie into which I'd slipped.

I stared at the dream-chaser demon. He'd been born to evil, and he'd made a choice. He'd chosen to stand on our side, to fight the menace. Was he good? Probably not. But he'd chosen to turn his back on a greater evil. Life was full of all shades between black and white.

With a sigh, I flashed him a faint smile. "I don't know. Good. Evil. Choices. It sounds like Hanna has dinner on, and here comes Trillian. Let's go eat." And with that, we all headed into the kitchen, to our own war council.

Trillian gobbled up the macaroni and cheese like he was starving. Along with the meat loaf, salad, and cherry pie, it was a full dinner and perfect on the drizzly October night.

"Kelvashan is destroyed. I have no idea of how many elves were killed, but the land is decimated. Almost all the villages are gone, and goblins swarm the lands. On the plus side, Tanaquar's warriors are numerous, and there are armies on the march from Svartalfheim, Dahnsburg, Nebulveori, and the Moon Mother's grove. Ceredream is holding its hand yet, which is not going over well among the northern lands. But we shall see. They're probably worried because they are an easy target from the Southern Wastes, and it's known that the sorcerers are based there."

He glanced over at Camille and me. "I have no idea how you escaped the destruction of the palace, but when I saw what was left, my heart was in my throat. You are lucky and cunning."

"We would have been trapped if it hadn't been for the unicorn horn," Camille said. "We couldn't get those doors open."

Trillian shook his head. "Well, the palace is obliterated. Sharah and Trenyth have their headquarters set up in a secret location and they put me under a geas. I couldn't tell you where it is, if I wanted to. The Knights were scattered, of course. I managed to find Amber and her child on the outskirts of the city, hiding in the woods. Luke was nearby."

"What about Tam Lin? Trenyth said he was captured?" Morio stabbed a piece of meatloaf with his fork.

"Rozurial was on the trail of Tam Lin when he saw a brigade of goblins swoop in and cart him away. They knew who they had, I'll tell you that, because they didn't hurt a hair on his head, even when he somehow managed to kill a good six or seven of them." Trillian stared at his plate.

"How did he do that?" Shade handed me the salad and I passed it over to Chase, who gave me a soft smile.

"Roz said there was some sort of blinding light . . . it came from the spirit seal. When it cleared, several of the goblins lay dead. But there were too many, and they overwhelmed poor Tom. I wish him a speedy death, because being carted before Shadow Wing?" Trillian shuddered.

The thought of poor Tom, as broken as he was, being dragged before the Demon Lord was more than any of us could handle. I could see it round the table, crossing everyone's face.

I spoke to break the silence. "You say Smoky and Roz are still hunting for Venus the Moonchild and Benjamin?"

Trillian nodded. "Yes."

"Venus is crafty and he's a shaman. Chances are, if anybody makes it out of there, he will. If Ben happens to be with him, so much the better." I sent a silent prayer to Bastus that my old friend, the former shaman of the Rainier Puma Pride, had made it safe. "One thing is for sure, if the goblins catch Venus, he'll take them down as hard as he can before he gives up the ghost."

We filled Trillian in on what had been happening with us as the evening wore on. Nobody wanted to leave the table—it was too safe, too homey, and for a brief moment, it felt like we could rest.

But as dinner came to an end, a terrific gust of wind passed over the house and the sound of breaking branches hit the roof.

Trillian wiped his mouth and stood. "Sounds like it's

brewing up a storm out there. I'll go and make sure there was no damage to the roof."

"I'll help." Morio followed him out.

Hanna began to clear the table and Nerissa jumped up to assist her.

Chase stood and yawned. "I guess I'll head back to Iris's and hit the hay early. I'm exhausted and we've all got a long day tomorrow."

Camille brewed a pot of tea while waiting for Morio and Trillian to return, and Menolly headed downstairs to keep Amber and Luke company. Shade and I said good night and wearily made our way upstairs.

Tomorrow, we'd have to start sorting out the pieces. Tomorrow, we'd face the mess we were mired in and figure out some way to deal with all of it. But tonight . . . tonight was for healing and resting, and hopefully, for peaceful dreams.

Chapter 20

❧❦❧

Shade closed the door behind us and turned on the music. As the strains of Leonard Cohen's "I'm Your Man" filtered through the room, we looked at each other. What could we say? So much had happened in the past few days, yet here we were, in a brief lull, not knowing how long the fragile moment would last.

He held out his arms and I slipped into them, leaning softly against his chest. He kissed my cheeks, brushing away stray wisps of my bangs. I caught my breath as his lips trailed down my face, softly pressing against my own. Melting into his arms, I inhaled deeply, the warm scent of his musk firing my hunger.

In silence, I reached down to unbuckle his belt. He held up one hand, and motioned for me to raise my arms. As I did, he lifted my shirt over my head, then softly turned me around to unhook my bra. His arms slid around my waist and he reached up to cup my breasts, breathing gently against my neck. I shivered at his touch, wanting him to throw me down, take me hard, make me forget the sorrow and tears and death that surrounded us.

Slowly, I pressed back against him, as he fingered my nipples, bringing them to attention. With a long breath, I unzipped my jeans and shoved them down, using my feet to kick them off. He slid his hands down from my breasts to slip his fingers under the sides of my panties, and with a smooth gesture, pushed them down my hips. Still with his arms around me, he traced his way across my stomach, his fingers tickling as he brought them down to finger my clit. I moaned gently, moving in rhythm to the music as he began to stroke me, circling softly at first, then harder as he picked up the pace.

I squirmed, letting out a loud groan, but still he moved with precision, not hurrying, not letting me hurry him. I could feel his erect cock through his pants, pressing against my back, and all I could think about was how much I wanted him inside me, filling me up, thrusting deep to take me out of my head.

"Shade—" I started to say but he shushed me.

"Quiet. Let me do this." Abruptly, he turned me to face him, and slid his arms around my waist and began to dance with me, his knee pushing between mine as we moved to the sultry music. I laughed, suddenly, and kicked off the panties from where they'd fallen to my feet.

"I want to feel your chest," I whispered, tugging at his shirt.

Still grinding against me, he let go and quickly divested himself of his shirt, then his arms were right back around my waist. I pressed my breasts against his bare chest, the coffee of his skin warm against my paleness. Draping my arms around his neck, I pressed my lips to his, my tongue dancing with his. We kissed, slow and long and deep, the fire kindling between us.

Shade chuckled, one hand caressing my lower back as he cupped my butt with the other. "Oh Delilah, you are ripe on the vine. You are my puss in heat."

I let out a little growl, playfully nipping him on the nose.

"What are you going to do about it? Going to scratch my itch? Going to give me a taste of what you have under those pants?"

"You want it, babe? You want it hard and fast?"

"Hard, fast, and deep." And the energy shifted again, from playful to serious as I pulled away, crooking my finger as I backed up to the bed. "Come get me if you want me."

He unbuckled his belt and slid it out from the loops, then stripped out of his pants. He was glorious, dark and rich skin shimmering in the dim light. I gazed at his cock, hungry and licking my lips.

Responding to my challenge, he strode over, grabbing me up and tossing me on the bed. The next moment, he landed between my legs, his lips fastening around one nipple to tease and nip at me. I let out a little cry as he lowered his lips to between my legs, and the next moment, he was licking me, his tongue creating delicious swirls. I could barely catch my breath as he continued, unrelenting, until I couldn't think, couldn't feel anything but the pulse of his tongue driving me higher. Panting, I let out a choked cry as I came, hard and sharp, and tears began to run down my face as the stress of the past few days let go in one long wave of release.

Shade immediately rose up to thrust his cock deep inside me, and I wrapped my legs around his back, rocking with him as we drove the demons into the night, pushing them away with our passion.

And, in the midst of death and destruction, there was this: the stroke of his cock, inside me, creating the union that made all the pain and worry worth it. As he came, I let go and, once again, tumbled into the minor death that is orgasm. And there, watching over both of us, stood my lord Hi'ran, Elemental Lord of the Harvest, the fire of passion crackling between the three of us even as the fires of war raged on in my homeworld.

CAST OF MAJOR CHARACTERS

The D'Artigo Family

Arial Lianan te Maria: Delilah's twin who died at birth. Half-Fae, half-human.

Camille Sepharial te Maria, aka Camille D'Artigo: The oldest sister; a Moon Witch and Priestess. Half-Fae, half-human.

Daniel George Fredericks: The D'Artigo sisters' half cousin; FBH.

Delilah Maria te Maria, aka Delilah D'Artigo: The middle sister; a werecat.

Hester Lou Fredericks: The D'Artigo sisters' half cousin; FBH.

Maria D'Artigo: The D'Artigo Sisters' mother. Human. Deceased.

Menolly Rosabelle te Maria, aka Menolly D'Artigo: The youngest sister; a vampire and jian-tu: extraordinary acrobat. Half-Fae, half-human.

Sephreh ob Tanu: The D'Artigo Sisters' father. Full Fae. Assumed deceased.

Shamas ob Olanda: The D'Artigo girls' cousin. Full Fae.

The D'Artigo Sisters' Lovers & Close Friends

Astrid (Johnson): Chase and Sharah's baby daughter.

Bruce O'Shea: Iris's husband. Leprechaun.

Carter: Leader of the Demonica Vacana Society, a group that watches and records the interactions of Demonkin and human through the ages. Carter is half demon and half Titan—his father was Hyperion, one of the Greek Titans.

Chase Garden Johnson: Detective, director of the Faerie-Human Crime Scene Investigation (FH-CSI) team. Human who has taken the Nectar of Life, which extends his life-span beyond any ordinary mortal, and has opened up his psychic abilities.

Chrysandra: Waitress at the Wayfarer Bar & Grill. Human. Deceased.

Derrick Means: Bartender at the Wayfarer Bar & Grill. Werebadger.

Erin Mathews: Former president of the Faerie Watchers Club and former owner of the Scarlet Harlot Boutique. Turned into a vampire by Menolly, her sire, moments before her death. Human.

Greta: Leader of the Death Maidens; Delilah's tutor.

Iris (Kuusi) O'Shea: Friend and companion of the girls. Priestess of Undutar. Talon-haltija (Finnish house sprite).

Lindsey Katharine Cartridge: Director of the Green Goddess Women's Shelter. Pagan and witch. Human.

Luke: Former bartender at the Wayfarer Bar & Grill. Werewolf. One of the Keraastar Knights.

Maria O'Shea: Iris and Bruce's baby daughter.

Marion Vespa: Coyote shifter; owner of the Supe-Urban Café.

Morio Kuroyama: One of Camille's lovers and husbands. Essentially the grandson of Grandmother Coyote. Youkai-kitsune (roughly translated: Japanese fox demon).

Neely Reed: Founding Member of the United Worlds Church. FBH.

Nerissa Shale: Menolly's wife. Worked for DSHS. Now working for Chase Johnson as a victims-rights counselor for the FH-CSI. Werepuma and member of the Rainier Puma Pride.

Roman: Ancient vampire; son of Blood Wyne, Queen of the Crimson Veil. Menolly's official consort in the Vampire Nation and her new sire.

Rozurial, aka Roz: Mercenary. Menolly's secondary lover. Incubus who used to be Fae before Zeus and Hera destroyed his marriage.

Shade: Delilah's fiancé. Part Stradolan, part black (shadow) dragon.

Sharah: Elfin medic; Chase's girlfriend.

Siobhan Morgan: One of the girls' friends. Selkie (wereseal); member of the Puget Sound Harbor Seal Pod.

Smoky: One of Camille's lovers and husbands. Half-white, half-silver dragon.

Tavah: Guardian of the portal at the Wayfarer Bar & Grill. Vampire (full Fae).

Tim Winthrop, aka Cleo Blanco: Computer student/ genius, female impersonator. FBH. Now owns the Scarlet Harlot.

Trillian: Mercenary. Camille's alpha lover and one of her three husbands. Svartan (one of the Charming Fae).

Ukkonen O'Shea: Iris and Bruce's baby son.

Vanzir: Was indentured slave to the Sisters, by his own choice. Dream-chaser demon who lost his powers and now is regaining new ones.

Venus the Moon Child: Former shaman of the Rainier Puma Pride. Werepuma. One of the Keraastar Knights.

Wade Stevens: President of Vampires Anonymous. Vampire (human).

Zachary Lyonnesse: Former member of the Rainier Puma Pride Council of Elders. Werepuma living in Otherworld.

GLOSSARY

Black Unicorn/Black Beast: Father of the Dahns unicorns, a magical unicorn that is reborn like the phoenix and lives in Darkynwyrd and Thistlewyd Deep. Raven Mother is his consort, and he is more a force of nature than a unicorn.

Calouk: The rough, common dialect used by a number of Otherworld inhabitants.

Court and Crown: "Crown" refers to the Queen of Y'Elestrial. "Court" refers to the nobility and military personnel that surround the Queen. "Court and Crown" together refer to the entire government of Y'Elestrial.

Court of the Three Queens: The newly risen Court of the three Earthside Fae Queens: Titania, the Fae Queen of Light and Morning; Morgaine, the half-Fae Queen of Dusk and Twilight; and Aeval, the Fae Queen of Shadow and Night.

Crypto: One of the Cryptozoid races. Cryptos include creatures out of legend that are not technically of the Fae races: gargoyles, unicorns, gryphons, chimeras, and so on. Most primarily inhabit Otherworld, but some have Earthside cousins.

Demon Gate: A gate through which demons may be summoned by a powerful sorcerer or necromancer.

Dreyerie: A dragon lair.

Earthside: Everything that exists on the Earth side of the portals.

Elemental Lords: The elemental beings—both male and female—who, along with the Hags of Fate and the Harvestmen, are the only true Immortals. They are avatars of various elements and energies, and they inhabit all realms. They do as they will and seldom concern themselves with humankind or Fae unless summoned. If asked for help, they often exact steep prices in return. The Elemental Lords are not concerned with balance like the Hags of Fate.

Elqaneve: The court city of Kelvashan—the Elfin lands in Otherworld.

FBH: Full-Blooded Human (usually refers to Earthside humans).

FH-CSI: The Faerie-Human Crime Scene Investigation team. The brainchild of Detective Chase Johnson, it was first formed as a collaboration between the OIA and the Seattle police department. Other FH-CSI units have been created around the country, based on the Seattle prototype. The FH-CSI takes care of both medical and criminal emergencies involving visitors from Otherworld.

Great Divide: A time of immense turmoil when the Elemental Lords and some of the High Court of Fae decided to rip apart the worlds. Until then, the Fae existed primarily on Earth, their lives and worlds mingling with those of humans. The Great Divide tore everything asunder, splitting off another dimension, which became Otherworld. At that time, the Twin Courts of Fae were disbanded and their queens stripped of power. This was the time during which the Spirit Seal was formed and broken in order to seal off the realms from each other. Some Fae chose to stay Earthside, others moved to the realm of Otherworld, and the demons were—for the most part—sealed in the Subterranean Realms.

Guard Des'Estar: The military of Y'Elestrial.

Hags of Fates: The women of destiny who keep the balance righted. Neither good nor evil, they observe the flow of destiny. When events get too far out of balance, they step in and take action, usually using humans, Fae, Supes, and other creatures as pawns to bring the path of destiny back into line.

Triple Threat: Camille's nickname for the newly risen three Earthside Queens of Fae.

Unseelie Court: The Earthside Fae Court of Shadow and Winter, disbanded during the Great Divide. Aeval was the Unseelie Queen.

VA/Vampires Anonymous: The Earthside group started by Wade Stevens, a vampire who was a psychiatrist during life. The group is focused on helping newly born vampires adjust to their new state of existence, and to encourage vampires to avoid harming the innocent as much as possible. The VA is vying for control. Their goal is to rule the vampires of the United States and to set up an internal policing agency.

Whispering Mirror: A magical communications device that links Otherworld and Earth. Think magical video phone.

Y'Eírialiastar: The Sidhe/Fae name for Otherworld.

Y'Elestrial: The city-state in Otherworld where the D'Artigo girls were born and raised. A Fae city, recently embroiled in a civil war between the drug-crazed tyrannical Queen Lethesanar and her more level-headed sister Tanaquar, who managed to claim the throne for herself. The civil war has ended and Tanaquar is restoring order to the land.

Youkai: Loosely (very loosely) translated as Japanese demon/nature spirit. For the purposes of this series, the youkai have three shapes: the animal, the human form, and the true demon form. Unlike the demons of the Subterranean Realms, youkai are not necessarily evil by nature.

PLAYLIST FOR *AUTUMN WHISPERS*

I write to music a good share of the time, and so I always put my playlists in the back of each book so you can see which artists/songs I listened to during the writing. Here's the playlist for *Autumn Whispers*:

A.J. Roach: "Devil May Dance"

Adele: "Rumour Has It"

Air: "Napalm Love; Playground Love"

Al Stewart: "Life in Dark Water"

Alice Cooper: "Welcome to My Nightmare"

Android Lust: "Saint Over," "God in the Hole," "In the Arms of the Heretic," "Here and Now," "When the Rains Came," "Vereor," "I Need to Know"

Asteroids Galaxy Tour: "Lady Jesus," The Sun Ain't Shining No More," "Sunshine Coolin'"

Awolnation: "Sail"

Beck: "Que Onda Guero," "Hell Yes," "Black Tambourine," "Elevator Music"

Black Mountain: "Angels"

Blue Oyster Cult: "The Reaper"

The Bravery: "Believe"

Broken Bells: "The High Road," "Your Head Is On Fire," "The Ghost Inside," "October"

Cream: "Sunshine of Your Love"

Creedence Clearwater Revival: "Run Through the Jungle"

David Bowie: "Golden Years," "I'm Afraid of Americans," "Without You"

Dizzi: "Dizzi Jig"

Don Henley: "Dirty Laundry"

Dragon Ritual Drummers: "The Fall"

Eastern Sun: "Beautiful Being"

Eels: "Souljacker Part 1"

Everlast: "Black Jesus," "Ends," "What It's Like"

Foster the People: "Pumped Up Kicks"

Gary Numan: "Petals," "Sleep By Windows," "Hunger," "I Can't Stop," "My Dying Machine"

Gorillaz: "Kids With Guns," "Clint Eastwood," "Feel Good, Inc.," "Stylo"

Gotye: "Somebody That I Used To Know"

Hanni El Khatib: "Come Alive"

Heart: "Magic Man"

Julian Cope: "Charlotte Anne"

Lady Gaga: "Paparazzi," "Born This Way," "Teeth"

Ladytron: "Black Cat," "Predict the Day"

Leonard Cohen: "I'm Your Man"

Lindstøm and Christabelle: "Lovesick"

Lou Reed: "Walk On the Wild Side"

Mark Lanegan: "Bleeding Muddy Water," "Riot In My House," "Phantasmagoria Blues," "Wedding Dress, "Methamphetamine Blues," "Like Little Willie John," "Riding the Nightingale," "Miracle"

Neil Young: "Cinnamon Girl"

Nick Cave & the Bad Seeds: "Red Right Hand"

Nirvana: "Come As You Are," "Lake of Fire"

Offspring: "Come Out and Play"

Pearl Jam: "Jeremy"

Radiohead: "Creep"

Screaming Trees: "All I Know," "Dime Western"

Soundgarden: "Superunknown"

Suzanne Vega: "99.9F," "Blood Makes Noise," "In My Movie," "Solitude Standing," "Straight Lines"

Talking Heads: "Burning Down the House," "Life During Wartime," "Take Me to the River," "Girlfriend Is Better"

Tangerine Dream: "Grind," "Burning Bar," "Dr. Destructo," "Gaudi Park," "Three Bikes in the Sky"

U2: "Elevation," "Vertigo"

Zero 7: "In the Waiting Line"

Dear Reader:

I truly hope you enjoyed Autumn Whispers, *book fourteen of the Otherworld Series. I love writing this world, it develops and grows with each book, and I see so many possibilities ahead for the D'Artigo sisters. This book expanded the war to a huge degree, and much of what was started here will play out over the next several books in the series. The next book in this series will be* Crimson Veil, *book fifteen, coming February 2014. And so, I'm including the first chapter here, to give you a taste of what's coming up for Menolly and her sisters.*

For those of you new to my books, I hope you've enjoyed your first foray into my worlds. For those of you who have followed me for a while, I want to thank you for once again revisiting the world of Camille, Menolly, and Delilah.

Bright Blessings,
The Painted Panther
Yasmine Galenorn

The sky was clear for once, though rain was forecast before morning. The moon glimmered, her faint sliver shining down over the cemetery. Soon she would be new, dark, and hiding her face. A steady flurry of gusts rocked the trees, the silhouettes of their boughs shaking like tall sentinels sounding the alarm. It was the perfect night for a funeral. A funeral none of us wanted to be at.

We were gathered at the Seryph Point Cemetery, around the open grave. A small group we were, not many there to send off our friend to the afterlife. There was me, Menolly, and my wife, Nerissa. My sisters Camille and Delilah stood beside us. Derrick Means was there—my bartender. And Tavah, Digger, and Kendra—all from the Wayfarer. Chase had joined us, as did Mallen. We had asked our men to stay home, to watch over the house. As I said, we were just a small group, but everyone here had cared, everyone was here because they wanted to be.

Chrysandra's casket rested in front of us, over the grave on the lowering device. Her body would fade back to the earth, even as we consigned her soul to the long nights of eternity. At the service—which we'd held in our house—Morio and Shade had worked their magic to seal her body in her grave. Nothing save the most powerful necromancer could ever raise Chrysandra's remains. She'd be free from the threat of being turned to a zombie. She'd never come back as one of the undead. Her soul was long gone and her body would be free to undergo its natural breakdown, undisturbed from the machinations of sorcery.

We had said our good-byes at the house. We had bid her farewell. Now we were here simply to stand witness to the final act. To the last chapter in our friend's life. Chrysandra Reece had been a waitress at the Wayfarer since I first came Earthside. She'd stayed on as I moved from bartender to owner. She'd helped me out, done her job and then some. But Chrysandra had been a private person. We still knew nothing of her family. It was like she'd left every trace of her past behind her, put it in a safe box and buried it somewhere to keep it hidden. Even now, in death, all we had left of her were these—her mortal remains.

I'd gone through her effects, helped Chase clear out her apartment after the fire that had destroyed my bar and the lives of eight people caught in the flames, including Chrysandra. We'd torn the place apart, but there had been nothing to indicate that she'd had any life before she first came to the bar. I was beginning to suspect she'd been in the Witness Protection Program, but if so, they seem to have left her unsupervised. Whatever the case, Chrysandra had died as she had lived—a private person, a loyal employee, and a woman I considered my friend.

As Gage, the funeral tech, lowered the casket into the ground, I closed my eyes. I'd cried myself out. I'd cried when I realized she was dying, in such horrible pain that she couldn't even scream at the hospital. I'd cried as I sucked the life out of her burned and crisped body, ending that pain. And I'd cried till my bloody tears left irremovable stains on my sheets. Now, the tears were gone, and I just wanted to find the arsonist responsible for Chrysandra's death, and the deaths of the others who had perished in the flames.

Gage glanced at me. He might as well be nameless and faceless, for all I knew him, though I knew he was a werewolf. He worked for the funeral home where we'd made Chrysandra's arrangements. We'd limited our transactions with them to buying her casket and paying for her care. She had told me once she wanted to be buried in a simple pine box, unprotected from the elements. She didn't want her body to outlast time. So we'd ordered a hand-carved coffin that was untreated, that would give her up to the earth as it broke down. We'd arranged for Gage to be there, to lower the casket, but we'd taken care of the service ourselves. The funeral director was a Supe, and he understood. He didn't try to push us into buying an armored casket that would last forever.

Silence hung heavy, like fog soup, as we watched the casket descend into the waiting grave. Delilah and Nerissa tossed roses on it. Derrick stared straight ahead, trying not to let anything crack his gruff demeanor, but I knew the werebadger was taking it hard. He and Chrysandra had gotten on, and I suspected they'd been on their way to a romance.

Tavah and Digger might be vampires, but they had also been friends, and now watched the proceedings bleakly. Camille stepped forward and gave me a nod. I took hold of her hand as we recited our prayer for the dead.

"What was life has crumbled. What was form, now falls away. Mortal chains unbind and the soul is lifted free. May you find your way to the ancestors. May you find your path to the gods. May your bravery and courage be remembered in song and story. May your parents be proud, and may your children carry your birthright. Sleep, and wander no more."

The words echoed in the night, punctuated only by the sound of the casket as it disappeared from sight. We stepped back and formed a circle around the grave, holding hands. And then, as a cloud passed over the face of the

moon, Gage pushed the button on the portable stereo, and
"Shuffle Your Feet," by the Black Rebel Motorcycle Club,
echoed into the night. It was Chrysandra's favorite song,
and it was the last time it would ever play for her in this
world.

I recognized the strains of the Stone Temple Pilots echoing
out from the crowded club. As much as I'd wanted to hole
up with my sisters and wife at home after the funeral, I had
an appointment to keep. Roman was waiting for me, and
with what had gone on this past week, there would be no
downtime for any of us—not for the foreseeable future.

As I threaded my way through the room, the scent of
blood hung heavy in the air. The Utopia was a new vampire
club. Shikra, the owner, managed to keep on the right side
of the Roman's rules, albeit by a narrow margin, so all was
good. No bloodwhores on the premises, but contracted private pets were allowed, and feeding on them was accept-
able. I still was squicked out by the thought of owning
someone just to drink off of them, but since the contract
was a two-way street and nobody was here against their
will, I couldn't very well impose my morals on the vamps
frequenting the joint. Hell, *I* fed on people—although they
were the dregs of society. Life was full of gray areas, and
black and white had ceased to exist for me the day Dredge
took my life and turned me.

Roman was waiting for me, looking gorgeous as usual.
He was wearing black leather pants, a shirt open to the
naval, and a burgundy smoking jacket. His long dark hair
was pulled back in a smooth ponytail, and his eyes were
almost frosted over, he'd been a vampire so long.

The Lord of the Vampire Nation, son of Blood Wyne—
the queen of vampires—Roman had chosen me for his official consort, and he had also re-sired me, taking over as my
sire to break a blood bond of which I had needed to divest
myself. So, while I was married to Nerissa and in love with
her, I was bound to Roman in an unbreakable fashion. And

to be honest, I didn't mind so much. He was ancient and dangerous, but seductive and passionate and though I didn't love him, I was able to fully be myself with him.

He stood as I approached, holding out one hand. I took his fingers lightly as he guided me to the booth. Every move he made was smooth and deliberate. Roman did nothing lightly, nothing without a reason.

"Menolly, love. Sit."

He used the word casually, but every time it still set off an uneasy feeling. I'd warned Roman not to fall in love with me—I could sleep with him but I couldn't return his love. Nerissa held my heart, and I held hers.

Roman motioned to the waitress. Only vamps worked at the Utopia; it was too dangerous to have living, breathing staff at a vamp club. But the fang girls and boys were out in droves tonight—FBHs who wanted to walk on the wild side. Full-blood humans here—Earthside—loved vampires as much as they feared us, just like they loved the Fae. We were all dangerous and held the promise of sex and passion, with an intensity that was sadly lacking in a lot of peoples' lives.

"Two bottles of your best, warm." Roman normally disdained bottled blood, but when we were out together, he drank it to appease me. I objected to his bringing members of his stable along on our dates. It wasn't that the other women bothered me—in fact, I wanted him to focus on other women. It was the whole bloodwhores thing again.

I slid into the booth, leaning my head back and closing my eyes for a moment. The silence of my pulse, the silence of my body echoed through me. I had gotten used to having no breath over the years, but there were times I missed the involuntary sigh, the rush of air flowing out as I let go of the stress.

"Was it so hard?" Roman's voice brought me back to the present.

I opened my eyes and gazed at him. "Rough enough."

He gave me a little nod. "I've seen so many people die over the centuries, so I suppose I'm used to it. But each

time a friend vanishes into time, into the past, it still hurts."
With a soft murmur, he reached out and stroked my face,
leaning in for a gentle kiss. "Poor Menolly . . . it has been a
harsh week for you."

I stared at the table. Harsh was an understatement. My
bar had burned down and eight people had died in the fire.
We were trying to break a daemon-run white-slavery ring
specializing in Supes, but were having a hard time figuring
out *how*. We'd just met relatives of our mother's, blood relatives at that, and had no clue how they were going to figure
into our lives.

And that wasn't the half of it. Back in Otherworld, the
Elfin city—Elqaneve—had been destroyed by the sorcerers and we'd been there for the direct hit. Delilah and
Camille had struggled to make it out of the war zone. I
counted myself lucky that I'd been trapped and rescued
without having to run the gauntlet of fire and destruction
that the sentient storm that had rained down on the Elfin
City. And now, Queen Asteria was dead, our father was
missing and presumed dead, and the spirit seals were in
jeopardy.

"Yeah, harsh is the word for it, all right. So, did you
draw up a list?"

The waitress brought our blood. It was bottled like beer,
only the bottles were red to mask the color for squeamish
bar patrons, and to differentiate it from the alcoholic bever-
age. Couldn't have a mix-up.

I cradled the bottle in my hands, then took a long swig.
A wave of hunger ran through me as I tasted the blood. If
that hunger gnawed too much, I'd want to go out hunting,
and right now, I didn't have the heart for it. Too much
death, too much anger and fear running rampant in my life.

Roman pulled out his tablet. He'd gone high tech when
high tech was still a baby and his ease with the computer
world confounded me the more I saw it in action. I hadn't
known that little fact about him, not at first, but slowly had
begun to realize just how savvy he was.

He tapped an icon, then another, and a document sprang

up. As he scooted close to me, my skin tingled. He was old—one of the older vampires, son of the queen. And his very presence exuded a magnetism hard to ignore. It made me want to run my hands over his chest, to slam him down on the ground and tear into him, fucking his brains out. That was one thing about being Roman's consort—it gave me the outlet I couldn't have with Nerissa. Roman and I could play rough without hurting each other. In a way, it let me keep my love and passion for my wife safe and secure, keeping her safe from my inner predator.

"Later," he murmured, feeling it too. "We'll play very soon."

"Count on it." I gazed into his eyes, the crackle of energy almost palpable between us. But then, bringing myself back to the task at hand, I took the tablet from him and scanned the document.

We really had no clue how many vamps frequented the Wayfarer, but there were some known regulars who had loved hanging out there since I'd become Roman's official consort. And that list ran to over forty names. As I looked it over , I recognized a number of them. Roman had rushed to pull this together, putting his best men on it.

The names had been highlighted with two colors. Green meant the vampire had been accounted for. Yellow meant they were missing and nobody had been able to get in touch with them. Out of the forty-two names, thirteen were highlighted in yellow. Their last known contact was listed, as well.

I winced. That meant we potentially had thirteen more victims. "Can you sort these out from the others and e-mail them to my phone?" I'd given in and accepted that I needed an e-mail address, as much as I hadn't wanted to go that route. Delilah had embraced her laptop. Camille had embraced her iPhone. I hadn't fallen in love with either one yet, though I had to admit, I loved my iPod, especially since I could plug it into my car.

"Hand it over." He tapped away while I sipped the rest of my blood.

"Should I track them down?" I didn't relish the legwork.

It wasn't that I was lazy, but we had so much going on that tracking missing vamps who might already be dead seemed like a colossal time suck.

"I've already got my men on it." He punched one final button and I heard a little swoosh sound. The next moment, my phone pinged and the list was in my e-mail inbox.

I played with the bottle, sliding it around on the table. "Thanks. By the way, in addition to trying to figure out who burned down the Wayfarer—they're pretty sure it's arson by now—I have the lovely privilege of having been served with a lawsuit. Don't know if I told you that. Add yet another thing to the week-from-hell list."

"What are you talking about?" Roman set down his tablet.

"I'm being sued for wrongful death or some such crap. One of the victim's families wasted no time in snagging a lawyer and slapping me with a lawsuit. Makes me wonder just how much they actually gave a damn for their daughter." Feeling terribly grumpy, I reached in my purse and pulled out the summons I'd received the night before and tossed it on the table. "Lovely, huh?"

Roman silently opened it, scanned it through—he read incredibly fast and I guessed his intelligence to be genius level—and then thoughtfully folded it back up and set it on the table.

"Bullshit. I'll have my lawyer contact you and we'll put a stop to this folly." He shook his head. "Money grubbing bastards."

"Chase said he'd find me a lawyer—"

"Nonsense. I have the best money can buy. You are my consort. That's all there is to it." He frowned, worrying his lower lip with his fangs. Then he placed his hand over mine. "I want to talk to you about something—two things actually. First, I want to pay for the rebuilding of your establishment."

Roman, pay for rebuilding the Wayfarer? As much as I cared for him and was bound to him, I still didn't fully trust him. I knew that Camille and Delilah assumed that

I'd given myself fully over, and it was true, now that he was my sire I *had* to answer to him. But that didn't stop me from keeping my eyes open.

I shook my head. "Thank you, but no. Smoky and Shade have already offered and I've accepted. Dragons horde treasure beyond even ancient vamps. They want to do this and I'd like to let them." It was, I thought, the most tactful way around saying, *"Thanks, but I don't want you having a stake in my bar."* Of course, Roman was smart enough to know what I was up to, but decorum had been observed and I knew him well enough to figure he'd accept my wishes.

He just laughed. "I know what you're pulling. Fine, then. Refuse my help. But if you need it, all you have to do is ask. I truly do not have a hidden agenda in helping you, you know. But Menolly, *we'll find out who did this.* I promise you all the help I can give to finding out who torched your bar. And when we do . . . they'd better pray to whatever gods they follow."

His voice was soft, low, and curled around me, inviting me in. I leaned closer to him and he wrapped his arm around me, pressing his lips to mine. I leisurely let his tongue dart between my lips and returned the kiss, melting into his embrace. It was long and slow, without pressure. We both knew that tonight was a no-go and that I needed to head home, so we left it at that. But it stoked my fire, and I knew that once I reached home, I'd be dragging Nerissa down to our lair, to fuck her brains out.

Finally, I pulled away. "What's the other thing you wanted to ask me?"

He cocked his head, the frost of his eyes glittering. "It's about your daughter, Erin."

I'd turned exactly one person: Erin Mathews. Former owner of the Scarlet Harlot lingerie boutique, she'd been captured when my former sire came looking for me to finish the job he'd started. Erin was almost dead when we got to her, and I'd given her the option of letting me turn her into a vampire. Otherwise, she would have died. She'd chosen eternal life, and, just like that, I'd birthed a middle-aged daughter. Erin was smart, and she was learning quickly how to adapt.

"What about her?" Erin had been working as secretary for Vampires Anonymous, a self-help club for newly minted vamps. Run by a friend—Wade Stevens, a vampire and former psychologist who had taken it upon himself to help the newly turned—the VA provided a place where the undead could bridge the gap with their living family and friends and learn how to coexist without giving in to their inner predators.

"I want to take her out of the VA. She's got the nature I'm looking for. I'd like to train her for my security department. She could rise quickly in the ranks." The tone of Roman's voice told me that he wasn't going to give up on this one without a fight.

I thought about the offer. Truthfully, Erin would probably love it. She wanted to be useful. Erin wasn't a woman who was happy sitting around. She'd hated the inactivity that Sassy had forced on her when I had left her with the socialite vamp. Sassy Branson had been a dear friend, but her inner predator had finally won out. I'd had to take her out—a promise I'd made when she was still in control of herself.

Erin's job she had now made her happy, but I knew she was itching for more to do, and she had too much talent and know-how to waste.

"I'll stop on the way home and offer her the opportunity. If she's up for it, no problem. Might do her a lot of good. If not, then you'll let her be."

He nodded. "Fair enough."

I paused, then decided to approach a subject that had been bugging me for a week or two. I hadn't even told my sisters about it yet. "You know . . . lately, I've had the feeling I'm being watched."

Roman cocked his head. "What do you mean?"

"For the past week or so, I have felt that somebody has been watching over my shoulder. But I haven't been able to pinpoint who it might be. Or, maybe . . . maybe it's just my imagination. Anyway, I'd better head out. They're waiting for me at home." I slugged back the last drops of blood and shook my head to clear my thoughts.

Before I could slide out of the booth, the owner of the Utopia—Shikra—glided up to our table. She was silent, like most vamps, and absolutely gorgeous. Her hair was full and thick, shoulder length and a tawny wheat color that reminded me of my Nerissa. Her eyes were icy blue—she had only been a vampire for five years, if I remembered right, but she had adapted quickly. She was wearing a PVC dress, with a zipper pulled down around her navel. She'd had implants before she died and her breasts were two glorious globes but they looked fake as hell. I wondered how being a vampire affected having implants, but decided to keep my mouth shut for now.

"I trust the service was good? And your drinks?" She gave a little dip, curtseying to Roman. Which was smart, considering his status.

He glanced at me and I nodded. It had become my place to answer the niceties such as questions like this when we were out. It was part of my job, and considered beneath Roman's stature.

"Wonderful, and great service." I gave her a toothy smile.

"I wondered . . ." Shikra paused.

"Yes?" Again, my place to answer. It was also my job to field queries coming at Roman when we were out together unless his bodyguard intervened.

"I need to ask Lord Roman's advice, if I may. Something has come up and I don't quite know what to do. I thought about approaching the police, but something just . . . is warning me not to."

She looked so worried that I motioned for her to sit down without asking Roman if he was willing to listen. But he simply waited for her to join us.

"What seems to be the problem?" Roman leaned forward, his elbows resting on the table, his gaze locking hers.

That was one thing that made him so popular—when he turned his attention to someone or something, he gave it total focus with an intensity that was almost frightening.

Shikra pulled out a letter and put it on the table. "I received this the other day. It was followed up by two anonymous phone calls. I think there's a connection but I can't prove it. I'll let you read the letter first."

The minute I picked up the paper, I recognized what it was. I'd seen the same thing come through my office—on the same letterhead. From some company called Vistar-Tashdey Enterprises, it was an offer to buy the Utopia Club from Shikra. Strongly worded, it was almost a demand, when I read through it again. There were no names listed, no signature other than that of the lawyer representing VT Enterprises. Same as the one I'd received.

On edge—the letter was as off-putting and self-important as the one I'd received had been—I held up the paper. "Can I have a copy of this? Do you have a copy machine on the premises?"

She took it. "Yes, I'll have one made. But this isn't the only problem. Last night, and then about an hour ago, I received two phone calls. Someone threatened to burn down the club. No reasoning, no blackmail demands. Just a gruff voice, making a death threat. I have no idea if the caller was male or female—the voice sounded disguised."

A shiver ran through me. "Roman . . . "

He seemed to be thinking along the same wavelength. "You're thinking there may be a connection?"

I nodded. "Could be. As far as the letter, can you think of some reason anyone would want to buy your club? No offense, but . . . are you making a ton of money?"

Shikra shook her head. "That puzzles me, too. Oh, I'm getting by—business isn't bad. But it's not the best, either. There's no real reason to buy me out unless they want the land the building is on, and I don't own that."

I didn't want to tell her about my experience—not yet. Not until we knew what was going on. "Make us a copy of the letter, please Do you happen to have a recording of the messages that came through?" I knew it was a slim chance, but thought I'd ask anyway.

As I thought, she didn't. "No, I took the calls when they came in. The voice was the same both times, and it sounded muffled, like whoever it was, was trying to disguise it. And both times, the calls were short. I asked questions—or tried to, but they didn't answer."

"What did they say, exactly?" Roman glanced around the club and I followed his gaze. The Utopia was unlike most vamp clubs, decked out in vivid crimson, green, gold, and black. The setup reminded me of a tropical lounge, with lush ferns and sprawling ivies spilling over the edge of built-in flower boxes. Booths, a muted crimson, were smooth and rounded, curving around dark walnut tables polished to a high sheen. The floor was a tiled linoleum, a black and white speckled pattern. There were no over-whelming drapes anywhere like in some vamp clubs, no highly sexual statues, or macabre images. For the most part, it could have been any upscale chic bar.

Shikra squinted. "Let me try to remember the exact words." After a moment, she shrugged. "He—or she, I have no clue why but I want to say it was a he . . . he said *'Better count your hours, blood sucker, because I'm going to send your fucking club up into flames.'* And then he paused. That's when I asked what the hell was going on. He hung up." She shivered, rubbing her arms. Vamps didn't feel the cold much, but I knew it wasn't a chill hitting her.

I closed my eyes. That almost mirrored to the exact word what my caller had said. The only difference had been, "Better count your hours, blood sucker, because I'm going to take you and your fucking bar down so hard you'll never get up."

That was all she could remember. Roman told her to put a recorder on the club phone and see if she could capture the message if the freak called back, and then she went to print out a copy of the letter for me.

As we headed out, I glanced back at the Utopia. "I hope it's just somebody's bad idea of a practical joke." But as I stared at the neon sign, I kept seeing the flames engulfing the Wayfarer. "I hope to hell that's all it is."

Roman walked me to my car. I stood by the Jag, staring into the night. "I'll drop by Erin's and ask her about the job opportunity. I'll call or have her call you tomorrow night." And then, Roman drew me in for a quick kiss. His body-guards were in the background, studiously ignoring us as his hands slipped over my body, cupping my butt. I moaned into his mouth, then pulled away.

"Night doll," he whispered, then ushered me into my car, shutting the door when I was in. As I drove off, he stood there, one hand raised, watching me go.

I stopped by Sassy Branson's old mansion—which was now both the headquarters for the Seattle Vampire Nexus, and Vampires Anonymous. Located on two acres, the estate was gorgeous and the mansion spacious. I stopped at the gate to show my ID. When Sassy had been alive, there had been a simple intercom system, but back then, nobody outside the vampire community knew she was a vamp, and she hadn't been all that nervous. Now, there was good rea-son to post armed guards around the perimeter, given the hate groups that were alive and thriving.

The guards told me that Erin was out for the evening—she was off to a movie with friends, so I left a message for her to call me when she got home, and pulled out of the driveway.

I glanced at the clock. Ten o'clock. It felt odd not be down at the Wayfarer at this time. I told myself not to, but I couldn't help it. I drove by the ruins of my bar and parked outside the burned out shell. Slowly, after a moment, I got out of the car and picked my way through the rubble, which still hadn't been cleaned up, and entered the hollow husk of the building. The sky had clouded over and the scent of rain hung heavy.

As I stood on the threshold of what had been my bar, my stomach lurched. The Wayfarer had become more than a business to me. It had become a friend. And now, that friend was as dead as Chrysandra. I started to turn away when I thought I saw something in the corner. I spun around, ready to defend myself, but there, in the murky pile of sodden wood and plaster, hovered a faint white light. I could swear a face stared at me from the mist, but then it vanished as lightning crashed overhead and the rain began to pound down in a steady stream. I gave one last glance in the corner, but now there was nothing there. Heading back to my car, I wondered if it had been Chrysandra's spirit—was she out wandering? Or one of the others who had died? Feeling numb again, and weary, I climbed back in my Jag and headed for home.

The road out to Belles-Faire was slick, the water beading across it as the steady rain became a downpour. My wipers were going full steam and I was doing my best to see between the streams of water racing down my windshield. As I neared the turn that would take me to our house, a blur emerged at top speed from one of the driveways.

Fuck! Another car!

I slammed on the brakes and the Jag began to spin. As I drove into the skid, trying to regain control, the other car loomed large and I realized I was headed straight for it. Holy fuck, this was bad—*this was so bad*. I considered jumping from the car—I could do it and live, but then my Jag would become a missile bearing down on the incoming vehicle without any constraint.

So I did what I could. Muscles and reflexes took over as I attempted to gain control of the spinning car. Closer . . . closer, the other car was in front of me now and also skidding into circles. And then, everything blurred as my Jag carried me into a crazy dance directly into the other car's embrace.

The crash was surprisingly muffled, but then a loud shriek filled the air as metal slid along metal and my airbag deployed. It was like being hit with a sledge hammer. As my Jag rolled to a stop, I realized that I was still sitting there, still intact. Instinct took over—and I forced my hands to unbuckle my seat belt, then struggled to open the door. I half climbed, half fell out of my car, stumbling out of the way. I'd seen too many movies where the cars went up in flames, but so far that didn't seem to be happening. After a moment when there didn't seem to be any flames, I patted myself down. I was okay. Jarred but all right. I turned my attention to the other car.

The heel on my boot was broken, so I limped over and yanked open the driver door, which was a mangled mess. My strength allowed me to pry it loose, though. With growing relief, I saw that the only occupant in the car seemed to be the driver—a youngish woman. But she looked unconscious, and I could only pray that she wasn't dead.